PRAISE FOR
THE CONNECTIONS SERIES

Mended

"Kim Karr is one of my few autobuys! Romantic, sexy, and downright gripping! I read it in one sitting because I just couldn't put it down!"
—*New York Times* bestselling author Vi Keeland

Torn

"I was riveted from the first line and couldn't put it down until the last word was read." —*New York Times* bestselling author A. L. Jackson

"After an edge-of-your-seat cliff-hanger, Kim Karr returns to beloved characters Dahlia and River. . . . Their passion is intense." —Fresh Fiction

"The story is fabulous, the characters are rich and full of emotion, and the romance, passion, and sexy are wonderfully balanced with the angst and heartbreak." —Bookish Temptations

Connected

"I was pulled in from the first word and felt every emotion . . . an incredibly emotional, romantic, sexy, and addictive read."
—Samantha Young, *New York Times* bestselling author of *Fall from India Place*

"Emotional, unpredictable, and downright hot."
—K. A. Tucker, author of *Ten Tiny Breaths*

continued . . .

T0200932

ALSO BY KIM KARR

FRAYED

The Connections Series

KIM KARR

New American Library

New American Library
Published by the Penguin Group
Penguin Group (USA) LLC, 375 Hudson Street,
New York, New York 10014

USA | Canada | UK | Ireland | Australia | New Zealand | India | South Africa | China
penguin.com
A Penguin Random House Company

First published by New American Library,
a division of Penguin Group (USA) LLC

First Printing, September 2014

 REGISTERED TRADEMARK—MARCA REGISTRADA

LIBRARY OF CONGRESS CATALOGING-IN-PUBLICATION DATA:
Karr, Kim.
Frayed/Kim Karr.
p. cm.—The connections series)
ISBN 978-0-451-47068-3 (paperback)
1. Man-woman relationships—Fiction. I. Title.
PS3611.A78464.F79 2014
813'.6—dc23   2014016750

Printed in the United States of America
10 9 8 7 6 5 4 3 2 1

Set in Bulmer MT STD
Designed by Spring Hoteling

To my three boys . . .
may you each grow up to be a strong and caring man

And hopefully some lucky woman's prince charming as well. <3

ACKNOWLEDGMENTS

My thanks to the artists and musicians who inspired me through every chapter. Music is a world within itself. It is a language we all understand. And although I hope the words in this book do not fail you, I also hope the music helps to enhance them. Music speaks to me and tells me a story, and when I listen to songs, I listen to that story. . . . I hope I have succeeded in telling you a story that was brought to life through both words and music.

This section is by far the most difficult to write because it is so very important to acknowledge all of those who have never wavered in their support of not only myself but of the Connections Series as well.

I would like to thank my beta readers, Mary Tarter, Jody O. Fraleigh, and Laura Hansen, for your endless help and suggestions.

To Amy Tannenbaum of the Jane Rotrosen Agency, who believed in me enough to sign me and then dedicated the time to help me throughout the writing of this series. You are such an amazing person, and I couldn't be more grateful to have you as my literary agent.

To Penguin. When I began this journey with *Connected*, I never imagined I would land a publishing deal. So thank you, Kerry Donovan and the team at New American Library for so eagerly and enthusiastically taking me on and helping get the Connections Series published.

To all of the bloggers who have become my friends—you're all so amazing, and I cannot possibly put into words the amount of gratitude I have for each and every one of you!

And finally, my love and gratitude to my family—to my husband of twenty years, who became Mr. Mom while continuing to go to work every day; to my children, who not only took on roles that I for many years had always done—laundry, grocery shopping, cleaning—but always asked how the book was coming and actually beamed to their friends when telling them their mom wrote a book.

Without the help of those mentioned above, plus all of the support from my readers, who have contacted me daily since *Connected*'s release, the writing of *Frayed* wouldn't have been possible—a giant thank-you to all of you.

"Nobody can go back and start a new beginning,
but anyone can start today and make a new ending."
                                                    —Maria Robinson

Frayed Playlist

Chapter 1

♪ Cage the Elephant—"Come a Little Closer"

Chapter 2

♪ Ke$ha—"Past Lives"

Chapter 3

♪ Lifehouse—"You and Me"

Chapter 4

♪ No Doubt—"Underneath It All"

Chapter 5

♪ Caroline Liar—"Show Me What I'm Looking For"

Chapter 6

♪ Lenny Kravitz—"Dig In"

FRAYED

CHAPTER 1
Come a Little Closer

Ben

The sign behind the bar reads:

WANTED . . .
THAT CRYSTAL ASHTRAY YOU FILCHED.
THE MONOGRAMMED TOWELS YOU
TOTED OFF IN YOUR SUITCASE.
THOSE SCOTTISH-MADE LINEN NAPKINS YOU POCKETED.
IF YOU TOOK ANY OF THESE ITEMS IN THE
LAST SEVENTY-FIVE YEARS . . .
WE WOULD LIKE THEM BACK.
PLEASE!

Resting my elbows on the slick surface of the bar, I gesture to the sign.

The bartender shrugs. "Don't ask me, I only serve the drinks."

A cute cocktail waitress slinks up beside me and slides her drink order across the bar. While she waits she crooks a finger and bends toward me at such at angle that her ample cleavage spills out. My eyes naturally fall to it, but I quickly force them away when the bartender's voice booms over to us loudly.

"Lucy, gin or vodka in the martini?" he asks her sternly.

"Vodka." But she doesn't let her gaze wander and crooks her finger at me yet again.

"Rumor has it that management is looking to open a museum," she whispers in my ear.

I straighten and lift an eyebrow. "Interesting way to go about filling it."

"They're even willing to give recognition to anyone who returns the items."

I raise my glass. "I'll keep that in mind."

"I can show you what they've collected so far if you're interested. I have time to take a break before dinner is served."

Her body language and the seductive tone of her voice tell me she's offering more than a quick glance in a closet. I admit to contemplating the offer. The devil on my shoulder reminds me what a bittersweet day today is and that getting lost for a while doesn't sound so bad. But another, stronger, voice declares that the days of needing to get lost in women are long behind me.

My foot taps the stool rung at an increasing speed. "Maybe another time," I tell her as nicely as I can manage, with a mental pat on the back.

A year ago I would have taken her up on her offer, unzipped my pants, lifted her skirt, and fucked her from behind without even thinking twice about it. She shrugs and bats her eyelashes at me as she puts her drink order on a tray. When she leaves she turns and winks, tossing over her shoulder, "I'll be back. Maybe you'll change your mind."

What is she, the fucking Terminator? I loosen my bow tie, not able to stand another minute of restraint. And once I can breathe, I blink away any second thoughts. At the sound of a soft sigh coming from the bartender, I lift my eyes toward him. He looks forlorn and so I'm pretty sure he's crushing on the cocktail waitress.

"She's never asked me to see the items in storage," he mumbles.

"Take the lead, man, and ask her."

He seems to contemplate the idea.

Leaving him to ponder my suggestion, I turn around and lean against the brass rail to survey the room. Legend has it that the Academy of Motion Picture Arts and Sciences was founded here, that World War II military men used it as their recreation facility, and that John F. Kennedy's nomination for president happened in this very space. The historic Biltmore Hotel has served great people who have done amazing things. And I can't believe I'm here.

Turning back around, I sip the rest of my sparkling water and push the glass toward the bartender. "Thanks, man."

"Anytime, and, sir . . ."

I look over toward him.

"Congratulations," he says.

"Thank you. And hey, think about what I said—take the lead."

He laughs before resuming his work. When he steps aside I catch sight of myself in the mirror behind the bar. For a minute I can't help thinking about how damn lucky I am to have gotten a second chance at life. I was a *dead man*, a man who then lost sight of what mattered and then fell over the edge. But somehow after everything I went through, I was tugged back up by life and able to land on my feet.

A beep from my phone alerts me I have a text. I pull it out and smile at the screen—Dahlia London. I know her name is Dahlia Wilde now, but to me she'll always be Dahlia London—the beautiful blond-haired girl with the tiniest of noses, heart-shaped lips, and a love of the beach that could only be matched by mine. She moved in next door when we were five and we spent our whole lives together. For the longest time I thought she was the one made for me. I even asked her to marry me. But then after things in my job went wrong, I entered the witness protection program . . . leaving her to think I was dead. When I came back years later, she was in love with someone else.

Time made me realize our love was one of comfort and familiarity, not true undying love. I don't think I've experienced the latter, but I see it in her eyes. Sure, I struggled for a while before coming to terms with the fact that she has moved on, but we're in a good place now.

I read her text.

```
I just wanted to say congratulations and
I was thinking of you today.
```

With a smile, I type out my reply,

```
Thank you. That means a lot to me.
```

Switching my phone to vibrate, I slide it back in my pocket. She'll always be important to me and I hope she'll always be in my life, as a friend.

A hand on my shoulder pulls me from my thoughts. "You ready for this?"

I glance over. "Couldn't be readier."

Then Jason makes his way to the front of the room and his husky voice is amplified to fill the space. "I'd like to have everyone's attention if I could please."

The room becomes eerily silent and my nerves start to buzz.

He clears his throat. "I'm honored to be here today to present this award. For those of you who don't know who I am, I'm Jason Holt, commander of an FBI special task force, and I am honored to be here tonight to present to you a man I know well—Ben Covington, California's Journalist of the Year."

The words of his introduction echo off the walls in the legendary Crystal Ballroom at the historic downtown Los Angeles hotel and it seems a little surreal. There's a round of applause as I cross toward the stairs with years of reflection sweeping through my mind. When I finally reach the stage, I take the steps two at a time and stride across it heading toward my ex-brother-in-law. His eyes lock on mine and then he extends his arm, handing me the glass typewriter award, and suddenly everything feels so . . . real. With a handshake and a nod, he clears the stage and I'm left standing at the podium alone. It's shorter than I had expected, and as I set the award on its shelf, I scan the room.

My eyes come to rest on the table before me. The circle of people sitting there are the ones who brought me home—not in the physical sense, but emotionally speaking. Serena, my sister, is seated front and center. Trent, my nephew, is at her side. Caleb Holt, my best friend for as long as I can remember, sits beside him. Then Kale Alexander, the mate I met in Australia who helped remind me of my love for writing. Beck Cavanaugh, who not only pulled me up from the darkness, but also shook me until I could see through it, is seated beside him. And finally closing the circle, Jason takes a seat beside his ex-wife, the same beautiful woman who is also my sister.

I clear my throat and begin. "In the movie *Citizen Kane* a reporter said, 'I don't think there's one word that can describe a man's life.' "

Lifting my eyes to the nods of people in the audience agreeing with me, I adjust the microphone and my voice grows stronger. "I'm sorry to say I don't entirely agree with that statement."

Nameless faces in the crowd furrow their brows, purse their lips, and stare at me. "*Rosebud* was the last word Charles Foster Kane muttered just before he died. In the movie a journalist tries to decipher what the millionaire newspaper tycoon meant. But in the end he gives up on his investigation and summarizes it by saying, 'Mr. Kane was a man who got everything he wanted and then lost it. Maybe Rosebud was something he couldn't get or something he lost. Anyway, it wouldn't have explained anything . . . I don't think any one word can explain a man's life. No, I guess Rosebud is just a piece in a jigsaw puzzle . . . a missing piece.'"

Long, rectangular white linen-draped tables outline the elegant ballroom with larger round ones filling its center. Journalists from all around the state occupy the many seats. Taking deep calming breaths, I continue. "And as we all know, in the end of the movie it is revealed to the audience that *Rosebud* was the name of the sled from Kane's childhood—it was a reference to the only time in his life that he was really happy. At the end of the movie we're left with the image of the sled being burned in the furnace because people thought it was just a piece of junk lying around."

Food is being ushered out to the tables around the perimeter of the room and I know my time is running short. With sweaty palms, I grip the wooden sides of the stand and try to clarify what I mean. "I've spent the past year thinking, what is my *Rosebud*? And although I agree one word cannot describe your whole life, I do think one word can describe your life in the here and now. I think that word will change throughout your life, but the important thing is not to dismiss what it represents. Don't let life pass you by."

Against the white backdrop of the walls and the golden reflection from the chandeliers above, a vibrant flash of red movement toward the back of the room demands my attention. But then again I always notice women with red hair. I squint, trying to see past the shadows of the bright lights. Suddenly my world stops and I hope I don't gasp out loud in the wake of all the air leaving my lungs. Is it really her?

My heart races and time stops as lust explodes within me. Red hair flows past her shoulders, and a tight green dress hugs her sexy body perfectly. I'd know her natural beauty anywhere—that knockout figure that is sexy as hell. No matter how hard I have tried, I could never seem to forget the way her body felt pressed up against mine.

I don't even have to see those otherworldly emerald eyes to know it's her, I can tell by the way she moves. She's S'belle Wilde. We shared only one unbelievable night together, but it's seared in my mind forever.

Wetting my lips, willing my heart to beat at a normal pace, I try to bring my thoughts back to why I'm here. But I'm having a hard time tearing my eyes from her—I'm drawn to her. I begrudgingly force my mouth to recite the rest of my speech. And even though the words that I've rehearsed flow out easily, I can't focus on them at all. My thoughts are locked on her.

I remember the night we shared together so long ago and how she rocked my world. I remember how we reconnected this past summer and how I screwed everything up by acting inappropriately with our mutual client. I remember it all as it flashes through my mind—the good and the bad, the hot and the cold. And I remember how much I craved her then, and I can't deny that I still do.

When I pause for a moment I'm momentarily distracted by the way she cocks her hip when she gives orders to the waitstaff. She marches to another table in those high heels, and my eyes sweep her body, from the curve of her hips, to the fullness of her breasts, to the pout of her mouth. With a pencil tucked behind her ear, she pauses, biting her lip as if assessing the position of everything on the table with a precision that is sexy as fuck. I suck in a breath and refocus on why I'm standing up here. "Sorry about that. I have to say I'm a little nervous. . . ."

I glance across the many faces in the audience as the words spill from my mouth and my gaze locks on hers. Her lips tip down into a frown when she notices my stare and she hastily averts her attention. Good. At least I can focus again. I continue, but I can't stop constantly canvassing the space around me for her position. When I spot her directing those around her at the carving station, my pulse thunders at the sight. I shift my gaze to follow her and notice some of the women in the audience dabbing their eyes with napkins. I can only assume my heartfelt words have moved them. When I notice S'belle pick up one of the black linen pieces of cloth and do the same, it takes my breath away. Not only does she seem to be impacted by my presence, but fuck me if she isn't wearing my watch, the one I left for her this summer after she told me hers had broken.

As I finish my speech, a strange feeling runs through me. I'm not sure if it's finality, closure, hope, or a sense of new beginnings, but whatever it is—I'll take it. It beats the despair and isolation that have kept me company for the past year. I raise the glass typewriter in the air. "I leave you all with these final thoughts. . . ."

My last words come out softer as the syllables catch in my throat. Applause reverberates through the grand ballroom and I close my eyes for a few moments, absorbing everything. When I open them a grin crosses my lips. But my smile isn't for the strangers who surround me or even for my friends before me. It's for the redheaded girl in the back of the room whose gaze keeps flickering over mine.

Exiting the stage, I keep my eyes locked on hers and can't help noticing that hers are locked on mine . . . blue to green, a reflection from so long ago, but a memory I've never forgotten. However, I can't read her. Each glance tells a different story. She seems to be shifting between emotions. Like to hate, disgust to admiration. She's a blend of confusion that echoes my own feelings. I'm pulled from my thoughts as I approach the table and my sister rushes toward me.

"Oh, Ben, I'm so proud of you. I wish Mom were here to see you."

"Yeah, me too," I say as I hug her. Again my words catch in my throat.

"Mom, don't cry," Trent calls over my shoulder.

I grab his head in a vise lock. "Glad you made it home, kid."

"I wouldn't fucking miss this for the world."

"Better lie low on the swearing or your mother will use the liquid soap in the restroom to wash out your mouth."

"Yes, I will," she adds.

I swing my arms around them both. "How do you hear everything?" I ask her as we approach the table.

"Superpowers."

And I think, *Oh yeah, just like our mom.*

Caleb extends his hand and pulls me toward him. With his hand slapping my back, he doesn't say a word, but I can feel what he feels. We had ridden this roller-coaster ride together. Both of our lives had changed once I started my investigation. I may have been the one who had to give up his identity, but a part of him was buried alongside me for those years. We both felt guilt, remorse, sorrow, but now was a time for celebration.

I push him away. "If you cop a feel I'm going to have to deck you."

His grin broadens. "I'll try to control myself."

On a serious note I say, "Thanks for everything."

His eyes dart to mine and I see the lump in his throat. "What are you drinking? I'll grab another round," he says.

"Sparkling water."

He rolls his eyes.

"I need to keep my senses around you. Wouldn't want you taking advantage," I joke.

Caleb hasn't been around much the past year. He hadn't seen how I let alcohol consume me. Let it erase the memories that were just too hard to bear. I don't consider myself an alcoholic, but I know I function much better when I stay away from it.

Kale and Beck are deep in conversation when I squat between them. "What am I missing that's so important I didn't even get a congratulations?"

Kale's eyes take on a glimmer. "Beck here is telling me about . . ."

My attention wavers the minute I see her again. She pulls her mass of hair back and bends down to examine one of the dishes being set out. When she straightens she catches me staring. We're close enough that I know she sees it when I smile suggestively, but she quickly cuts her eyes elsewhere. I narrow in on the vision before me. I can see her flawless skin left uncovered by her sleeveless dress. I notice the way her neck and arm flow into a sea of glimmer from the sparkling lights above. I imagine grabbing her, pulling her to me, and bending to nip the smooth hollow where her neck and shoulder meet. She looks back at me and this time a slight smile crosses her lips. I'll be damned if it doesn't light up the whole fucking room.

"Don't go there, man," Caleb's voice warns.

"Hmm?" I turn to look at him.

"Here's your drink."

Turning back toward Beck and Kale, I clasp Kale's shoulder. "Great work. Stop in my office Monday. I want to hear all about it."

"I see the way you're looking at her." Caleb won't drop it.

"I'm not looking at her in any way," I deny.

"The fuck you're not. You're practically licking her off the rim of that glass."

"You don't know what you're talking about."

His hard glare cuts across the room to where she stands. "Yeah, I think I do. Just remember she's forbidden fruit. Leave well enough alone. You're in a good place right now—you don't need to go down that road."

"I hear you."

He looks at me skeptically.

Glass in hand, I sip my drink and crunch on one of the ice cubes, thinking past wrongs and forbidden fruit—none of that matters when I remember the night we shared. I also know that my insides hum with every move she makes. But I don't say anything else to Caleb, because he's right; going down that road won't lead to any place I need to go.

The night passes quickly with so many conversations with people I've never met. Beck left to pick his girlfriend, Ruby, up from work, and Kale followed him out, discussing whatever they are working on. Caleb was taking a red-eye back to wherever it is he goes, but said he'll be back next month. And per his advice, I've gone out of my way to avoid

S'belle, but it's killing me to do it. I know there's a huge chance she wouldn't talk to me anyway after what happened this summer, but I also think there's a chance she would and with Caleb's words echoing in my ears, I'm not sure I should go there.

When my phone rings with a call from Aerie Daniels, I take the opportunity to slip away from the crowd. "Hello."

"Hi, Ben. It's Aerie."

I open a door marked EXIT and end up in a quiet service hallway. With no one around I lean against the cool stainless wall behind me.

"Hey. Everything okay?" I ask.

Not only is Aerie my ex-fiancée's best friend but she also works for me.

"I just wanted to apologize for not being there tonight. I'm leaving in the morning for that quick trip to New York City I told you about and thought I should get everything together for the November issue and go through it one last time."

"Aerie, it's going to be fine. Don't stress about it."

"Are you sure you don't need me to stay?"

"I'm sure. Stop stressing. It's all set and there's nothing to worry about."

"Okay. It's just I've never been out of the office on trigger day. My plane lands first thing in the morning, so if anything—"

"Let's bring out the desserts all at once."

I hear a familiar sound—soft and sexy—nearby. Jerking my head to the right, I greedily take S'belle in. The way her body moves with each movement, I can't suppress the memories that always surface when I see her. I remember everything about that night. Her perky tits that hardened the minute I caressed them, the way her mouth opened and her eyes closed when I touched her in the most intimate places, the feel of her hands seductively sliding over my body, the way she smelled, the raspy tone of her voice when she pleaded for more. My head begins to spin with fresh justification about why it's okay to just talk to her.

She exits the small space quickly, though, through the next set of doors, and again the hall is quiet once more.

"You there?" Aerie's voice calls through the phone.

"I'm here." I manage to make my own voice sound normal.

"Okay, then. I'll check in when we land."

"Sounds like a plan. And, Aerie, for fuck's sake, have fun."

She responds with a laugh, "Language, Ben, language," and then she hangs up.

I shake my head and shove my phone in my pocket. Just as I'm about halfway to the door, it swings open again.

"Ben," she greets me in a velvety soft voice.

I can't even tell whether I'm more startled or happy to see her there. But when a flush runs up her neck and her breathing steadily picks up, I want to think she's as impacted by my presence as I am by hers. Her reaction surprises me, but I'm even more surprised to see warmth in her gaze. My eyes drink her in with a thirst—her hot body, her beautiful stare. My nose catches a faint whiff of her lemony scent. She smells amazing and I almost spasm on the spot. Just as I open my mouth to speak, the door opens again.

"Did you find the serving spoons?" a guy much too young to be in charge asks.

"Grabbing them now," she answers, chewing on her lip before moving across the hall to the counter and picking up a handful of silver ladles.

He holds the door open for her and she glances at me one last time before walking toward him. And as I watch her, the way her body moves with ease as she leaves, I can't help thinking back to that night so long ago. The fantasy come to life that I've never been able to forget.

I filled my hands with her beautiful breasts as I slammed into her from behind. Moans of passion that I weren't sure if they were hers or mine. My body shaking, hers quivering. I had been drunk, but I felt com-

pletely sober when my hands roamed her body and my lips followed. Her pussy was so sweet and I wanted more. Without any inhibitions, a string of my deepest darkest sexual desires left my mouth. I saw her smile at my words. She whispered how she wanted to answer them. And as I stood, I grabbed her neck and brought her mouth to mine. I felt my dick throb and I wanted more.

The way I felt when I was inside her was unlike anything I had ever experienced. But I force myself to blink the thought away. It's not how I should be thinking. But fuck, seeing her again makes me horny as hell and makes me think about things I know I shouldn't.

As I head back to the party, I tell myself that I need to leave the past in the past. But the words just don't feel right.

CHAPTER 2
Past Lives

Bell

At first glance he had me aching for him. Just one word from him and I was purring. He exuded passion—I felt it the first time he touched me. If you met him, he would make you feel the same way too. I promise. Charming, elusive, full of sex appeal—nothing has changed. One look from Ben Covington and I know what he wants, and it's not as though I don't want the same thing too. But I also know all too well the pleasure I would feel would only be followed by a stabbing pain in my heart. That's just the way it is with him. The only way it can be after everything we've been through.

I try to shake the memories he evokes, but they won't budge. They just keep rushing back, flooding me further with want and need. I can't help remembering how he made me feel. How I thought I ruled the world. How I even thought I had a superpower. It wasn't as glamorous as Emma Frost's telepathic manifestation or Wonder Woman's ability to fly, but it was cool nonetheless. My superpower was that I had a way

with words. Somehow my uncanny ability allowed me to talk myself
into or out of just about anything—an extension on a late paper, a cita-
tion for illegally parking, admission into a sold-out club—it didn't really matter what it was; if I wanted it I got it.

But I cursed that ability after the night I spent with him. Cursed
him for everything, but especially for leaving an impact on my soul that
felt as if it would last forever. Yet on seeing him tonight, hearing his
moving speech, the feelings tumble through me as I set up the dessert
table, making me question everything. I'm beginning to think I was
wrong. Maybe wiggling my way into the fraternity party as a makeshift
sorority sister and then into his bed wasn't actually a curse. But if it
wasn't, then what was it?

"*Bonjour!*" *I said to the girl with a name tag that read Claire
pinned to her white lace blouse.*

*Medium-brown hair tumbled to her shoulders in smooth waves and
was held back by a black ribbon headband. She wore a very short plaid
skirt with red tights and ankle boots. Flawless and polished, she was
perfectly put together. I had to blink twice because she looked so much
like the character Blair Waldorf from* Gossip Girl. *She stood with a
huge grin on her face behind a pink-draped table with a golden triangle
and the letter Z emblazoned across it in the student center at the University of Southern California. It had only been two weeks since I
traded in the City of Lights for the City of Angels. The night was cool,
but since the rain had let up I had decided to get out and stop by the
recruitment fair. Clubs, fraternities, and sororities populated the
room. With so many choices, I had no idea which booth to visit first. I
stood back and watched and it was Claire's enthusiasm that caught my
attention. So I moved closer and stood in line as she talked to a group of
girls about joining her sorority. They giggled and jumped up and down
when she gave them a piece of paper with an address on it and told them
she'd meet them there.*

Her gaze lifted at my greeting and she quirked a smile. With a gleam in her eye she said, "Hi. Are you from France?"

I gave a slight laugh. "No, California but I spent my freshman year in Paris."

"Ah . . . you're new. I am too. I just transferred in from New York University."

I felt a spark of excitement. "Are you a sophomore?"

She straightened her shoulders. "No, actually I'm a junior."

"Has anyone ever told you that you look like a character from Gossip Girl?"

Her smile grew bright. "All the time and I love to hear it. She's my idol. I fashion my wardrobe after her."

I nodded. Not certain of what to add to that, I quickly glanced down at the table of pamphlets and asked, "So, you were in a sorority at NYU?"

I was somewhat curious only because she was obviously the quintessential prep school girl turned college sorority member. I knew them well. I had gone to a prep school and I was sure all the girls I graduated with had joined sororities. But for me, the preppy schoolgirl look was never my thing. I liked to think my look was more Kate Moss. I mixed fashion-forward clothing with vintage. I wasn't afraid to throw any two pieces together and put my own spin on an outfit. My mother liked my edgy wardrobe but warned me to avoid anything too revealing. That made me laugh because guys never looked at me that way anyway. I was always just the cute little sister.

"How did you know? Delta Zeta!" She beamed with pride, pointing to the flattering propaganda spread out in front of her.

I bit my lip. I had considered joining a sorority for the sheer purpose of making friends, but I wasn't certain if I had the time with my heavy course load.

She must have noticed my eyes flicker in contemplation because she asked, "You are a PNM, aren't you?"

"A PNM?" I questioned.

"A potential new member," she clarified, leaning closer to me.

I shrugged. "Well, yes. I guess I am."

"Great," she said, assessing my outfit—a short cropped jacket, skinny jeans, low-heeled boots, and my grandmother's always-present layered gold necklaces.

"What does a PNM have to do?"

"Depends on what you can offer and who you know."

"I'm new, so I haven't met very many people."

She frowned as if reconsidering if she should have asked me.

Not wanting to feel rejected, I threw out, "But I have a brother in a band and another brother who's a graduate student here."

Her eyes twinkled with excitement. "Are they hot?"

I shrugged again. "I guess so."

"Then you're a PNM."

I clasped my hands together in excitement at having a title and making a new girlfriend.

"We need little sisters to help at the Kappa Sigma's Pledge Night tonight."

"I'm not really a little sister, though."

"Oh, I'm giving you temporary membership. Raise your right hand and repeat after me to accept and we can move on to the hazing," she said in a serious tone.

My mouth dropped open.

"I'm only kidding."

Not quite sure I believed her, I did as she instructed, trying to recall movies I had watched with sororities, but my mind went blank. I finished repeating the words.

She skipped around the table. "Done!"

I felt nervous and excited at the same time.

She grabbed her materials up off the flat surface. "Let's go."

I patted my hair. "Now?"

"Yes. Inspiration period is about to begin."

I slanted her a questioning look.

"Hell week," she mumbled.

"Oh, but I'm not sure I . . ."

She put her hand up and ignored my concerns as she filled her purse with the brochures and swung it over her shoulder. "But first you need to change your outfit. Come with me; you look close to my size."

She took me to her dorm room, gave me a change of clothes, and we were off. It was dark and streetlights lit our way. The shoes she had me change into weren't exactly made for walking long distances. I wore heels all the time, but those must have been five or six inches high. My hair blew in my eyes and I pushed it behind my ears. Claire had tried to tame it, but it was still a frizzy mess.

"What am I supposed to do tonight?" I asked, trying to keep up with her pace.

She rolled some lipstick on her lips and smacked them. "Be bitchy and nice, ugly and pretty, stupid and smart, innocent and slutty, blond or brunette."

I looked at her in confusion.

She laughed. "It's easy. You just tend to one of the fraternity brothers' needs." With a silver tube in one hand she air-quoted the word needs.

I wasn't quite sure what she meant, but I suddenly felt like a call girl in her short skirt and tight top and I started to think twice about going. My stomach lurched. I wasn't really a partyer. I'd lived with my aunt in Paris and didn't often participate in the college extracurricular activities. I always had tons of guys who were friends and I called them boyfriends, but I don't think I ever had one in the true sense of the meaning. Girlfriends, on the other hand, those were harder to make and I wondered if I was a bit too quirky for most girls' liking. But since Claire had brought me under her wing, I didn't want to blow my opportunity.

"Ne . . . needs?" I stuttered.

She peered at herself in a compact mirror. "You be whatever he wants you to be. You know, make sure his cup is full, flirt with him, tell him what he wants to hear. Make yourself his dream girl for the night. But never, ever let him know it's your job. It should seem natural and real—like you really like him."

I stumbled on a crack in the sidewalk.

She looked over at me. "You can do that, can't you?"

"Of course." I swallowed, thinking maybe my silver tongue had gotten me in over my head this time, but then I thought no, I had read many books where girls molded themselves to be what the guy wanted and ended up liking who she became. With that thought I knew I could be the kind of girl she was talking about—strong and confident in her sexual prowess. I could be just like one of the heroines of my romance novels.

"Great! Just relax. Enjoy the free booze and man candy. I promise it'll be fun."

I bit my lip, hoping my brother Xander wouldn't be there. He'd kill me not only for not telling him where I was going or for what I was wearing, but more so for what I was going to be doing.

She pushed her boobs up. "Oh, and if he wants a blow job, make sure you give him one."

My eyes widened and my mouth fell open.

"Only kidding. But you should have seen what I had to do!"

"What?" I asked, once again stifling the urge to turn back around.

"I was forced to dance on tables for all the fraternities on campus to absurdly sexual songs."

Oh God, *I thought.*

"So, tell me about that brother of yours that's in the band."

I couldn't look at her. I was still trying to process what I had gotten myself into. I finally took a deep breath and said, "His name is River and he's coming to visit in a few weeks. His band is actually going to play on campus."

She tossed her hair over her shoulder. "Oh, I love rock stars. You have to introduce me to him."

"Um . . . sure, I can do that." But I already knew she wasn't his type.

"Does he have a girlfriend?"

I laughed. "No, he says he doesn't do girlfriends." And I air-quoted my last word as she had earlier.

"He sounds dreamy," she said.

Again I cursed my silver tongue.

When she opened the door to the frat house, all I could do was stare. People were everywhere. Music played loudly from the speakers in every corner, silver kegs lined one wall, and large plastic bowls overflowed with food on the tables. She led the way and when she stopped abruptly, I ran right into her.

"Sorry," I hollered over the pulsing music.

She ignored me and moved forward, but I stood glued to the spot I had stopped in. My pulse was racing. My cheeks prickled with heat. There he stood, Ben Covington, just a few feet away—tall, beautiful, messy blond hair, a body that made mine tingle everywhere, and a smile that caused me to melt without even knowing why it formed on his lips.

Claire doubled back. She noticed my stare.

"Can I be assigned to him?" I pointed, my stomach fluttering.

She made a low dismissive noise. Waving her hand, she said, "He has a girlfriend."

"So you don't assign guys with girlfriends?" I asked a little too sharply.

She raised an eyebrow. "Sure, he's all yours. But you should know he never really pays attention to any of us."

I shrugged and resumed my staring.

She shook her head at me. "I have to say you really are a strange one."

Lightly laughing at her comment and trying not to take offense, I kept my eyes glued on him. He was across the room talking to some younger guy rather animatedly, and when he stretched out his hand with a red Solo cup in it, I straightened my shoulders. "I'm off."

She pursed her lips and grabbed my arm. *"Do you want any pointers?"*

Knowing I must seem like a contradiction, I met her eyes. "I got this, Claire."

She grabbed my elbow as I started to walk toward him.

I twisted to look at her.

"Honey, my name is Stacy. Claire is my dream girl name. What's your name, by the way?"

"Bell Wilde."

"Oh, I like it. Is that your dream girl or real name?"

I gave her a blank look. "Real."

"So what's your dream girl name?"

A smile crossed my lips as I looked over to the guy who had captured my attention since I first saw him just a few weeks ago. Xander had taken me to a frat party but made me leave when he saw me drinking a beer and staring at Ben. The guy across the room was also the same guy I had been obsessing over since he talked to me in the library a few days ago. I couldn't believe he was here.

"S'belle," I said to her, more sure of that than anything I had since I met her. At that moment, I stood tall and strode across the room chanting, I can be his dream girl for the night over and over.

My insides froze when I stopped in front of him. I was so nervous that when I wrapped my trembling hand around his cup, I thought I might be sick. Then I thought, I can do this. It's my job, after all. But when our fingers touched and a heat spread throughout my body, my nerves were back.

He grinned down at me with eyes that had to make every girl look twice. He shuffled his feet and for a second I thought maybe he was nervous too, but only for a second because when I looked up into the smoldering heat of those blue eyes, I saw nothing but confidence. That one look gave me strength and I suddenly found my words. "I've been assigned as your little sister," I said, feeling as if my tone came out more little girl than dream girl. But the way he looked at me, I didn't think that was what he thought at all.

"Bell, you okay?" Dino asks, and pulls me from my memories.

"Yes, I'm fine," I reassure him as he places the last of the food on the table.

Dino works for Tate, my boss from my day job, and for me on occasion. I glance away from what we're doing and catch sight of Ben. He looks almost edible in his tux. He's talking to his sister and when he lowers his chin in an almost shy fashion, I have to look away. He's just too much to take in.

With my heart pounding, I race out onto the terrace for some air. I have to stay away from him. The way he looks at me, I know what he wants. And I can't control the way my body reacts when he's near. I know he's not good for me, and that nothing but heartache can come out of the attraction between us. There's just too much in our past to ever make this work. Two wrongs will never, ever make a right.

CHAPTER 3
You and Me

Ben

As the night draws to an end, people start funneling out of the ballroom, stopping one last time to congratulate me. With each good-bye I look around, trying to spot her, but she's nowhere in sight. It's probably better that way. Once most of the guests are gone, I make my way toward the bar for some refuge. It's been a bittersweet night and I'm ready for the memories it's awoken to once again become dormant.

"The same?" the bartender asks me.

I nod. "With a lemon slice if you don't mind."

I'm leaning over the short glass filled with ice, sparkling water, and the scent of citrus—the scent of her—chewing on a cube, thinking about my speech and the haunting sadness that Kane, with all his money and power, died with no one by his side.

When he died no one knew the one simple important fact that mattered most to him—the one thing that made him happy. Am I headed down that same road? Fuck. Recently my sister and I came into a ten-million-dollar inheritance, and since then I've done nothing except build my company. Put the pieces in play to establish what I hope will become a lucrative publishing holding company.

Staring at the lemon floating among the melting ice cubes, I can't help thinking how much things have changed over the past year. I came back to California looking to reclaim my life. But that life was long gone before I ever returned. My childhood sweetheart, the girl I was engaged to, was already in love with someone else. Then before I could even accept that and move forward, my mother died and I don't remember much of what happened after that. I know I spent many long months drowning my sorrows and making one poor decision after another. But I was serious about no more looking back. I need to move forward.

Jason slides in beside me. "Everything okay?"

Sitting up straight, I turn to face him. "Just thinking about a girl."

"Dahlia?" he asks.

"No, actually not her. We're in a good place as friends now."

"Good, I'm glad to hear it. Want to talk about the girl, then?"

"Jason!" We both turn in the direction of the voice. Serena walks toward us with her hands on her hips and a frown on her face. Her eyes narrow on the bar in front of us.

"What, baby?" he asks, pulling her toward him and kissing her lips.

She lifts my glass and sniffs it. Setting it back down, she looks between the two of us and smiles. "Nothing."

"Ready to go?" he asks.

She nods, her long earrings swinging along her jawline. "If you are," she answers, folding into his side. She looks toward me. "Come home with us?"

I can't help noticing how much she looks like our mother tonight. Her hair is pulled back, she has makeup on, and she's wearing a long black dress. She looks beautiful.

"I think I'll stay a bit longer. When is Trent leaving?"

"You should tell him now," Jason mumbles in her ear.

"Now now." Twisting, she says to me, "In three days."

"There might not be time," Jason says louder.

"Come on, you two, I'm right here. Just tell me."

"I don't know how to say this," Serena says, looking nervous and inhaling a deep breath.

Seriousness overtakes me. "Say what?"

"Baby, just tell him before you give him a heart attack," Jason pushes.

She blows out the breath she was holding. "Jason and I are going to take Trent back to the University of Hawaii together."

I give her a blank look. "Okay, have fun. When are you coming back?"

"It's more than a vacation. We're going to get remarried while we're there."

I stare at her for a long beat. Then I stand up and open my arms. My sister collapses into them. "I'm really happy for you," I say.

She wipes away some stray tears and I offer my hand to Jason. "Congratulations, man. I know it's been a long road."

"I'll take care of them better this time," he promises.

And I believe him. I've been on this roller-coaster ride for three years, but he's been on it for five. He distanced himself from his family to keep them safe as he pretended to be a dirty detective, all the while working under a special task force. He joined forces with a drug cartel to learn their inner workings and let his wife and son believe he was on the take. He sacrificed a lot to bring the cartel down. He deserves this second chance. But what's most important to me is that my sister and Trent are happy. And as long as they are, I'm happy for them.

"What do you say we grab the boy and all stop for ice cream at that place he likes with all the toppings?" Jason says to Serena.

"I don't eat that shit anymore," Trent says, joining us.

I try to hide my smile but can't. Instead I cross my arms and watch.

"Trent Holt, that's enough of the potty mouth!"

"Mom, I'm not four. You don't have to say potty mouth."

"Son, let's just humor your mother and leave the foul language for your uncle."

I shake my head and laugh. "Have a good night, everyone." I hug them all good-bye and watch as they head out the door, hoping that this time maybe they really can be one happy family.

With the room almost empty, I stare at the buffet tables that have already been broken down.

"Can I get you anything else?" the bartender asks.

I shake my head no and toss a fifty on the bar. "Have a great night."

My fingers curl around the base of the crystal typewriter with the words *California's Journalist of the Year* scripted across it. Despite the glamorous surroundings, a sudden wave of loneliness floods me as I exit the now-empty Crystal Ballroom. I can't shake the feeling as I make my way out. I consider stopping in the lobby bar when I see the cocktail waitress in there but decide I'd better go home. I don't want to do something I'll be kicking myself for tomorrow.

Next I take my time wandering the corridors of the grand hotel and by the time I find an exit door, I notice I'm in the staff parking lot. Just as I'm about to turn around, I spot S'belle's car. The little cabriolet sits among a few other stray automobiles. My spirits suddenly lift at the sight and I have a driving need to see her. Thoughts of her—her smile . . . never forced but always bright, her hair . . . red like fire, her body . . . hot and sexy—have flooded me with need all night, yet it's her attitude . . . sassy but somehow innocent . . . that has made me burn for her.

For the longest time I stare up at the abundant stars in the clear night sky. I undo my bow tie and take it off, shoving it into my pocket as I question whether I should even be attempting to talk to her. Just then the sound of the side door opening startles me and I stand up straight. I nod toward the two guys wearing white server jackets and black pants, each carrying large silver trays. The taller one is the one who came to get S'belle earlier.

I relax back against the brick wall and consider just going home. But when the door swings open again and I spot that distinctive curtain of red hair, it's too late. Her arms are loaded with smaller-sized pans and her attention is focused on the two guys, so she doesn't notice me. I stand back and Caleb's words echo in my head—*leave well enough alone*. The parking lot lights cast shadows over her as she walks farther away from me into the darkness. That's what I decide to do—leave well enough alone.

"I'm parked over to the right," her sweet voice calls to the guys ahead of her.

She fumbles in her purse while trying to balance the load in her arms. She seems to be losing the battle. And then without thinking, I rush over toward her, trying to grab what I can from her hands, but I'm too late and it all crashes down. Pans bounce off the blacktop, denting and skidding as they land, but our eyes aren't on the fallen items— they're on each other.

"Hi," she says in a voice that screams innocence.

"Hi there," I answer back.

The faint freckles on her nose are something I don't remember. But the warmth of her breath whispering against my cheek makes my body come alive—need instantly floods me. Her smile gleams and I smile back. I study her. Her eyes are a liquid green that reminds me of emeralds; the color's richer than I remember. Her red hair seems brighter than I recall it being and her curls are gone, but her mannerisms, her quirkiness, they're all still the same.

"Need help?" one of the white-coated guys calls.

"I got it," I yell back.

With the moment broken, we both squat to pick up the items and when we grab for the same tray our fingers touch and I feel it— electricity bolting through my body. She yanks her hand away as if electrocuted and I know she feels it too. And this time when our eyes meet, I am certain of what I see—desire. It's then that my confusion fades and I know what I want.

Knowing what I want and getting it have usually gone hand in hand for me, but I'm not so sure that will be the case when it comes to the spitfire in front of me. Our history is sordid, maybe even tainted, but in this one moment of clarity I don't give a shit. The attraction between us can't be denied. And really what does it matter that we spent one night together when I was with someone else, or even that her brother is now married to that same girl? After all, two consenting adults should be able to have sex without the past being an issue.

Her fingers are shaking as she busies herself grabbing at the trays. "I got them." I cover up her hands with mine.

She stands quickly while I stay crouched gathering the last of the silver dishes from the ground. I've thought about being with her again for so long, and the attraction only grew when we worked together this past summer. And right now I'll do whatever it takes to have her. I'm on my knees and I consider groveling, apologizing for my lack of morals when I messed around with the bride whose wedding I was reporting on and she was coordinating, but with two dudes watching over me, there's no way in hell I'll ever do that.

When I stand up, she tucks her hair behind her ear and my breath catches. Her face is strikingly beautiful—eyelashes longer than I've ever seen, wide green eyes with a look of innocence about them, ivory skin with faint freckles on her dainty nose, and full lips that I want so much to have on mine.

There's a shift in her gaze as I stare at her and the warmth suddenly disappears. She pouts her lips and then attempts to take the trays from me.

I'm bemused by her mood swing. "Let me help you to your car." She turns on her heel and leaves me standing there.

My lips twitch. "I guess that's a yes?"

She walks toward her cabriolet and clicks her key fob to open her trunk while nodding. The guys holding the larger pans are already beside the car, where they help her deposit the items.

"See you, Bell," one says.

"Good night, Matt," she answers.

"Night, Bell. You sure you're okay?" the other asks.

She looks at me. "Yes. And thanks for all your help," she calls as they both walk toward their own cars.

They seem young, yet hot for her just the same. But I can't help wondering if the taller one is having a thing with her. The thought makes my stomach churn. Ignoring it, I set the stuff I'm holding on top of the others and close her trunk. I'm relieved that she doesn't hurry to get in her car but instead stays where she is. My hands feel a little wet and sticky from the dishes, so I rub them together.

"I have something to clean your hands with in my backseat. Hang on," she says, and opens her car door, pulling out a pile of black linen napkins monogrammed with a BH in the corner.

I raise an eyebrow. "Contraband?"

Her mouth falls open. "No! I grabbed what I could find quickly from the ballroom when I brought the food in. I used them to wipe up the juice from a tray that spilled on my seat on the way here. I'll return them the next time I come."

"Isn't that what they all say?"

She places her hands on her hips. "I will!"

"I believe you," I say with a grin.

She hands me one of the napkins.

"You know there's a reward for items like those."

Her eyes narrow. "You're lying."

My smile grows smug. "No, I'm not. Well, there's a reward for seventy-five-year-old items like them. Come on, let me show you."

"I don't know, it's late."

"It's not far, and who knows, we may even run into the ghosts who are said to haunt the place."

I finish wiping my hands and reach for her elbow. She doesn't flinch, so I let my fingers slide down her arm and rest on her tiny waist. Heat flares between us. "Come on. I'll keep you safe."

She slants me a look, her eyes settling on the position of my hands. She steps back. "This isn't going to be like one of those Alfred Hitchcock movies, is it?"

I snort. "No, I promise."

She shrugs. "Sure, okay, why not?"

As we walk side by side, I find that my glance keeps shifting down to her shapely legs and then up to her full breasts. She's such a knockout. I blink a few times rapidly to erase the images playing in my mind and ask, "You watch Hitchcock movies?"

She clasps her hands together in the cutest fucking way. "Yes, I love old movies. I used to watch them with my dad all the time when I was a kid."

I open the side door, which is surprisingly unlocked. "Me too."

She seems to consider this for a moment before she steps back into the building.

In the hallway of the hotel she's very quiet. "Everything okay?" I ask.

"Why do you think this hotel is haunted?" she asks, and I think she might actually be a little scared.

"It was built on a cemetery and it's said you can hear laughing inside the Crystal Ballroom, but when one opens the doors, no one is in there. Some people have even claimed to have seen a ladylike shape walking through it."

"How did you become such an expert on the place?"

"I'm not really an expert. I bought a book over the summer about the history of LA, and haunted locations was one of the chapters."

"You mean there are others?"

I step aside as I open a door for her to yet another hallway. "Yeah, like twelve more. The Roosevelt is one. Marilyn Monroe lived there for a while. In fact, her first magazine spread was shot there. It's rumored that people who stay in room 1200 can see her. I guess that's the room she lived in."

Her eyes widen. "See her how?"

"They say they see her living in the mirror."

The hallways are dimly lit, so I do my best to lead us back to the Crystal Ballroom. The sound of a door slamming makes her jump.

I stop to look over at her. "Hey, Red, you're not really scared, are you?"

She looks a little pale and I take a step closer to her. She closes her eyes and I follow the line of her jaw to the peak of her collarbone, gently brushing my fingertips up that same line. "Hey, look at me."

She opens her eyes and there is no denying it. It's the way she looks at me, has always looked at me. As though she gets me. It makes me want her as I've never wanted anyone.

"What are you two doing in here?" a husky voice calls from the end of the hallway. "This is for staff only."

The trance is broken and she finds her voice. "Oh, I worked an event earlier and left something behind. I'm just going back to get it," S'belle tells the man.

"Oh, okay, then. Make it fast."

"Did you just lie to that man?"

Her eyes cut to mine. "It wasn't really a lie. Just a half-truth."

"There's a difference?" I feign ignorance.

"Yes, now come on before he catches up with us," she says nervously.

I laugh and her eyes stay locked on mine. Her initially hard stare softens second by second and then just like that she shoves me forward and takes the lead. I follow her and the next door takes us right into the Crystal Ballroom.

I scratch my head. "How did you know how to get here?"

"I just mapped the location out in my head and followed the service corridors."

I raise my eyebrows. "I'm impressed."

"We're closed," the bartender calls.

"Hey, man, I just popped in to show this nonbeliever your sign behind the bar."

"Mr. Covington, I didn't realize it was you. Come on over."

"Mr. Covington," she scoffs, and straightens her shoulders as she strides toward the bar. "Hi, Ryan. How was your night?" she greets him.

Shock overtakes me. She knows him too?

He smiles at her. "Busy," is all he says when he catches the look on my face.

She takes a seat and I move to stand behind her, making sure he knows she's with me. But with being this close, all I can think about is wanting to press myself against her.

He lifts the framed sign from behind the bar and hands it to S'belle.

Her laughter jolts through me. She looks over her shoulder at me. "You're not going to turn me in, are you, Mr. Covington?"

I wink at her and lean down to whisper in her ear, "Not if you behave."

She sits perfectly still.

I watch in the mirror as her eyes close. I stay close just breathing into her ear and inhaling her lemon scent.

"Funny, right?" Ryan comments as he takes the sign from her and puts it back, making himself scarce at the other end of the bar.

S'belle twirls around to face me. "Your speech told such an emotional tale. I never thought about all you went through. I'm really sorry—"

I place a finger over her lips. "Shhh . . . no sorries. That part of my life is over and I'm moving forward. But I want to apologize to you for the last time we spoke. I really should explain—I wasn't thinking clearly then. I was in a really bad place and—"

She repeats my action and places her finger over my lips. "Shhh . . . we've all made mistakes. I shouldn't have judged. So let's just let it go."

She's letting me off the hook for my lapse in judgment. Good. Working as a wedding columnist over the summer and fraternizing with the bride is not anything I'm proud of or even want to ever think about again.

We lean toward each other, drawn together like two magnets. I place my hands on either side of her. This close there's no denying that we are two people who want each other. Lust, fire, desire erupt between us.

"I'm sorry, Mr. Covington, but I have to close the room down now."

The weight of his gaze as he takes us in tells me he wants to be me. A smug satisfied smile spreads across my lips that he isn't.

"We'll get out of your hair and thanks for letting us in."

"Anytime," he says.

I pull myself back to look at her.

She tries to step from the barstool, but one of her heels gets caught in the rung. I catch her splaying my fingers across her hipbones and guide her to safety. "You okay?"

She blinks but doesn't answer.

When I assess her body for signs of injury, the only thing I notice is gooseflesh up and down her arms. "Ready to head back?" I ask her softly.

She nods, still unable to speak, seemingly in a daze. I find it rather adorable. But that feeling passes quickly when she raises her eyes and they meet mine. In them I see no need for words. I recognize the look— one of pure hunger.

CHAPTER 4
Underneath It All

Bell

I'm not going to try to deny the desire burning within me. Heat flares as he leads me out of the ballroom, and it only seems to get hotter with each breath I take. I am, as always, completely under the spell that is Ben Covington—whenever he is near me now, then, and dare I say forever? The thing is that I can also tell he wants me just as much as I want him.

He turns around, walking and talking at the same time, his eyes drinking me in all the while. "Can you lead us back this way or should we take the main hallways?"

From the intense look he gives me, the same memory that was interrupted earlier assaults me.

At the frat party his eyes drank me in as if he had been in the desert for days and I were his first cup of water. Shivers went down my spine and I lost my ability to speak, but I didn't really need to because he com-

municated with me by trailing his gaze slowly down my body. He stopped on my low-cut shirt and I was sure he could see my nipples popping out of the thin fabric. My breathing picked up as he lowered his eyes to the short hemline of my skirt. I had a feeling he knew my panties were already soaked, because I saw him swallow a few times.

When his eyes returned to my face, it was my turn. I scanned him in the same way he had swept his gorgeous blue eyes over me—from head to toe. His mop of shaggy blond hair was even more of a mess than usual. I wanted to run my fingers through it and comb it into place. His tall, lean, muscular body looked tan. I wanted to touch it to see how smooth it felt. He wore a white button-down shirt; he seemed to wear those a lot. This one was frayed around the untucked edges, which made it look comfortable—I wanted to wear it. I smiled and with a wicked grin he smiled back. He seemed to understand the purpose of my presence before him, but he didn't release his hold. Something passed between us and then his stare went blank and he finally let go of the cup.

I twirled in a half turn and bounced over to the keg. I was extremely uncomfortable in this overtly short skirt and tried to shimmy it down with one hand as I walked. Claire's shoes were too big and I kept slipping out of them, so I had to walk slowly. On my way back I saw Ben motion as if he was unzipping his pants and make a sucking gesture to the guy he was talking to. At that point I wondered if Claire was wrong about him. Maybe he didn't have a girlfriend? Maybe he liked guys? I wasn't close enough to hear what he was saying, but in the next moment he was laughing hysterically. The sound of his laugh made a heat creep up my chest.

Just as I approached him he turned around. I was sure I had a look of horror on my face because he said, "What?" with another laugh.

"That's not really a part of hazing, is it?" I naively asked, wondering if Claire wasn't kidding after all.

"Fuck no. I was just busting his balls," he said, taking his beer. Then he said, "Thank you . . ."

"S'belle," I finished for him.

"I know your name."

The sound of his voice caused a tingle between my thighs.

That tingling only magnified with the grin he wore. I was surprised he'd remembered. But before I could say anything else, he excused himself and walked away. I tried to mingle, but my eyes kept roving back to him. Claire checked on me. "I told you he was a dud."

I didn't think that at all.

"Do you want to be assigned to someone new? A few guys just arrived and I'm pretty sure they're looking for attention."

"No," I immediately protested.

She raised her hands. "Okay. Your boredom, not mine. I have to get back to it."

I nodded, glad for her to be gone. During our brief conversation, I had lost sight of Ben in the crowd. People were pushing and shoving or maybe they were dancing I couldn't tell. All I knew was the majority of them were drunk. The place stank of cigarettes and beer, and even more disgusting sweat. Even in heels, I was shorter than most of the people and they kept running into me. I threaded my way through the crowd but tripped when one of my heels caught in the fringe on a throw rug. I fell into someone's hard chest and his girlfriend or dream girl looked as though she wanted to kill me.

"Watch where the fuck you're going!" she snarled.

My eyes widened. "I'm so sorry!"

She looked as if she wanted to punch me.

"Relax, Ella, it was an accident. Don't get your panties in a wad." His voice boomed over the music.

I looked up into Ben's eyes. My hero had saved me. He took my elbow and tried to steer me away from the crowd, but the center of the room had turned into a mosh pit and I kept getting dragged behind him. That's when he grabbed my hand. He moved fast and with my pulse pounding he guided me to the safety of the wall. But as soon as we reached it, he *released his grip on my hand. I felt an immediate loss, and my body temperature seemed to dip, as the heat that was there between us had suffused me and I missed it.*

He shoved his hands in his pockets. "Some chicks are vicious," he commented.

I giggled, using the wall to support myself as I recovered.

"I like your laugh," he said, his eyes unknowingly or maybe knowingly scanning the length of my body.

I melted on the spot.

He leaned forward to whisper in my ear, "You look a little shaken. Let me get you a drink."

I was shaken, that was for sure, but not from what had just happened. I snapped out of it and grabbed his arm. "No, let me get you a drink. That's my job." I slapped my hand over my mouth. "Shoot, I didn't mean my job. I didn't mean it that way."

He smirked and then winked. "I won't tell anyone you said the forbidden word. Don't worry."

I swallowed deeply and tried to gather myself as I watched him saunter across the room. God, everything about him was so electric.

When he returned with two cups of beer, he clinked his to mine. "To making it through rush—unscathed," he joked.

His voice was warm, seductive, and I wanted to hear it again. I smiled at him, but before I could say anything else that blank look crossed his face once more. Then just like that, he nodded and turned back around, getting lost in the crowd. I made sure not to lose sight of him again. I refilled his beer whenever it was empty for the rest of the night and he thanked me, but the conversation never went any further. He laughed and carried on with pledges and brothers as I admired him from afar. I couldn't do any of the things Claire, or Stacy, had encouraged, because he didn't give me the opportunity.

The night ended before I expected when all of a sudden Ben stood on a chair and announced to the new pledges their task. They were to comb *the campus for pink lace panties. If I could have run home and changed my underwear, I would have, even though the thought was so unlike me. Once everyone took off, the house was practically empty. Claire had disappeared with one of the guys and so had the other girls I had seen earlier at her table. I had only consumed a few beers, but since I really never drank I was feeling a little tipsy and quite bold. I stared across the room at Ben. He looked insanely gorgeous with one foot propped against the paneling, lazily leaning against the wall while talking on his phone. He flipped it shut and slid it in his pocket and then stared into his red Solo cup. It was then that I made my move because I knew it was now or never. My legs were trembling, so I approached him slowly. I stood in front of him and took his cup again. He glanced up and I swear his eyes were bluer than any ocean I'd ever seen.*

"I'm good," he said. His languid eyes stared into the depths of mine.

The trembling made its way up my body and my fingers started shaking. But when I looked up at him and his hand covered mine, I felt it all over again—the electricity that passed between us. I batted my eyelashes even though I felt ridiculous. "Are you sure?"

He chuckled. "Yeah, I'm sure."

My cheeks flamed because I was pretty sure he was laughing at my attempt to be a dream girl and I decided to drop that act before it even started. He could obviously see through it.

"Did you have fun tonight?"

"What's not fun about naive college freshmen?" He laughed. "What about you?" he asked, low and slow, with a huskiness to his voice that made my nipples harden.

"I've had more fun," I answered, reaching inside myself to find a flirtiness that I never knew I had.

He raised an eyebrow. "Oh yeah? Do tell."

He caught me off guard. I wasn't expecting him to ask me that. I sucked in a breath and reeled for what to say. My eyes darted around the room and landed on a poster on the wall that read LA CÔTE D'AZUR and

I made something up quickly about the place that I knew would turn any guy on. Of course, it was something I had never actually done.

I summoned all my courage and said, "I spent my freshman year in France, and the French Riviera had so many nude beaches that were always fun." I made sure to say it in a sultry seductive tone. And technically what I told him wasn't a lie. I was sure they were fun.

His eyes may have been unfocused, but he straightened his stance and stared at me.

I moved even closer, trying to remember how to breathe.

His mouth quirked and he asked, "When you went to the beach did you do the American thing and wear your bathing suit?"

Something came over me and I became someone else entirely. I wasn't someone made up, but rather someone that knew what she wanted, and suddenly any apprehension or nervousness I had slipped away. I leaned in and whispered, "No, I didn't even bring one to France." My voice sounded saucy.

His eyes widened and I couldn't believe what I had just said. But I wanted him. I wanted him as I'd never wanted anyone else before. I felt different with him and I liked who I was. I was pretty sure he liked it too because when I glanced down at his jeans, there was no mistaking he was turned on. Needing to keep his attention, I bit my lip and averted my gaze, trying to summon the confidence to seduce him. I took a deep breath.

"Everyone was completely nude. There were a lot of beady-eyed older men conspicuously peering over the top of their newspaper."

"And you?" he asked.

"I stripped it all off," I answered confidently.

He swallowed. "You weren't alone, I hope."

Shoot, who was I with? "No. My friend brought me. She was obsessed with staring at naked men." What?

"Were there more men or women?"

"Oh, many more women." I had no idea.

The more detail I described, the more his gaze shifted from my eyes to my body. When I noticed he was interested, that he was paying attention, I became S'belle. I let my inner vixen reign and continued to paint the picture—making it as hot as I could.

Suddenly he cleared his throat. "Excuse me, I forgot I have something I have to do." He turned and walked away without even glancing back.

I couldn't let him go, so I followed him. He went into one of the downstairs suites, but no one answered when I knocked, so I turned the knob. It was unlocked. He wasn't in there, but a light from a corner room told me where he was. I heard the water running and knocked again. I didn't hear any protest, so I walked in and there he was, leaning over the sink, looking at me in the mirror. I quickly closed the door behind me and locked it. I was his dream girl and I wasn't going to give him a chance to ask me to leave. I summoned all my inner strength and went for it, tugging my skirt down and standing before him in my black lace panties. The way he looked at me gave me all the strength I needed to proceed. I had never stood in front of a guy with the confidence I felt with him that day. It was because of the way he looked at me.

His lips parted and he watched me with a reckless abandon that made me yearn for him. I slowly unbuttoned my low-cut blouse that was already partially undone anyway. When I finished with the buttons, I glided my palms down my stomach. I was so nervous that when I slid my fingers in the waistband of my panties, I scratched myself. But the way he watched me in the mirror made excitement surge through me.

"They aren't pink, but will they do?" I asked, finding that same flirty voice I had used earlier.

He turned around to face me but said nothing. I didn't move. His eyes locked on mine and he licked his lips as though he was hungry for me. I took my shirt completely off and then quickly removed my bra. I still wasn't sure if he was going to stay. I thought maybe his girlfriend would win out in the internal battle he seemed to be waging within himself.

But once I twirled around slowly and said, "This is how I looked on the French Riviera," I knew he wanted me as much as I wanted him.

His eyes held me in his stare.

My heart pounded from the heat I saw in his gaze. He strode across the room and caught me by surprise when he stopped short. He stood in front of me and drank me in but didn't move. I looked up at him, but at the want I saw in his eyes, I was done waiting. I tugged on the waistband of his pants and pulled him toward me. His soapy scent smelled fresh and clean and I breathed it in—knowing I'd never forget it.

In a flash he grabbed the back of my neck and found my mouth. His tongue licked my lips. I opened my mouth, allowing him entrance. His lips were warm and soft. My stomach fluttered from the contact. The tingling between my legs became almost painful as electricity surged through my entire body. I kissed him back with the same urgency he kissed me with. The kiss felt different from anything I had ever experienced before; he felt different. He kissed me with a need no one had ever shown me before and I knew then that what we were doing couldn't be wrong.

What I didn't know was that one kiss would change the rest of my life.

Both of us breathless, he pulled back and just stared at me for the longest time. Then finally he touched me. His fingers brushed the lace of my panties. He moved them back and forth, up and down—it was slow, it was torturous. When he slipped his hand inside them, my blood rushed through my veins to that very spot and I was sure he could feel it.

"Are you sure you want to do this?" he breathed against my neck, his fingers right where I wanted them.

My pulse pounded and this time I was certain he could hear it. "Yes," I answered without hesitation.

His small featherlike touches made me gasp.

"Take them off," he ordered.

His tone, his demanding demeanor, made a thrill erupt inside me.

I felt as if my blood were boiling. No one had ever spoken to me like that. He crossed his arms and leaned against the counter to watch me. My pulse raced as I slowly pushed the fabric down my hips and over my thighs, letting it fall to the floor.

"Come over here," he commanded.

I was far too excited as I stepped out of my panties. My breasts had already swelled and I could feel the arousal between my legs. I did as he said. I thought I might do anything he asked. His tone was so deep and sultry that it oozed sex appeal. He swooped me up and set me on the counter. There I sat, naked, before him and I used the same force he had used just a few moments earlier and pulled his head to mine to kiss him. He returned the kiss, his hands sliding down my chest. The heat of his touch erased any doubts I had that he might leave. My nipples pebbled at his touch and when he bent down and sucked on one I thought I might explode.

I had my heels on and ran the toe of my shoe up his thigh.

"Take those off," he told me, his voice sounding raspy.

I quickly kicked them to the floor and this time ran my bare foot back up the same path, curling my toes around his hard cock. He groaned and I wanted to hear that sound again. My hands flew to where my foot had just been and I traced his erection with my fingernails, eliciting another groan from him.

Then he stood back and toed his sneakers off. He stripped out of the rest of his clothing before his eyes cut to mine. His lids were partially hooded, but I could still see the deep blue. God, his eyes were gorgeous. God, was he gorgeous!

He lowered his head. "You sure you want to do this?" This time his tone was soft, sweet, unlike the way it had been up until now.

There was no doubt I wanted this. I nodded and reached my hand back down to stroke his throbbing cock.

"Say it," he said with the force back in his voice.

I bit my lip. "I want you."

"You want me what?"

"I want you to fuck me," I breathed.

When the words left my mouth, there was no question who I was. I wasn't the dream girl I had been told to be—no, I was the real me and I wanted him, all of him. Everything he had to give I wanted to take. The hunger inside me was nearly unbearable. Thank God it didn't take long before he was inside me. He made love to me as no one ever had. I became his dream girl at some point during the night because I wanted to give him everything he didn't even know he wanted. I wanted to do things to him I had only heard about.

The things we did would become a memory that stayed with me for a very long time. When he took me it wasn't with an urgency to just fulfill his own need. It wasn't fast and quick like with other guys I had been with. Rather, it was a night filled with passion, lust, with our deepest, darkest desires being met. It was a dream, a fantasy—one I wanted to live out over and over for a very long time. He must have fallen asleep around five a.m., but I didn't want to close my eyes. I watched him, thinking how perfect he seemed. He was a mix of good and bad, salty and sweet, all of which left me wanting more. I wanted to be his dream girl—always.

But he belonged to someone else and who was I to take him from her? The sudden realization shattered me. I knew I should leave before morning came, to make this easier for both of us. So while he slept, I gathered my things. Before leaving, I picked up his shirt and breathed in the scent and stared at Ben for the longest time. I'd remember him like that forever— all long and lean, suntanned skin, mess of blond hair covering those eyes that were bluer than any ocean. I covered him with his shirt, the one with the frayed edges. When I looked down at him one last time, I couldn't help thinking it looked the way I felt.

Walking backward toward the door, I stumbled over his sweatshirt on the floor. I couldn't resist it. I wanted to keep a small piece of him, so I slipped it on. He stirred, mumbling, "S'belle" as he slept, but he never woke. I crept out of the room, thinking to myself my name was Bell, not S'belle. My Paris high was still strong and even though I had told a few people my name was S'belle because I thought it sounded sexier, I knew he would be the last. I wanted him to own it.

"*Red?* Did you hear me?" he asks, pulling me back to the here and now.

He calls me Red because I flat-out told him when I saw him this past summer to never call me S'belle again. That's not what I wanted at all, but it was for the best. I draw in a shaky breath before I can find my voice. "I know the way back. Follow me."

In the dark corridor he takes my hand in his. An innocent gesture, gallant even—guide a woman through a dark hallway. But to me, there's more to it. *Don't read too much into it,* I remind myself. I squash the emotions entering my brain that can only lead to false hope. But when he squeezes our laced fingers, my stomach immediately starts to flutter. Sex, I tell myself. That's all this could ever be. That's all it ever was. And besides, there is too much baggage between us for there to be anything else.

"You know this hotel is not only rumored to be haunted but has a monumental place in movie history," he says so matter-of-factly that I'm wondering if maybe the attraction I thought was mutual isn't.

"No, I didn't know that. What do you mean?" I try to mask my anxious breathing the farther into the darkness we step.

"The hotel was used to film the prom scene in *Pretty in Pink*. A boxing ring was set up in one of the ballrooms for *Rocky III*. The *Ghostbusters* movie used the Music Room to catch Slimer. Eddie Murphy—"

I interrupt his list of credits, thinking maybe he might be a little nervous after all. "Oh, my brother Xander loved *Ghostbusters*. I used to watch it with him and his girlfriend all the time when we were younger."

We enter into the stainless steel food prep area, where I had seen him earlier tonight. Suddenly a noise, sounding like a loud whisper, echoes through the room and I jump at the same time a scream escapes me. "Oh my God, this place really is haunted." My heart thumps at the thought.

It's kind of hard to make out in the dim lighting, but I know I catch sight of a smirk on Ben's face.

"Hey, it's okay. It's not ghosts, I promise. It's probably just the mice."

I shriek this time. "Where are they? I hate rodents."

He presses me against the cool stainless steel wall before murmuring in my ear, "They live in the walls. They can't hurt you. And even if they could, I'm here."

I'm not sure if he means the ghosts or the mice, but honestly, I don't care about either with the warmth of his body pressed so close to mine. Even in my heels I have to tilt my head to see his face. "I'm not a damsel in distress, you know."

He slides his tongue along his lip before answering me. "Maybe you could be," he whispers.

Lust, want, and need for this man purge themselves from every single one of my pores. I swallow hard, then lean in and breathe him in. It's the same scent I remember from so long ago—nothing more, just soap. Fresh and clean.

"Did you just smell me?" he asks.

"I did," I purr.

"Fuck."

And with his curse his lips crash to mine. His mouth is soft and warm; his tongue is slick and wet. It's a heady combination, but this kiss is anything but sweet. It's frantic, dark, deliriously delicious. Sweet—definitely not. Ben draws me closer and I can feel his hardness against my belly. The thought that I can do this to him so quickly enables me to be bolder. My fingers move to his shirt and I pull it out of his pants. "I thought you were here to save me," I manage between frantic kisses after deciding to be that damsel in distress after all.

Before I can even undo the first button, his hands encircle my wrists and lift them over my head. "I am," he says, obviously spurred on by this little charade. He holds my wrists with one hand, and the other effortlessly unzips my dress and it puddles at my feet. He's good. A lot of practice, I think.

He breaks our kiss and leans back, not letting go of my hands. He hisses in a breath through his teeth in a way that tells me he likes what he sees. I take a second to look around at our surroundings.

"What if someone walks through here?" I'm standing in my black strapless bra and hose before him.

"No one is around this late at night. And besides, remember, I'm here to protect you?" His voice is more of a rasp. "God, you're so fucking sexy."

I look at him. Lips parted. Eyes hooded. And a grin that pierces every nerve in my body. "Take your shirt off," I tell him.

His grin grows wicked. But he doesn't do as I instructed. Instead he glides a hand down the side of my body. His touch leaves an ever-burning flame in its wake. His mouth finds my neck to sprinkle hot, wet kisses up to my ear. "I'll take my shirt off but because I want it off," he growls.

He lets go of my wrists and they fall to my side. I can feel my body tremble as I watch him slowly unbutton his shirt. I can't help remembering the bad boy that rocked my world that one night. My heart pounds louder and faster with every passing second. As the consequences of our night together fade from my mind, I let the joy of this moment consume me. Why? Because in all the years since him, in all the boyfriends I've had, no one has ever made my body tingle with anticipation like him. No one has ever made me feel the way he did.

"Do you feel safer now?" He's got a cocky grin as his shirt falls to the floor and he unbuckles his belt but doesn't undo his pants.

I'm completely absorbed in following the lines of his body. From his biceps, where his muscles flex every time his arms move, to his perfectly defined smooth chest. A six-pack worthy of tracing, with my tongue or my finger. His pants hang low and I can't help staring at the muscles that connect his hipbones or at the thin line of fine hair that trails down and disappears into the waistband of his pants.

"See something you like?" he asks.

His devilishly handsome features have already shifted into a knowing grin when I raise my eyes to him. I swallow, suddenly feeling shy.

His fingers caress my face. "You sure about this?"

I bite my lower lip and nod, once again unable to speak.

His expression grows dark and within seconds I lose sight of those blue eyes that I could look into for hours. He bends to kiss the exposed skin of my chest while his hands go to my thighs. My nipples tighten beneath the lace of my bra as his mouth skates over my breasts and my core aches when his fingers dance in between my thighs.

I mirror the position of his fingers and slowly pull his zipper down. As soon as I do his dress trousers slide even farther down his hips. His hands quickly slide up the silk of my hose, and his palms come to rest between my legs. "Fuck, you're drenched," he pants.

I throw my head back and find my courage to talk dirty. I can do it. "I'm not wearing underwear and I started dripping the moment I saw you."

His guttural groan echoes through the room and in a flash he rips the crotch of my stockings and tugs down his boxers. He pulls his wallet out and once the condom is in place his eyes darken. The tip of his cock presses against me in the very next moment, but then he scans the area and hesitates.

I don't give him time to second-guess things. This is what I want. I wrap my arms around his neck and arch my hips into his. By now our breathing is out of control.

"Take me," I moan.

And that's just what he does.

CHAPTER 5
Show Me What I'm Looking For

Ben

We make our way back through the dark corridors and a little thing called guilt settles in my mind. This girl does crazy things to me and I want her. I've always wanted her. Every time I see her I think about what it felt like to be buried deep inside her.

I lean down and whisper in her ear, "That was unexpected."

She lowers her gaze, allowing her hair to shield her face. "Was it?"

Heat rises in my body as I consider her response. Suddenly a sound of pipes clattering above us has her raising her hands over her head. I pull her close. "Hey, the plumbing here is old. It's nothing to be scared of."

I walk faster and with her hand clutching mine, I open the door and we step outside. This time I not only notice the stars but see the moon is full, bright. The air also seems cooler. Good. I glance around the now-vacant parking lot, then down at her. "Where's the Tate catering truck? Why were you squeezing pans into your car anyway?"

Her lipstick is a little smeared and her hair disheveled, but she's still a knockout. "Tonight's event was all me," she says, beaming.

"All you? You don't work for that asshole anymore?"

She giggles. "I do, but since Tate only does weddings now, he's fine with me venturing out on my own. I just recently started my own event-planning company."

"Tate's cool with that?" I have to say I'm surprised. From what I saw of him over the summer, he seemed like a complete dick-wad.

"His only stipulation was that I not include weddings as one of my offerings, so I've been concentrating mainly on business events. I usually have everything delivered, but the peppered beef skewers from Pebbles are my favorite and they don't deliver."

"Ah . . . I definitely ate my fair share of those."

"Right! They are so good you can't have just one."

I laugh.

She smiles.

The sight triggers something odd inside me, something that I haven't felt in a very long time. Maybe it's just that I don't want to say good-bye to her. I'm not ready for the night to end and I don't think she is either. I consider my options as they run through my mind. But in the end I decide to do the gentlemanly thing rather than what I really want to do—again. I have this strange feeling that she's struggling with her emotions and I know what that's like, as I seem to be doing the same.

"What do you say to a cup of coffee?"

She scans the parking lot. "How did you get here?"

"My bike. Why?"

"I'll agree to go for coffee, but only if you let me drive."

"Are you scared?"

"No!"

"Then what is it?"

"I don't want to get pulled over for not wearing a helmet."

"That didn't bother you the time I drove you home when you'd locked your keys in your car."

"I was in a hurry then. It was different."

I refrain from scoffing under my breath. "Different how?"

"I don't know. If I had to explain to a policeman I'm sure I could think of something."

She's serious. I have to hide my laughter at how fucking cute she is. "Ah . . . those half-truths are easier to tell than lies."

"Yes. That's it." She's got a glow about her that's not from the parking lot lights above us. "And, Ben"—her tone drops to a whisper—"I never got to say thank you for changing my tire." Then she lifts her wrist. "And for the watch."

"It was no big deal. Glad the watch has come in handy." I decide to make light of it. I'd helped her out over the summer by changing a flat and giving her my watch when hers was broken. But I'm glad she seems to have appreciated it. I want to kiss her. I want her to come home with me. But I settle on trying to turn the quickie in the prep kitchen into something more and ask, "You hungry?"

"A little." She smiles with that look of innocence she has about her, and the heat between us is almost unbearable.

I avert my gaze and bob my chin toward the sidewalk. "Come on, I know a great little coffee shop right around the corner with the best homemade pies. We can walk."

Four & Twenty Blackbirds seems straight from a 1950s sitcom, all decorated in red gingham. And in keeping with the nostalgic theme, the homemade pies taste as if they've just come out of Grandma's oven. The mom-and-pop place is dimly lit, but the carousel of pies is lit up in a way I've never noticed.

S'belle rushes over to it and splays her hands across the glass. She points to a slice. "What's that one?"

I step close enough to whisper in her ear, "Oh, that would be their signature triple-crusted berry pie. I know it well."

"Triple crust?" Her eyes are wide as she turns to glance back at me and licks her lips. Fuck, that's hot.

"It's really good." I pat my stomach.

From this angle over her shoulder, my eyes go directly to her ample breasts spilling out the top of what I know is a black lacy strapless bra. My cock throbs at the sight—again. She turns her head in time to catch my stare. Her breathing picks up as if she's reliving things too. I can see it. The light of the case highlights her freckles. I think about the way her eyes drift downward when she talks and how she lets her hair cover her face when she answers me—she's got a quirky, sassy personality, but there's also an innocence there.

"What's that one?" she asks, twisting back toward the case.

"I think that's the sweet potato pie."

She wrinkles her nose. "Vegetables should not be put in desserts."

I raise an eyebrow. "You have an issue with vegetables?"

"I just might," she says sassily.

A smile tugs at my lips. "Me too."

She's flirting with me. I haven't flirted with a girl in . . . Fuck, I'm not really sure I've ever actually flirted, except with her back in college. My pulse is racing and I think it's time to leave the pie display before I push her up against it. I glance around. Only a few people are sitting at the communal table, so we have our choice of seats.

"Come on. The booth in the front has the best view of the street."

We sit by the window and I notice her shiver when our thighs touch. I remove my jacket and stand to drape it around her.

"Thank you." She pulls it closed around her body.

I catch sight of her sniffing it and although I want to bust out laughing, at the same time I find it really endearing and don't want to ruin the moment, so I keep my mouth shut and glance down at my menu instead.

The waitress doesn't wait for us to go to the counter to place our order. Instead she comes over to our table. "Haven't seen you around here in a while," she says.

"I know. I've definitely missed the food."

"Ruby just left."

"That's too bad. I haven't caught up with her in a while."

The waitress whose name I don't know pulls out her small pad of paper. "What are you two having?"

I look across at S'belle and motion for her to go first.

"Coffee with cream and sugar—oh, make it decaffeinated—and whatever pie he's having."

The waitress glances over to me. "Coffee, but not that decaf crap, and two slices of the triple-crusted blackberry pie."

The waitress closes her pad. "Coming right up."

My eyes lift toward S'belle's, and a smile crosses her face. "Good choice."

"Yeah, I've been known to make a few." I grin at her.

A yawn escapes her mouth.

"Am I boring you?"

"No, it's just been a long day."

"Well, drinking decaf isn't going to help that."

"Yes, it is."

I give her a questioning look.

"Coffee is coffee."

Man, this girl is quirky . . . it's such a turn-on.

The waitress returns with our coffees and I watch as S'belle turns hers into a cup of steamed milk. A few minutes later the pie arrives and we sit happily across from each other drinking coffee and eating pie. Glances swap back and forth and there is no doubt what we're both thinking about.

She pushes her half-eaten slice of pie in front of her. "I'm so full. That was delicious."

"Next time we come, you have to try the apple. It's just as good. I promise."

Twirling her spoon in her coffee and staring in her cup, she asks, "Who's Ruby?"

"She's a waitress here I met last summer. I helped her out with a few things and we got close."

"So she was your girlfriend?"

I raise my eyebrows. "No, she's dating my buddy now. I introduced them."

"Oh," she says, and I notice she hasn't looked up from her cup yet.

Hmm . . . she's not jealous, is she?

I feel the need to explain further.

But then she looks up with a raised brow and says, "I would never have pegged you for a matchmaker."

I shrug and grin back at her.

Her cell phone rings and she takes it from her purse. "Excuse me, I have to take this."

I nod.

"Hello," she answers. "No, I didn't forget about it. I'm going to drop it off tomorrow."

There's a pause and her whole body tenses. "Okay, I'll meet her first thing in the morning."

Another pause and her eyebrows scrunch. "I didn't know she wanted to see it first. I'm sorry."

Without a good-bye she presses END on her phone.

"Everything okay?" I ask.

She nods and I swear I see tears welling in her eyes. "That was Tate. We miscommunicated about the bride approving her cake topper for her wedding tomorrow."

I raise an eyebrow. "Did he hang up on you?"

She lowers her gaze. "He was done talking."

Exasperation clear in my voice, I ask, "Why are you still working for that asshole?"

"He's not that bad. And not only do I need the experience, but the connections I'm making are invaluable. My plan is to quit by the end of the year."

"At least you have a plan that includes dumping him."

She looks a little forlorn and rests her elbows on the table with her chin in her hands. "Can I ask you something?"

"Sure."

"Why did you quit your job this summer?" she asks me.

I sit forward and reach across the table for her hands. "Are you serious? That job was never for me."

She giggles. "I was very surprised when you told me you were the wedding columnist for the *LA Times*."

"I hated every fucking minute of it, but like I told you, I was in a bad place. I needed money and wasn't thinking clearly. I didn't realize staying at that job was only adding to my unhappiness."

She sips her coffee as a couple of minutes of silence pass between us—and with all that cream in it, by now it must be cold.

"So, how did you end up acquiring both *Surfer's End* and *Sound Music*?"

"Ah, now, that's a story. . . ."

Time rushes by as I open up to her in a way I haven't opened up to anyone in a very long time. I tell her about my time in Australia—which led to my freelance gig for *Surfer's End* magazine and my eventual takeover of it once I had the money. I explain to her why I finally wrote the piece about the drug cartel that I had investigated—because people deserved to know. I even tell her about training Trent before he went off to college in Hawaii with hopes to compete in surf competitions.

The large silver-rimmed clock on the wall has ticked past two a.m. when I notice her glance up at it.

"Hey." I point to the watch I gave her. "Doesn't that work?"

She glances down at it. "No. It's stuck on seven o'clock."

"Is the battery dead?"

She shrugs. "I'm not sure. It just stopped working, but I can't stand not having it on my wrist."

Cocking my head to one side with a bemused expression, I find I have no words.

"Closing time." The waitress slides the bill across the table.

S'belle grabs for it.

"I got it."

"No, really, let me pay my share."

"Um . . . really, I got it."

She tosses her napkin on the table. "Thank you."

"Not taking that one?" I point to the frayed white cloth near the pie plate.

She stands and pushes her hand against my chest. "No, it's not monogrammed."

Playfulness. Physical contact. Heat, lust, want, and need—all bundled into that one innocent touch. I drop my gaze to where her palm rests, but this time before I can grab her hand to lead her out the door, she pulls it away.

I toss a twenty on the table and walk backward toward the exit. "I got your number now. A discriminating thief."

"I didn't steal them. I borrowed them to clean up my car because I couldn't find any towels. I told you I'm going to return them."

I open the door and let her pass. She takes the lead and I catch up. I make air quotes as I say, "Discriminating borrower."

A frown forms on her lips.

"I'm just screwing with you."

"I know," she says, but I can see a sadness dwelling in her eyes.

The walk back to her car is short. She unlocks her door as soon as we arrive. When I open her door, she hurries to get in.

"Red . . ."

She twists before sitting. "You do know my name is Bell? Don't you?"

I shake my head in disbelief. "Yes, I know that." Of course I know her name, but she told me not to call her S'belle the last time I saw her, so I came up with another suitable name for her.

"Okay, just checking." She turns back around in her seat.

I hover inside the car door, feeling a little nervous for some strange reason about what I'm about to say. Finally I push it out. "I want to see you again."

The lampposts above us cast shadows over her face and I'm unable to read it. She hesitates for a beat before saying anything. But just then our eyes find each other and something passes between us. "You can call me, but I'm not looking for anything but sex right now," she says.

If I said I wasn't shocked as shit by her words, I'd be lying. I mean, what guy doesn't want to hear that? But for some reason I wasn't jumping out of my skin at her offer. The attraction between us is undeniable, and in fact I can feel the heat getting hotter with each passing moment— the way her body reacts when I'm close to her and the way mine aches to draw her near. But there's more than just a physical attraction. I can see she feels it too. It's in her eyes—the way she looks at me.

As I'm standing in her car door staring at her, trying to figure out where she's coming from, I realize what I saw in her eyes earlier wasn't hatred or loathing; it was trepidation. I know because I'm looking at it again right now. And I understand that she has reason to be scared. I can't deny it. So I nod and whisper in her ear, "Who am I to turn down an offer like that?"

CHAPTER 6
Dig In

Bell

In a tangle of sheets, I toss and turn, stuck somewhere between the dreamworld and the real world. I can't get Ben Covington out of my mind. His intense blue-eyed stare. The black tuxedo tailored to his perfect body. A missing bow tie—displaying a glimpse of a rebel. The man knew how to use his hands and mouth and I was completely charmed by him. I wanted more of what I know I couldn't have—a bad boy my family would never accept.

My phone shrills from my nightstand. I jump, blindly reaching for it. Four rings later I finally grab it.

"Hello?" My voice sounds raspy with sleepiness.

There's a slight sigh along with barely audible breathing, and a push of a button that alerts me that I'm being taken off speakerphone. "Bell, are you still sleeping?" Tate's voice asks in an eerily seductive tone.

I look around my dark room but see faint light through the blinds.

I whip my head around and my eyes race to the digital clock beside me. It reads eight forty-five.

"Yes, sorry. Late night."

I hear a squeak of the chair. "Baby, I miss you. Tell me what you have on."

"Tate, that's completely inappropriate."

"I know but I'm desperate. When are you going to forgive me? Please give me another chance."

I sit up and draw my knees to my chest. "We've discussed this. We're over, Tate. We've been over for a long time. Where is this coming from?"

"Dino told me he saw you in the parking lot with some guy last night. Did you let *him* fuck you?" His voice is cold and his question crude. One I would never answer truthfully to him, especially put like that.

"Tate, I'll be by in an hour to pick up the cake topper and bring it by Caroline's for her approval before I drop it off at the bakery. Do you need anything else before tonight?"

"You should have been here already. It's almost nine," he hisses.

I bow my head between my legs, so tired of the temper tantrums and mood swings. I think to myself, *Not much longer. You can do this. Failure is not an option.*

"I'll be there as soon as I can," I say, keeping my anger at bay and then hanging up.

Working for him has been a roller-coaster ride. It certainly didn't help that I mixed business with pleasure and started dating him— made him my boyfriend. Almost a year ago now I came to work for him. Shortly after, right about the time my brother got married, he started asking me out and I didn't see any harm, so I said yes. By New Year's I was over him. We went on dates that always ended with make-out sessions in the car and good-byes at the door. I just wasn't attracted to him enough to sleep with him. One night he pushed for more. I threw him out and told him I would never go out with him again. The next day he apologized profusely and said it wouldn't impact our working relationship. And for the most part it hasn't. He's moody, sure, but he was like that before. He's also brilliant at his job and I've learned so much from him.

Although to be honest I don't love event planning the way he does. At first I thought maybe it was just weddings I didn't care for, so I started my own consulting business. When I started out, I used to think of event planners as the man behind the curtain like in *The Wizard of Oz*. Magicians tasked with creating something fabulous out of a myriad of details, all the while making it look effortless for the client. However, it turns out that I'm more like a firefighter dousing flames in every direction. But since failure isn't an option, I'm going to stick with it. I finally found direction in my life and I'm not going to let myself or my family down.

Rolling out of bed, I know I have to start my day. As I walk slowly toward the kitchen, I pray I have enough cream left for one cup of coffee. Then I can't help grinning. One very large cup of Starbucks coffee sits on my counter with a note in my mother's handwriting.

> *I was in the area, so I stopped by to check on you and drop a few things off. I didn't want to wake you. Pop the coffee in the microwave. Enjoy your day. Call me later.*
>
> Love, Mom

My family is amazing. I don't know what I'd do without them. My mother and my stepfather, Jack, are always stopping by with things for my apartment, food, or just to check on me. I love the company. Leaving home wasn't as easy as I thought it would be. My mother knows what a hard time I've had adjusting to living on my own, and since I haven't tried very hard to make this place a home, she's done it for me. She used to call first, but I told her she didn't have to. It's not as if I have anything to worry about. I haven't dated anyone since Tate. I decided to give up *boyfriends* and concentrate on myself for a while.

My brother River and I have always been close. I'd go as far as to say he was my best friend for the longest time; maybe he still is. We were together so much when we were younger, people used to think we were twins. His wife, Dahlia, and I are also really close. In fact she is the only one who knows about what happened with Tate and also how I really haven't found my dream job. She wants me to quit and has been trying to get me to move in with her and my brother until I figure out what I want to do but um . . . no, thank you! I love them both to death but they are way too cutesy to live with full-time. I'd be pulling my hair out. Actually, who am I kidding? I'm jealous as anything and would love a relationship like that.

And my brother Xander, what would I do without him in my life? He's my rock, my voice of reason. He's always looked after me and guided me when I thought I was lost. But he's also stern and a bit of an ass at times. I have to say now that he has a girl in his life, he's softened . . . slightly. Ivy though, she's amazing and the best thing about her—she makes Xander unbelievably happy and he deserves it.

Yep, I'm the baby in my family, and they treat me like one . . . but I wouldn't trade any of them for the world. I pop my coffee in the microwave, and after it's warmed up, I truck to the shower to get ready to start my day.

Once I'm dressed, I hop in my car and drive to work. My mind keeps wandering back to Ben, to last night. To his delicious body, what I saw of it, and the heat between us. To the way I wanted to touch him everywhere. How fast he got turned on and the things he whispered in the dark—dirty, hot words in the heat of passion. And to how hard I came with him inside me. That had only happened once before—and it was with him.

The Wyatt Events office isn't far from where I live in West Hollywood and I make it there in less than fifteen minutes. Even as I walk down the street, Ben's still on my mind. I wonder if he'll even call me. And if he does, what will I say?

As soon as I step through the modern space, I'm startled out of my thoughts when Tate's voice booms loudly, "Bell, I need you in my office. Now!"

I glance up at the clock—ten after ten. I'm really not late considering that I won't be home until at least ten o'clock tonight. My gaze swivels to Josie, Tate's assistant. She's tall, almost as tall as my sister-in-law, Dahlia. She's waiflike with blond and blue hair—her hair complements her pale blue eyes perfectly. She has a punk rock style that is killer. She took my place when I got promoted to consultant. Her eyes lock on mine and she ever so slightly shakes her head and mouths, "Piss-ass mood."

"Great," I mutter under my breath as I pass her and linger in the doorway.

"Come in and close the door," he says.

He checks the time on his watch, then looks up at me sharply before his eyes drift down my gray dress all the way to the red patent leather pumps I'm wearing. "What are your plans after you go see the bride?" His voice is calm and I'm surprised.

"I thought I'd come back here and gather what we need for the venue."

He nods. "I'd like to take you to lunch. To discuss the evening's schedule of events."

"Sure, of course."

"Okay, then. Thank you for taking care of Caroline's insecurities about the topper. I'm sure it will be fine."

"It's not a problem, Tate."

Just then my phone rings. I never switched it to vibrate because being summoned into his office was unexpected.

"That's all. I'll see you back here around noon and you pick the lunch spot." He slips on his reading glasses and directs his attention to the stack of papers on his desk.

"Hello?" I pull my phone out of my purse to answer as soon as I step out of Tate's office.

"Hi there." Ben's voice flows through the line, warm like molasses, and I melt a little right there in the hallway.

"Hello," I say again before realizing I already said that.

He chuckles. "I want to see you tonight."

"I can't. I have to work."

"Then tomorrow night." He's not asking.

I know that we can't go any further than what happened last night. It's just not possible. But I already told him that. So like last night again—sure, why not? One more time. Sex only. I can do that. "Sure, tomorrow night. I'm at work now, so can I call you tomorrow with the details?"

A laugh echoes through the line. "I'm calling you. How is it you're the one deciding on the plans?"

"Oh, I think you'll like what I have in mind," I coo to him. Josie's head snaps up and I drop my gaze to the floor, unable to look at her.

"When you put it like that, how can I say no?"

"Okay, I'll be in touch tomorrow. I have to go. Bye." I hang up and rush to my desk.

In a matter of minutes fingers are tapping on the wooden surface. "Spill it," Josie says.

"I can't right now. I have to go out to meet a client. But I'll catch you up on Monday, I promise."

She smiles at me. "Please tell whoever that was he is one lucky guy, because I've never seen a look like that in your eyes before."

I shake my head and grab the topper before heading out the door.

After lunch with Tate, we arrive at the hotel to supervise the vendors setting up, answer questions, and discuss the couple's grand entrance, first dance, cake cutting, garter toss, and other details. As the time for the ceremony approaches, we head to the church to distribute the flowers and organize the wedding party. Tate cues the music to begin the ceremony while I keep the processional flowing.

From the ceremony we move quickly to the reception venue to ensure that the wedding party is in their appropriate places for photos to begin. I have to admit that when Tate is in the right frame of mind, we work well together. There's dinner, dancing, cake cutting, and finally the night comes to a close without any complications. One good thing about all the work has been that it's kept me from daydreaming about Ben. The way one hand expertly pinned me to the wall and the other roamed my body. The way he filled me, stretched me, and covered my mouth when I screamed out in ecstasy.

"Want to grab a drink?" Tate asks, tearing me away from my erotic memories.

"Not tonight. I'm really tired. It's been a long day."

"Are you seeing someone else?" he asks.

Exasperation overtakes me, but exhaustion overrules it. "No, Tate, I'm not. My feet hurt. My calves ache. And I just want to go home. I'll see you Monday." I don't bother to explain that it wouldn't be someone *else* anyway since he isn't someone I'm seeing. But that would just trigger his temper. I don't need that.

He nods affably, although his eyes pry into mine, looking for a lie. But there isn't one. I'm not seeing anyone, by definition anyway, and I really am wiped out.

The funny thing about exhaustion is that it plays with your mind. I fall asleep easily but wake up constantly, each time after another dream about Ben. I'm a damsel in distress and he saves me. I'm a patient and he's my doctor. I'm a naughty girl and he's my master.

The next day I decide to sleep in and spend the day lying around trying to keep my mind from wandering—trying not to dwell on the incredible sex Ben and I shared the other night. How he took control, how he set the pace, how much I enjoyed that. How different he is from anyone I've been with and how much I want him. I'm obviously failing at erasing him from my mind and decide to get out for spin class to help chase away some of the pent-up energy I'm feeling.

I come home and make my typical round of calls—Mom, River, Xander—and then I decide it's time for the not so typical call. With a shaky finger I find his number and tap it. Not even one full ring and Ben's voice, smooth and velvety, seduces me through the line. "Hi there."

"Hi," I say, losing my ability to think coherently once again.

"We're on for tonight, right?"

"Yes."

"What time do you want me to pick you up?"

"Oh no, you can't pick me up."

He chuckles. "Okay, then, what is your plan?"

My voice is shakier than my legs at this point. I know I don't have the courage to tell him my idea. "I'll text you the details."

"Sounds mysterious."

"I have to go, but I'll be in touch soon."

"Okay," he says, and it almost sounds as if he's laughing.

I hit END and cradle the phone in my hands. I have to shed the sixteen-year-old smitten girl and be the woman I know he wants. I can do that. I know I can. So with renewed determination I type out what I was unable to say on the phone.

```
Since you seemed to enjoy saving the dam-
sel in distress so much the other night,
maybe you wouldn't mind helping a student
out with a failing grade.
```

His response is immediate.

```
Are you asking for a favor? A grade re-
versal perhaps?
```

Good, he's going to play along.

```
I am and I'm willing to meet you in the
USC Library, fifteenth floor, third room
on the right, to discuss my grade at nine
tonight.
```

```
Just so you know, I don't change grades
for just anyone or anything.
```

I didn't think he'd have a problem with my little game. Ben has always been about sex, and since I can't seem to shake him, or get him out of my system, I'll give him what he wants one more time and then I'm sure he'll never call me again. And even if he does I'll be able to say no— I have to.

I hop in the shower, scrub, shampoo, condition, shave, and moisturize. Once my body is smooth and silky, I pull my long locks into two low pigtails, find a white button blouse, a plaid skirt, a pair of low flats, and I'm ready. I skip the underwear—top and bottom.

I arrive on campus a little early and make my way to the study units. The first thing I notice when I enter the room is the glow of the moon and how it lights up the sky. My eyes adjust quickly to the darkness while I cross the small space to the window overlooking the city, leaning my head against the glass, trying to find the stars. But there are none to be seen tonight. I close my eyes and conjure up my own—they look a lot like the ones in the sky the first night I spent with Ben so long ago. It was a night that changed everything but also a time when things felt much simpler to me.

"Beautiful view," he whispers from behind me.

I jump at his voice, surprised he's already arrived.

"Turn on the lights," he demands in a raspy, husky tone that makes my body clench with need.

I pause for a moment, drawing in a deep breath before moving back toward the door and flicking on the light. I also quickly lock the door. In the bright room my eyes dart to him hungrily. How could I think this time would be the last time? Whenever I see him I only want him more. He gives me that grin that makes my heart stop and I know immediately I won't be saying good-bye at the end of the night.

I take him in a little at a time—he's perched with his broad shoulders leaning against the wall, hair rumpled but looking perfect nonetheless. His arms are crossed over his already unbuttoned shirt, displaying his lean, chiseled abdominal muscles. His jeans hang low, undone but not unzipped. Scrumptious, delicious, and mouthwatering. The tingling between my thighs signifies how ready I am for him.

"Did you not like receiving a failing grade on your paper?" he asks, keeping his voice low and steady.

My eyes lift back to his blue ones—as calm and tranquil as the Pacific Ocean on a clear day. I swallow hard a few times before shaking my head no. Where are my damn words? Oh yeah—stuck in my throat along with the lump from his imposing presence.

His mouth lifts up in a sexy grin and my toes curl from the look alone. This is dangerous territory. The more time I spend with him, the more time I *want* to spend with him. I can't seem to stop myself, but I know that soon enough I'll have to say good-bye.

He scans my body and his tongue flicks out in a way that not only sends a shiver down my spine but causes an almost unbearable ache between my legs. "I can't seem to get enough of you."

I want to tell him he's out of character, but I can't. I want to say something back, but there are no words. Instead I just stare at him, already knowing I'll mourn his absence once we've parted again. But I want him to remember me—that's what this meeting is about.

He saunters over toward me. My nipples peak into tight, hard buds and I'm sure he can see them through the fabric of my blouse.

"What grade do you want your paper changed to?" he demands, standing right in front of me but not touching me.

I squirm at his tone, unable to believe how much it turns me on. "An . . . an . . . A."

He fondles the collar of my shirt. "An A? You're willing to work for this A?"

I nod and stare into his eyes, already wild with desire.

He grins and unbuttons my shirt. "I'm going to kiss you slowly . . . starting with your neck . . . moving down your chest, then your tits . . . where I'll lick your nipples. Do you think you can handle that?"

"Yes, sir. I can handle that," I answer in a mousy schoolgirl tone I'm surprised I found.

"Good, that should raise your F to a D." His mouth twists into a smile that I can't resist returning. He brushes my lips with his but quickly buries his head in my neck. I breathe in his clean soapy scent again and I feel his smile grow wider. His tongue drags across my skin, torturously slow, until he flicks his tongue around my nipple and finally laves it into his mouth. The fabric of my blouse hangs to the side and bares both breasts.

I can't help moaning as he hungrily takes possession of my lips. Wet, hot, scorching, his mouth plunders mine and his tongue strikes against mine greedily. He's aggressive. Taking everything I have to give.

I kiss along his neck and drag my teeth across his shoulder. His fingertips trail up my leg and under my skirt. "Fuck," he mutters. "You're not wearing any panties again."

He's out of character again, but that's okay. I kind of like that he can't keep his mind focused on the role. I've never done anything like this and although it's hot as hell, concentrating on being his student is getting lost in the passion. It's being sucked up by the throbbing between my legs that I want satisfied by him.

When his fingers dip inside me, my moan is drowned out by his louder groan. "You're a good student. Are you only doing this for a better grade or because you're really bad underneath it all?"

"No, I'm a good student who hates a bad grade," I say softly. I'm finding it easier to talk seductively in role-playing mode than as Bell Wilde.

He moves closer to the table and kicks the rolling chair out of the way. He tugs his jeans off and then his boxers. "Come here," he demands.

I stare at him, in all of his glory. He's big, as I remember. I felt it the other night but didn't see it. Thoughts of taking him in my mouth empower me and I walk toward him, etching his naked body into my mind to keep it harbored in my thoughts forever. When I'm close enough he takes my hand, but I reach for him instead. I want to feel the length of him, his girth as it grows larger. I want to taste him. I drop to my knees, but he immediately pulls me back up.

"No, I don't want to do that like this," he whispers in my ear. His voice is soft and normal. He's out of role again and it puts a more serious note in the encounter that I'm not ready for. I have to get us back to playing.

"Okay, but I really want that A."

He grins. "I think you're well on your way to earning it. Sit on the table. Spread your legs," he says, his voice deep again. As soon as I'm in position he pulls me to the edge. The length of him rubs against my belly, stirring the resting butterflies that always seem to be there ready to take flight. He takes his time—milking the moment, drawing out the anticipation of what's to come.

When he pulls away I reach for him and he gives me a single moment of contact where I'm in control. "Wrap your arms around my neck," he demands.

I do as he instructs, but in that second I felt his body tremble—I saw the excitement clear in his eyes.

"A nice girl like you shouldn't be taking my hard cock inside yourself for a better grade."

"I told you I want an A. I'm determined."

"Are you sure?" he asks, and I know he's out of role again, but I pretend he's not.

"Oh, professor, I'm very sure."

In the next moment he reaches for his jeans and pulls out a condom. Once he rolls it on he plunges inside me and positions my hands in his on either side of us, flat to the table. Something about being restrained makes every thrust feel deeper, more intimate. Maybe it's because I'm vulnerable, both physically and emotionally. Again he's in control, setting the pace, but I don't care. I just want to feel him.

"I love fucking you like this . . . you look so hot when your tits bounce up and down."

I wrap my legs around his waist and move as close to him as I can. I think I'm practically off the table.

He gently licks my ear and blows his warm breath over it. His words come faster now. "Your pussy wraps my cock so tight, your legs feel so good around me . . . and you like my tongue licking your ear, don't you?"

"Yes, yes," I pant.

Whether or not we're still role-playing doesn't matter to me anymore. I lose myself in him. In his dirty mouth. He tugs at my lip and I tug back. Then I press my mouth to his and attack it as hungrily as he has attacked mine. I've heard girls say, "I fucked him with my mouth," but I never knew how that could make sense—until this moment. I moan loudly and call out his name a few times and I'm pretty sure he's just as far gone as I am.

In fact, I know he is when he stops my assault on his lips to whisper in my ear, "I'm so deep inside you, so close, I want to fill your pussy up with my hot come. . . . Would you like that?"

I wet my lips, my chest rising and falling rapidly. I nod and answer truthfully, "Yes, yes!" Goose bumps form all up my arms. I cry out this time more frantically, "Yes, yes, yes!" and he does the same as we ride out the wave of unbelievable pleasure we've found together.

CHAPTER 7
Maybe Tomorrow

Ben

I can hear the sound of the seagulls above me as my feet hit the sand. I feel the burn—five miles barefoot on the beach has never felt so good. I take the steps two at a time and plop myself on a lounge chair up on the deck, watching the tops of the palm trees sway back and forth and the waves crashing against the shore. I'm drenched with sweat and decide a shower before coffee is in order.

Opening the glass door to my house, I catch my reflection and think about how the last couple of nights have been somewhat of a mind fuck. While I thought I would be closing the book to my past, instead I opened a new chapter. It feels ironic that the first time I'm more than just hot for a girl she shuts me down, only offering sex. I know I'm not the most romantic guy on the block and haven't always taken women's feelings into account, but something doesn't feel right about a sex-only relationship with S'belle. There's something else there; I can feel it between us. But she keeps pulling back and distancing herself. And since I'm no expert on women, I'm at a loss as to figure out what comes next.

I hadn't been with a woman since the night I was arrested. And being with S'belle—well, felt fucking amazing. Although I hadn't counted the long days, I do the math quickly—yeah, that's seven months without sex, a shit ton of time. Celibacy wasn't a conscious goal. But I'd had my share of too many faceless women. Booze and random hookups, they always went hand in hand. Give up one—you give up the other. The drinking clouded my judgment, and the women were just warm bodies. I wasn't moving forward living that life. I knew I had to stop and I did.

I had pulled my shit together. I started my own company, one with a goal I'm passionate about—helping struggling publications. I want to breathe life back into words, making magazines that improve people's lives relevant. And I hope that's what I'm doing.

Now I have this crazy, absurdly sexy goddess wanting to role-play with me and no strings attached. I know that she's been trying to appear tough, but I've seen the vulnerability clear in her eyes. I know it has to be either because she doesn't trust me or maybe because she doesn't see me as dating material. Fuck.

I look up at the towering fifteen-year-old ficus tree in the middle of the two-story atrium and think, *Am I dating material?* What the fuck? Now I'm asking a tree. But it is what sold me on the place. Well, the tree and the carefree beach vibe—they make the house feel alive. From an outsider's point of view, it must look like the perfect bachelor pad. A circular sofa, a sunken dining area, and bleached walnut floors surrounded by shaggy Moroccan rugs and alabaster lights. Stylish, rogue, sophisticated. The Realtor said it would make any woman's heart skip a beat. Funny, the only women I've had here are my sister and the housekeeper.

I make my way into my bathroom, thinking about when I should call S'belle and whether to tell her I want more of a relationship. The shower tile feels cool underneath my toes and I turn the water on. Muscles aching, I bend my neck to let the hot water massage away the tension. As the warm heat sprays down, I close my eyes and see her. Red hair tumbling over her shoulders, an effervescent smile that does something to my chest, small but fierce—she's got an innocent quality, but it doesn't diminish her seductive allure at all. She's many things and I can't quite determine which of them I'm more fascinated by.

I shut the water off, towel myself dry, and slide on a pair of sweats—thankful it's Sunday. Fuck, I'm horny just thinking about her and I start to second-guess myself. Maybe a casual affair is just what I need right now. My cock grows hard at the memories and demands my attention. Fuck, I've been having sex with myself for so long, it's strange to think I have someone to call. And not just someone—the woman I've never forgotten since our first time together.

I pull my sweatpants down and kick them off. Running my hand down my stomach, I wrap it around my dick and think of how it felt to be inside her. I stare at the ceiling and pump slowly from my balls to my tip, thinking of the noises she made when I touched her, how she screamed when I fucked her.

My breathing comes in short bursts as the past blends with the present and images of her then and now pass through my mind. Her tongue, her mouth, her sweet pussy. My bed is still unmade from my restless night's sleep and I settle my head on a pillow, bending my legs to push my hips up and pump my fist harder, faster. After a few minutes, I slow my hand to prolong the pleasure, but thoughts of her thrusting her hips into mine rush my need for release. I arch my back and tip my head, letting the feeling absorb me as I come. But it's not even close to how I felt last night when I was with her.

Rising from the bed, I hop back in the shower. This girl does crazy things to me. I can't get her off my mind, and just thinking about her gets me all worked up. Thinking what the hell? I open the shower door and grab my phone off the counter to text her.

```
I want to take you out tonight.
```

Her response is immediate.

```
At brunch with my family. I'll be in
touch in a bit.
```

I take a deep breath. *Okay, focus, Ben.* I try to think about all I have to accomplish in the next month before the announcement of my takeover, but my mind keeps reeling back to her. Something is going on in my head. I have an urge to fill the empty void of loneliness that has loomed within the depths of my soul for far too long. Fuck, that's dramatic. What the hell is wrong with me?

I hurry out of the shower and get dressed for the second time in thirty minutes. If focusing won't work I'll refocus. I grab my laptop and take it outside and attempt to throw my mind as far into my work as I can. I finish up the draft press release announcing my company, Plan B, and its holdings to the public. Then I glance down at my phone to make sure I haven't missed a call or a text. I stare at the screen waiting for her to get back with me—if this isn't a chick move, I don't know what is.

"I knocked," a voice says over my shoulder.

I glance up. "I didn't hear the door. Sorry."

"No worries, I let myself in," Serena says.

"You on your way to the airport?"

She puts her hand on my shoulder. "Yes, Jason and Trent went ahead to get the luggage checked in. We were running really late but I had to stop and say good-bye."

"And check on me?" I shoot my sister an inquisitive glance.

"No, well, yes." She looks down at me.

"I'm fine. Really I am. I'm glad that part of my life is behind me."

"Is it?"

I set my laptop on the table beside me and plant my feet on the floor. "Caleb talking to you?"

"Maybe."

I roll my eyes.

"I'm not going to tell you what to do, Ben. Just think about it first."

I study her expression. No judgment, just concern. "Fair enough."

"I can't believe you're doing work on a gorgeous day like today."

"Well, if you'd stop stalling and come to work for me, I wouldn't have to."

"You can hire anyone. You don't need me."

"But I do. Your mind is like a computer."

"No, it's not."

"Yes, it is. I mean, come on, you have a love affair with the number twelve."

Her hands go to her hips. "You know it's my lucky number."

Laughing, I toss my phone on the chair. "Yes, and why exactly is that? Because you're the biggest geek on the planet. And I need the biggest geek to work for me. Social media and apps. Think about it."

"I'm really not that savvy. I just like numbers, especially even ones. And come on, I'm thirty-six and this is turning out to be an amazing year."

I raise an eyebrow, questioning what that means.

"Thirty-six is divisible by twelve." She beams at me.

That sounds like something S'belle would say, and the thought makes me laugh. "Like I said, you're the biggest geek on the planet."

"Gotta run," she says, kissing my cheek and avoiding my umpteenth request for her join me at Plan B.

I shove my hands in my pockets and shake my head, watching her take off down the wooden steps. "Tell Trent to call me," I yell after her.

"I will," she calls back.

I rush to the railing. "And, Serena . . ."

She stops in the sand and raises her hand over her forehead to shield herself from the sun's glare.

"I love you."

"I love you too."

My sister and I have always been close. I know why she loves the number twelve. It's not because it's an even number or because she loves how divisible it is—it's because that's how old she was when our father was killed. I was only five and my memories of him aren't really that clear, but my sister's are. She always told me stories about how much fun we had together, and I think a small part of her will remain twelve so that her memories stay alive. Every day that passes I see how very much like our mother she is and I hope that I'm just a little like my father.

With the sun directly overhead, I realize it's past noon and I should figure out where I want to take S'belle on our date tonight. I snatch my phone and pace the planks of the deck. Fancy restaurant might be too stuffy. Casual might look as though I'm cheap. Bringing her here will definitely look as if I just want to get in her pants. But she did say sex only. Having no fucking idea where to take her, I decide I'm done waiting for her to call. It's not as though she can't take a call in front of her family.

I squint at the screen and press her name. When she answers on the first ring, I know I made the right choice.

"Hello?"

"Red, it's me."

"Me who?" But she asks in a way that I know she knows it's me.

"Ben . . . Ben Covington," I say to humor her.

There's silence for a few moments. "Oh, hey, Ben." She tries for casual, but there's something more than casualness in her tone.

"I haven't heard back from you."

"Oh, right. Sorry."

Is she blowing me off? Well, she'll have to do it to my face. "I want to take you out to dinner."

"When?"

"Tonight." I think I already mentioned that in my earlier text.

"I'm not sure. I have a lot to do."

"I thought we could talk about this thing we have going on."

"Oh, um . . . ," she stutters, clearly not expecting my comment.

"I was thinking Pebbles," I add. Where the hell did that come from? It's the perfect spot.

She's quiet for the longest time, but I don't break the silence. I can play along a little too.

"Sure, I can probably make it. What time?"

Now I know I hear excitement in her voice. "Seven. I'll pick you up."

"Seven thirty and I'll meet you there."

"Okay, but I want you to know, I like to pick a girl up when I take her out."

"We're meeting for dinner. You said you wanted to talk. This isn't a date."

"Call it whatever you want."

She's silent but still there.

"And, Red, I'm looking forward to it."

All she says is "bye" before she hangs up.

I'm not at all surprised she said yes. I know she wants to see me too. If she's scared about going out with me, I'm confident I can prove I'm worthy. As soon I suggested we go to what she had already told me is one of her favorite places, I swear she purred at the mention. I've got this.

CHAPTER 8
Run Run Run

Bell

The mental anguish and sleepless nights have left me exhausted. So I decide on a quick nap after brunch to try to rid my mind of the thoughts I know I shouldn't be thinking, the idea of the two of us as a couple. However, my nap turns into an all-day siesta full of dreams of him. As I bury my head into my pillow, the sound of his voice keeps ringing over and over in my head. *Red, it's me. Ben Covington.* His voice through the line melted any resistance I was feeling toward the idea of seeing him for another date.

I still remember the first time the same thing happened in college. It was our first official conversation. And it was the first time he had strung those two perfect words together, his name, in a way that reverberated through the library and slid into my soul—forever.

The library was filled with people. Hushed voices echoed through the huge space. The enormous arched windows in the back gave the vast space a feel of magnificence while also allowing a powerful amount of light to shine in. Rectangular wooden tables and artificial trees were scattered around, giving the place a more homelike feel. I spent a lot of time there and appreciated those touches. I was premed and biology was kicking my ass. So I often sought refuge in the library to study and help drill everything I needed to know into my brain. Deep within one of the stacks of books, I spotted him. He stood in one of the aisles, lost in his novel. He was the same guy who had captured my attention one night at a party, but who didn't even know I existed.

With his mop of shaggy blond hair and tall, lean, muscular body, he looked like a sexy, younger version of Ocean's Eleven's Rusty Ryan, and my pulse raced at being close to him. Something made me stop; I was frozen in place and couldn't pass him by. He seemed at ease leaning against the shelves, tapping the heel of his black suede sneaker against the mass of books behind him as he read. I wanted to see his face, so I lifted my sunglasses and let them rest on top of my head. Then I ambled along the aisle pretending I was looking for a book. I thumbed one out and slid my finger down the smooth binding, then shoved it back. I repeated this gesture, swinging a glance his way with each push and pull. I got closer to where he stood with every repeated motion. I was an arm's length away before I knew it, but he hadn't noticed. He was lost in his reading, blond hair falling over his eyes. He wore a plaid button-down shirt, untucked, and a pair of worn khaki shorts. Plaid would normally have been a total turnoff to me, but on him it just seemed to fit. Crazy thoughts whirled in my head of skimming the frayed edges of his shirt with my fingers or maybe even unbuttoning it.

A snort, almost a snicker, escaped his throat and I bit down on my lip at the sexy sound. He was laughing to himself about something he was reading. Watching his slow, easy grin made my pulse race. It just seemed so natural, without any pretense. When I ceremoniously took out my next book, I accidentally dropped it, I was so lost in watching him, in watching the seductive way his mouth tipped up at the corners. He *glanced at me, meeting my gaze as he effortlessly bent to retrieve my book. I stared into his blue eyes, but only for a moment. His eyes were intense and I felt magnetized by his proximity. I could tell by the way he moved that he was sure of himself, full of confidence, but it seemed less like arrogance and more of ease. His hands gripped the book on the floor while my eyes swept up to his other hand, to the spine of the book he was holding. He was reading* The Adventures of Huckleberry Finn, *and seeing its title rendered me utterly speechless. What an odd book to be reading with such in-depth interest, I thought.*

That slow, easy grin that had to melt every girl's heart turned into a smirk. "Kama Sutra," he said, raising an eyebrow.

I wasn't really listening. I didn't hear what he said. My heart pounded as my gaze swiveled from his book to his face—tanned skin, eyes bluer than the sky, cheeks flecked with just the right amount of stubble. He was rugged and handsome and hot.

My voice sounded dry. "What?"

"The Illustrated version of A Lover's Guide to Kama Sutra. *You're looking for help? In a library?" he asked in utter seriousness.*

"No, no. No, I'm not." Horrified, I grabbed the book from him and shoved it onto a shelf. But I noticed that my skin tingled where it had brushed his. Of all the books in the world, that's the one that I had to be touching—are you kidding me? It took me a few seconds to collect myself, but somehow I kept the conversation going.

I pointed to his book. "Homework?" I asked, raising an eyebrow.

He lifted his hands surrender-style, the book still gripped tightly. My eyes shot to the bare skin that showed between his shirt and shorts and I began to feel flushed when an ache radiated between my thighs.

"No. You caught me. Just hiding out reading one of the classics. Fucking Huck Finn. Something he said turned my mind in a way it shouldn't have." He laughed.

"What?" I asked. My curiosity had been piqued.

"Have you ever read it?"

I shook my head no.

"You can't judge me, then," he said, his voice deep and husky. He opened the book and recited the line that had him cracking himself up. "'That is just the way with some people. They get down on a thing when they don't know nothing about it.'"

The way the words rolled off his tongue—it was hot; he was hot. I knew what he was laughing about and my heart thudded in my chest as I tried not to giggle. I moved closer, drawn to him. As soon as our eyes locked again, there was a moment of pure vulnerability, and the silence that wrapped itself around us seemed to speak volumes. Or that was what I thought until he blinked and handed me the book.

"You should read this if you have time. It really is one of the best books ever written."

I did giggle at that. "Right. I'm sure it's up there next to Tom Sawyer."

"How'd you know?" He winked.

My stomach fluttered with desire and I couldn't help grinning.

He started to walk backward and I really wanted him to stay. When he stopped at the end of the aisle, I thought he'd changed his mind. But instead what he did captured my heart. He put both feet together and leaned forward slightly to gesture that he was tipping an imaginary hat and said, "It was nice talking to you . . ." He paused, waiting for me to fill in the blank.

"S'belle," I finished for him, not knowing why I'd gone with my nickname from my time abroad.

"S'belle." He grinned, the upward tilt of his lip making him even more charming. He stood straight again and I swallowed, meeting his gaze. I breathed out a sigh and before I could even ask his name, he disappeared around the corner.

I yelled, "Wait, I didn't catch your name."

From someplace in a distance I heard his deep husky voice call, "Ben, my name is Ben Covington."

. . .

"*Ben,* Ben Covington." They are the same words that traveled through the Crystal Ballroom and back into my heart a few nights ago. The same words that melted through the phone line a few hours ago. And the same words that make my body mold to the mattress right now with a want I shouldn't be feeling.

My fingers slide down my stomach on their own. My body trembles at just the thought of his kisses and the way his tongue flicked against mine with urgency. I circle my warm flesh and think about the desire that flows between us, the way he looks at me with those languid blue eyes, and his charming demeanor. And I know I have to satisfy this longing before I see him. A sigh escapes my throat as I apply pressure where I need it because there's no way I'm sleeping with him at the restaurant. And there's no way I'm bringing him back here or going to his house. All of those places are too intimate. No, we'll eat dinner together tonight and I'll plant the seed for one more rendezvous before I say good-bye.

CHAPTER 9
Towers

Ben

I cruise into Brentwood on my bike with plenty of time to spare. The town isn't that big and I locate the restaurant right away. The sign in front reading Valet Parking throws me for a loop. The name *Pebbles* had me envisioning a BBQ pit with picnic tables, but what I'm looking at is anything but. A large curved window gives me a peek into the intimate setting inside. It looks pretty nice, which I'm relieved about because I would have hated to take a girl to a dump on a first date.

I skip the valet since I don't like anyone touching my bike. I find a small parking garage around the corner and pull into it. I've been to this town a few times, but the only thing I really remember about it is the white dogwood trees that line the streets. With my bike secure, I walk slowly down the street looking around at the small shops, all very different but inviting to passersby. The old-fashioned streetlights display banners that read MERRY CHRISTMAS. It's a little early for that—isn't it?

The town looks to be a little larger than Laguna, and a bit quainter, but nowhere near as trendy or diverse. I pass a florist, some retail shops, a few galleries, and many restaurants and bars. People are walking as though they don't have a care in the world, just browsing, talking, and laughing. One store in particular catches my eye. It's a bookstore named Fiction Vixen. My love for old books draws me toward the two stacks in the large windows located on both sides of its front door. The books are displayed in a Christmas-tree-like fashion with strands of lights wrapped around them.

Arriving at Pebbles, I pull open the heavy glass door only to find that the place is crowded. I weave my way through the people waiting in the entry and stop at the hostess station.

"Can I help you?" the cute girl says.

"I'd like a table for two."

"Do you have a reservation?"

"No, do I need one?"

She glances down at the book of names in front of her. "I'm sorry but you do. We're full tonight."

I lean down. "Are you sure you can't find a small table for two tucked away somewhere? It's just that this is my first date with a girl and I was really hoping to impress her. I don't want to look like the jackass I am for forgetting to make a reservation." I quirk a smile and stand a little closer.

She glances up at me and her eyelashes flutter. "That's really sweet. Let me see what I can do."

She scans the seating chart before her.

"How about right there?" I point.

"One of the window tables? Those are always the first ones requested."

I shoot her a wink. "So my date would be really impressed if I got us one of those?"

She smiles at me as she erases the name printed above the table. "Your name, sir?"

With my biggest shit-eating grin I say, "Ben. Ben Covington."

As she leads me to the table, we pass a granite-topped bar where a few couples perched on the stools are lost in deep conversations—hands on knees, faces a little too close, hooded eyes. I remember thinking just recently the only girl I ever came close to flirting with besides my long-term girlfriend was S'belle. But maybe that wasn't entirely true. Then again, it depends how you define flirting. To me it means you have game in mind. With the hostess I was just pouring on the charm, not trying to bed her. So I stand by the idea that I've never really put myself out there in flirting mode. But something tells me I'm about to before the night ends.

"Let me know if I can help you with anything else," the hostess says before leaving me at a table near the window with two menus.

I check the time on my phone; it's seven twenty-seven. I sit here wondering if maybe S'belle isn't going to show and find my nervousness disconcerting. Not a minute ticks by before I spot her. Her back's to me and she's talking to the hostess. The lights from the street cast shadows on her long red hair. But it's as vibrant as ever against her bare back. She pulls it to one side as she laughs at something the hostess says. Oh, fuck, is that girl blowing it for me? She twists in my direction as the hostess points over to me. Fuck, I think I'm busted.

I stand up and she smiles at me. My body hums at the sight of her approaching me—she's wearing a halter top that reveals a hint of cleavage and tight jeans that hug her shape perfectly with the highest fucking heels I've ever seen. She sashays toward me and the thin gold chains hanging over her shapely chest swing back and forth. She isn't a girl anyone could pass by without drooling over. I consciously close my jaw that I know is hanging open. At our table her eyes look me over—head to toe. I see it plain as day and I have to pull back the knowing grin from my lips.

"Hi there," I say with a grin, and lean in to kiss her.

"Hi," she answers, turning her face so my mouth lands on her cheek.

"You look beautiful." I'm trying my best not to be affected by the kiss snub.

"Thank you," she says softly, and there it is—that look of innocence that sets my body ablaze. Okay, I'll let the snub pass. Who knows? Maybe she has some crazy role-playing game cooking in her head.

I extend my hand and she places hers softly in my palm so that I can bring her hand to my lips and kiss it. Her smile is wide and bright as I let her hand go.

"Madam," I say as I pull out her chair. Maybe I could be the maître d' and she could be a demanding patron?

She sits and sets her phone on the table and her purse on the floor. When she sits back up, I breathe in her scent as I take her napkin and place it on her lap. Leaning down, I let my warm breath caress her neck. "In case you want to add it to your collection before it gets dirty."

She looks up at me. "Very funny."

"I try to be."

"Oh, I think you try to be more than that."

I raise an eyebrow. "Please explain."

"Kelsie told me how charming you are."

There must be a puzzled look on my face. "The hostess," she clarifies.

I shake my head. "Ah yes. She was very . . . helpful."

Her mouth tilts with the beginning of a smile.

I lean even closer, hovering just above her lips. "I can be . . . very helpful too. Especially to damsels in distress and failing students."

A slight pink blush colors her skin, and it's such a turn-on that she can play dirty but gets embarrassed talking about it.

Our eyes lock for a few intense moments until I break the spell. "So, how was your Sunday?" Just like that the night begins like a real date. The funny conversation leads into discussions about our day, and when the waitress approaches to take our order, we both ask for sparkling water with lemon and peppered beef skewers.

S'belle looks over toward me when the waters are placed in front of us. "You don't drink?"

I cast her a tentative look. "I do. Well, I don't."

She scrunches her eyebrows in confusion.

I laugh. "That sounded moronic. What I mean is I don't have a problem or anything. I just think it's healthier for me to abstain."

She doesn't laugh or question why, but instead she says, "I get it. Same here. I had fallen into a rut where I was drinking more than I should and I found I wasn't moving forward in my life."

I nod and swallow the lump in my throat at how much what she just said mimics my life over the past three years. I look at her and raise my glass. "Perfectly said."

We end the topic there, but that short conversation tells me we might have more in common than either of us realizes. I look across the table at her. The glow of the candle, the intimacy of the small space, the seductive outfit she's wearing—everything makes me want to get closer to her.

Her phone buzzes and I can see the name Tate Wyatt flash across the screen. She silences it and switches her phone to vibrate. "Sorry. We have a big wedding next weekend and I'm sure Tate is already pondering the to-do list."

I try to read her. She seems nervous or maybe just uncomfortable. "Well, that only proves my point—he's an asshole."

"Ben. You don't even know him."

"I've seen and heard enough."

She shakes her head. "Tell me something about your job."

"Well, I got awesome news today. My buddy Beck finally found someone to run his father's bar and is coming to work for me full-time this week." I lower my voice as I finish the sentence. It's a casual move. Almost too smooth. With the overhead music providing ambience and the bar so close to us, it is loud and I'm keeping my voice softer than I normally speak.

She leans forward. "I'm so sorry, but I can't hear you very well."

I slide into the empty chair next to her and repeat myself. "My buddy Beck finally found someone to run his father's bar and is coming to work for me full-time next week." This time I speak directly into her ear and savor the closeness. I'm supposed to be flirting with her, in charge here, but her scent overwhelms me and the thumping in my heart seems to have spread throughout my body. She's turning me on beyond control.

She inches away from me, but I can see her pulse beating in her neck. "What does he do?" she asks a little hoarsely. I've heard that tone before.

Her hands are on her glass gripping it tightly. One slides to the table.

I grab my water and our hands graze but don't fully touch. The heat of her hand seeps down my arm—electric. "He's a whiz at social media. He's just what I need to push forward and embrace the technology side of journalism."

Her breathing picks up and her green eyes bore into me. "You mean like apps, Twitter, and Facebook—social media?"

"Yes. Both *Surfer's End* and *Sound Music* are so behind they don't even have issues available online or apps to accompany them."

"Oh, you don't know how to do that yourself?"

Our salads arrive. I take my fork in my hand. "No, I have no idea how to do something like that."

She stabs her fork into a cherry tomato. "I do. I taught myself. It's really fun. Last week I created one for my event-planning company," she says, and this surprises me for some reason.

I lean forward on the table, bringing our bodies even closer together. "Are we role-playing?"

She breathes a breathy sigh. "No, I'm serious."

Now I'm really curious. "I'd love to hear about it."

"It's no big deal. I designed an app for clients to download so they can create their dream event. I use it as a start for planning. Most of the time clients have no idea what they want, so the app helps me understand them a little better."

I ponder what she's talking about for a moment. "So you know what your clients want before they do?"

A huge smile crosses her lips. "Yeah, I guess I do."

"That's fucking brilliant."

She shrugs. "It was easy."

"Maybe I should hire you, then?"

"I'm not interested in running a magazine."

I nearly spit a piece of lettuce out of my mouth. "I mean to help launch Plan B's holdings into the social media arena."

"Oh, I could show Aerie."

A devilish smile crosses my lips at the thought of the outburst that would come if I gave Aerie one more thing to be responsible for. Rattling her can be so much fun. "I think she has enough on her plate."

S'belle sets her fork down. "You get along with her?"

I nod. "Yes, we work well together."

"Have you met Jagger?"

"I actually met him when I lived in New York City. Small world that we're both here now."

"He's my cousin."

"I know." I smile.

"You do?"

"Yeah, he told me. He stops by the office once in a while to have lunch with Aerie, so we've kind of reconnected."

"How did you meet? In New York City, I mean."

At this point I'm not sure how much to tell her but decide to just tell the truth. "He was dating the sister of a girl I was somewhat seeing back then."

"Oh." Her face drops. Then her phone vibrates on the table and she glances at the screen. "Excuse me one minute. I really should take this."

I nod, thinking I'd love to know what that asshole's problem is.

She gets up and walks over toward the bar. I watch her body tense, but she quickly ends the call. When she comes back to the table, she doesn't make mention of him but resumes eating her salad quietly and I do the same. She squeezes more lemon into her drink and then onto her lettuce. I'm so intrigued by her I can't resist staring.

"What?" she asks.

"It's nothing."

She sips the glass of sparkling water and her head tips back slightly to expose the seductive lines of her throat and chest. I think for a moment she's moving that way on purpose—maybe flirting with me.

I drag my mind off her body and bring my eyes back to hers. "So, you're pretty busy at work?"

"Busy isn't even the right word. It's crazy right now. So many weddings and Tate keeps pushing more onto me. Plus, I'm trying to get my own business off the ground."

"Do you have a name for it?"

She laughs. "Believe it or not, no. I'm not so sure it's what I want to do. Giving it a name and then abandoning it somehow seems more like a failure. I have one more event planned for the rest of the year and it's Ivy's release party. And I got that job because she's my brother's girlfriend. I actually got the job with Tate because he knows my stepfather."

"But you love it? Event planning?"

"It's what my family thinks I'm good at."

"What about you? What do you think?"

She shrugs. "Some direction is better than none."

At that I want to take her into my arms, to reassure her that she should do what she wants. She's strong, confident, and has what it takes to succeed in anything. But just as I reach across the table, two steaming plates of peppered beef skewers and island rice are placed in front of us. We both push our salads to the side.

"Smells so good," she says, and from the look in her eyes she's hungry for more than food.

"You just ate them a few days ago," I point out. "I hope you aren't going to be sick of them."

"Oh, I never eat the food I cater in."

I nearly choke on a piece of pineapple in my rice. "Why is that? Because I have to say now I'm almost afraid to ask. And even more afraid to eat this."

She giggles. "It has nothing to do with the food. I just have to smell it all night, so by the time I get a chance to eat, the last thing I want is what's been under my nose for hours."

"I get it. I guess. So, who are the guys who carried the empty pans to your car?"

"Matt and Dino? They work for me when I need help."

"The taller one, I think he has the hots for you," I tease her.

Her eyes dart to mine. "We're just friends. He's not interested in me."

I nod, thinking she must be blind if she doesn't see it. "So you don't have a boyfriend?"

She bites her lip. "No. I wouldn't have . . . well, you know . . . if I did."

"I do know." I give a low laugh, trying not to growl at the visions her words elicit.

She drops her gaze and her hair falls across her face. "Do you have any specific fantasy you'd like fulfilled?" she asks. "Working girl, sex slave, nurse?"

Her words come out fully charged, arousing me instantly. Fuck me if my cock doesn't start to throb beneath the denim of my jeans. But as I sit here looking over at her, my answer on the tip of my tongue, the reality of it all comes crashing down on me. I suddenly see through the curtain of red. She's trying to be who she thinks I want her to be. Just like her job. She's doing what she thinks she should do. And I don't know if I'm insulted or flattered, but I do know the games are over.

My words come out in a biting tone. "What if that's not what I'm looking for?"

Her brow creases with tension as her eyes lift back up to my face. "What do you mean?"

"What if I want more than a game and a quick fuck in a secluded location?"

"Well, that's not what I'm looking for. I told you that."

"What are you looking for?"

She shrugs. "Not something I know will never work."

"How do you know that if you're not willing to see what happens?" I try not to sound insulted.

"Come on, Ben. We both know the only thing that will work between us is sex."

"Well, shit, I guess you have it all figured out. Okay, then, I choose the john. Why don't you go on into the bathroom and I'll be in in a minute? Just tell me how much up front."

She gapes at me in disbelief.

"What? You asked. I'm telling you. No need to finish dinner. Let's fuck and get it out of our systems—for today anyway."

She shrugs again with clear disappointment. "I'm not fucking you here."

"Good, then. Can we finish our dinner and our date?"

"Are you testing me?"

"No. I'm trying to show you that maybe there is more and maybe you could at least give me a chance before you make assumptions about me."

"Okay, then, so if sex isn't the only thing you're after from me, how about we start over?" There's a strange twinkle in her eyes that looks a lot like a challenge.

"There's nothing I'd like more," I say, suppressing the urge to reveal the satisfaction I feel at her words.

"As friends only," she adds as if it just occurred to her.

I try not to let my jaw drop. Obviously she thinks I can't go without sex. She doesn't know me as well as she thinks she does. "Fine. Friends only."

"Since we agree, I think we need to set some guidelines."

"Guidelines?" I raise an eyebrow in challenge.

She nods and her hair bounces effortlessly over her shoulder with her movement. "Yes, guidelines."

"Do you set these guidelines with all the men you call friends? Matt? Dino?"

"No. But I haven't slept with them either."

"Okay, then." It's easy to agree because I'm beyond relieved to hear that.

She eats a few bites and I watch her, waiting to hear these guidelines, mostly because I'm intrigued.

"Are you going to tell me what they are?" I finally prompt.

She pats her lips with her napkin. "Oh yes, of course. One," she says, holding up her thumb, "we can be friends as long as we keep it between us."

I guess I understand. Only two people in my life know I'm interested in S'belle, and I got all kinds of warnings from them. But really I want to laugh that I've become a dirty little secret.

"Two." She holds up her index finger. "We will not talk about my brother or his wife."

She licks the sauce off her finger when she's done speaking—and if she only knew how turned on I am watching her. This friends thing might be harder than I think. But I keep quiet and don't argue. And besides, I have no intention of discussing my ex-fiancée and her husband with her anyway.

However, I do have to stop her before she moves on.

"Red, you can say Dahlia's name. I'm fine with it and I think she'll be fine with us as well." I assume S'belle already knows Dahlia and I have talked and that she's come to terms with the fact that I cheated on her with S'belle in college.

She shakes her head fervently. "I mean it, Ben. My family is not to know."

I hold my hands up. "Okay, okay. I get it. What else?"

When she puts a third finger up and it's her middle finger, I can't contain myself. I don't want to appear immature, but she is being so serious—setting guidelines for a friendship that we both know is much more than that. I can't hold back as laughter escapes my lungs and I have to rest my hand on my stomach to try to stop myself.

She looks over at me before setting her hands on the table and pushing up. "You're so immature," she huffs.

"Wait, go on, I'm good. I'm sorry."

She narrows her eyes at me. "I'm not joking around. I just got my life on track and I can't be derailed."

Okay, so again I'm going to be the bigger person and not take offense, but why does she think I would derail her life? I run a hand through my hair as I consider how to respond. "I hear what you're saying." I bring my hand down and rest it over hers on the table. "But, Red, you and I both know a friendship-only relationship isn't going to be easy." I inch forward and close my fingers around hers. Sparks ignite between us, and any anger I might have been feeling dissipates.

She pulls her hand away after a few seconds, but her trembling body tells me she feels what I feel. "And three, no touching," she says quickly. Almost as though, if she didn't say it right, then she would change her mind. She goes on to add to her list that we can go out but we will meet each other in public places only.

I have to commend her; she's tough. But I can do this. I can see through it. She wants me to prove to her that I'm looking for more. And I will. Who knows? It might even be fun. For sure, it will be a challenge.

She bites her lip and returns my stare. She's nervous. I shake my head and draw in a deep breath. "I know you better than you think, you know."

And although I'm not at all sure that her guidelines are realistic, I see them as her security blanket and for that reason I decide to accept them . . . for now.

She drops her eyes again.

"Red, look at me. I know you bite your bottom lip when you're nervous. I know you're smarter than you like people to know. And I know that I'd like nothing more than to prove to you that I can be your friend. So I'll agree to take it slow, but I can't agree to the no touching." My eyes skim her face and fall slowly to her chest before rising back up. The tension builds between us as the evidence of her arousal spreads across her chest in the form of a flush.

She stares at me for a while before speaking. "It's all or nothing," she says, her tone lightly squeaky.

I inhale a deep breath. "Lucky for you I'm an all-or-nothing kind of guy."

Her eyes sharpen and she starts to sputter in a way that makes no sense. "So, um, is that a yes, a no . . . ?"

I'm pretty sure I've flustered her. I sit back in my chair and try to figure out what we just agreed to, because like her I have no fucking idea. Then finally I give her a pointed stare. "What happens to your guidelines when you change your mind about only being friends?"

She swallows. "I don't see it going that far," she says firmly.

I'm okay with letting her think that . . . for the time being.

CHAPTER 10
I'm Ready

Bell

Today is Monday, and with no events until Friday I need to get to the office on time. Maybe if I pull the covers over my head, time will reverse and give me another hour of dreaming. No such luck, I know. I stretch and stifle a yawn before swinging my bare feet down onto the hardwood floors. This morning feels particularly cold for California in October.

I pad to the bathroom and blast the hot water, brushing my teeth while I wait for it to warm. By the time I finally slink into the shower, the small bathroom has already filled with steam. If only the water could knead away all of my tension, but with a low-pressure shower and so many knots, my chances are slim. I don't know what I'm doing with Ben anymore. How could I have thrown a friends-only relationship out there last night? First of all, that's not what I want and second, I should stay away from him. And what was he doing accepting my challenge? What if this fortifies our relationship instead of destroying it?

No, that won't happen. Chances are he'll never call me again after last night anyway. I reach for the shampoo and scrub my head before conditioning. I skip the shaving—no need for that and I'm the only one to blame. Rushing around, hoping to put some distance between myself and my thoughts, I concentrate on getting ready. I slide into a pair of comfortable underwear and a no-frills bra, pull a dark gray jersey knit dress over my head, and slip into a pair of black boots, skipping the hose. I run to the kitchen to check the time and decide to go light on the makeup to have time for Starbucks. I dry my hair into a sleek curtain, swipe some blush on my cheeks, a little lip gloss and mascara, and I'm ready to go.

With my leather jacket in hand I grab my keys and rush back to my room for my phone. I hear the beep from it before I even cross the threshold—two missed calls. One from my mother and the other from Ben. I head toward the door, thumbing to my voice mail and listening to his first.

"Look, I thought we could maybe go out tomorrow night with Aerie and Jagger. Friends do that, right?" A few seconds of soft breathing. "Go out with other friends, I mean. Just to clarify. Let me know what you think. In the meantime I'll plan something."

I try not to stumble down the flight of stairs while I listen to the message. I play it again as I walk through the courtyard, this time absorbing the sound of his voice. Again I wonder, what was I thinking last night? Spending more time with him was just going to make this harder.

I listen two more times before moving on to my mother's message. She was just checking on me and wanted to know if I was interested in coming over for dinner tomorrow night. While I walk to my car I call my mother back to tell her I can't make dinner—that I'm having dinner with a friend. I just have to find a way to make sure Jagger doesn't tell my mother who the *friend* is and Aerie doesn't tell Dahlia either. Things are already getting messy. This is exactly what I didn't want. I should have just said no.

My phone rings as I circle the street looking for a close parking place. Working in West Hollywood has its advantages and disadvantages, and parking is definitely a disadvantage. I don't even look at the screen as I hit ANSWER on my steering wheel.

"Hi there." Ben's voice exudes seduction.

"Hi," I manage in a much more friendlike tone.

"Did you get my message?" His voice is low and sexy.

"Friends don't talk to friends like that," I blurt out.

"Like what?" He laughs, and the sound is almost like a caress that wraps around my bare legs and up my dress like a gust of wind.

"Sounding like sex."

He laughs even louder. "No one has ever told me I sound like sex, but I'll take that as a compliment."

"You're doing it again."

"Is this better?" This time his voice is deeper, richer, but it still sounds velvety smooth to me and full of promise—promises I've taken off the table.

"Yes," I agree because I think that even if he sounded drunk, exhausted, or disoriented, I'd still feel the dampness spread between my legs from his voice alone.

"Good. Okay, then." A soft chuckle escapes his throat. "Tomorrow night I'll pick you up at seven."

"I'll meet you," I insist.

"Red, that's ridiculous."

"Ben, I'll meet you or I'll pass."

"Fine, I'll let you know where."

"Okay. I have to go before I'm late for work."

"See ya, Red," he says, and hangs up.

"Bye, Ben," I breathe over the empty line.

I find a spot a little farther away from the office than I'd like and park. Grabbing the tray of coffees, I walk fast and pull open the showroom door. I look around in shock. It's a complete mess. Walls are down, drop cloths are everywhere, and Tate is leaning against my desk with his arms crossed. His face is unreadable. Tall, dark hair, suave, and always put together, he's a man of style and confidence, but he's also very self-absorbed and, as Xander says, a bit of an asshole.

I stop quickly to drop a coffee off to Josie. "Good morning."

Her back is to Tate, so she mouths, "Thank you. Piss-ass mood," while she rolls her eyes. I pass her desk and approach Tate with apprehension. I want to look at my watch, but it stopped a long time ago and pulling my phone out would be way too obvious.

I raise the tray. "Coffee." I offer it to him with a smile.

He straightens and his suit hangs perfectly, tailor-made, I'm sure. He looks at his watch before taking the coffee and then smiles. "How'd you know I needed this?"

"Intuition."

"Or ass-kissing."

I shrug and let that pass without commenting on it. "What's going on in here?"

"Time for some renovations. The place needed a pick-me-up. I'm thinking of trading the Harrods look for something more Vera Wang."

"So you're trading the black-and-white toile for platinum modernism?"

"Exactly." He grins and raises his cup. "I knew I hired you for a reason."

I toss my purse in my desk drawer and take a seat.

He walks toward his office and then turns. "I'll be out of town until Friday. We have a new client coming in on Thursday that I'd like you to take care of, so be on time."

"Sure, who is it?"

"Romeo Fairchild, the governor's son. His fiancée is a wreck and he wants us to handle the entire wedding."

"That shouldn't be a problem."

"He wants the event to take place the day after Thanksgiving," he says, and his grin is lascivious.

Yeah, he can be a bit of an asshole.

I watch him slam his door and catch Josie's glare. She averts her eyes to the break room and stands, heading that way. I nod and wait a few minutes before taking my coffee and joining her. The break room doubles as a meeting spot when the conference room is taken, so it's decorated to the nines—bright orange focal wall, dark wooden table, white leather armchairs, and a large vase filled with artificial birds-of-paradise adorning the corner. I close the glass door behind me and take a seat, sipping my coffee while Josie stares at me.

"What?" I ask.

"There's something different about you." Her eyes flicker over me.

I roll my eyes. "You're so dramatic."

"Oh, that's the pot calling the kettle black."

I laugh. She's right. I usually am up and down with Tate's moods, but today I didn't let him bother me and it paid off. "So, what spurred the décor change?"

"Don't change the subject. Now spill it. Who were you talking to that got you all hot and bothered the other day?"

"I was not hot and bothered."

"Oh yes, you were."

I smile. "Well, there's this guy I've known for a while. The thing is, we have a sordid history and I didn't think getting involved with him was a good idea."

"Did you fuck him?"

"Josie!"

She twirls a piece of blue hair around her finger. "Well, did you?"

I don't answer and let my silence speak for itself.

"Hey, if he's good in bed and gives you that glow, I say screw the rest."

I laugh. She makes it sound so easy—if only she knew.

Acabár isn't that far from my apartment. In fact, it's even on Sunset, so I decide to walk. The two days since I've seen him have felt more like two weeks and I can't wait to see him again. The sign is in my sights when I see him walking my way and smile broadly. White button-down shirt, slightly faded jeans, black boots, and that smile that makes the apex of my legs pulse. His mop of shaggy blond hair is disheveled and my guess is he rode his motorcycle—as if he's not hot enough, visions of him riding his bike only send my body into overdrive.

"Hi," I say, trying to keep my voice even.

His eyes sweep me from my open-toed pumps, up my tight leather pants, right through my sheer silver top, to my straight hair with a few carefully placed waves. "Hi there," he says, and a slight growl follows his greeting.

I labored a long time on what to wear—casual, businesslike, or dressy, but in the end decided on sexy.

"You didn't have to meet me outside," I say.

Before I can move back, lips land on my cheek. My mouth falls open at the sudden scorching heat between us and I stare at him, unable to speak.

His eyes drop and he shoves his hands in his pockets, but his lips quirk up. "Friends wait for friends. Friends kiss each other on the cheek."

He's pushing it, but I secretly don't mind it at all—not that I'd let him know that.

I push his shoulder back. "I don't think friends let their tongue leave their mouth during a slight peck on the cheek."

He shrugs. "So I have a few things to learn."

I nod in the direction of the stretch of sidewalk leading us to the restaurant and smile. "Come on, let's go."

He tries to grab my hand and again the gesture sends butterflies bouncing off the walls of my stomach, but I pretend not to react and tuck a piece of hair behind my ear. "Did you use your charm to get reservations here? Because I've heard it takes months just to get an eleven o'clock reservation." I glance over at him while waiting for a reply and notice that his profile is just as alluring as the full-on view.

His lips twist into a smile and his eyes shift to mine.

I can't help wondering if he can see the butterflies escaping my mouth and swarming around him.

"You know, as much as I'd love to say my charm works wonders, I can't lie. Jagger used his hobnobbing connections to get us a table."

I flinch because there it is, looming over us. Smack in my face it hits—reality. Lies, half-truths, what he doesn't know. What I'm afraid to tell him—not only because I have no idea how he'll react but because reliving our past is just too painful. It's the very reason this, him and me, can never work.

He bumps my shoulder. "Hey, sorry to disappoint you."

I paint a fake smile on my face. "Actually I'm kind of secretly enjoying the fact that you don't always get what you want."

He reaches for the tall brass door and places his other hand on the small of my back. "That happens more than you'd think," he whispers in my ear.

A shiver runs down my spine. The meaning of his words is clear—he wants me. I wish I could be honest and tell him that I want him too, but I know I can't. We're friends. I'll take that until he can't take it anymore. Something is better than nothing.

"Wow, this place is amazing."

He agrees with me and says, "I know, it's like being transported to another time and place."

The grand space is very lavish with a bar in the center and a dining room and lounge flanking each side. Intricate tile-work, carved plaster columns, and a beautifully ornate hand-painted ceiling set the mood perfectly.

"I've never eaten at a Moroccan restaurant," I say a little more breathy than I'd like with his hand still searing my skin.

"Should I have checked with you first before letting Jagger pick the place?"

I laugh, and my nerves settle as I realize he's a little nervous too. "No, I'm sure I'll love it."

"There they are." He points to a booth in a dimly lit corner with a bottle of wine on the table and flickering votive candles in the center. Jagger has his arm stretched across the back of the brown-leather-upholstered bench with his mouth hovering over Aerie's ear. A huge smile is plastered on her face.

Jagger spots us and rises to his feet, waving us over. He's dressed similar to Ben, in a gray button-down and black jeans. He's my cousin and although it seems I've known him forever, we only just met less than a year ago. Jagger's mother is my mother's sister. She lives in Paris. She never married Jagger's father and allowed his father to raise him in New York City. River actually met Jagger for the first time on his honeymoon in Paris and they hit it off so well Jagger decided to move to LA. Lucky for all of us and especially for Aerie. She captured his heart from their first meeting, and after a few bumps in the road they are a full-fledged couple. I'm surrounded by adorable couples lately.

Aerie stands as well and Ben ushers me into the booth, his hand still resting possessively on my back. Aerie leans over to hug me and Jagger kisses my cheek, nothing like the one Ben had placed there earlier. Ben's hand casually drifts up my spine and back down, and visions of his lips doing the same pop into my mind. I try to push away the primal response his physical presence elicits from me. Ben removes his hand to shake hands with Jagger and says hello to Aerie. I notice there's no kissing between them. I guess when two people work together, any such physical contact is awkward.

We all sit down as I try to wrap my mind around this—a double date? No, it's simply friends sharing a meal together at a very expensive restaurant.

"I'm sorry I'm late," I ramble, feeling nervous with Ben so close. I wasn't this nervous when he took me to the diner for pie. But then again we had just screwed each other's brains out. This is different. The sexual tension between us is overwhelming, but we said we'd be friends. He'd agreed. There would be no screwing afterward. Just a friendly good-bye. It's what I said I wanted.

"You're not late," Jagger answers. "Aerie insisted we would be late, so she made me pick her up at work a little too early."

"There's always so much traffic coming into LA at rush hour," she defends herself.

I giggle a little. She's not a fan of LA and she convinced my cousin to move to Laguna. He doesn't seem to mind the commute, though. I can see Jagger's arm moving and I know he's caressing his fingers up and down her leg. She's wearing a cute suit. I saw it when she stood up. Short red skirt, black-and-red-checked jacket, and a black silk top with a slight V neck. Her jewelry, though, is absolutely fabulous. Small red sparkling hearts circle her neck with crystal leaves peeking out here and there. She has the most exquisite antique pieces—hand-me-downs from her grandmother.

"I love your necklace."

"Thank you. Jagger bought it for me for my birthday."

"It's beautiful." I offer my cousin a look of admiration. "I thought it was a piece from your grandmother's collection."

"I know, right?" she says, gushing over him. "It couldn't be more perfect." Her hand fingers the crystals as they sparkle.

"Not only does my cousin have swagger, but he has awesome taste." I smile at them.

He shrugs off the compliment.

"Swagger?" Ben chokes, pretending to pound his chest with his fist.

"Watch it, man." Jagger points to him with a grin that tells me they're joking with each other.

I was a little nervous when Ben suggested we all go out to dinner because I wasn't sure how the dynamic would be between the two men. But I guess since they had already forged a relationship in New York City through circumstances I'd rather not think about, they get along.

The waitress approaches and greets our table. "What can I get you both to drink?"

I start to answer, but Ben orders for the both of us. "Two sparkling waters with lemon please."

My heart starts to steadily pound. He remembers what I drink and he now adds lemon to his own drink. I try to rein in my smile, but it's too late.

"You look really happy today, Bell," Jagger muses, his eyes drifting between Ben and me. He's obviously trying to gauge the situation.

"Oh, I got a new client that I'm excited to work with," I lie. Well, it's not really a lie—I am excited about working with the governor's son, but that's not why I was smiling.

"Who?" Aerie asks, genuinely curious.

"Romeo Fairchild."

"Oh, that should be exciting. He's notorious for being a ladies' man. I can't believe he's settling down."

"He's getting married late next month. The day after Thanksgiving."

"Shotgun wedding?" She quirks an eyebrow.

I shrug. I can feel Ben's stare burning me. I lift my eyes to meet his and I'm not sure what I see brewing in them.

"Have you met him yet?" he asks.

"No, we have our first meeting later this week. I guess his fiancée is so nervous she's left the whole thing up to him."

"Oh, sounds like you're in for a treat," Aerie says.

"How's that?" Jagger asks, his own eyebrow rising now.

"Well, he's stunning and if the fiancée doesn't want anything to do with the wedding planning, I'd say something isn't right."

Ben's whole body goes rigid. "I went to high school with him. But how do you know him?" he asks Aerie.

"His parents had a house on the bluff near my uncle's. Rome and I used to build sand castles together."

"Rome?" Jagger clears his throat.

"Well, yes, that's what we called him. I haven't seen him for years, though. Just his picture in the paper." She squirms a little under the scrutiny of both men at the table.

"I'd like to hear a little more about how stunning he is," Jagger says, his lips turning up in a teasing fashion.

Aerie's cheeks blaze. And Ben is unusually quiet.

"Well, not as stunning as you, of course." Her eyes lift to Jagger's.

He leans over and whispers something in her ear and all I can hear is the word *sand*.

She whispers something back that I'm pretty sure is "I can't do that."

His mouth quirks up in a *we'll see* kind of way.

Ben clears his throat and opens his menu.

So while Aerie and Jagger share an intimate moment, I look down at my own menu. The inscription on the front reads *A culinary journey that will lead you through the Spice Trail . . . Indochina . . . Franco-Afrique . . . The Levant . . . Southeast Asia . . . La Méditerranée.*

I lean toward Ben. "What does this mean?"

He leans closer to me. "I think it means the food is really spicy." He laughs. His warm breath feels amazing on my neck and he doesn't move back. Instead he stays close enough to me that our thighs touch.

"Oh." It's all I can say because once again his physical contact has rendered me speechless. My stomach is fluttering, my pulse is racing, and my body is doing other things that aren't appropriate at the table.

"So, what's good?" Ben directs his question to Jagger, who reluctantly pulls himself away from his private conversation with Aerie.

"The chicken and lamb are my favorites. Or the camel, rabbit, and mutton are also really good. The lemon pickling is really good."

I gulp, not liking the sound of any of that.

Ben's eyes drift toward me, and his shoulder bumps mine. "You like lemon."

My gaze latches on to his as Jagger continues to give us a rundown on the use of unrefined olive oils and dried fruits in the Moroccan cooking processes. Ben's eyes don't wander and my pulse races from his gentle but concerned stare.

"Oh, and the sherry cobbler is the best you'll ever have," Jagger says, drawing my attention back to the conversation.

The waitress returns with our drinks and refreshes Aerie's and Jagger's wineglasses before asking Ben and me if we'd like a glass. We both shake our heads no. "Are you ready to order, then?" she asks.

"How about we start with the les olives *maison* and rustic loaf?" Jagger says to the waitress. He looks at the three of us. "Anything else to start?"

I shake my head no and Aerie does the same.

"Sounds good," Ben answers for all of us.

The waitress walks away and Aerie looks at Jagger, a little horrified.

"What?" he asks.

"That's not going to taste like the artichoke bread, is it?"

He laughs. "I hope not. We'll see when we try it."

"Artichoke bread?" I can't help asking.

"Long story," Aerie says. "But Jagger always wants to try new things and—"

Ben busts out laughing and so does Jagger.

Not getting what is going on, I say, "I hate vegetables."

Everyone's eyes go to me.

I sit straight. "What? I do."

Ben shakes his head and Jagger does the same. Aerie just smiles at me.

"So, what are you having?" I ask her.

She clears her throat. "I don't know."

Jagger taps his menu. Her eyes go to where he's pointing on her menu and she ferociously shakes her head no.

The waitress returns. "Have you decided on your main course?"

Ben looks around the table and then up at her. "I think we need a few more minutes."

"No problem." She smiles at him.

Oh my God, is she flirting with him when I'm sitting right next to him? Is he flirting back? Was that a wink I saw? Okay, I need to calm down—I'm just friends with him after all. Except telling myself that doesn't help at all.

"Hey, where are you?" Ben asks me

My eyes meet his ocean blue gaze and I try to push my haze of green jealousy away.

"Trying to decide what to order." I smile.

He points to the twenty-two-ounce cauliflower steak on my menu. "I guess you won't be ordering this," he whispers in my ear.

"I'm thinking of eating dessert for dinner," I whisper back.

"I'll take you for a juicy burger when we leave here. And I promise, no vegetables will be on it." This time his mouth actually touches my ear.

A shiver that feels more like a yearning courses through me. "Excuse me, I need to use the restroom."

I get up quickly and walk as fast as I can to the bathroom. He remembers everything. Guys never remember details like that. I try to gather my wits. With my head bent over the sink, I take deep breaths, but tears are still prickling my eyes. I never knew how sweet he really was, and every minute we spend together just makes me want him more. What am I doing?

"Everything okay?" Aerie asks me, and I look up to see her perfectly polished, beautiful reflection in the mirror.

"Oh yes. I just really needed to use the restroom," I lie.

"It's none of my business, but what's going on between the two of you?" she asks.

And there it is—judgment.

"Nothing," I quickly answer. "We just ran into each other last week at his awards banquet and started talking. It's really nothing. In fact, if you could not mention it to anyone I'd really appreciate it."

Her hand covers mine, gripping the bathroom counter. "Bell, I'm not judging. I've just known Ben a really long time and have to tell you that I like how he is with you."

I turn around. "What do you mean?"

She smiles. "Nervous, eager, maybe happy. I've seen many sides of him, but this one suits him. I don't know how to describe it."

"Well, we're just friends."

She raises her palms. "Remember, I'm not judging. And if you don't like the restaurant we can go somewhere else."

I smile at her. "Oh no, we're staying. I'm pretty sure I saw Theo James in the corner on my way in here."

"Come on, let's go see." She takes my hand.

We walk slowly through the dining room staring at the table and when we get to our own table, Ben looks at me with concern.

"Are you okay?" He moves aside for me to take my seat.

I nod.

"I don't think that was him," Aerie says, helping to lift the sullen mood at the table.

"Who?" Jagger asks.

"Theo James," she says enthusiastically.

Jagger hovers over her in the booth. "That's enough talk about other men." Then he kisses her and practically pins her to the wall.

When I look over at Ben I decide I'll take this piece of him while I can because he makes me happy.

He opens his menu again and points to an item. "What do you say to the *côte de boeuf* for two, minus the winter root?" He grins at me in his irresistible way.

I allow my finger to trace the words on the menu where his hands lie. "That sounds really good."

CHAPTER 11
Show Me

Ben

One of the perks of owning your own business is making your own schedule. I can come in as early or as late as I want, but I'm always here by seven. I can also take a long lunch or skip it in favor of working. And I get to leave at four or stay until I'm done, although I'm always here well past eight. But what I like most is that I can work out at any time of the day. And today I've been feeling a lot of tension that needs to be relieved, so I decided midday works best.

The treadmill beeps and I slow my pace.

Kale throws me a towel. "Speed it up, man. I've been done for more than five minutes."

"I didn't know I was running a marathon."

"I don't think you knew you were running at all."

I grab my water bottle and guzzle it down after wiping the sweat off my brow. "Do I want to know what you thought I was doing?"

"Yeah, you just might. I think you were trying not to get a hard-on thinking about that girl you've been besting up to." His Australian accent stresses the word *hard-on*.

"Besting up to? What the hell does that mean?"

He hooks his feet under the padded bar of the bench next to me. He pauses mid-sit-up to answer me. "Come on, man, you've got it bad for that girl, but besties don't fuck."

I shoot him a glare. "You don't know shit." I refuse to tell him I fucked her twice before the friends-only rule was invoked.

Huffing and puffing, he continues his count and I head for the door, my muscles still tight and tensed, not in the least bit relieved from running.

"Don't be pissed," he calls to me. "I'm just looking out for you. Maybe she's getting it elsewhere."

I shove my middle finger up in the air as I enter the locker room of the small gym on Plan B's floor. His comment cuts deep. It's been a few weeks since I found out she'd be working with Romeo Fairchild. I've brought him up a couple of times since then and all she talks about is how well the wedding planning is going. I know him, though. He was a snake in high school and I have no doubt he still is. The thought of him alone with her drives me fucking crazy. Then there's that asshole boss of hers calling her night and day. Maybe she was all about the fun we were having and when I said no to any more role-playing—to fucking in public places—she just wasn't interested in me and this friends thing was really her way of trying to get rid of me, not trying to get to know me.

Just as I'm changing into a clean shirt, my phone beeps—a text from S'belle.

You're not going to believe this. Xander's going to propose to Ivy the night of her release party. I'm so excited but have to add some special touches to the event now. One week! I can't wait.

My fingers hover over the keyboard, but I don't respond. I've seen S'belle almost every night this week. We've texted and talked on the phone more than I've ever done with anyone, in fact, more than I've probably done in my lifetime. Our conversations have been deep at times and lighter at others. She hasn't laxed on her friendship guidelines, yet my attraction toward her has steadily grown. The quirky, funny things she says get me in the gut and do strange things to me. But Kale hit a sore spot. The whole "friends" dating thing is growing tiresome. Don't get me wrong, I've enjoyed getting to know her and having someone to talk to, but I think Kale might be right. I respond with a quick note.

```
Great news. Hey, I'm going to have to
cancel tonight. Something came up at
work.
```

Her response is immediate.

```
Okay. Hope everything is all right. Call
me later.
```

I shove my phone in my pocket, grab my shit, and head back to my office. Once I'm there I drop it all on my desk and pace to the window. Plan B headquarters is located in the Jamboree Business Center in Irvine, a quick hop on the freeway from Laguna. It's also a fast drive to LA.

I can see the calm Pacific framed in the distance through my large window and long to be out there, but I have work to do. I think about all I have to accomplish before the announcement of my takeovers is made public. *Surfer's End*'s migration to this building is finally happening this week, and I am so fucking happy—the transition has been a nightmare. Their offices will occupy the floor below me, whereas

Sound Music occupies the one above. Both publications should be ready to upload their online issues early next week. And I just need to hire a few more people and we will be hitting the modern world of technology with a boom.

In order to concentrate on work, I have to avert my eyes from the California view. Just as I head toward my phone to text her again, there's a knock at my door.

"Come in," I call.

The door opens and Kale stands there. "Just checking on you. I didn't mean to piss you off."

As soon as I sit down my speakerphone buzzes. I raise a finger and answer it. "Yeah, Beck?"

"I need to go over this budget with you. Is now okay?"

"Sure."

"On my way."

I glance back over to Kale. "I'm not pissed, man. I think you might be onto something. I may have become her 'girlfriend' as hard as that is for me to say."

"What do you say to grabbing a beer tonight?"

"Yeah, sure, why not?"

Before I can finish asking where, Beck is standing behind him.

Kale turns. "Hey, how's it going today?"

"Better than yesterday," Beck responds.

Kale grins. "Always good. Catch you both later. I'll stop by before I leave."

"You're not going out tonight, are you?" Beck asks me.

My eyes cut to his. "I can go out for a beer on a Friday night. I'm not an alcoholic."

"Ben, why would you do that now? What's going on with you?"

"Nothing."

"Is it that girl you're into? The one you like?"

"I never said I like her. I'm not fifteen."

"You don't have to say you like someone for it to be apparent that you're interested."

"You know what, Beck, no offense, but I don't want to talk about it."

He raises his hands. "Look, man, not trying to get in your business. I'm just looking out for you."

Sighing, I slouch over, resting my forearms on my thighs. "Yeah, I know. I appreciate it. How about you show me what you've got?"

He hands me a stack of papers—Beck's budget seems doable. "Looks great, man," I say after a quick perusal.

He nods. "I'll leave them with you. I'm heading out for the day."

"Thanks. And see ya."

I swivel in my chair and decide to look over the *Sound Music* budget Aerie gave me yesterday. Time flies as I spend the rest of the day analyzing it.

There's a light tap on my door before it opens.

"Ready to go grab that beer, mate?" Kale asks.

I glance at the clock on my desk. "Fuck, it's already seven?"

"Yeah, it is. What, did the day get away from you?"

"It did. I think I'm going to pass tonight. I want to finish this budget shit up and be done with it."

"No worries. Take care and call if you change your mind."

"Thanks, man. I will." But I know I won't. Beck is right. I don't need to fall back into that scene again.

It's not quite six a.m. and I'm feeling restless, staring out in the darkness of my room. I pull out my journal to record my thoughts, but I can't get them down because I don't know what they are. I've never been at a loss for words before—but today I am. After an hour or so I toss my journal aside and decide to go on a run.

By the time I hit the main road, the sun has already risen. I slow down and make my way through town and to the corner coffee shop. Grabbing a paper and a cup of coffee, I sit outside under one of the umbrella tables and catch up on the news. Once I've scoured the paper I decide to people-watch. I haven't done that in a long time. Time slips away from me and when I glance at my phone it's almost eleven.

Tossing my shit in the trash, I take the beach path home. When I pass the little run-down surf shack, I decide to stop in. It doesn't look like much from the outside, but what Noel has done with the inside is fucking amazing. Blondie's, the shop that used to belong to my dad, always feels like home away from home to me. My father named his business after his pet name for my mother, but back then it was no small operation. I don't remember coming here before Noel bought it, but I know my father not only sold boards of every size and design, but also owned a fleet of boats that he chartered, along with any and every apparatus made for the sea. Sadly, it was his thirst to try out everything and anything new under the sun that killed him. My sister and I had recently discovered that his death resulted from taking a new sailboat out alone—the police reports said his death was due to a piece of malfunctioning equipment that hanged him by the ropes. My mother never told us what happened to him.

My sister thinks it was because she didn't want us to picture him that way; I'm not so sure. She also never told us she had been awarded ten million dollars as a wrongful death settlement. Again, I don't think it's for the reason my sister believes. I shake my dark thoughts away. Inheriting that money hasn't changed me at all, but it has given me direction. It's given me the ability to do something I never would have been able to do without it—start my own business.

Taking one step at a time, I glance around the outside of the shack. It looks the same as always—wind chimes everywhere, peeling green paint, a weathered roof that needs replacing, a ramp that has long since collapsed. I walk in and as usual my head circles the perimeter. Surfboards line the arched ceiling, covering every inch of it.

"Just a fucking brilliant way to expand the merchandise," I say to Noel. I say it every time I walk in because I'm so impressed.

He beams from behind the counter. "Hey, Benny boy. What brings you by?"

Noel's an out-of-shape, middle-aged man who at one time was the undisputed ASP World Champion. My dad was also a member of the Association of Surfing Professionals and that's how they met. Noel bought the shop from my dad's business partner a few years after my dad died, and he's run it ever since.

"Just out for a run and passing by."

"Sure you're not checking on your board?"

"Ha, you caught me," I joke. "I've got a car now, so I won't have to leave her here much longer. I just have to have a rack put on."

"She's not bothering me. At least I know you'll be stopping by once in a while with her here."

"Noel, come on, man. I stop by as much as I can."

"I haven't seen you in three weeks." He scrubs his beard. "Something tells me you're chasing tail."

I shake my head. "I never chase anything but a wave. You know that."

He looks at me with sincerity in his eyes. "Sometimes you have to chase what you really want because everything in life worth having won't fall into your lap."

"You're awful philosophical for this early in the day."

"I always think clearer before five." He laughs.

The ding of the door alerts us to a customer.

"Hey, I gotta run but I'll be by soon."

He moves forward to hug me. "It was good to see you, Benny."

I hug him back. "You too, Noel. Tell Faith hello for me."

He nods. "Will do. She'll be sorry she missed you."

His attention is diverted to the dude checking out the boards overhead and I slip out, deciding to take it easy and walk the rest of the way home rather than run. My phone vibrates and I stop, pulling it from my sock. In my rush this morning to escape the silence, I left the house with no earphones and no armband. It's a message from S'belle. I have to squint to read it since I forgot my sunglasses as well.

Is everything okay?

Three little words and my heart falls in my chest. *Am I wrong about the sexual pull I thought we both recognized? Am I just her friend and along for a ride going nowhere?* I drop in the sand and scroll through our messages over the last few weeks. I stop on one from when I asked her to go to the Hollywood Forever Cemetery Screening with me. She had said yes. She always says yes. She was a little startled at the thought at first, but once I assured her it would be a blast, her anxiety eased. I told her I'd pick her up and as I read her response now, I can't help laughing.

I'm more than capable of driving in the
dark and I didn't invite you over to get
me anyway.

That night I met her in the front of the cemetery. She was late and I paced the sidewalk. When she finally arrived, she seemed exasperated.

"What's wrong?" I asked, scrutinizing her demeanor.

She frowned. "I'm so sorry I'm late. Tate needed to review next month's wedding schedule and had a bit of a meltdown over everything still left to do."

"Wyatt is an asshole."

She stared at me with something in her eyes I couldn't quite figure out. "He can be."

"You should quit," I grunted.

She ignored me, but she always does when I tell her what she already knows. The guy is a dick—there are no two ways about it.

"A picnic?" she asked, changing the subject with her green eyes alight.

I had a bag of sandwiches and two slices of pie from Four & Twenty Blackbirds in one hand and a blanket in the other. Her brow quirked as she assessed my wares, and her mood went from dark to jubilant just like that.

"Yeah, I can put a pretty cool party together too."

"I bet you can," she said, grabbing the blanket, and I sensed a hint of another meaning in her response.

"Just call me Martha fucking Stewart," I snorted.

We both burst out laughing.

"C'mon. I want to get a good spot."

S'belle followed me past the line of people that wrapped around the block and into the iconic cemetery. Thank fuck I had bought tickets online. I'd never been there but always wanted to go and didn't want to miss my opportunity in case of a sellout. I glanced around and gave a low whistle. "Cool place."

She clutched the blanket and moved closer to me. The air seemed filled with intrigue. The cemetery shared a wall with Paramount Studios. Music was being played by a DJ and a projector from somewhere in the distance cast music videos upon it. We passed the tombs of Hollywood legends Peter Lorre, Victor Fleming, and Norma Talmadge as S'belle stared in awe.

"Want to go in?" I asked, leaning down and whispering in her ear.

Her eyes closed and I knew she was trying to compose herself. "Nope."

I grinned at her. "Nope? Not sure, why not, or maybe later?" I said, bumping her shoulder.

"Nope," she said again. "Too creepy for me." And I covered my mouth to stifle a laugh.

"Don't laugh," she huffed.

I placed my hand on her back. "I'm not. I think it's cute. You know I'll keep you safe."

She picked up the pace. "Where do you want to sit?"

"That way," I said, pointing to the sign with an arrow that read
FAIRBANKS LAWN.

"Didn't Douglas Fairbanks play Zorro?"

*I flung her a look, amazed she knew that. "Yeah, he did and Robin
Hood too. Have you seen them?"*

"Both versions."

"Ah . . . we both loved marked men."

She nodded. "I didn't see, what was playing tonight?"

"Dial M for Murder." I smirked.

"Alfred Hitchcock?" Her eyes glittered.

"That's why I picked it."

She tipped her head up toward the stars. "Beautiful night."

*"It is," I agreed, and stopped at the perfect location. It wasn't in the
middle of the thousands of people already sitting in rows, but rather it
was off to the side with the cemetery just behind us. Setting my bag down,
I laid out the blanket so we could both sit.*

*We ate and watched the movie. She moved close to me when she was
scared and I tried hard to keep my hands off her. Just before the final
credits rolled, I stretched my arms over my head and brought one down
behind her back. It was a classic guy move, one I had never attempted on
a girl before. I practically rolled my eyes at my own ridiculousness, but
she didn't say anything, so I left it there.*

She turned toward me. "Ben . . . ," she whispered.

*"Yeah." Her face was so close to my lips and I couldn't resist lower-
ing them slightly and brushing my mouth over hers. Heat filled the air
between us, but I hesitated a little too long about deepening the kiss. I
didn't want to make a move until I was sure she wanted me to.*

*"It's over," she said, jumping to her feet. She stood there visibly
trembling.*

*I stayed where I was, motionless, as lust flooded me and I cursed
myself for hesitating.*

A gust of wind blows sand in my face and I snap out of it. What the fuck am I doing ignoring her? I know she feels what I feel. I said I'd give her time. I can do that. I continue scrolling through more of the old text messages between us, and stop on another one from her.

```
Do you think we'll be climbing a lot of
stairs at Hearst Castle?
```

I had typed back a question mark.
She responded with what I've labeled a Bellism.

```
Heels look better with the outfit I'm
wearing, but I'm not sure they're all
right for climbing stairs.
```

I answered with the following.

```
I don't think you have to worry about
stairs. It's not a tower. Wear your heels
and if I have to, I'll fucking carry you.
```

I didn't carry her, but I did stare at her ass as we climbed the stairs of the castle. I scroll down and stop on the one that reads:

```
What should I wear to the rock climbing
gym?
```

I have to laugh out loud. I had responded:

```
Surprise me.
```

And she did. She showed up in jeans and high heels claiming she thought she'd just take her shoes off. We bought her a pair of appropriate shoes in the lobby. After I tortured myself not only ogling her ass but also pushing it upward for an hour, I had to stop. The blood kept rushing to my cock and I was so uncomfortable after a while there was no way I could climb. I called it a night early.

I spend another five minutes going through messages just like those and think about the places we've gone and the connection we've shared. I feel the grin building on my lips with each passing one. And I know what to do. I dial her number.

"Hello," she answers on the first ring.

"Hey, how are you?"

"Good. How are you?"

I look out over the ocean. "Better now that I hear your voice."

"Is everything okay?"

"Yes. Just had a lot of shit going on."

"I missed talking to you."

Now I wish I could pull her through the phone. "What are you doing right now?"

"Nothing. I just got home from helping Tate set up for a wedding."

"What, the prick can't lift the silverware himself?"

She giggles. "No, just some coordination issues that needed to be worked out."

I bite back what I want to say about her boss. "I'm coming to get you. I have something I want to show you."

She starts to argue.

"I'll pick you up at five. I don't want to hear another word about it. I'm not taking no for an answer this time."

"Okay."

I'm surprised she gives in that easy. "See you in a bit, Red."

"Bye, Ben," she says, and her tone is quiet. I can picture her face, all innocent and beautiful, and my stomach does that thumping that I can't figure out. I don't know what it is about her that affects me so much.

I take off for home, shower, get dressed, and make a stop along the way before heading to her place. As soon as my hand reaches out to lift the bar to the gate, I spot her. She's sitting at one of the tables and quickly hangs up her phone. She's wearing jeans, a tight sweater with a scarf wrapped around her neck, and high-heel boots.

"What are you doing down here alone, beautiful?" I ask as I open the gate.

"I'm waiting for you." Her green eyes gleam and her mouth lifts up into a smile that I can't resist returning.

But she seems a little shaken.

"Everything okay?"

She nods. "Of course." But she's not in the least bit convincing.

I move closer, close enough to smell her lemony scent, even though normally I keep a small distance between us. But I have this over-whelming need to feel her warmth, so I hug her—nothing sexual, just a friendly hello. She's receptive to it and hugs me back. I disengage from her quickly. I don't want to trigger her alarm. The one where she backs away when she thinks I'm too close.

I stare into her mesmerizing eyes. "Have you ever seen the view from Carl's Curve at night?"

"Up on Mulholland Drive?"

"That's the place."

"No, I haven't."

I extend my hand. "Well, come on. We should be able to make it before sunset."

Her fingers entangle with mine and they fit perfectly in my hand. When I open the gate I cover her eyes.

"What are you doing?" she asks.

"You'll see." I lead her to my bike and grab the helmet off the seat before I remove my other hand.

"We're not riding on your bike up there. I told you . . ."

I pull my hand from my behind my back and hand her the green helmet I stopped and picked up on my way over. She jumps up and down and the excitement she exudes over the smallest things—the way she clasps her hands together and bounces when something makes her happy—it gets me every time. I wish I knew how to get that reaction all the time.

Stepping closer, I push away the hair from her eyes and slip the helmet on her head. Once I do I dip my head down and kiss her, but just her cheek. I pull away before the urge to slide my lips and cover hers becomes impossible ignore. Then I strap my own black helmet on and hop on my bike. She circles to the left and does the same. When she gets on she wraps her arms around me so naturally my heart rate speeds at the contact.

With a quick turn of the ignition switch, I shift into neutral and kick-start her to life. S'belle breathes loudly in my ear and I can sense the rush she must be feeling. The short ride up the curvy road urges her closer. It makes me feel that she's finally living in the moment, not overthinking everything. Each downshift is met with just the right amount of throttle as I carve each turn perfectly and her body sways into mine. I can smell her lemony scent, hear the puff of her breath, feel the warmth of her body against mine. My muscles tense with each movement she makes.

She holds me tight as we ride like the wind up to what has become one of my favorite places. When I feel her resting her chin on my shoulder, I suck in a breath. But when her hands slide down to my thighs for a moment before she realizes it and pulls them back up, I grin like a fucking idiot because I know the walls are finally coming down.

CHAPTER 12
Still Into You

Bell

The sun is shining bright and there isn't a cloud in the sky. I take my time walking down Hollywood Boulevard looking around at the many businesses and shops. Funny thing is I'm not really looking at them, though, because all I can see is Ben. I can't get him out of my head. We talk all the time, we text all the time. Up until this week, we've spent all of our free time together. What was supposed to be a friends-only relationship to ward him off seems to have spurred him on.

Today it hit me that it seems like forever since I last saw him, which was Sunday night. He picked me up and took me to gaze at the view of LA from Mulholland Drive. It was stunning and riding on his bike was absolutely dreamy. He's told me many times he's not a romantic, but he doesn't see what I see.

I pull on the showroom door and step in, looking around. It's all put together in a very trendy modern metallic palette. My gaze darts to a blur of waving arms, and Josie's wide eyes direct me to the break room. I look at the time—ten thirty. I lift the coffees and nod to my desk. She shakes her head. That can only mean trouble. I follow behind her, noticing Tate's door is shut.

"What is it?" Quickly, I close the door behind me and set my stuff on the table.

"He's on the warpath."

"Why?" I ask mildly, leaning back against the glass door.

"Romeo Fairchild is in his office. He came in for his meeting with you thirty minutes ago. But, um . . . well, you weren't here. I tried to call you."

I set the coffees down and pull my phone from my purse. Shoot, she did call. I must have been on the phone with Ben and never noticed. I set my phone on the table. "The meeting is tomorrow, not today," I insist.

"Well, tell that to Mr. Eleven."

"What?"

"He's an eleven on a scale of one to ten. You should go out with him."

I gape at her. "Josie, are you out of your mind? You call me in here like I'm about to get fired and then tell me I should date our engaged client. The one whose wedding we're planning."

"Oh, Bell, I see how he looks at you. He practically fucks you with his eyes every time he's in here."

"Josie, honestly. And besides, I think he screws anything that moves."

Her hand flies to her mouth. "Bell Wilde, I've never heard you talk like that. I like this new wild side."

I laugh at her. "You should have known me before I found direction."

"Is that like finding God?"

I ponder her question. "Yeah, I guess it is."

She blows a piece of blue hair out of her eyes. "Oh, and I almost forgot, that really hot brother of yours, the one who's, you know . . . married"—she rolls her eyes—"stopped by already too. He said to let you know he had a few things to take care of and would be back to take you to lunch."

Suddenly Josie's eyes grow even wider than when I first walked in and then there's a slight tap on the glass behind me.

I swallow and mutter, "Is that Tate?"

Her eyes confirm my suspicion without her having to say a single word.

My nerves start to buzz as I turn around and push the door. There stand Tate and Romeo.

"Miss Wilde, you decided to join us at work today. I'm so glad," he says sternly but he's still conducting himself civilly.

My eyes shift to Romeo's. Aerie is right—he's a stunner. And Ben is right too—he's a snake. His look is aristocratic but bad boy at the same time. Dark brown wavy hair, a sexy, slender frame with broad shoulders, and boy, does he know how to dress! I thought Tate dressed with style, but Romeo is in a whole other league. Today he's wearing a black suit with a white shirt, his gray tie crisply knotted around his neck, and he looks every bit as put together as Tate if not more so.

He speaks before I do. "Bell, I have to apologize. I realized after I arrived that our meeting is tomorrow, but Tate insisted I wait for you to get here."

My eyes shoot back to Tate's. He's a man who gives his work more than one hundred percent, but the problem is he can't give any aspect his one hundred percent attention. So he has me take on the more complex clients—the needier ones. And Romeo, he's needy all right. But I'm not sure if his need isn't to get me into a bathroom and have his way with me.

"Even though our appointment was for tomorrow morning, since you're here we can go over any of your concerns now if you'd like," I say to Romeo.

"Excellent. Today is a much better day for me and Laney is driving me crazy over selecting a band. She's practically terrified that if we don't nail one down we'll be stuck with a DJ."

Tate nods. "I'll leave the two of you to iron out your fiancée's concerns. And, Josie, has the announcement been sent to the paper so the wedding columnist can be notified?"

Josie's blue hair moves like a wave as she skirts past us. "Mr. Wyatt, that is next on my list of things to do." She doubles back and grabs the cup marked MOCHA off the table. "Thank you," she mouths, and hustles out of the room.

"I'll be in my office if you need me for anything, Bell. And, Romeo, it was a pleasure talking to you."

Romeo smooths his tie between his thumb and finger. "As always, Tate."

"Why don't we go to the conference room?" I ask him when it's just the two of us.

"I think here is fine."

"Okay, let me go grab your file and I'll be right back."

"Of course," he says, his eyes staring at the ruffled edges of my chiffon blouse that just happen to be right over my breasts.

I scurry out of the door. The conference room is visible from the showroom with a glass wall as the partition, but the break room is around the corner and not visible. Josie's comments have me all kinds of paranoid now. I take a deep breath—he's just a client. *Stop reading more into it.* Tate's door is closed—thank God. I pass Josie's desk and she shoots me a wink. I roll my eyes.

My desk is cluttered with linen samples, venue décor photos, centerpiece ideas—all pertaining to the Blair/Fairchild wedding. Laney Blair has yet to set foot inside this office. I haven't even met her. It's all a little strange that Romeo is my only contact, but he seems determined to pull off this wedding in record time. I grab the folder marked BANDS and my wedding file and head back toward the break room.

This time when I enter the room I can smell coffee percolating and my eyes flare to the counter—he made coffee? Wow, that's a first. A client making his own. The beep of my phone rivets my attention to the table and right to Romeo's prying eyes.

He knows I caught him and with a smile says, "Would that Ben Covington happen to have gone to high school in Laguna?"

I feel myself flushing. Why? The heat between Ben and me has to be evident on my face. "I think so," I say, my voice shaky.

"He's your boyfriend?" he asks inquisitively.

I drop my phone into my purse. "We're just friends."

"Right," he says with a smirk that says *friends with benefits*. What the heck did Ben text? And up until now Aerie and Jagger are the only people aware of whatever is going on between Ben and me. Talking to Romeo about it doesn't seem right.

I carefully place the folders and files in my hands on the table. "So bands, your fiancée has a valid concern—"

He cuts me off. "I went to high school with Ben. He was a surfer, had a girl, and seemed like a rebel. He had one guy friend I remember him hanging with, and he stayed clear of my crowd."

I feel an anger rise inside me and I want to tell this arrogant guy that Ben's not pretentious, and image has never mattered to him. But I don't—of course instead I try to drop the subject. "I didn't know him then. But anyway, there are only a few bands that have your wedding date open. Do you want to listen to them with your fiancée and let me know what you think?"

"Sit down. Please," he says.

When I do he stands and goes over to the coffeepot, opening the cupboard above and pulling out a mug. "Would you like a fresh cup?"

I pull my own coffee from the tray and take the lid off. "No, I'm good, thank you."

"Do you have sound clips for us to listen to now?"

I do, but they're on my laptop, which is at my desk.

"I'm not in a hurry," he says, taking a seat next to me.

With my purse in hand I again leave the room, but this time I make a stop in the restroom. I grab my phone from my bag quickly and read Ben's text.

```
I'll be by to pick you up at 7. And if
you even think of saying no, I'll still
come by to swing you over my shoulder and
carry you to dinner. I might even have to
spank you.
```

Oh my God, Romeo read that! The air flies out of my lungs, but it's not from embarrassment. A sudden burst of excitement hums through me as I read his text again. I have no idea what I'm doing anymore. I don't know where the lines are. I entered into this determined to push him away, but all I've seemed to do is pull him closer. And that makes me happy, really happy.

The rest of the morning moves at a snail's pace. Romeo and I listen to the available bands, review the other finer details, discuss songs, and the cake—ultimately he leaves the decision making up to me. It's as if I'm planning my own wedding.

Toward the end of our meeting, Josie pokes her head in the door to get my attention.

"Your brother's here to take you to lunch. Do you want me to tell him to wait?"

"No, that won't be necessary," Romeo says. "We're finished here. I think I've taken enough of Bell's time."

We leave the break room together. I gather what I can and he kindly takes the rest. My brother is sitting on the other side of the showroom in one of the chairs at the table set for two looking down at his phone with a smirk on his face that tells me he must be texting Dahlia.

I plop my stuff on my desk and Romeo does the same. Tate's still in his office with his door closed—I can only imagine what storm is brewing. I look up at Romeo and extend my hand. "I'll be in touch as soon as I hear back from the bands."

He eyes dance with amusement as he leans in a little too close and then shakes my hand. "Sounds like a plan."

I look over my shoulder in time to catch my brother's assessing eyes. He gets up and strides in our direction.

"Hey, I was hoping you have time for lunch." River grins at me.

"Sure. I'd love to." I smile back at him.

"We were just saying good-bye." Romeo turns on his heels, but he stops. "Son of a bitch. You're River Wilde, aren't you?"

River nods.

"We spend all morning looking for bands and you neglected to tell me who your brother is?" Romeo says to me.

River's look turns questioning. "What am I missing?"

"Bell has been trying to find a band for my wedding on really short notice and I never put two and two together."

"Romeo, my brother isn't in a band anymore," I hiss in his direction.

"Such a small world. I went to high school with your wife," Romeo says to River, ignoring me.

Oh my God, he's going to tell River about Ben. My body tightens and suddenly the room seems to be shrinking.

River grabs my hand. "Hey, Bell, are you okay?"

I blink up. "Yeah, yeah, I'm fine."

"You look really pale."

"Honestly, I haven't eaten yet today."

River shakes his head at me. "Come on, let's get you fed."

He extends his hand to Romeo. "Nice to meet you, man. Good luck with your wedding."

Romeo nods and River puts his arm around me, knuckling my side. "You need to take better care of yourself." And when we get outside he turns to me and asks, "Who was that asshole?"

"He's a client and the governor's son."

"Well, I didn't like the way he was looking at you."

I sigh, just thankful Romeo didn't let Ben's name roll off his tongue.

I'm distracted all through lunch with my brother and when I finally get back to my desk, I plop down exhausted. As I browse through my e-mails, my mind wanders to Ben and the reality of the situation. He will never be welcome in my family—there's too much baggage there, not just Dahlia but with me. So what the hell am I doing with him? Why can't I just break it off? It's time to find a way to let him go.

CHAPTER 13
Kinks Shirt

Ben

Life has a way of sneaking up on you. I've been content focusing on my career ever since I started Plan B. It keeps me busy and keeps my mind on what's important and off the things that aren't. But this week I've had a hard time concentrating. My mind keeps wandering to her. I know we can't keep going on like this. We can't keep walking the line between friends and more, because if we do the both of us will explode.

Walking to her apartment building, I spot her immediately. She looks like a burst of sunshine on a cloudy day. She's sitting at one of the tables in her courtyard waiting for me, and when she stands to open the gate I quickly reach around and open it first just to be closer to her faster.

She rolls her eyes at me and says, "Such a rebel."

I shrug. "Takes one to know one."

She laughs. "Touché."

"You look fucking fantastic," I say, purposefully dragging my eyes up and down her body.

Her smile grows even wider and the air suddenly becomes denser.

I draw her in and embrace her. She lets me, even allowing my lips to linger in the crook of her neck. I can hear her breathe me in and I have to stop myself from grinning like a fucking idiot.

I slide my palms down to her ass, touching every curve I can along the way. With a slow hiss of breath I say, "Hi there."

"Hi," she says with that innocent voice that always seems to come out of nowhere and jump-start my already aching need to take her. Which is what I want to do right now, right here.

"Pizza?" she says, pulling away just as my fingers start to circle around to her hips.

Fuck! I need to play it cool. *Don't chase her away now.* Rechanneling my thoughts, I rub my stomach. "Sure, sounds good. I'm pretty hungry."

"I know a great place and we can even walk." Her voice tapers off and she seems distracted.

"Everything okay?"

"Just a crazy day. Glad it's over."

I straighten and look in her eyes. "Want to talk about it?"

She stiffens. "No. Not now."

I nod and grab her hand to lead her out of the courtyard. We eat and end up meandering down Sunset for a bit afterward. Just as the sky turns dark we head back to her place with coffees to sit in the courtyard.

"So, what happened at work today?" I ask.

"Oh, really it's nothing. Tate has me doing two really big weddings next month and the clients are very needy," she says, sipping her decaffeinated coffee with so much milk and sugar I doubt it even tastes like coffee.

"I thought you were going to quit soon."

"I was planning on it at the end of the year but haven't really gotten my own business off the ground. And these weddings are huge. I'll have the potential to make so many contacts through them I really want to impress them."

"I don't doubt you will."

"Tate is just such a micromanager that sometimes I feel like the clients know he's babysitting me."

"Tell him to go fuck himself."

She laughs. "I wish I could some days."

"He's such a dick-wad, I wish you would."

She shakes her head. "You don't even know him. Why do you dislike him so much?"

"I don't have to know him. I don't like the way he treats you or the sadness I see in your eyes when you get off the phone with him. And besides, he has the hots for you."

"No, he doesn't. We broke up over a year ago."

My eyes shoot out of my head and before I can stop myself I'm bolting out of the chair. "Are you fucking kidding me? You slept with him!"

She squishes her lips together in displeasure. "No. Just because I date someone doesn't mean I sleep with him."

My blood pressure is boiling. Yeah, I guess I already know that. I look up into the night and stare at the stars, taking deep calming breaths. "I should be going," I say.

She grabs my wrist. "Don't be mad. Don't go. Isn't it still early?"

Her hand slides to my hand, but I don't grab it. "Yeah, it is but I took tomorrow off and I'm hitting the surf at sunrise."

"Really? I'd love to join you." She takes my hand in hers since I wouldn't take hers, and electricity jolts me.

I let my annoyance with the jackass go as best I can and grin at her. "Don't you have Ivy's release party?"

"Yes, but not until later."

"Are you sure? You'll have to get up really early."

She nods. "I'm sure. I'll be there," she says, standing up and staring at me for the longest time.

I kiss her on the cheek, letting my lips linger and start for the gate. I turn around. "The main beach at six thirty," I say. "In the morning," I clarify.

"I know that," she calls before reaching her top step and then disappearing around the corner.

I stay where I am, buzzing from the high of knowing the walls she's erected between us are crumbling. She has never agreed to come to Laguna—to come to me. Tomorrow should be a whole lot of fun.

Breathe in. . . . now exhale. Feel it. Enjoy it. Don't rush it. Prolong the awesomeness for as long as possible because while it's happening you experience only one thing—pure joy. It becomes an addiction . . . you can't help wanting to do it over and over again. There's no greater feeling in the world than being one with her. And in that single moment she becomes everything you want and everything you need rolled together. There's a weightlessness that exists between us as I move quickly—up and down, hovering over her. I gain speed and it's thrilling, exhilarating, liberating even. I can feel her everywhere—the salty, tangy taste she leaves in my mouth, the way my feet shift to accommodate her size, her cold spray on my body. I break through her ledge and position myself on her peak. She's large and hollow and I have to move forcefully to stop from getting caught in her lip, but I do it and just like that—I'm riding the best fucking wave.

The sun rises on this anniversary of sorts and there's a haze hanging in the air as I enfold myself inside the wave's whirl. I look ahead and can't help thinking that for the first time in a long while I'm focused, I have no doubts, and I know where I'm going. It hasn't been easy. It's been a long road. I wince at the memories of how poorly I acted—how badly I handled everything. Blinking my sad thoughts away, I look up as the swell emerges from more than one-hundred-foot depths and watch as the silver-tinted waves of the Pacific roll in at a lightning-fast rate. Then I ride her out like a master. When I know my time is up, I take a full breath, all the way from my stomach to my chest, tilt my head back to open my lungs, and take in more air until it happens—the water cascades all around me and I'm completely submerged. Time stands still while I swim through the blur and toward the light. I reach the surface and blinking, I see the clear day that is beckoning on the horizon.

Chest to board, I paddle in and watch the shore come alive in the early morning hours. As I scan the beach, my eye catches a reflection of sorts in the sand. I strain to see what it is and that's when I see her. Cupping the water faster, I pick up speed and hit shallow water. I can't help grinning at the sight of her. Last night I was pissed as hell at her, but now seeing her—it all just slides away because the sexy, sassy, and funny-as-hell girl that won't let me call her mine is waiting for me. Waving a hand in the air, I shake the water from my hair and tuck my board under my arm.

"You made it," I yell as I emerge from the water.

"I did," she says, shading her eyes with her hand.

"Where's your board?"

She shrugs. "I don't have one."

"All right, then—it looks like we'll be taking turns."

My gaze sweeps the length of her and once my body stops humming in desire, I curl my fingers over my mouth to stifle my laughter at what she wore to surf in—a flowered green bikini with gold strings at the neck and hipbones, earrings, and even a necklace. She looks fucking beautiful, like Miss America. She's even wearing sparkly sandals. And even though today isn't about winning a beauty pageant, I can't help approaching the unrivaled winner with a cheerful smirk.

As I close the distance I feel something shifting between us. It's in the way she's looking at me. Her alluring features come clearly into focus—the long strands of her red hair blowing in the wind, her full breasts popping out from beneath her tiny top, the curvy shape of her hips, and fuck me, she has a belly button ring. I try to tame the thudding of my pulse, but it isn't easy. It's been hard enough keeping my hands off her, well, semi off her, with her clothes on—this is going to be hell.

Kicking the sand up beneath my feet, I lift my gaze upward, where I notice the sparkle in her emerald green eyes. A slight sense of pride overtakes me because her eyes are shimmering. I think they might even be dancing with anticipation. It thrills me that she's here this early to surf and happy about it. Just a few short weeks ago I wasn't sure what I saw when I looked into her eyes. At first I thought maybe hate, anger, disgust—or possibly a combination of just about every negative emotion. But it was fear and I've been taking the time to make it clear that she's mine. I've been doing it subtly, but I will do it.

When a cool breeze presents itself on the shoreline, I stop on my heels and dig my board into the sand. I move a little closer but know I should keep a healthy distance between us. Although it doesn't seem to matter how close or far away she is, I haven't been able to stop thinking about her. She bends down to rub some sunscreen on. When she does her breasts spill out farther from her top and I have to suppress a groan. I take a deep breath and sure enough, it's there—that lemony citrus smell that's everywhere when she's around.

I lean down and reach for the bottle. "Here, let me help you."

My guess is she'll say no, so when she hands me the bottle I'm shocked.

She stands straight and turns around, lifting her hair as she does. "You can do my back."

"I was thinking I'd start with the front," I say, my voice going deep all on its own.

I notice her stiffen before she hands me the sunscreen over her shoulder. It's cool in my hands and I rub my palms together to warm it. My fingers cover her shoulders and the back of her neck. I knead her skin ever so slightly and slide down under the strings in the front a little. She gasps and I'm pretty sure it's not from the chill of the lotion. Her skin is soft and I notice a few faint freckles I never knew she had on her shoulders—they're sexy as hell. Her head drops as I rub down her back. When I get midway I caress the skin spilling out from the sides of her tiny top, and again a slight shiver rocks her shoulders. I grin to myself like a Cheshire cat.

"You're full of tension. You could use a massage," I whisper in her ear, moving down her back a little more until my fingertips rest on the fabric of her bottoms. I let them slip inside teasingly and pull them back out.

She jumps and turns around. "I'm good. That's enough," she says, sounding a little flustered.

I grin and hand her back the bottle. "If you say so. I just didn't want you to burn."

"I won't," she says. "It's not that hot today anyway."

As the words leave her lips and I'm just about to tell her the temperature has nothing to do with the strength of the sun's rays, I notice she's wearing makeup and I have to try hard to suppress my laughter.

Squinting, she puts her hands on her hips. "What is so funny?"

I shake my head. "Nothing."

She purses her lips and narrows her eyes.

I just smile at her and pull her sunglasses from atop her silky soft hair and place them on her face. I let my thumbs linger for a few short seconds and caress her cheek.

"There, now you don't have to squint."

She touches their sides. "Thank you," she says, and I can see her nipples protruding in hard nubs.

I'm not sure if it's from the water I dripped on her or my touch, but I'm going with the latter. I've behaved myself for much longer than I ever thought I could. But I know she wants me and if she won't admit it, I'm going to have to push her along a little. The old me would already have done that. Hell, the old me would never have allowed a girl to call the shots.

But I've made too many wrong decisions in my life and have too many atonements to make. And she deserves one of them. The fact that she's even talking to me is enough reason to stick around.

She smooths one last squirt of sunscreen over her chest and my eyes drop again to her hard nipples beading through the fabric of her bikini top. Fuck, now I'm sure I'm popping out too.

Averting my eyes in a useless attempt to tame my dick, I have this sudden realization. "Red?" I ask.

She looks up at me.

"Have you ever surfed before?"

She scrunches her brow. "No. But how hard can it be?"

I try not to choke on my laughter. "Maybe just a little harder than you think."

"That's why I'm here. So you can teach me."

"Right," I say, scratching my head because it's just that easy.

She smiles.

I take a deep breath and rub my hands together. "Okay, let's do this."

"Yeah." She beams at me and does a slight jump into the air. Her earrings bob and her necklaces jangle as she heads toward the water.

I love how excited she gets and really hate to disappoint her, but I grab her hand and pull her back. "Whoa, where are you going?"

She whips her head around. "To surf."

"Yeah . . . not quite yet." I give her a serious look.

She looks at me, confused. "Okay, what is it?"

I step toward her and even with the chill in the air, a heat flares between us regardless of what "guidelines" have been set. Today the attraction feels stronger than ever. But now that I have a mission, teach S'belle Wilde how to surf, I have something to take my mind off it—for now. I push forward and answer her question. "You can't surf with your jewelry on. You have to be able to move without restraint," I tell her.

"Oh," she says, shrugging before circling her hands around her neck. The wind catches in her hair, and the necklaces seem to get caught in it.

"Look down," I say.

She does without question and I carefully untangle the necklaces from her hair and remove them from around her neck. When she raises her head, her eyes lift to meet mine and we stare at each other for a few short moments. My heart is beating wildly and I have to cut my glance sideways to slow its pace. With the necklaces gripped firmly in the palm of my hand, I step closer and pinch my fingers around her earlobe to gently remove the hoop from her ear. "These too."

Her breathing quickens, I can see it in the rise and fall of her chest. With almost no space between us, her eyes meet mine again and we speak to each other clearly without words. We seem to be able to communicate best that way, or maybe we are just more honest about our feelings with our silent acknowledgments? I'm not sure. But our relationship began with unspoken words and has moved painfully slowly in the very same manner.

The sun beats down, but that's not where the heat I feel is coming from. When the rays become even brighter as the morning clouds burn away, I blink rapidly at the sudden abundance of light shining on us. The magnetism between us is undeniable and I have to remind myself of what I am doing. Glancing down, my eyes hit my board. Yes, right, getting her ready for our surf lesson. Shifting my gaze, I catch the sparkle in the sand and grin before saying, "One last thing."

She watches as I drop to my knees. I let my fingertips trail down her legs on the way and notice the deep breath she draws in. I motion for her to lift her foot and set it on my leg. When she does she braces her hand on my shoulder and her touch sears me, makes me ache for her. I try to catch her gaze, but my eyes dart to the gleam in her belly button. The ring pierced inside it is a four-leaf clover fabricated with gold and green emeralds.

Glancing up, I ask, "Are you Irish?"

"A little. My grandfather was Irish."

"Is that the significance of this?" I point to the clover.

She stiffens. "No, it's not."

My eyes are pulled back to it. I want nothing more than to run my tongue around it: it takes every ounce of control I have not to. I have to keep reminding myself I'm supposed to be teaching her how to surf. Focusing on the task at hand, I glide my fingers across the top of her foot as I slowly unbuckle the sandal strap. Her leg quivers slightly from the contact. I run my palms up the back of her calf. Her skin is soft and smooth and feels so good. I grip her calf tightly as I raise her leg slightly and slowly remove her sandal. Brushing some of the sand off her perfectly painted toes, I drop my knee to the ground and to steady herself she rests her other hand on my bare shoulder. Her body cages my head. With her stomach so close to my mouth, I let my lips skim the ornament. Nothing that seems obnoxious, just enough to let her know that I want her.

Her whole body trembles and she quickly stands up straight. "I can do the other one."

"No, please let me," I insist with a devilish grin.

Once I've repeated the process, I can only hope that it turned her on as much as it turned me on. With my heart pounding and my pulse racing, I stand up and take a deep breath. Letting it out, I let my eyes rove over her one more time—she's so fucking sexy. When they land on her face, I pause and allow our eyes to lock. Then I force myself to shake away the thoughts of what I want to do to her and instead lift the large bag she's got draped over her shoulder and dump everything I'm holding in it. "There, now you're almost ready. Just tie your hair back so it doesn't catch in the wind."

While she fumbles through her bag, I take a moment to pull myself together. When I agreed to this friends thing, I knew I was agreeing to take it slow, but it feels like utter torture with her standing in front of me practically naked and I can't help blurring the lines a little. In the past if a girl I was interested in had ever thrown out the *friend* word, I would have deleted her number from my phone. But there's just something about S'belle . . .

She lifts her arms and pulls her hair up off her shoulders. She smiles at me as I watch her. Yeah, there's something about her. *Everything* about her is sexy as hell—the way she moves, the faces she makes when she's concentrating on something, even the way she stands.

"Ready," she says with a small bounce.

Does she have any idea what that does to me? I scan her body again as I pick my board up, and this time I notice the hint of a scar peeking out from her bathing suit bottoms.

I point to it. "What happened?"

She glances down and quickly adjusts her bottoms.

She blows some stray pieces of hair out of her eyes. "Are we going to start this lesson today or what?"

I laugh and toss my board to the ground. I sit on it and pat the empty space beside me.

She stares at me.

"Sit down."

She does but makes sure our bodies don't touch.

I smirk over at her. "Let's go over the guidelines."

She blinks at me without speaking.

"The guidelines of surfing."

"Surfing has guidelines?"

"More like generalities, things you should know. But I'll call them guidelines."

She rolls her eyes.

I grin and raise a finger. "Number one, the instructor must always be respected."

She laughs and shoves my shoulder. Again her skin against mine feels anything but wrong.

I raise an eyebrow.

"Go on, I'm listening," she says.

"First, do you know what a rip current is?"

She shakes her head.

Five minutes into my guidelines, it's apparent she has no knowledge whatsoever about surfing and there's no way I'm letting her go out there on a board today. When she asked to come surfing, I assumed she knew how—but she doesn't even know how to stand on a board or which end is which.

We need to start with the basics. I find a stick to draw in the sand. She pays attention and her eagerness to attempt surfing does nothing but fuel the fire between us. I point out to the water. "She's in charge out there. You have to respect her. Know what you can handle and what you can't. No two waves are ever the same."

An hour of Surfing 101 later, we both need a break. She takes a sip from the water bottle I hand to her, and some spills from her mouth down to her chest. Immediately I have a vision of licking the drips up for her. When she bends over toward her giant purse, I follow the lines of her body and notice the sand sticking everywhere and think I should wipe it off for her. But she stands with a cup of grapes in her hand before I get close enough.

I bite down on my lower lip instead. "Do you have a picnic lunch in there too? Because if not we need to take a break and eat."

She pops a grape in her mouth. "No." She laughs. "I stopped and grabbed these with my coffee this morning, but I think I should have picked up some sandwiches too. I didn't know it was going to take this long to learn to surf." She blows some hair out of her eyes.

I can't help laughing at her. "I'm only kidding."

She extends her hand, offering me the cup. "Want some?"

I flash her a boyish grin. "Yes, I want some." I move closer and tuck that same strand of hair back behind her ear before curling my hand around hers and pinching a grape from the container.

Our faces are so close that it's hard to tell whose breathing is louder. But I'm sure it's mine when she lowers herself to the ground and brushes against me before she takes a seat. She wipes her face and drinks thirstily from the bottle.

"You all right?"

"Yes, I think I just need a breather. This is hard."

I plop down beside her. "Want to go grab some food? Call it a day?"

"No. I'm having fun." She buries her toes in the sand and I mimic her action.

"Okay, but let's take a short break."

She nods.

We sit on the shore in comfortable silence for a bit and both watch the way the waves break. I assess the wind conditions as she studies the current rolling in. But I also find myself glancing over at her and thinking about how much fun I've had with her over the past few weeks. And even though we haven't had sex, I've enjoyed her company. I seem to want her near me all the time. It's not a feeling I'm used to. But sex or not, things have definitely progressed between us since our first date. And I haven't pushed her. I've let her set the pace for the most part. And the fact that she joined me this morning in something she knows I love triggers an odd feeling in my stomach.

CHAPTER 14
I Choose You

Bell

It's a beautiful day for the beach. The sun is shining, there's just a slight breeze, and he's here sitting next to me.

He leans in close and startles me. "Look over there. Watch what he does."

With a grin, we both watch the guy as waves rise from under him and he catches one just right. "It looks like heaven."

He jumps to his feet and pulls me up. "Come on, let's do this. Lie down on the board on your stomach."

"Shouldn't we be in the water?"

"Red, you have a few dry land lessons to complete before we take you out there."

My hands go to my hips. "What do you mean? Surfing is done in the water, not on the beach."

"Yes, it is. But not for us—not today."

I pout my lips but mostly for show because dry lessons means his hands are on me, and I can't deny how much I like his touch.

He drops down on the board and all his muscles flex in the most delicious way. "Like this. See, you have to move fast." He snaps from his stomach to his feet. "It looks easy but it's not. Speed is what matters. And as simple as it sounds, the less time you spend trying to get to your feet, the more success you'll have staying up. Do you know how to stand on the board?"

My eyes are ogling the ridges of his abdominal muscles and I fear I might be drooling.

"Red? You got that?"

I start to shake my head mostly because I haven't tried to process what he said, not because I don't understand it. I was too busy looking at what I haven't seen in what seems like a very long time.

"Come here." His tone is commanding and his voice deep.

I take a step and position myself right in front of him where he wants me. He nudges my feet apart with his, and the friction between his toes and my skin makes my pulse throb in places I didn't even know it could.

"This is the tail," he says, pointing to where my back leg is.

I shift my eyes and curl my toes into his. "Got it," I say as my mouth goes dry.

"And this is the midpoint," he says, trailing his fingertips down my thigh and peering over my shoulder.

By now I'm unable to speak and we stay like this for a few heartbeats—he's standing close behind me in a provocative way. When his hands go to my hips, I have to close my eyes. He adjusts my stance so that my back is flush with his stomach and all I can think about is how much I need to have him.

"Just like this," he whispers in my ear. His voice is hoarse.

His fingers glide up my skin from my hips to my waist as he realigns my stance. I wonder if he can feel my racing heartbeat. I can't help myself and I lean into him, pressing the small of my back into what I already knew was there—his erection. He pops off the board like a rocket. My eyes snap open and his gaze follows every curve of my body before landing on my face.

He clears his throat. "Okay, so next you'll move from a horizontal position up to your feet. Got it?"

I chew on my lip. Does he have any idea how crazy he's making me? I swear he's doing it on purpose. But I do as he instructs and lie on my stomach. When I swivel my gaze, I notice he averts his stare toward the water.

"Okay, Red, snap," he snaps.

I hop to my feet but lose my balance and stumble down on top of the sand. He dashes to catch me but ends up landing on top of me instead. His body molds to mine perfectly and the closeness and familiarity make me crave him in a way that's painful. I don't push him away and he doesn't move. Both of us are breathing hard and I can feel his heart beating as erratically as mine.

After a beat, he rises to his elbows and looks down at me. "Are you okay?"

I nod and watch as his eyes dart to my lips, then to my eyes. My hands move on their own and when I grasp his jaw a guttural moan escapes his mouth. I can no longer fight the feeling. I no longer want to. He lowers his head and hovers his mouth over my lips. I want him to kiss me. I know he wants to. But when the coolness of the water surrounds us, I scream. He quickly stands, grabbing my arm and bringing me with him. The tide rolls in and he laughs as I brush water from my face. I pull the tie from my hair and discover that the water has brought back my curls.

He twists a piece of my hair around my finger. "I like your hair curly. I remember it this way."

I blow some stray strands out of my eyes as he runs his fingers through my hair.

"Really?" I ask, surprised.

He moves closer to me. "Yes. I do. I really do."

I smile and tuck a piece of my wild locks behind my ear. I stare up at him into those blue eyes. "Why can't we take the board into the water?"

He grabs my hand and points out into the vast ocean with it. "Because that out there is dangerous and I don't want you to get hurt. I'll let you know when you're ready."

"So we'll do this again?" I ask.

"I hope so. I'd like to think I'm a good teacher." He smirks at me.

Moments pass without words while I stare at him, but I think he knows what I'm thinking. I step closer to him and grab his other hand.

He moves into me, leaving no space between us. His eyes are locked on mine.

"Remember when you asked me what would happen to my guidelines when I changed my mind?" I ask.

His thumbs skim over my thighs with our fingers still laced at our sides. "Yeah. Yeah, I do." He offers me a sexy grin. "You said you didn't see it going that far."

The heat between us is almost unbearable as he gazes into my eyes. He closes the final space that separates us.

I run my palms up his chest. "Well, it's every girl's prerogative to say those words and to change her mind after. You told me to tell you if I changed my mind and . . . Ben, I have."

"Fuck," he groans.

I nod with a glimmer in my eye because that's just what I want to do.

"Fuck," he groans again.

A few more moments of silence pass as we communicate without words.

He places his hands on both sides of my face. "What made you change your mind?"

I push the hair from his eyes. "You."

With a devilish grin he asks, "Would you care to elaborate?"

"Later," I say, making my voice sound low and enticing.

He nods and then tangles his fingers in my hair, pulling me so tight against him I know he can feel my hard nipples against his bare chest. I caress the skin of his back and when his fingers sneak beneath the golden string of my bikini top, I shiver. My hands move to his shoulders, his neck, his hair. He looks down into my eyes but still hasn't kissed me.

"Why haven't you kissed me?" I ask in a breathy voice.

The corners of his lips quirk up. "I'm enjoying watching you," he says.

But I think it's more. I think he wants to make sure I want this. And I do. I don't care about anything other than him right now. So I make sure he sees nothing but absolute certainty in my eyes. And then just like that, he grabs my face. Our mouths meet, our tongues collide, and we breathe each other in. We kiss with a hunger that I'm almost certain can never be satisfied. Time slips away as our hands move freely roaming over each other in ways they shouldn't in a public place. With my heart thundering in my ears, my pulse racing, and my breathing out of control, I never want this moment to end.

Then just like that, he breaks our connection. My mind is whirling with how much I want him, right here, right now. The beach is fairly secluded, even if it's not private.

"Come back to my place with me," he whispers.

And I want to. I really do. But I can't. I run my palms down his chest, trying to soothe the sting that's about to come. "I can't. I have Ivy's release party tonight. I should have left already."

He rests his forehead against mine and grabs my fingers, lacing our hands together. "Later tonight, then," he says, and kisses me once more.

CHAPTER 15
Show Me

Ben

Having the freedom to finally touch her makes me feel like a kid in the candy store. The beach is quiet, with few surfers in the water and even fewer cars in the parking lot. I've thought about her, remembered what she felt like, ached for her body to touch mine for so many weeks you'd think knowing we will finally be together in just a few short hours would be enough, but it isn't. I don't want to wait.

But I walk her to her car with my hand resting on her ass, all the while whispering things in her ear that I'm going to do to her. She looks up at me, a glimmer in her eyes, and I swear I growl at her.

When we reach the parking lot I step in front of her and lift her chin, forcing her eyes to mine. "I want you wearing this when I see you later."

She pushes up on her toes and bites on my lip. "I thought you'd want me wearing nothing."

"Fuck," I mutter. "You're killing me."

She smiles in that sexy way she has.

I can feel myself turning predatory. With a slide of my hands into her bikini bottoms, I palm her ass. We walk the rest of the way like that to the car with our lips locked. Only when she fumbles for her keys in her purse do I remove my hands. But when I hear the click of the lock, I open the door quickly and push her up against the opening. She gasps and threads her fingers through my hair. Then I kiss her hard. Her lips are soft and taste like mint—I've never forgotten their taste. I run my hands over her bathing suit top and then down her bare stomach, where I stop to finger the clover I saw earlier. "You're so fucking sexy," I murmur.

She freezes for a moment but then lets out a soft moan when my fingertips graze the edge of her bikini bottoms. I twist my head to survey the area. Her car is parked at the end of the lot and we seem fairly isolated. If I could fuck her here I would, but we've already gone down that road. The next time I have her, I want her in my bed. But that doesn't mean I won't settle for leaving her thinking about me until she sees me again.

"Red," I whisper over her mouth.

"Hmm . . . ," she breathes, nipping at my lip.

I don't say anything else. Instead I rub the heel of my palm over her pussy.

Her lips part and she makes that quiet sound again.

"Do you like that?" I ask her.

"Yes," she answers, her breath blowing hot against my neck.

I slide my fingers inside the golden string of her bottoms and stroke them up and down before stopping to massage her clit.

Her eyes widen and her head bobs side to side.

"It's okay. Don't worry, no one can see you with me standing in front of you," I whisper in her ear. "Do you like how this feels?"

She gasps, nodding and digging her fingers into my flesh.

I kiss up her neck and stop to whisper in her ear, "You're so wet."

My cock grows so hard it throbs almost painfully as I watch her—the way her eyelids close, the way her mouth parts, and how her hold on me tightens with every move of my hand. I want to touch her everywhere. I want to kiss every spot on her body and then sink deep inside her. But here in the parking lot there's no way I can do that. With one arm shielding one side of us and her car door shielding the other, I move my fingers mercilessly in and out of her, wishing they were my cock. My pulse pounds in my ears when she buries her head in my neck and whispers something I can't hear. The waves crash against the rocks, the wind whistles as it blows, but there is no mistaking her muffled cries of pleasure. She nips at the skin on my neck while digging her nails into my shoulders, but I don't stop. I want her to remember me. Her body pulses against my hand and only when her body shudders and a much louder "Oh God, yes" escapes her lips do I stop.

"You make me so hot," I murmur in her ear.

"That was nothing," she purrs.

"I can't wait to see something, then."

She cups my face and pulls me in to look at her. "I can't wait to do *something* to you."

Fuck. She can't wait. I can't wait. I slide my hand out of her bottoms and around to her ass, pushing her into me so she can feel how much I want her. Her hands slide down my chest to my board shorts, but I grab them.

"Later," I whisper in her ear.

"I can't leave you like this," she giggles, pushing her hips into my erection.

"Don't you have to go to work?"

She nods. "I'm probably already going to be late."

I pull both our hands to my mouth and kiss hers. Then I smack her ass. "So get going. Now!"

She rubs her ass but I didn't hit it hard.

I smile. "You like that, don't you?"

Her head drops and her hair covers her face so I can't see it.

"You don't have to answer. I already know you do."

She collapses into the seat of her car but pulls me down for one last kiss. "Ben . . ."

I pause and look at her.

"It really will be worth the wait. I promise."

I shake my head and stand there as she puts her car in DRIVE. Then something occurs to me and I chase after her, pounding on the door.

She stops and opens her window. "Are you crazy?"

"No, I just wanted to tell you, don't let the past dictate the future, okay? We'll work it out. I promise."

A mix of motions drifts across her face but none I can nail. She nods and closes her window and I watch as she drives away. With a grin I wouldn't want her to see in the mirror, I think how much I like the way she kisses me, the way her lips taste, how much I love touching her—everywhere. Then when her car disappears around the bend, I take off toward the cold water of the ocean to ease the pain of my throbbing cock.

The sun is just beginning to set once I decide to pack up and head out, so it's not too blinding. Blondie's is just a few feet away. My feet kick up little bits of sand as I walk down the familiar beach with my board tucked under my arm and think what a big day tomorrow is for me. November first marks the day the announcement of both takeovers will be made, but more important, shares of Plan B will be available to the public. It's a huge financial risk as well as an excellent opportunity for me.

"Hey, man," I greet Noel.

He beams. "Hey, Benny boy. How was it out there?"

"Fucking amazing. I haven't spent the whole day out on her in months."

He smiles, baring his yellowing teeth and pride at the same time.

"I didn't expect to still see you in here this late. Faith isn't going to be happy if you miss dinner." I wink at him.

"Fuck, what time is it?" he says, looking at his watch.

I shrug as I lean my board against the wall. "The sun's just about down, so it must be close to your dinnertime."

"Fuck. Come home with me. Have dinner with us. Then Faith can't be pissed off at me for being late," he begs.

"Can't tonight. Sorry, you're on your own."

"Damn, boy, way to make a grown man beg."

I just shake my head.

He opens the avocado green fridge and pulls out two cold ones. He tosses me one and I catch it but shake my head no and place the can on the counter.

"Don't be a fucking pansy ass." But Noel says it with a grin.

"I'll give you pansy ass," I tell him as I grab a long board hanging on the wall. I skateboarded all the time as a kid, so I have no doubt my agility will prevail. I give this bad boy a spin around the shop worth my time. I move fast. Of course the adrenaline coursing through my body certainly helps. When I stop, I flip the end and push it his way. "Your turn."

His hands go up surrender-style, as he shakes his head no, then strides over to lock the front door.

"Come on," I coax. "Who's being the pansy ass now? I thought the coolest thing about long boards is that you could even sell them to dudes' grandmas."

We both laugh again but this time at the sales spiel he gives the kids in his shop who come to work for him. I know it well. I spent so many hours here as a teenager. As he closes the place down, I pull my shirt from my bag and slide into it, tugging my jeans over my board shorts before slipping into my boots, not bothering to tie them. "Thanks for letting me leave my shit here. I still haven't had a rack put on my new car yet."

"So you keep saying. And I'll keep saying anytime, you know that. And, Ben, Faith would really love to see you."

I nod. "I'll call you next week. I might just come and bring a guest."

"Oh yeah? You decided to chase some lucky girl?" he asks.

"You know what, Noel, I did."

He slaps his hand on my shoulder. "That's the way, boy."

We both walk out the back door together and as he hops in his truck he yells, "Don't forget to call me."

I wave good-bye. "I won't."

The shiny black paint of my BMW touring bike is gleaming off the reflection of the streetlights. Its low silhouette and sleek shape are all that remain in the parking lot at this time of night. I can't stifle my smile when I see her green helmet with sparkles enameled in it strapped on its back. As I hop on I catch sight of where her car was parked earlier and remember what it felt like to touch her again, but for some reason it felt different this time—even better if that's possible. The next few hours can't fly by fast enough. I pull my phone from my pocket and scroll through my short list of contacts until I find her name—then I send her a quick text.

```
I'll pick you up. I don't want you driv-
ing back here tonight so late.

I'm more than capable of driving in the
dark and I didn't invite you over.

I'll be there at eleven.

I said I didn't invite you over.

I said I'd be there at eleven.

Fine. But don't come in.
```

I stare at my screen and shake my head. I'll be patient and wait until she's ready to tell her family, but not for too long. Of course I understand her hesitation. I'm done with secrets and hiding things. I've had enough of that shit to last a lifetime.

With the handlebars beneath my palms, I grip tight as the wind whips all around me and the dark sky meets the horizon before me. My intent when I took today off from work was that it would be a day of reflection. It's Halloween, which officially marks one year to the day that my downward spiral into oblivion began, which eventually resulted in me hitting rock bottom—hard. I was lost for many long months, but I've since found myself . . . becoming a better person.

Aside from walking around constantly feeling I'd been stabbed in the heart and punched in the gut at the same time, I was down and out with no one to turn to. My relationship with my sister had suffered from my blatant disregard of anyone else's feelings but my own. My friendship with Caleb had been strained from my deceitfulness, and even though we seemed to be back on track, he wasn't around. He was away training to become an FBI agent. And honestly, aside from Dahl I had no one left in my life. That's when I took off for Australia.

I spent four months there and loved every minute of it. When I returned to California I decided to live in LA in hopes of getting my old job back. But that too didn't go as planned. Not only did I live in a shithole motel for way too long, but I ended up as the wedding columnist for my old editor. I wanted my investigative journalist job back, but since I wouldn't play ball and divulge my source for the piece on the drug cartel or turn over the article I had written more than three years ago but never published, she pigeonholed me into a job she knew I'd hate. But I couldn't give her what she wanted. First of all, I no longer had any of that shit. I had given it all to Caleb. And second, my journalistic code of honor prevented me from divulging my sources. Taking the job she offered was just another poor choice I made in a long list of poor choices.

But I had already been down so many twisted roads I couldn't see straight anymore. Pinpointing a single catalyst is hard, but if I had to choose one I would say it was the investigation. And although the investigation might be why I had to leave my old life, it's not why I lost myself. But for the longest time I used it as the reason. Why wouldn't I?

The whole thing was so fucked up. It started out as a simple task—publish an article on drug trafficking. Easy enough, I thought . . . just research it, write it, gain critical attention, rise to the top—and I'd be the next Anderson Cooper. Well, that's not how it went down. The story I was investigating was not only way bigger than I ever could have imagined, but also much more dangerous. Dangerous enough that my subject wanted to kill me and threatened to kill my girl if I didn't stop. But even when I did stop, that wasn't enough—they were coming after me. So I faked my own death and disappeared for what I thought would be the rest of my life.

I defected to New York City and lived there for three years as Alex Coven. The first two years were rough, but by the third year I started to make a life for myself. I was hanging out with a girl I liked, started swimming and running again, stopped the excessive drinking, and even made a few friends. But that life seemed small and worthless the day the FBI knocked on my door and told me I could go back home to California. I didn't even have to think about it. All I knew was I had a second chance to get my old life back and I wanted it . . . all of it, including my girl, Dahlia London.

But three years was a long time to be gone, and things change, people change. Dahl wasn't the same girl I left behind. She was harder, maybe stronger, maybe more broken . . . I don't know exactly, but I do know she wasn't in love with me anymore. I tried to get her back, but it didn't take long to figure out I couldn't. I stopped my worthless efforts after my mother died. It was never going to happen anyway, especially after Dahl found out I had cheated on her in college and wouldn't you know it—it was with the sister of the guy she now loved.

Then as if that wasn't enough, my beloved mother suffered a stroke and passed away. After that I didn't give a fuck about anything anymore. I just wanted to forget everything . . . who I was, what I'd done, what had happened to me. Forget it all. And I can wholeheartedly say that no longer caring about anything was when I lost myself. I hit rock bottom because I didn't give a shit about anyone, not even myself.

My final wrong step came the day I watched Dahl's attacker and my shooter, Josh Hart, being found guilty of a pony charge. I couldn't take it anymore and as I was drowning myself in a bottle of Jack, my ex-girlfriend from New York City called me. Kimberly was looking for company and since I was too, I went to her. She was drunk, I was drunk, and I fucked her as if she were someone else. Of course Kimberly threw my ass out. I left her apartment full of guilt and not paying the least bit of attention to how much alcohol I had consumed.

That night I was pulled over and arrested for driving while intoxicated and had no one to call—Caleb was MIA, Serena was in Hawaii with Trent, and my only friends, Beck and Ruby, were out of town. That left me with only Dahl. And when I called her I was shocked that she came and bailed me out. My life changed after that. Maybe it was the arrest that scared the shit out of me, maybe it was closure—I had felt nothing but friendship toward Dahl when she drove me home—or maybe it was knowing I owed my mother more than the life I was leading.

But I turned things around after that day. I quit the job I hated, I let go of the loose ends to the investigation that I hadn't been able to put to rest, and I reconciled with my sister. I moved back to the place I loved—Laguna. And in the process of moving back into my mother's house, my sister and I discovered that my mother had been awarded a ten-million-dollar settlement for my father's wrongful death and had willed it to us. With that money I knew what I wanted to do with my life—help magazines suffering rejuvenate themselves.

I blink away the memories and look up. The stars above me are bright, the night is clear, and the air is warm, but I won't be taking my bike to pick up Bell tonight. I'm not sure she'd appreciate climbing on the back in a dress and heels even though I wouldn't mind. Hmm . . . maybe I should reconsider? Cruising up the hill to my driveway, I stop and put both feet on the ground—my intent was that today would be a day of reflection, but now I see it as another new beginning.

CHAPTER 16
What Now

Bell

Magic is in the air. The Amazing Grace Sound Studios have been transformed into a place fit for a princess for the unveiling of Ivy's new album, *My Mended Heart*, and by none other than myself. I couldn't be prouder of how it turned out. Elation is buoying me and nothing is going to squash it. I can't believe how much one day can change everything—put things in perspective. I shouldn't have been so worried about the past. I need to concentrate on the future . . . as Ben said. Because really—that's all that matters.

I breathe in the scent of the flowers that fill the room and then shift my gaze to admire the glimmer of light from the crystal chandeliers. The room looks magical, just as I envisioned. Amazing Grace has been transformed from a concrete hangar into a glittering nightclub. With six crystal chandeliers, dozens of round tables, and more than a hundred vases of purple dahlias and, of course, a splash of ivy.

I'm not late, but I'm by no means early. Jack and my mom drop me off before they park the car because they know I'm fretting. I have so much to do in so little time. Ivy and Xander are right on my heels and they try to catch up with me, but all I can squeeze out is a quick hello and congratulations. I have to run to make sure the food has arrived, and the table centers are just as I described, not to mention make sure Nix and Garrett get off the stage and stop fooling around. I'm feeling a little overwhelmed and I also feel bad for not bringing Ben, but we had discussed it last week. I'd told him I'd be too busy to bring a guest. That was the truth, but not the whole truth.

He had laughed and said, "Sound Music received an invitation, but Aerie will be attending since my ownership of the company won't be made public until the following day."

Admittedly I was relieved. I still am. I'm not ready to tell my family anything—there are just too many variables. And thank God ownership of Sound Music has never come up so I haven't had to feign ignorance or lie.

"Garrett, get off the stage and stop goofing around," I scold.

His brow creases. "What's wrong with you? You look really red."

I feel my forehead. My temperature seems normal, but I'm burning up. "No, I don't. Do you think you can help me out and find Leif? I want to make sure he has everything set up for Ivy to take the stage."

He scuffs the carpet with his foot and offers me a bright smile. "Anything for you—tomato face." He grins.

I shove his shoulder. "Cut it out."

He strides toward the bar area but stops and tosses over his shoulder, "Red and green." He points to my shorts romper. "You're practically ready for Christmas."

I chase after him grabbing a napkin off the table, ready to swat him.

"I better make like a hockey player and get the puck out of here." He laughs.

I really missed the gang while they were gone on tour. I'm glad that even though the Wilde Ones broke up they are all still working together at the studio. And of course we have the addition of Ivy now and her bassist, Leif Morgan, both of whom I adore. Speaking of adoring—in walk my brother and Dahlia.

Dahlia looks amazing. She's wearing a pewter-colored halter dress with a chain neck and a large brooch at the center of the deep V. River looks pretty good himself in a suit much like Xander's, and he has opted for no tie. He and Dahlia are fashionably late as always, but since today is their one-year anniversary and I was practically late myself, I think it's perfectly acceptable.

I watch as River and Dahlia meet up with Xander and Ivy. I notice River search Xander's eyes, and if I hadn't been looking, I would never have noticed the slight nod Xander gives him. River grabs Xander around the neck and pulls him forward. Oh my God, the engagement. And it's River and Dahlia's anniversary too. What's wrong with me? I rush over but it's too late. The four of them are huddled together. I move fast, as fast as I can in these heels, but still Garrett beats me to them.

"Aw . . . I missed out on the hugs and kisses. What, because we all work together now I get shafted?" he says.

I try to push forward to congratulate my brother, but there's a tap on my shoulder.

"Hey, Dino, everything all set with the food?"

"Well, there were a few changes to the menu," he says softly.

"Like what?" I ask sternly.

Out of the corner of my eye, I see Garrett grab River by the collar and jerk him backward. "Dino, I'll be right back."

I head over to Garrett with my hands on my hips.

"You're late, dick. Come on," he quips to River. Then he starts to shake his hips and sing, "LA, let's get this party started!"

I guess the old band is going to have a jam session, because when I look toward the stage they're all up there—River, Leif, Garrett, Nix, the drummer, and even Zane, River's replacement before Ivy. Since the crowd rushes the dance floor and throws their hands in the air, dancing to a cover of "Hands All Over," I decide to leave them alone. It's a record release party after all. It's then I notice I still have the napkin clenched in my hand, and thoughts of Ben instantly surface. His hands on my body, the way he knows just how to touch me. The way he made me come right there on the beach with firecrackers behind my eyelids.

"Bell, do you want the trays of champagne brought out now or after Ivy sings?" Matt asks.

I blink away my dreamy state, a little embarrassed that Matt might have just gotten a glimpse of what I was imagining. I shake away the thoughts for now and decide it's also time for me to get this party started.

"After, I think," I say, and then go in search of Ivy.

"Finally," I say when I find her. With my nerves calmed I get to look at her for the first time tonight. She looks utterly beautiful in her short dark blue sapphire satin dress. I'm shocked that Xander hasn't had a heart attack yet over her wearing it—it's not only sleeveless but backless as well. He's very protective over, as he says, what is his. But since the dress matches the color of her eyes as well as her sapphire star earrings, he must have let it go or maybe he's just more secure. Her earrings glitter from her ears like shooting stars from the sky. They make me smile every time I see them. They were my grandmother's and Ivy always admired them when she wore them. It seemed fitting that Mimi gave them to her, because she always thought Ivy was going to be a star.

"Come with me," I tell her. "So?" I ask.

She looks at me blankly.

I grab her hand and turn it over and there it is—the engagement ring my father gave to my mother. I hug her tightly and whisper, "Congratulations."

"Thank you, Bell."

I pull away. "Now come on, we have things to do."

I drag her over to the photo booth I rented. I have her pose a few times, well, maybe more than a few. Next Dino captures my attention and points to the table centers. They are missing the silver stars I asked to be confettied around the flowers.

"I have to go," I say, running off to place some of the photographs in the centers instead.

Aerie sashays up to me as I'm fixing the tables. "Bell, you look amazing. I love your outfit," she says in a really bubbly manner.

"Thank you. I love your look too." She looks very businesslike with a touch of sass—her hair is in a bun and she's wearing a purple pantsuit with pumps, but surprisingly it's low-cut and shows a hint of cleavage.

She smiles. "So, how are things?"

I know exactly what she's asking and I can't take the chance of discussing Ben here, so I deflect the question. "Where's Jagger?"

She gestures toward the makeshift bar with her wineglass. "Oh, Jack caught him on our way in and they're huddled somewhere."

"Film talk?" I roll my eyes.

"Yep."

"That's so Jack. So, how's the movie anyway?"

"Still hasn't started filming. Production issues."

"Sorry to hear that."

She shrugs. "I'm going to get another drink before I tell Xander and River about Ben acquiring *Sound Music* magazine."

I gulp. "Oh." I want to say thanks for the heads-up because I plan to be nowhere near either of those conversations. I watch Aerie approach Xander and quickly avert my gaze, not even wanting to witness his reaction. When I scan the room, my eyes land on not only Tate but Romeo too. Romeo grins with a slight wave and I wave back, then head toward the hallway and into one of the offices we've turned into our prep room. I suspect Tate brought Romeo as his plus one. Tate has been a friend of Jack's for a while, so I knew he'd be invited. His father was Jack's business associate many years ago. But when did he become buddies with Romeo?

Once I have everything as organized as possible, I check my phone. No texts from Ben since before I left. I can't understand why. I feel so disappointed I could have invited him to come with me—but I was too chicken. The thought of Ben in the same room with River and Xander seriously makes me almost break out in hives. In fact, my skin is itchy just thinking about it.

But Ivy and Xander offer the perfect distraction when I meet them in the hallway. We haven't spent that much time together since I've been living in Ben World, but I've known her since I was ten, so I feel a connection to her.

"No more pictures, Bell," she jokes.

I have to laugh. "Oh God, no. I think Xander might lose it if I ask him to smile one more time."

"What's so funny?" Xander asks, putting his arm around Ivy and pulling her to him. I love seeing him like this—happy and in love.

"Nothing. Nothing at all," we both say in unison.

My phone dings and I quickly pull it out of the pocket of my little romper. Finally . . . Ben. Why is seeing him in such a short time making me so nervous? It's not as if we haven't sleep together before. I read his text.

```
Did I tell you how much I enjoyed the
noises you made in the parking lot
earlier?
```

A slight rosy color blooms on my cheeks—I can feel it. My body already feels ten degrees hotter than it should, and his message only intensifies the heat.

"Who's that? A guy? Maybe a boyfriend?" Ivy teases.

Xander snorts. "You don't know Bell well enough yet—she always has a boyfriend."

I try not to let his quip jab me in the heart, but it does. Yes, I always *had* a boyfriend, but they were never really boyfriends, not that he'd understand that. I've always had this overwhelming need to make men happy. It's deep-rooted, my therapist said—stems from feeling that I couldn't make my father happy so I was trying to make up for that. But I've worked through those issues now.

I redirect my attention to my brother and put my hands on my hips. "I'll have you know, brother of mine, I have not had a boyfriend since Tate almost a year ago."

Xander raises his arms in surrender. "Wow, calm down. I didn't know. But I'm just teasing you."

I roll my eyes at him and quickly text Ben back.

> Did I tell you I make those sounds when I
> eat my favorite foods?

I slide my phone back into my pocket and watch Xander slip a stuffed mushroom in Ivy's mouth.

"Um . . . these are so good," she says, and I want to gag. Fungus with bread crumbs is definitely not something I had selected for the menu tonight. I wonder what else got messed up.

"Hey, little sis, aren't those your favorite?" he asks, pointing to a silver tray with scallops wrapped in bacon.

"Very funny."

"Why don't you try one of them for old times?" Xander asks.

"No, thank you," I say almost menacingly.

"I dare you," he challenges.

My gaze flits over him in an assessing manner. In our family we never shut down a dare. So I reach for the appetizer. I squish my nose in disgust and pop it into my mouth, swallowing it without even chewing. Then I cover my mouth to stop from gagging.

"Happy?" I wave my hands in the air at me.

"What? Are you going to throw up?" Xander asks, now with concern in his voice.

I cover my lips again, not really sure if I'm going to, and decide I'd better hurry to the bathroom just in case. "I just remembered. I forgot the Bellinis. I'll be back."

I make it into the bathroom and I'm fine by then. There's a chair in the corner and I take a seat, pulling out my phone to see if Ben responded. He did.

```
Do you forget, I've heard the sounds you
make when you've eaten and they are noth-
ing like what I heard today. Just admit
it, you want me.
```

I smile hugely and my cheeks prickle when I do. Quickly I text him back.

```
That's a fact I've never denied. You just
never asked.
```

```
I was being respectful of your "guide-
lines." But tell me now, "Do you want
me?"
```

```
I've always wanted you.
```

```
Fuck me.
```

```
That's the plan.
```

My stomach flutters and I'm feeling pretty proud of myself for my wit. I shove my phone in my pocket and stop to look in the mirror. When I do I'm a little shocked by how red my skin is. I splash some cool water over my face, but my discomfort level is starting to rise. A dab of powder takes away the shine and dulls the color.

A few hours later, I'm tired but happy watching everyone enjoying themselves. I'm also feeling eager for it to end.

"Perk up," Tate whispers in my ear.

The hand he places on my waist starts drifting down to my rear. I jump and turn around with a glare that should remind him where things stand between us. The dilation of his pupils tells me he's had way too much to drink.

He lifts his glass. "You know how to throw a great party."

"Thank you," I say curtly.

He frowns at me. "You don't look happy."

I step back. "I am . . . about the party."

I glance around, trying to avoid his scrutinizing stare. Romeo is dancing extremely close with some woman. Their bodies are rubbing against each other in a way that screams *we're having sex tonight*—I'm not sure whether it's his fiancée, because I've never met her, even though this woman does look familiar to me.

Jagger and Aerie are dancing in the same way, but the sight of them together makes me smile. And River is kissing Dahlia while Garrett stands next to them as if waiting for him to finish. Garrett really needs a girlfriend of his own. I thought he was into Ena, Xander's assistant, but it seems she's with Leif. I can't keep up.

"You're extremely moody," Tate says.

"Me?" I say, trying not to sound as offended as I am. My grin fades. "I'm not the moody one," I say in a bold tone I haven't displayed in a while.

He clams up.

"I have a few things to take care of."

He grabs my arm before I can walk away. "Dance with me."

"No, thank you."

"Who are you seeing?" His short, sharp tone isn't the normal one I'm used to. This tone is laced with menace.

"Oh, there you are," my mother says, oblivious of the scene before her.

I try to smile at her, to make everything seem all right.

Her eyes zero in on my face and I know it must be flushed with anger. "You look like you got too much sun today."

"Yeah, I think I did—"

I'm interrupted by the sound of Xander's voice in the microphone. "Here she is, everyone—Ivy Taylor," he announces.

"Come on, darling, we're going to miss it," my mother says, reaching for my hand. I take hers and despite myself I feel guilty I haven't told her about Ben.

We press our way over to the stage and listen to a medley of Ivy's new songs. I close my eyes and sing along, but all the while visions of Ben kissing me, putting his hands on my body, feeling me in the most intimate places are all I can think about. I open my eyes when everyone applauds, smiling when I see the look on Xander's face. He holds out his arm for Ivy to join him and then does something completely out of character and jumps onstage, swinging Ivy around. I look at my mother and we both have tears in our eyes. She pulls me in for a hug and her slight touch feels like pinpricks against my tender skin.

"Don't cry, Mom."

"I'm trying not to, but seeing him so happy makes me so happy."

"I know, Mom. I know."

She takes a deep breath and whispers, "It's what I want for all of my children."

I pull away. "I have to go check on Dino and Matt."

She nods.

I spend what's left of the night talking to the guests and trying to avoid both Tate and Romeo, who have approached me numerous times

together and separately. My phone vibrates in my pocket. I pull it out
and read the message.

```
I should be there in about twenty min-
utes.
```

I text back.

```
I can't wait to see you.
```

```
I can't wait to do a lot of things.
```

My nerves flutter like the butterflies in my stomach, but I don't
have much time to think about them because the music begins and I
know it's time for the engagement announcement. Keeping my mouth
shut has been difficult but I managed it. River starts to sing "Marry
Me," the No Doubt version, of course—Xander always said Ivy looked
like Gwen Stefani. As River sings, Xander braces his arms around Ivy
and they dance. My mother has tears streaming down her face and
when they finish she goes to hug them.

A tinge of jealousy flares within me. River and now Xander—both
of my brothers have found their happily ever after. Will I ever find
mine? But I push that aside because I couldn't be happier for my
brother. Our family has been through a lot, but I think Xander has
been through the most. He deserves this. I notice Jack flash a grin at
them and then engulf Ivy in a huge embrace.

Dino elbows me. "Didn't you want these?" he asks.

"Yes, oh yes." For the first time as I thank Dino I think Ben might
be right—he's interested in me. I'm flattered, but it's almost laughable,
as he's so young.

I wave my hands toward River and he crosses the room to grab the
champagne.

"You're on fire," he comments.

I laugh. "I'm prepared."

"No, for real. You're so red. Are you okay?"

I jab the bottle at him. "I'm fine. Let's get a move on."

Dahlia is at his side, snapping pictures, and I trail behind with the tray of champagne flutes.

"Pssttt," I say to her.

She looks over her shoulder.

"Happy anniversary."

She smiles. "Thank you."

We all circle around Xander and Ivy, and River tugs on the cork and it goes flying. I jump, startled by the noise. Laughter fills the room when he spills a little on the floor and flashes a grin. "I always say I'm not much of a bartender."

Xander whispers something to him that I can't hear. River nods and then the two embrace, pulling me in as well. Now tears well in my eyes. I love them so much.

River turns back to the crowd and hoists a glass high for a toast. "To Ivy and Xander. To true love."

We all clink our glasses and my tears of joy spill over.

I make a toast next. "To Ivy and Xander—if I ever doubted fate you've changed that for me. Because of you I believe in fairy tales, butterflies, and destiny."

Everyone looks at me questioningly. I shrug with a smile and they all let it go and start sipping their champagne.

When everyone starts to converse, I whisper in Ivy's ear, "I have to leave, but I'll be calling you to plan the wedding." And with that my heels click the floor as I dash as fast as I can toward the door.

CHAPTER 17
Navigate Me

Ben

The road between Laguna Beach and LA is once again becoming very familiar territory to me. In my BMW X-5, I head toward the City of Angels. I have a thing for BMWs—always have. I remember my father driving the oldest, ugliest orange BMW when I was a kid. They're some of the clearest memories I have of him. I'd be sitting in the backseat on the perforated black leather and watching as my father jammed his foot up and down when he tried to unstick the clutch or when he'd pound his fist against the stick next to him because he couldn't get the gears to shift. We'd almost always roll out of the driveway backward and my dad would yell words my mother would scold him for. I didn't understand why either of them seemed upset when to me it was nothing but fun. I'd sit in the backseat and laugh at them both.

Approaching the seemingly infinite lights that twinkle all around me, I find it odd to feel the start of a smile when I look ahead. I've always hated LA, but for some reason I don't see it as pretentious anymore. Instead it reminds me of Bell. The music in the car is low because I don't need to blast it to ease my thoughts as I careen through the streets. The night seems oddly quiet. But as I coast onto the streets of LA, the quietness fades. The tree-lined streets become lively, but it's not with cars. Trick-or-treaters fill the sidewalks—pumpkins, ghosts, goblins, and even a few Batman costumes parade door to door. I pass the *LA Times* building lit up in orange and remember how excited I was to start working there so many years ago. So much has happened since then. But I've put the past in the past and I'm moving forward.

The traffic light turns red and I stop and take the time to reread our texts from earlier. My anticipation of what the night is going to bring only grows by the moment, as does the size of my cock. The light turns green and I drive even faster to get there. Cars are emptying out of the parking lot as I pull in. I had considered attending a million different times, but each scenario ended with putting S'belle in an awkward situation and I didn't want to stress her out when this was meant to be a happy time for her family.

Putting my BMW in PARK, I look toward the car in front of me. The license plate reads T WYATT. What the fuck is that asshole doing here? I swivel my gaze toward the building and I'm caught off guard by the sign before me. Dahlia had told me what she named the company she started with her husband. But hearing about it and seeing the evidence in person are entirely different. Erected to the side of the pathway leading to the building's glass doors stands a huge rectangular concrete sign with the words TYLER RECORDS AND AMAZING GRACE STUDIOS scripted across it in rose letters.

This gesture rocks me more than I thought it would. My mother's name scripted in her favorite color makes everything suddenly seem more real. Maybe I was wrong about not caring if our relationship would be tainted by how it first began? How will my connection to the people inside affect a possible future with S'belle? Would her family ever be able to let the fact go that I cheated on Dahlia with S'belle?

If it was just about me, I couldn't give a shit. But I know how important her family is to her. I know she doesn't think they can accept me and my part in her past and that's why she hasn't told them she's been seeing me. Not sure anymore if I should go down this road with her, I shift my car into DRIVE, but before I can take my foot off the gas, the passenger door opens and S'belle slips inside.

Her lemony scent immediately assaults me. I breathe deep and glance at her. She's so fucking sexy wearing a green strapless shorts outfit with metallic flowers on it, and the same wisps of thin gold chains that I untangled from her hair this morning are wrapped around her neck. Her eyes sparkle as she leans toward me and I'm greeted with a breathy "Hi."

"Hi there, beautiful," I say, letting my doubts go as I stare at the girl sitting beside me.

Her smile widens.

"Did I mention I can't wait to strip your clothes off?"

She leans over toward me and slides her hands up my thighs, and my cock is just as excited as I am. I clear my throat, knowing we need to get out of the parking lot and back to her place . . . quickly.

She hovers over me, her hands on my legs. "Did I ever mention I took a striptease class a few years ago?"

I swallow. "A striptease class?"

"Yes, it was great exercise."

"Fuck," I mutter.

She sits back in her seat and when she attempts to strap her seat belt on she says, "Ouch."

"What is it?"

"Nothing," she responds.

"How was the party?"

Something flickers in her gaze. "It was . . . fun," she says. "But it would have been more fun if you were there."

"You didn't invite me," I joke.

She catches me off guard when her hands grab my face. And then her soft lips are on mine for a moment before she speaks. "You know it's complicated."

I do actually. We did discuss the event; we have yet to discuss just how complicated the situation is. But now is not the time. I grab the back of her neck and pull her even closer to me. When her soft lips meet mine I wonder what the hell I was thinking when I almost left without her. My tongue finds hers and I kiss her with the hunger I seem to feel for her all the time. When we finally break apart and neither of us is able to breathe, I look at her, into her eyes. "Do you know how much I want you?"

She nods, her eyes glimmering. "As much as I want you." She smiles.

I put the car in reverse and catch her gaze. "Are you ready?"

"More than ready." Her voice is hoarse but definitely not weak.

I put my foot on the brake and place my hand on her thigh. She jumps a little when I circle my thumb over her bare skin and after a few minutes she grabs my hand.

"Everything okay?" I ask, shooting a glance her way as I hop on the freeway.

"Yes," she says with forced exaggeration.

"Really? Because it doesn't sound that way."

"I'm fine," she says, moving our hands over to my leg.

I exit the freeway and stop at the light. "Come here," I tell her, and grab her shoulder, pulling her over to me. Again she jumps. I let go of her and take her chin in my hand. "Okay, what's the matter, Red? Do you not want to do this?"

"No, that's not it at all. It's just . . ." She pauses.

The light turns and I drop my hand. "Just what?" I ask, twisting to see her.

Her eyes widen like saucers. "You have to promise not to laugh."

I want to promise, I really do, but the face she made makes a memory flash through my mind. The first time we talked in the library at college and she dropped the Kama Sutra book on the floor.

Her lips purse and her eyes narrow on me. "I just asked you not to laugh."

"You haven't even told me anything," I say, holding my stomach to control my own laughter. It's so strange how she can lift my mood so quickly.

"I know, so why are you already laughing?" she scoffs.

"You made a face that reminded me of the first time I saw you in the library when you were randomly shuffling through books and you dropped that book on the floor."

Her gaze softens. "You remember that?"

"Yeah, I do."

Pulling up in front of her nicely kept Spanish-style apartment complex, I turn the engine off. Twisting toward her, I run my fingers down the bare skin of her arm and again she jumps. All remnants of laughter dissolve as I turn toward her in the dark of the night. "What's going on?"

"Nothing really. I just feel a little sunburned."

I flick the dome light on in the car. Fuck me, she's the color of a lobster. "A little! Have you put anything on it?"

"No, not yet. Honestly, I didn't start to feel it until I got to the party."

"What kind of sunblock was that you put on?"

"Actually I didn't have much sunblock left, so I poured a little moisturizer in the bottle. It said it had SPF in it."

I shake my head at her in disbelief. "Come on, let's go put something cool on it."

I'm careful to only touch where her clothing is, but even then I see her body tighten in discomfort. She leads me up the stairs and to the door of her apartment that from the outside I know so well. When she opens it and walks through, I catch sight for the first time of where she lives. Candles are scattered all around, a bottle of sparkling water with two glasses sits on her coffee table, and her bikini is thrown on the back of her sofa. I try to ignore the intimate setting that she has set and swivel my gaze over the rest of the room. There isn't much furniture—the sofa, the coffee table, a television, and a small stereo unit on the floor. I look over toward the kitchen—a few barstools, but no table under the light in the corner. I know she's lived here for a while, but it looks as if she just moved in.

"This is really nice," I say, closing the door behind me.

"Thanks, I'm not done with it yet, but it's getting there."

I walk up behind her. "It looks like you were expecting company."

She tosses her keys and twists her head back to rest on my shoulder. "Well, someone who wasn't invited was making a nuisance of himself."

"Is this the way you greet all nuisances who invite themselves over?" I bend down to kiss her lips and rest my hands on her shoulders.

"Ouch," she exclaims loudly.

I glance around, looking for a light switch, and flick it on. "Turn around, let me see you."

"I'm fine," she says, kicking her heels off.

I circle over to her and take a look. "You have blisters on your lips."

She slaps her hand to her mouth. "Oh my God, did you give me herpes?"

I should be insulted, but instead I'm laughing so hard a few tears drip from my eyes.

"It's not funny," she says, running down the hall. "Oh God, they're huge."

I walk down the hallway and see her looking in the bathroom mirror. "Let me see."

She turns toward me.

"You don't just have a little sunburn, you might have sun poisoning."

"Do you think so?"

"Do I think I didn't give you herpes? Yes."

"I know you didn't," she says, rolling her eyes. "I'm talking about sun poisoning."

I mimic her and roll my eyes. "Yes, I'm pretty sure. I've taken care of sun poisoning a few times before. You need to take some aspirin, put some cold compresses over those blisters, and drink a lot of water. So let's start with where I'll find the aspirin."

"I have Midol. Will that work?"

I laugh. "No, but I'll run out to the store and pick some up along with some aloe because I'm going to guess you don't have that either."

She shakes her head no and turns back toward the mirror.

"Don't keep touching them," I yell as I walk into the kitchen and open the refrigerator, looking for a bottle of spring water. It's completely empty except for a large bag of lemons. I close it and open a few cupboards until I find a glass. I fill it with water and when I turn she's standing behind me. "Drink this. Get changed and put some cold washcloths over the blisters. I'll be right back. Okay?"

She runs her hand down my chest. "Thank you."

Our eyes lock and I grab her hand and kiss it. "You don't have to thank me."

"I'm so sorry. I was really looking forward to tonight."

I kiss the top of her head, the only place I know won't hurt her. "There will be other nights."

She drinks the water, sets the glass down, and opens the refrigerator, removing a few lemons from the bag. She sniffs them and I pause to watch her. She sets them on the counter, cuts one in half, and squeezes the juice up her arm. I watch her curiously as she repeats this process on the other arm and winces.

"What are you doing?" I ask.

She turns toward me. "Cleansing my skin. I usually rub them up my arm, but I think that might sting more than it already does."

I bunch my eyebrows.

"What?" she asks. "It's common knowledge lemon juice is good for your skin, so it should help with sunburn too."

"Yeah, but don't most people squeeze them into their water?"

She shrugs. "I'm not like most people."

"No. No, you're not." I laugh.

As I walk out the door now knowing why she always smells of lemon, I'm surprisingly not thinking about how our night has been ruined but rather about how I'm glad I'm here to take care of her.

The grocery store is quiet at this time of night as I push my cart through the aisles. I've decided to pick up a few things since I'm not sure she'll be going out this weekend. My phone beeps and I slide it out of my pocket. It's S'belle.

Did I say thank you?

You did and I told you you didn't have to say that, but I think I've changed my mind.

Did I tell you I was really looking forward to tonight?

You did. Don't you want to know why I changed my mind?

Did I tell you I really wanted to have sex with you tonight?

I nearly drop my phone. Fuck, she must be trying to kill me. I hurry up and pay for my cartload of shit and throw the bags in the car. By the time I get in my phone has beeped again.

Did you get my last text?

I did. And I think you're trying to kill me.

No, I'm not. And I really do want to know what changed your mind.

Because whenever you get over this sun-burn, I have a few ILLUSTRATED ways in mind that you can say thank you. Do you get my drift?

I capitalized *illustrated* so she might pick up my hint. When she doesn't respond right away, I put the car in DRIVE and head back to her place, assuming she didn't get it.

When I get back to her apartment, I pull the chain lock across the door and yell out, "Red."

"I'm in my bedroom."

"Can I come in?"

"Yes!" I can hear her laughing from here.

Setting the bags on the counter, I glance around again. I see a few personal things but not much, not even pictures.

"Are you coming?" she calls.

"I'll be right there." I throw the cold things into the fridge and freezer, grab a few water bottles from the pack I bought, the bottle of aspirin, the aloe, and walk down the hall. I know which room is hers immediately because there's a candle glow from the doorway. Her bed-room is much like the living room—plain with very little in terms of dé-cor. She's lying on the bed with practically nothing on—as I said, she's trying to kill me. She's in a loose-fitting pair of lightweight sleep shorts and a thin-strapped tank top. Both are white. Both see-through.

"Hey, I got some stuff that should make you feel better."

She glances up at me and I can tell there's something bothering her. I take her phone from her clutched hand and when I do it chirps—a text from Tate Wyatt. I set it on the night table. "Wyatt? At this time of night?"

She shrugs. "He must have a question."

"Well, it's after hours, so you can contact him tomorrow, right?"

She stares at me as if contemplating what I just said but doesn't move to grab her phone.

"Everything all right?" I ask as I set the things in my hands down on the nightstand.

"Yes."

When I sit beside her, my stomach jolts. I want to hold her, to kiss her, to fuck her. But when I pull her chin toward me and stare into her eyes, I see tears.

"Why are you crying?"

"I'm being stupid."

"About?"

"I'm just surprised you ever gave me a second thought."

I gently kiss her lips and whisper to her, "You're the fucking sexiest thing I've ever seen. Yes, I gave you a second thought." Then I add, "Many second thoughts."

Silence overtakes us as we both seem to get lost in our memories. When my lips graze hers again, she flinches. I pull back and take the aspirin bottle, pop the cap off, and pour out two. Then I twist the top of the water bottle off and hand her both. She swallows the pills. After I kick my sneakers off, I crawl up next to her so we're face-to-face. I run my fingers through her strands of red hair and notice the blotchiness on the skin of her shoulders.

"Bell," I say, caressing her cheek. "I remember the first time I saw you in the library. I remember every single detail about the night we spent together. And if you want to talk about it, I will. But there are some things that I think are better left in the past. I have this need to have you in my life. I don't understand what it is, but I know I haven't felt more whole or more alive in a very long time than I have with you these last six weeks."

A few stray tears trickle down her face. "You called me Bell."

"That's your name."

"I know but you've never called me that."

I shrug and carefully wipe her tears away. I pull myself up on the bed and lean against the headboard. Patting my stomach, I say, "Come here."

She moves over to me.

I understand where her sadness is coming from. Where we started is complicated, confusing even. I was with Dahl then and there's nothing I could say to make what we did right, no, what I did, right. I try to calm her by combing my fingers through her hair. I would hold her, hug her, if I could. When her sobbing eases I lean over and kiss her head. After a few long silent minutes I say, "Sit up. Let's put this aloe on you."

She slides across the sheets before settling with her back to me and I lean over to whisper softly in her ear, "Lift your hair."

I take a moment to collect myself, trying to control the impact she's having on me. She's barely dressed and it's hard to control my desire. I open the bottle and rub the cool liquid in my hands. "This is going to tingle at first, but you'll feel much better, I promise." I carefully pat it on her shoulders and just feeling her smooth skin makes me want to do so much more.

She screams, "Ouch," and I can hear a sob and with that any sexual thoughts I had disappear. Fuck, I hate this. I don't want her to cry. "I'm sorry, baby. Almost done." I pat her shoulders, her back, her chest. She's beyond sunburned everywhere. When I'm done I stand up. "I'll be right back."

She nods, taking another sip of water.

I leave the bathroom with a washcloth soaked in cold water. I place it on her forehead and she grabs it. Her fingers touch mine and an electrical current exchanges between us. Emptying my pockets, I lie down next to her and she moves to my chest. She fits perfectly there. She rubs her fingers over the buttons of my shirt and I resist the urge to touch her. I settle for running my fingers through her silky-smooth strands of hair and breathing in her lemon scent.

Exhaustion hits quickly and just as I start to drift off she softly says, "Ben."

"Yeah," I mumble.

"You can call me S'belle."

I kiss her head one last time and grin before closing my eyes.

CHAPTER 18
Dirty Laundry

Bell

$\mathscr{A}$ tingle radiates all the way from my head to my toes as a vision of his lean and sinewy muscled body standing behind me on his surfboard with his very erect penis pressing into my back awakens me from my dreamlike sleep and I float back to earth.

"Hmm . . ." The noise escapes me involuntarily.

I knew I was a goner yesterday the minute he strode out of the water. There he was—a vision of utter perfection with his tight stomach muscles on display. He has stunned me into silence many times over the past weeks with his charm, the funny things he says, and his utter good looks, but when I saw him on the beach—his lean form, the faint line of hair that disappears into the waistband of his shorts, the dips and ridges of his half-naked body, then when his laugh dipped from his throat, everything just seemed so right. And lying here knowing he shared my bed last night for the first time, I can't contain my glee.

Squeezing my eyes shut, I can't help feeling amazed that the man I dream about is the one I'm waking up next to this morning. But then a sudden fit of anxiety bounces through me. I'm still a little scared. That hasn't changed. It's not a frightened kind of scared, though. It's the same feeling I got when he first looked at me across the room almost a month ago. It was the same way he looked at me the night we were together so long ago and it thrills me, excites me, and scares me at the same time.

We are different people now than we were when our bodies first collided into a passion that consumed us. Sure, we've fooled around twice since, but it wasn't like that night. I know he wants me in that way again, I can tell, and I want the same thing. But so much has happened— and there are still things that need to happen, truths to be told, for this to mean something. I am afraid it might be too much for him, or maybe too much for me. Yet the past few weeks have shown me that the pull between us is too strong to deny . . . I have to give us a try.

Deciding to wake up, I let my fingers creep across the sheets, inching their way around so I can feel him. But he's not anywhere in the bed. Last night we hadn't had sex, but it was still somehow unforgettable. The way he took care of me, how sweet he was, his concern for how I was feeling. The way my head fit perfectly in the crook of his neck and how I fell asleep in his arms. It all felt so real, so right . . . there was nothing wrong about any of it.

With the light streaming through the blinds, my eyes slowly blink open. I look around my room for him. My lips curl into a smile when I spot his sneakers on the carpet. As the smile spreads across my lips, my hand flies to my mouth, and although a few small bumps remain, they don't hurt. Thoughts of my feelings for him bubble back to the surface. I locked them away for a long time, but no matter how hard I tried to forget him I couldn't let him go.

I ached for him when I saw him in my brother's house last year. Having no idea who he was, I felt hope cascading through me. I thought it was finally our time. Memories of how he'd brought me to climax over and over were all I could think of. I'd blocked out everything else. But when I found out he was Dahlia's Ben, her long-lost fiancé thought dead, I was sickened, horrified even that she had been the one whose boyfriend I had taken without regard and I knew the flame he had lit inside me needed to be doused. Thank God Dahlia didn't hold on to angry feelings. Thank God she couldn't see inside my head. But she was in love with my brother and nothing else mattered. She was willing to move forward. She accepted what I had done, what Ben and I had done, and I was so very thankful

Then when I saw him again I wasn't worried about Dahlia, or River, or even my mother; I was worried about myself. No matter how hard I tried to shut him out I, couldn't. When I looked in his eyes the past became a blur; the only thing I could see were the memories of how he made me feel. So I let him in. I couldn't help myself. More than anything I wanted to feel that way again. But this time I knew I needed to proceed with caution. And that's what I've done—until now.

I sigh deeply at all the memories. The issues are still there, but this time I feel strong enough to face them, to throw caution to the wind and accept the consequences. I twist my back and stretch my neck, happy to be feeling only a fraction of the pain I felt yesterday, and a huge grin crosses my lips. It's Saturday and I have no plans. Hopefully Ben and I can spend the day together—alone. I'm particularly thankful right now that I told Tate I couldn't work today. I knew after Ivy's event I'd be wiped. He was upset, but the event he had planned for today wasn't mine; it was his. He just wanted me there.

It was time for me to start pulling back on assisting him with events so I could spend more time on my own planning. Part of me wishes I could just leave, but I'm not ready to quit, although I'm not sure how much longer I can take it. He's becoming more and more demanding of my time, and his advances toward me since our breakup last winter aren't letting up.

Sliding my feet to the floor, I spot Ben's keys and wallet on my nightstand. And then I start second-guessing myself, wondering if moving forward with him right now is what I should be doing. My goal for this year was to focus on myself. Get my life on track. It didn't include a relationship—that wasn't in my plans. But everything about him seems so right this time. And even the repercussions don't seem overwhelming. Sure, my family's issues will be abundant. But Dahlia has accepted Ben in her life and I'm sure she can help me with River. Xander will be an ass, but I can handle him. The biggest issue of all will be my mother. But once I explain to her what Ben said last night, that he wanted to leave the past in the past, I know she'll understand.

Looking down at the clover I've worn for the past six years, I can't help thinking . . . why tell him? What's done is done; there's no undoing it.

My nose starts to twitch, tearing me from all my thoughts as I catch the faint smell of sizzling bacon in the air. I sniff again, thinking about my empty refrigerator. Ambling out of bed, I make a quick stop in the bathroom before I patter down the hall in search of him and the delicious smell. My heart leaps at the sight in the kitchen—Ben, messy blond hair, muscled, skin tanned, barefoot, standing at my stove in front of a frying pan. With a fluttering stomach, I lick my lips wanting to just taste him. He looks nothing short of edible in his white shirt and faded jeans that hug him just right. His pants are hung low, frayed at the hem just like his shirt. He is the sexiest man I've ever seen. He has always been.

I watch as he flips the slices before him and remember the last time we spent the night together—and how it ended. I blink that sad thought away. And again needing to make sure this is real—I step closer.

"S'belle, you're awake." He grins while dropping a piece of bacon onto a plate.

My pulse races. Those two syllables that I've longed to hear from his lips for so long and suddenly any doubts I had are gone—I know

I'm ready to take this leap with him. I lean against the kitchen doorway and I smile. "Good morning. You went shopping?"

He laughs. "I picked a few things up while I was at the store last night. I noticed you were a little on the empty side." He points to the fridge.

"Yeah, I haven't gotten the living on my own thing down yet," I respond, but really I have; I just hate it.

"Are you hungry?"

"Starving," I answer. My voice is low and seductive.

He turns. "Good. It's almost done. How's the sunburn?" he asks, sweeping the length of me with his eyes as he cracks an egg into a bowl.

I raise my arms in a catlike stretch, making sure to pull my hair up off my shoulders so it tumbles down when I let it go. Then I run my hands down my body.

His eyes flicker over me.

"It's much, much better," I purr.

"Fuck," he mutters.

I nod and smile, slow and sweet.

The most devilish grin forms on his lips and he quickly tosses the eggshell into the sink. Then he turns the stove off and transfers the pan to the burner beside it.

"Come here," he demands, then adds, "Now."

Not only do his words and his smile send tingles to every nerve in my body, but the sound of his voice and the anticipation of what's to come make me quiver with need. I saunter into the kitchen in my best attempt to be as seductive as he is. And it works, because in a heartbeat he grabs me and pushes me up against the counter. His hands cup the back of my neck and he pulls me to him. Heat and his hardness assault me immediately. Just the feel of his lips on mine sweeps me away—lust and need the only things I can think about, the only things left in the room. I fall into his kiss, whimpering at the way his tongue presses against mine, the way it searches my mouth, demanding all of me. The kiss is warm, deep, and desire floods me in a mad rush.

Leaving me breathless, he pulls back and studies my face. His fingers move to gently stroke my shoulders beneath the straps of my tank top. "Does this hurt?" He dips his head to kiss my shoulder.

I shake my head no because I can't speak. The feel of his skin on mine causes my breath to catch in my throat and I'm rendered speechless.

"Good." He peppers light, soft kisses up my neck and back down.

I toss my head back.

He pushes my straps farther down and his dips even lower.

"This?" he asks as his lips touch my nipple and circle it while his hand cups the other one.

"N . . . n . . . no," I stammer.

He licks and sucks one nipple while he rolls the other between his thumb and finger.

I press my hips forward. "Oh God, Ben."

I can feel his lips tilt up into a smile. He looks up at me from underneath his lashes. "You like that?"

I feel my legs start to tremble from just the look he's giving me.

"I didn't hear you."

"You know I do," I pant.

Both of us are breathing loudly and I'm not sure whose breath is whose anymore. His grin grows wide as he drags his hot mouth up my chest to my jaw. He nips my lower lip with his teeth and presses his very erect penis against me. I whimper at the contact.

"You want this." His voice is husky.

"Yes," I say more quickly and more clearly than I have answered any of his questions since coming into the kitchen.

He groans, almost roars in response. In a beat he lifts me and sets me on the counter. His palms press down on either side of me and I feel his closeness even with the small distance between us.

I stare at him, drinking in the sight—hooded lids, parted lips, chest rising and falling.

His deep blue eyes sweep me. "You know I think you're hot as fuck."

I love his dirty mouth and his commanding tone. His forcefulness turns me on so much. I've never been with a guy like him. Something about him makes me want to give myself over to him in any way he wants. I want to be anything he desires, everything he needs—I want to be his dream girl.

I lean forward and begin to undo his buttons. "I think the same thing about you. Yesterday after I left the beach, all I could think about was your cock inside me. I might have had at least three mini orgasms at the thought."

"Fuck," he mutters, biting down on his lip. His hands slide to my breasts and he cups both of them. Feeling almost dizzy, I press myself into his palms and drop my hands from his shirt, letting the sensation of his touch slide through me. My nipples pebble into hard peaks as he squeezes them and I can't help moaning even louder.

He pushes the spaghetti straps of my tank farther down my arms to uncover my handful-sized breasts. His breath hitches as his mouth dips to mine. "Did you wear this to drive me crazy last night?"

I shake my head and try to catch his lips with mine, but he maintains a slight distance between us.

"And without a bra to kill me." This time it's not a question.

But I shake my head no again.

His hands move up my thighs and his fingertips dance under the flimsy cotton of my bottoms. "Fuck me, you're not wearing any underwear."

Again I try to press my lips to his, but he keeps drawing back. He lets his fingers only lightly graze over me and I brace my palms on the counter to keep steady. When he presses them a little harder I moan, but he pulls his hands away. He covers them over mine, lightly caressing his thumbs across my skin. "Tell me and I'll put my fingers inside your sweet pussy."

I'm tingling everywhere as I mumble, "No, I didn't, I promise. I was trying to keep anything from touching my sunburn and besides, if I wanted to drive you crazy I would have worn that." I lift my hand from underneath his and point to the skimpy swimsuit I laid out perfectly yesterday before I left for Ivy's release party.

The wickedest grin crosses his lips. "Put it on now."

I bite my lip. "Whatever you say, Mr. Covington."

He catches my mouth with his and finally kisses me again. I rub my naked chest against his and I think he might be panting. I clutch his shoulders under his shirt and scoot off the counter. He presses his fingers into my hips and guides me down.

I saunter across the room, pick up the suit, and hold it in front of me. "Is this what you want to see me in?"

He bobs his chin, but his smoldering eyes stay locked on mine.

"I'll be right back," I say, sashaying toward the bathroom.

"No, don't leave the room. Show me a little of that striptease you said you learned."

I shrug as if it's no big deal, but really I want to be as sexy for him as I can be, and the thrill of being able to give him what he wants makes my stomach flip. I pull the straps of my tank top back up and turn around. Just as I glance over my shoulder and start to slowly lower the straps back down, his eyes shift from ocean blue into midnight sky before me.

"But just know I'm fucking you in your bed—all day," he growls.

A sudden throbbing expands from my heart to my fingertips to my core but just as suddenly dissipates when there's a knock at my door and I hear the jangling of my mother's keys and very familiar voice.

"Bell, honey, are you up? Jack and I went to the market this morning and brought you a few things," she says as she tries to open the front door, but the chain prevents her.

"Fuck, not how I want to meet your parents," Ben mutters under his breath.

I quickly pull my top back down. Ben is fast too, moving to redo the buttons I just moments ago undid. Patting my hair and taking a deep breath, I walk toward the door and unhook the chain.

With bags blocking their view, my mother and stepfather come in.

"So glad you're finally using that lock I installed," Jack says.

I smile. Ben must have used it last night. Honestly, I always forget.

"Oh, good, you're already up. I thought we'd have breakfast together. You left so fast last night I didn't get a chance to ask about your day at the beach," my mother says.

"And, missy, how did you get home anyway? Xander told us you'd left. I was worried about you," Jack scolds.

"Oh, Jack, a girl is allowed some secrets." My mother winks at him.

He shrugs. "Charlotte, you know I can't help it. I worry about her on her own."

My mother dismisses his comment, but I know she worries about me too. "It smells like you're already cooking breakfast," she says.

As they move toward the kitchen I know I have to say something. "Actually Ben is making breakfast."

"Ben?" my mother questions.

"Yes, Ben Covington. He stopped by to check on me."

My mother's face drops and she stands frozen just looking into the kitchen.

Jack sets his bags on the counter, grabbing my mother's from her and doing the same. Ben moves toward them and extending his hand first to my mother, he says, "Mrs. Tyler, it's a pleasure to finally meet you. Bell has told me so much about you."

Surprise and shock seem to swamp her, but she eventually smiles and extends her hand.

Ben turns to Jack and does the same. Jack is more cordial. When he extends his hand he says, "Ben, I heard the announcement this morning. Congratulations on the acquisition of *Sound Music.* I hear you have some terrific ideas for how to boost the publication. I'd love to hear about them."

"I do, sir. And I'd be happy to share them anytime."

I can't decide whether I want to hide underneath the sofa or jump on top of it in celebration at the effort Ben is making.

My mother clears her throat as she turns to me. Her eyes scan my flimsy attire that is not at all appropriate for visitors. "You said Ben was checking on you. What's the matter?"

"I took her to the beach yesterday and was worried she might have gotten too much sun," he rushes to answer.

"Oh, you're the friend who was teaching Bell how to surf?" Jack asks.

Ben's hands go to his pockets and he nods with a smile.

I've kept my mother and Jack in the loop on my "dates" with Ben. I just failed to mention his name. And now I wonder if that was worse than not telling them. I'd painted a picture of a proper suitor pursuing me, and he was one and he did pursue me. They just didn't know the guy was Ben Covington. But they were both really happy for me that I was finally spending time with someone I liked. So why should it matter who it is?

Jack even mentioned that since I called my new suitor a friend and not my *boyfriend*, it must be serious. And I was planning on telling them as soon as I knew for sure Ben wanted more than just sex from me, so that should count for something. Not that I'd tell my parents that.

My mother's eyes dart to me again. "Oh my, you are really burnt. You looked pink last night, but today it's much worse. Did you put something on it?"

"Yes, Ben brought over some aloe," I answer, rushing toward the bags that Jack set on the counter.

"Oh, let me," my mother answers as I start unloading the items.

"Bell, I should run. I have some calls to make at the office," Ben says, and I notice the use of my real name. I don't like it.

"I didn't realize you had to work today. It's Saturday." I know I'm frowning but I can't help myself. He's trying to ease out of an awkward situation, but I really don't want him to go.

"With the announcement I really should head in and return a few calls," he says. "Mr. and Mrs. Tyler, it was a pleasure to meet you."

"Call me Jack."

"Oh, and I'm Charlotte of course," my mother adds, rounding the counter and making her way into the kitchen.

"What about breakfast?" I ask, hoping he'll stay.

"I made it for you," he says.

I stop unloading the goods from the bags that my mother has already started to put away and follow him to the door. My mother and Jack begin their own conversation and Ben points to his feet. *Crap, crap, crap.*

"Let me get you those books you asked to borrow before you leave." I don't know what else to say. Honestly I don't care if you're sixteen or twenty-six; getting caught by your mother with a boy in your room is just plain embarrassing.

Ben covers his mouth with his fingers in a move I've come to love but right now hate. I know he does it when he's trying not to laugh. I scowl at him and he pats his pockets. I get it—don't forget his keys and wallet. I make the walk of shame to my room as my mother and Jack act as if they don't know what's going on. Entering my room with a deep sigh, I gather everything. I come back with a brown-handled shopping bag, knowing my mother and stepfather must have noticed Ben didn't have his shoes on. I hand him the bag filled with his stuff and some random romance novels I grabbed off my floor. When our hands connect he brushes his thumb across the top of mine. Electricity shoots through me and I finally smile at him.

He opens the door and once again says good-bye to my mother and Jack.

"Bye, thanks for stopping by to check on me."

A devilish grin crosses his lips. "Anytime. Call me later if you need anything," he replies with a wink.

When he leaves I collapse against the door. My body is taut with tension but also tingling at the same time.

"Bell, I think we should have a talk." My mother's voice is stern, but soft. And I hope to God she doesn't want to give me the sex talk again. She gave it to me when I was sixteen and again after I told her I was pregnant. I think I get it.

Jack busies himself putting the fruit in Tupperware containers my mother also brought over. Even though he isn't my father, he has always treated me like a daughter. His love and concern have meant a lot to me, but he also knows when to keep quiet—like now.

Standing straight, I slowly make my way to the kitchen. "Mom, I'm sorry I didn't tell you I was seeing him. I just didn't want you to judge him."

My mother stops what she's doing. "Bell, I would never judge him. I just don't want you to get hurt."

"But you are judging him. I can tell by the look on your face."

"Charlotte, he seems like a nice boy. Respectful, concerned about Bell," Jack says, and my mouth drops. I wouldn't have counted on him as an ally.

"I'm not judging him." The tone of her voice rises. She glances at me. "I am not one to judge anyone. What happened years ago when he was with Dahlia is for you and him and your brother to come to terms with, and I'm sure you know that isn't going to be easy."

"Ben and Dahlia have talked. They've made peace."

She raises her hand. "Like I said, that is between the four of you. My concern right now is only for you. Have you told him about the baby?"

I shake my head no.

She levels with me. "Secrets become lies."

"I'm not you," I snap back.

She ignores me and I know I shouldn't have said that.

"Bell, honey, not telling him isn't any way to start a relationship. You can't keep a secret like that. It's not fair to him. Everyone in our family knows. You know I think you should have told him years ago, but since he wouldn't return your calls I let you make the decision not to."

I tremble at the painful memory.

She reaches across the counter to grab my hand. "I just don't want you to get hurt."

Tears spill from my eyes. "But, Mom, I'm hurting now. Every time you bring it up, it hurts me. Don't you get it? I want to forget it."

"I'm sorry, honey, but you can't and I can't let you—not this time."

I run to my room crying and throw myself on the bed. My hand goes to my belly button, then to my scar, and the memory comes back as if it were yesterday.

There were no breathing exercises, no Lamaze classes. It was nothing like Rachel giving birth on Friends. *I had been diagnosed with pre-eclampsia and was being monitored closely. Corticosteroid shots were part of my daily regimen to help mature the baby's lungs. Magnesium sulfate also became part of the ritual to help prevent seizures, but that drug wasn't an easy shot; it was given in IV form and I hated it. I was warned that when delivery time came the magnesium sulfate dosage might need to be increased. I didn't understand what that meant, but the nurses looked as though they felt sorry for me.*

On March seventeenth, almost eight months after the baby had been conceived, I understood why. My already high blood pressure had risen to an unhealthy level, putting the baby's life in danger. The doctors had decided it was time to induce me. So with Pitocin in one IV and mag in another, I was in pain, burning up, and dry-heaving in a basin my mother held for me. Her tears only made me cry all the more. The contractions came on quickly. They were nothing like what I thought they would be. They were the worst kind of cramps and so painful I was screaming before I was even close to being fully dilated. I had opted to remain drug free, but the pain was so bad I begged the nurses to call an anesthesiologist. The fear of a needle stuck in my back seemed so small compared to what I was feeling.

However, before relief could even arrive, I was being wheeled down a sterile hall with the words emergency C-section *being thrown at me. My blood pressure had reached an alarming level and the doctors could no longer wait for the birth-inducing drug to kick in. My mother wasn't allowed in and I was terrified. With fear and pain all I could fathom, a mask went over my face and as I counted backward, blackness came. I awoke sometime later in the recovery room. I patted my stomach but couldn't feel anything. I looked around for my mother, my brothers, but sleep called to me. The next time I woke up I was in a different hospital room. It wasn't the same one I had been recovering in since the accident. The one I had to stay in even after the trauma had passed while we waited for the baby to come.*

I remember the nurse asking, "Do you want to see the baby?"

"I don't know," I cried out.

I had told them I didn't. All I could think about was why were they asking me? The adoption was already arranged—I had selected the people I thought would make the most perfect parents, but having my baby taken from me before I expected left me empty, wondering. I started to second-guess myself. I became hysterical and screamed for my mother. The nurses brought her to me.

"Is the baby okay?" I asked.

She cried, nodding.

"Did you hold it?"

She cried even harder, nodding again.

Once I knew the baby was safe, my doubts were no more. I couldn't hold the baby, because if I did I just knew I'd never be able to give it up. So on that day I signed my child over to its new parents, never seeing it, never knowing if it was a boy or girl because it didn't matter. All I knew, all that mattered was that my child would be raised by two people who would forever love him or her. What I didn't know is I would never stop loving that child either.

A familiar comforting hand runs up and down my back and I twist around, wiping my tears away.

"Bell, you know how much I love you. I want more than anything for you to be happy. And if you think this man will make you happy, I will accept him with open arms. But you have to be honest with him. I've been through a lot in my life and learned from my mistakes. I never told your brother who his real father was and I could have lost him because of that. I'm not trying to hurt you. I know thinking about the baby is painful, but please think about what I've said. I won't bring it up again. How you move forward is your decision."

With the memories so vivid and painful, I sit up and pull my mother to me. Eventually my cries muffle into familiar sobs as everything I've tried so hard to forget circles around me.

CHAPTER 19
Pain

Ben

The beach is quiet as I sit outside on the deck and sip a cup of coffee. After I left S'belle's house I decided to come home and change quickly and then head into the office before going back to get her.

I can't help thinking about her while I scan the ocean view. She's just so fucking sexy all I have to do is glance at her and I'm hard. Everything about her captures my attention—from her cute quirky personality to the sex kitten underneath it. I'm so hot for her I can hardly stand it. The strange thing is our day at the beach was so much fun and last night, although not what I planned, was still memorable. And I actually think that running into her mother and stepfather this morning didn't turn out to be so bad. She's been so determined not to tell her family that maybe this was the best way for them to find out about us.

Heading inside, I rinse my cup and walk into my bedroom. My dirty clothes are in a pile on the floor and I stop while picking them up to look at the picture on my dresser—my mother, my sister, Trent, and me just before my mother died. It's hard to believe she's been gone a year. I pull my phone from my pocket with an urge to talk to my sister.

"Hello," she answers sleepily.

"Hi, it's me. Did I wake you?"

"It's okay. I have to get up anyway."

"When did you get back?"

"Late last night."

"How was Hawaii?"

"Oh, Ben, it was beautiful, fun, and amazing."

"So, how does it feel to be a married woman again?"

She sighs happily and I can feel her smile through the phone. "The same but different."

She's always so matter-of-fact.

"Why don't you come by for dinner tonight?"

"I can't. I have plans," I say.

"Oh yeah, what kind of plans?" she asks curiously.

"How about lunch tomorrow and I'll catch you up?"

"That scares me."

"Why?"

"I wasn't gone that long and I talked to you a number of times. So the fact that I am unaware of something and need to be caught up kind of scares me."

I chuckle. "I'll call you tomorrow morning. I gotta run into the office now."

"Okay, Ben, love you."

"Love you too." I hang up and can't help wondering how she's going to react to hearing the news.

Typing a response to one of the dozens of e-mails in my in-box, I click SEND and close it down. My crystal typewriter award is sitting on my desk and the way the sunlight hits it creates a mock rainbow around it that mesmerizes me. But no matter how hard I try, I can't keep my glance from shifting to the screen of my phone for the umpteenth time. S'belle hasn't contacted me yet and it's killing me. It's been more than six hours—I ran home and showered, came here expecting to stop in for only a few short minutes, and hours later I'm still here.

"Hey, man, you're here," Beck says from the doorway just as I pick up my phone to call S'belle.

"Technically I'm not." I shove away from my desk.

"Yeah, right. Well, anyway, I want to show you this. I came up with it yesterday but couldn't get it quite right until this morning."

He sits down with his laptop in front of him at the conference table in the corner of my office.

I join him. "Okay, show me what you've got."

"Be prepared for your world to be rocked," he gloats.

I shake my head, thinking how much my world has already been rocked and how right now I'm tipping over the edge waiting to talk to her. As Beck walks me through a very detailed and complete design of how he plans to simultaneously launch all of Plan B's holding into the social media arena, I sit back in awe, genuinely impressed by not only his skills, but his visionary talent. But when my phone chirps from across the room, my attention wanes.

"Hot date?" Beck asks as he catches my gaze drift to my desk.

"I hope so." I grin. "Give me a minute." I cross the room to grab my cell.

"No worries, mate, it's not like it's a Saturday and I am working or anything."

"You've been spending too much time with Alexander. Only difference is you sound like a douche bag using the word *mate*."

"Fuck off, at least I'm not a pansy ass who can't go after what he wants."

I sit back in my chair. "Ah . . . that's where you're wrong. I have been going after what I want."

"Glad to hear it. All right, then I'll leave you to it. I'm heading out, working a shift at my old man's tonight. Need anything before I go?" Beck asks.

"I'm good."

"And, Ben," he says.

I look over at him.

"If I were you I wouldn't take too much longer. She's liable to move on to a douche bag like me who never would have taken six weeks to close a deal."

"Thanks for the advice, mate."

He throws me the finger.

"Close the door."

He laughs and walks away, leaving it open. Fucker. I read the message from S'belle.

Can you meet me at Pebbles?

I can pick you up and take you out to dinner.

I'd rather meet you there.

Okay, but I'm pretty sure we broke through that wall yesterday. What's going on?

Can you just meet me there?

You're not fucking with me, are you? 50 First Dates is not what I have in mind for tonight.

Please.

Sure, when?

Two hours?

See you then. And, S'belle, I can't wait.

I want to fuck with her some more, but something doesn't seem right. Her text messages are too straightforward, too direct, so I stop. After I read through a few more work e-mails and forward some of them on to Aerie for her to follow up on, my attention level is close to nil and I decide to call it a day.

Once I open the glass doors, the cool, crisp breeze assaults me. The air is much cooler than yesterday. Fall is definitely here. With plenty of time to spare, I zip up my jacket and decide to cruise up to Mulholland Drive. Having switched to my bike when I went home, I take the winding roads at a speed I've come to love. It looks so different up here during the day but equally as breathtaking as when the sun falls off the cliffs and into the ocean at sunset.

Stopping at my favorite overlook, I take the time to get off my bike and climb the two flights of wooden stairs to the top. From up here I have to admit glancing around downtown Los Angeles during the day is a sight. It's one huge conglomerate. Tall buildings, freeways that sprawl for miles, homes, trees—it's a view one could get used to. But I've lived there and good and evil lie hand in hand—although I suppose that might be true of anywhere. Shaking away the thought, I stride back down to my bike and head into the city.

The parking garage is empty, but the streets are full. I make a quick stop in Fiction Vixen for a purchase and then head to my destination. I'm one of the first patrons to arrive at the restaurant, so getting the same table as our first date is easy enough. I set my package on it and order two sparkling waters, with lemon. The thought of her squeezing the juice over her arms last night makes me laugh to myself. Moments later the door opens and there stands the hottest little number—her red hair tumbles in waves around her shoulders, her short green dress is anything but modest, her gold necklaces drape her neck, and she looks sexier than hell. Fuck me. I have no doubt now she's trying to kill by asking me to meet her in public—yet again.

Trying to vanish my shit-eating grin, I rise from the table and stride over to greet her, but some older guy has his hands around her before I even make it over to the door. With the giant's arms still enveloping her tiny body, I clear my throat. She breaks free of his hold and with a glint in her eyes she looks at me.

"Ben, this is Pebbles. Well, really his name is Rocko and he owns the place," she says with an upward tilt of her lips.

I begrudgingly extend my arm. "Nice to meet you."

He nods. "Same here. Heard a lot about you."

"Really, don't believe it all." I grin.

"It's all good, man," he says as if I need the assurance.

Dropping my eyes to S'belle, I bend my elbow toward her. "Shall we?"

She gives a little wave to Pebbles or Rocko or whatever he goes by and then wraps her arm through mine with the most effervescent smile.

"Who is he?"

"A friend," she answers.

"You know I'm jealous as fuck, don't you?" I growl in her ear.

She tilts her head and lifts her hand to my face. Cupping my jaw, she whispers, "You have no reason to be."

Heat surges between us before I even pull her chair out and I wonder why she insisted on meeting at a restaurant. As she sits, I lean forward and brush my mouth over hers. A slight tremble rocks her shoulders. "S'belle, what are we doing here? I thought the next time I saw you you'd be in that bikini sprawled out on your bed."

She tosses her head from side to side as if trying to break free of the vision I just created. "I need to tell you something and wasn't sure how or where to do it. This place just seemed right."

She sets her napkin on her lap and immediately starts nervously clicking her fingernails against the tabletop.

I take a seat and grab her hand. "Okay. We're here now, so tell me, let's eat, and then I want to take you home and fuck you."

She swallows and I notice her hands trembling.

"Maybe that was a bit crass. Let me try again. Okay. We're here now, so tell me."

She grabs for the water in front of her and drinks it down, all of it. Her eyes lift to mine. "I'm not sure how to tell you this."

I can feel confusion wrinkling my brow.

Her gaze falls. "But I know I have to. I have a confession to make. Something from a long time ago. And I'm not sure how you're going to react."

My fingers creep up her arm to her chin.

She leans into my touch and her face looks almost pained.

"I already know what you're going to tell me." I try not to laugh as I reach for the wrapped brown package I set on the table.

She stares at it.

"Since you lent me some of your books, I thought it was only fair I return the favor. Although I'm not sure reading *Fifty Shades of Grey* is my thing," I chuckle.

Her eyes widen like saucers as I hand her the package. She takes it with trembling fingers.

"It's safe, I promise. You can open it. I'm cool with your half-truth."

The waitress approaches our table and refills both our sparkling waters. "Are you ready to order?"

"Two peppered beef skewers with rice," I tell her, and turn my attention back to S'belle. "So, go ahead, open it."

Tearing open the wrap, she stares at the first book, *Everything You Ever Need to Know About the French Riviera*. Her eyes dart to mine.

"I know you never went there."

She sits motionless.

"That first night we were together, when you told me all about what it was like on the French Riviera, I knew you'd never been there as soon as you said you went."

She scrunches her eyebrows and purses her lips.

"It was written all over your face."

Tears fill her eyes as she sets the stack on the table. "You're right, I never went to the Riviera."

Feeling like a real asshole, I pull her to me. "Come here. I'm only playing with you. And I got you some other books as well."

She sits on my lap and buries her head in my neck, not even looking at the other titles. Her lemon scent assaults me and her mess of wild hair brushes across my skin. I breathe her in. "Don't cry about it. It's nothing to cry over. I think it's funny."

She buries her head farther in my neck. "I'm not crying about that. But I can't believe you knew the whole time. You should have said something and not let me go on and on."

"But that wouldn't have been nearly as much fun."

She gives a faint smile and wipes her tears, but then she stands up and goes back to sit in her chair. She takes another gulp of her water and then looks at me.

I soften my voice. "Please tell me."

She nods. "Do you remember yesterday when you asked me what the shamrock I wear is for?"

My mind recalls vividly the green emerald in her belly button and the thoughts I had about running my tongue around it. With a devilish grin I answer, "Yes."

She sets her glass down. Her hands are shaking and she's unable to speak.

I suddenly lose any sense of fun in this conversation. "Hey, look at me," I say, leaning over the table and taking both her hands.

Her eyes cut to mine, the fire now dulled and consumed by sadness.

"What is it? Just tell me."

She stays silent and draws in a breath as if gaining courage.

"S'belle? What the fuck is it?" My impatience is getting the better of me.

Her stare searches the table. "The shamrock represents St. Patrick's Day."

I nod, agreeing with her that it does.

Silence falls again for another few short moments and then she looks up at me. "That's the day I gave birth to our child." Her voice is shaky and broken. Her words come out in alternating whispers and squeaks.

The floor drops from beneath me. My ears ring and the room doesn't seem quite so square anymore. I take a deep breath, replaying what she just said in my head, but it doesn't make sense. I sit there motionless. I couldn't have heard her correctly. When my senses recover, I flash her a look that seeks answers.

Through gritted teeth I ask, "What did you say?"

She squeezes my hands, but I jerk them away. Unbearable silence passes between us, and nothing except the overhead music of Frank Sinatra crooning a love song can be heard. There's a look of desperation on her face, but there is no way I can help her.

"What did you just say?" My voice takes on an aggressive tone I've never used with her as her words register in my brain—I have a child out in the world.

Tears now slide down her face. She leans forward and through sobs says, "On March seventeenth, almost six years ago, I gave up my child, our child. I gave it up for adoption. That's why I wear the shamrock. It symbolizes the love I have for the baby I wish every day I never let go."

My body goes limp. Looking around, I can't figure out why she'd tell me this in a public place. Oh God, my stomach lurches when I think about how I wanted to run my tongue over the sparkling green emerald in her belly button. I start to get up but sit back down, needing a chance to understand what she's telling me. The words catch in my throat and nothing comes out. I stare at her in disbelief for the longest time, trying to see anything but the truth, but I can't find it. I glance around at the empty restaurant and feel as if I'm suffocating.

"I . . . I . . . didn't want . . . I didn't want to have to tell you, but I knew I couldn't start this relationship with a lie. That's—that's why I wanted to keep it casual. I . . . I thought you'd get me out of your system and move on," she stammers.

My eyes flare to hers, but the fire I feel is not from want or lust. "Why didn't you tell me then? Why?"

She holds my gaze. "Because I didn't think you'd care."

"Then you don't know me at all," I spit out.

"No, I do know you. I do."

"So what? Is this one of those half-truths? Because I'll tell you something—you're only fooling yourself."

Standing up, I reach in my pocket and toss a fifty on the table. With her chest visibly rising and falling, she watches me silently. She stares at me with a blank expression and says nothing else. I look at her one last time and then walk away, leaving her sitting there. As soon as the cool air hits my lungs, I feel I can finally breathe. I pace the sidewalk with my hands behind my head and stare through the glass at her. A few seconds later she's standing in front of me.

"Ben, let's talk about this. I want to explain everything. It's not easy for me, but I understand you're upset."

My eyes burn into hers with an anger I've never felt for anyone. "What exactly are you going to explain? Explain how you had a baby, my baby, and gave it up without ever telling me?" I hiss.

"It's not like that. It wasn't that easy."

"Really? What part wasn't easy? The part you skipped about informing the father?"

Her eyes drop. "Please, Ben, let's go back in and sit down."

"Why would you think you should tell me something like that in a public place?"

"You said you wanted to put the past behind you. I just wanted to meet somewhere neutral and do the same."

"Are you fucking kidding me? That is not the past."

"It is. It's mine." Her voice is a whisper.

My voice is tight. "How could you not tell me back then?"

"I tried. I called you twice."

"I remember your calls. You called and left a couple of messages that said to call you back. There was no urgency in your tone. You knew I had a girlfriend. I couldn't call you back. That wasn't trying."

"I called," she cries again, her voice fading.

I throw my hands up in the air. "You knew I couldn't see you again. You had to know that's why I thought you were calling. So you may have called, but you didn't try to tell me this. Don't fool yourself."

"What difference would it have made if I had told you?"

"What difference?" My voice spikes up in anger.

"It wouldn't have changed anything."

I stare at her with coldness in my eyes. "Fuck, is that another one of your half-truths?"

"No guy wants to hear he got a girl pregnant," she says, her voice raspy.

"How would you know what I wanted to hear when you never gave me the chance?"

"What would have been the point?"

"The point in telling me we conceived a child? The point in telling me there's a part of me out there in the world? I don't know, maybe that I deserved to know."

"I'm sorry," she cries, and closes her eyes.

I stare at her, my heart feeling pulled in so many directions I don't know what to do. Then without another word I turn and walk away.

CHAPTER 20
Little White Lies

Bell

The dogwood trees blow in the wind and their white blossoms whirl in the air. One sticks to my arm, but I swat it off. I don't want to make a wish on it today. I watch him, following his back as he walks away from me until I can't see him anymore. I bolt down the street as fast as I can, running nowhere. When another blossom blows in my path, I pause for a brief moment and decide to make a wish after all. I wish for him to understand—even when I know that's impossible. Still, I'm not sorry I told him. I know I had to. I am, however, sorry I didn't do things differently from the start. I'm sorry about how I messed my own life up again. I'm sorry I can't go back in time and change everything.

Feeling defeated, lost, and disheartened, I turn around and go back to the restaurant to get my things. It's quiet inside and thank God Rocko is nowhere to be seen. Pebbles has always been a place of comfort for me. That's why I flock here whenever I'm nervous. It's kind of like a home away from home. When I was little, my dad would bring me here after school sometimes, just him and me. We'd sit and talk about my day, about music, and about my brothers. Rocko would join us sometimes and they'd talk about when they were younger. They were good friends, attended high school together and Rocko even played the drums for my dad when he was on the road. So after my dad died I came here a lot. I'd take a bus after school to just sit and talk to Rocko. He's told me so many stories about my dad, good ones, happy ones—it was the way I wanted to remember him.

A brief bittersweet smile passes across my lips as I walk by the bar and look at the picture on the wall of Rocko and my dad among all the other celebrity photos. My dad was famous even if he never thought so. More tears fill my eyes and I don't even know who they're for any-more—my dad or Ben. I grab the package of books off the table and fumble for keys in my purse. When I go back outside I hand my keys off to the valet and wait while he quickly pulls my car up. He opens my door and I seek refuge inside. The sound of the car engine helps to muffle my loud cries.

You knew better, I cry to myself. *You did.* I slam the steering wheel. I thought he'd be mad, but I didn't expect disdain from him or his disgust. The flame of attraction that burned in his deep blue eyes whenever he looked at me was extinguished the minute my words registered.

The drive home feels too short and the walk up the stairs even shorter. The longest part of the day is yet to come—the night I was supposed to spend with him. I throw myself on the couch and lie here for the longest time. My phone rings and I glance at it, knowing it won't be him. It's not. It's Tate. Why won't he leave me alone? I ignore it and resume my blank stare, not wanting my numbness to vanish because the pain will be too much to bear.

I must have fallen asleep, because the sound of my phone ringing again wakes me up. I sit up and look around before reaching for it. Romeo Fairchild flashes across the screen.

"Hello," I answer.

"Bell, it's Romeo. Sorry to bother you at home but that band you recommended is playing tonight at a bar not too far from the showroom and since you told me you lived close by I was wondering if you would come over and tell me what you think."

I contemplate the idea. Maybe some distraction is just what I need. Maybe a drink wouldn't be so bad either. I need to get Ben out of my system. To not let this bring me down. I knew better than to go down this road with him. I knew there was nowhere else for it to end up. Ben just isn't the kind of guy to open his arms and say I forgive you, it's okay. Somehow I hoped it would be different, yet in my heart I always knew things would end up like this.

"What do you think, Bell? Tate said he'd try to make it too."

His voice over the line jolts me from my thoughts. Something doesn't feel right with this invite. I remember when I was leaving last night in a rush to see Ben that I saw Tate and Romeo and that girl I feel I've seen somewhere before standing together, the three of them at the makeshift bar.

"I'm sorry, I can't tonight, but I'm sure you and Tate will find your own kind of fun."

His laugh is a rumble. "Guess you're not interested in our kind of fun. Sorry to hear that. But if you change your mind we'll be at a place called Beck's. It'll be fun, I promise."

"I have to go."

"Yeah, no worries," he says, and hangs up.

I stand up and pace the room. The brown package is on the couch where I threw it. I open it up and place both books on the coffee table, *The Adventures of Huckleberry Finn* on top.

I decide to call my mother. I can talk to her about this.

"Everything okay?" she answers.

"Yes, but you sound like everything isn't."

"I'm talking to Aunt Celeste. Jagger's father is really sick and Jack and I are going to fly out in the morning to be with her. Can I call you back?"

"Of course. No rush. I hope everything is okay."

"I'll call you back," she says, and hangs up.

I try to call Jagger but there's no answer. I try Aerie but no answer there either. My aunt and Jagger's father were close; at least they were when I spent a year with my aunt in Paris. She spoke to him every day. I felt they were in love, but they were two ships that passed in the night, star-crossed lovers, I remember thinking.

With sadness for my aunt and Jagger in my already broken heart and no one else to talk to about Ben, I head for the door, leaving my cell phone behind. I need to chase away the dark clouds storming in my head—a few bottles of wine, maybe even a bottle of vodka can certainly help me do that.

CHAPTER 21
Away from the Sun

Ben

The winds have picked up as I tear down the road. I haven't wanted a drink in a long time, but I do now. I ride like hell to get out of town. I don't pay any attention to where I'm going, turning right or left depending on which light is green. A few hours later I end up far from where I started, in West Hollywood, only a few blocks from Beck's. The traffic is fucking bumper to bumper and I can't sit in it. I park in the first open spot I find and walk the rest of the way to his place.

The sign above the door is lit in neon red. It's like a beacon lighting my way in a storm. I slip inside the hole-in-the-wall bar and look around. The place has really changed. The jukebox that sat in one corner is gone, as are the few booths that used to line the wall to the right. They've been replaced by a stage and a dance floor made out of parquet wood. The few bunches of tables that used to be scattered throughout have multiplied into many. The giant L-shaped bar is the same and the wall of beer taps that rests behind hasn't changed. I sit at the end of the bar and a chick I don't know approaches me.

"What are you having?"

I scan the more than one hundred beers behind her. "Whatever you want to give me," I answer, unable to decide.

She pours a beer and sets it in front of me. I stare at it for the longest time as she tends to some other customers. Then I pick it up and down it.

She bends down in front of me to wipe a few too many times around where the condensation from my beer mug dripped on the bar. "Another?"

I nod. "Beck around?"

"Senior or Junior?" she asks, twisting to refill my glass.

"Junior."

"No, he's not around much anymore." She bounces her tits in my face.

"Who are you?" I ask her.

She smiles. "I'm the new manager. My name is Kate."

I lift my glass. "Nice to meet you, Kate. The place looks great."

"Yeah, the band Echo starts tonight. They're really good. You sticking around?"

"I might be."

Beer after beer . . . I chug them down and before I know it I've moved on to my trusty old Jack. She pours me another drink and I hazily stare at what she's wanted me to notice all night. Her tits hang out of her tight T-shirt nicely. They're not bad-looking and neither is she—short blond hair, medium height, about forty.

"How do you know Beck?" she asks over the start of the blasting sound of the bass.

I glance around and notice the band is onstage and the dance floor is full. "I met him here. He works for me now."

She smiles. "You're his new boss."

I try not to slur my words. "That would be me. I'm Ben. Ben Covington." I reach for her hand.

She extends hers. "Nice to meet you."

A redhead I hadn't noticed before calls her over to the other end of the bar. When I look over toward her, she winks at me and I can't keep my lips from pulling into a frown as I think of S'belle's red hair. My mind wanders back to what she told me today—I have a child out there somewhere in the world. A child that is about the same age I was when my father died. My mood turns dark.

"She's bad news," the bartender says.

I turn to look at her. "Makes no difference to me."

She nods. "Trust me, it should."

I shrug. "A chick's a chick."

I stand up and gain my balance, needing to hit the restroom. To get to the back hallway I need to weave my way through the crowd. The number of people has multiplied tenfold since I arrived and everyone seems to be in their own world, caught up in the music and seduction of those around them. The band is pretty decent and I catch the sound of horns in the background, which even in my state draws my attention. The bartender chick was right, they are pretty good.

When I come out I run right into the redhead from the bar. Her gaze traces me and I allow mine to do the same to her. She's tall, really tall. Her features are attractive enough and her body isn't bad. I zero in on her ample chest and catch sight of her nipples pebbling through her sheer top. Fuck, she's not wearing a bra.

"Fancy meeting you here," she says, her eyes locking on mine.

I allow a smirk to cross my lips. "Something tells me you planned it."

She raises an eyebrow. "Cocky, aren't you?"

I shrug. "Can I buy you a drink?"

She smiles and steps a little closer. "I'd love that."

I sidestep her to head to the bar. The place is so packed there's nowhere to move. I turn toward her. "Stay here and I'll grab us a couple of drinks. What are you drinking?"

She tugs the collar of my shirt. "We could go somewhere . . . quieter," she whispers in my ear as she leans forward.

I pull back and stare at her, considering the possibility of forgetting everything and just getting lost in her. "How about a drink first?"

"Sure, vodka cranberry."

Just as I pass the dance floor I come face-to-face with not only Tate Wyatt but fucking Romeo Fairchild. I try to ignore them both, but as soon as I walk past them one of their hands is on my shoulder.

"Ben, man, it's been far too long."

I'm in no mood for this guy's shit. I turn to look at him. My eyes take him in—dressed in a suit with a smug-ass look on his face. I really want to deck him. "Not long enough," I mutter under my breath, and keep walking.

"I saw your name on your *friend's* phone not too long ago. Shame you're just friends because she's a hot piece of ass."

"Why the fuck is she showing you her phone?" I don't even give him time to explain because I don't give a shit what he has to say. I just turn around ready to pound him to the floor like the piece of shit he is. This arrogant son of bitch and I were never friends, but his superiority complex isn't why he hates me. He hates me because he couldn't get the one thing in high school he wanted—Dahlia.

A hand grips my shoulder a little too tightly and draws my attention. I twist around, ready to deck the guy getting in my space.

"What's going on?" Beck asks.

My teeth are gritted and the anger is all I can feel. He steps between me and them. He whispers something to them I can't hear and they make their way toward the door.

"Yeah, you better leave," I spit out.

Beck grabs me. "Shut the fuck up."

I take a step back. "Yeah, sorry, man."

His lips settle into a thin firm line. "Come on, man, let's get out of here." He pulls me toward the back door and Ruby is right behind him. I nod in her direction. The fraction of a smile graces her lips in return.

I look at Beck. "You two just got here. Don't you want to stay and celebrate with me?"

He furrows his brow. "Let's get you home and you can tell me all about what you're celebrating."

"Fair enough."

"Hey, what happened to that drink?" the redhead asks, pulling on my shirt.

I turn around. "Yeah, sorry about that. I have to go."

She stands there pissed as hell looking at me. I shrug, not really caring about being cordial right now.

"You're an asshole," she mutters.

"Yeah, I am," I toss back at her.

We hit the outside a few seconds later and the sudden burst of air makes my stomach turn. Beck and Ruby walk in front of me not saying a word. They turn into the side alley where Beck's Jeep is parked. I start to feel sicker with each step. I stop at his car but have to brace my hands against the brick of the building and hang my head. Inhaling and exhaling over and over, I catch my breath.

"You're not going to barf in my car?" he asks.

I shake my head no and climb into the backseat with my head spinning.

Over his shoulder as he drives he asks, "Where are you parked?"

"I have no fucking idea." I laugh.

"Are you for real?"

"What crawled up your ass?"

He slams his foot on the brake and jerks the car into PARK, then turns around. "I don't want to see you ruin everything you've worked so hard to accomplish."

His words are sobering. "I found out today I have a kid out there somewhere that I never knew about."

Ruby's head snaps in my direction.

Beck's eyes soften. "Let's get your vehicle and get you home and I'll throw on a pot of coffee and we can talk about it."

"Okay, man. I think my bike's down on Melrose somewhere."

Beck rides my motorcycle and Ruby drives his Jeep to Laguna. I fade in and out of consciousness until we hit the beach. The smell of the sea air awakens my senses. I stare out the window and into the vast body of water. Childhood memories assault me one after another— making sand castles, flying a kite, shell hunting. My phone is vibrating like a motherfucker, but I ignore it. When we get to my house, I sit at the kitchen table and cradle my head in my hands.

Beck makes the coffee and pulls three mugs from the cupboard.

Ruby sits beside me. She takes my hand. "Do you want to talk about it?"

I take a breath. "You know the girl I told you about?"

"The one with the French name?"

I can't hold back a slight smile. "Yeah, S'belle. Well, her name is Bell."

She nods, obviously already knowing this.

Beck sets three cups of coffee on the table and has a seat.

I take a sip of mine. "I . . ." I ponder how to say I fucked her one night without a condom and never thought twice about the lack of protection.

"You slept with her and she got pregnant?" Ruby asks.

I stare down at the table. "Yes, I slept with her one night my senior year of college when I had a girlfriend."

"Dahlia?" she asks.

I nod, not really remembering how much I told her during any of my previous drunken ventures but ascertaining that I blabbed about plenty. "She told me today . . ." I tell them both everything that happened earlier this evening. They listen, no judgment or comment.

When I'm finished baring my soul, Ruby asks, "Do you know if it was an open or a closed adoption."

My eyes rise to hers. "I have no idea. What does it matter?"

"An open adoption usually has an option of contact."

I shoot her a quizzical look.

"I'm adopted. I've known since I was six years old, but my adoption was closed."

"Your parents told you when you were young," I comment.

"Yes, they didn't want me to feel any less loved and I didn't. In fact, I grew up feeling extremely special. But a part of me wanted to know who my birth parents were. I went through the whole nature-nurture debate in my mind and when I turned eighteen I paid a woman five hundred dollars to locate my biological parents. She wasn't able to find my birth father, but she gave me the address and phone number of my birth mother."

"Why couldn't she locate your birth father?"

"His name wasn't recorded on the birth certificate."

With my elbows on the table, I steeple my hands together and then look over toward Ruby. "Did you contact your birth mother? Did she tell you who he was?"

She shakes her head. "I love my parents—my adoptive parents, and once I had that piece of paper in my hand, I decided I didn't need to know."

Beck stands, lifting his empty cup. He looks down at Ruby. "We should go."

She glances up at him and nods. She rises and shifts her eyes to me. "Ben, if you ever want to talk, call me."

I walk them to the door and Beck leans over toward me. "You call me first the next time you feel the need to go to my bar. You know I'm always here to talk."

I nod sincerely, shooting him an appreciative glance.

Staring at them as they walk to their car, I think about what Ruby said. Then I stand there wondering if someday in the future I'll be sitting across from a person with a piece of paper in her hand with my name on it.

He runs down the stairs with a football tucked under his arm. He's wearing a Chicago Bears football helmet and a blue jersey that's too big for him. It looks so familiar.

"Hey, champ, slow down," I call as he hurtles past me.

"Daddy, Daddy, I did it," he says as he comes to a stop next to me.

I look down at his flushed face and brush his blond hair from his eyes. "What did you do, champ?"

"I roared. I roared," he says with a gleam in his eye.

With a huge grin on my face, I bend down to pick him up. "You scored, little lion, you scored."

The little boy's laughter morphs into mine. His eyes look just like mine. His voice sounds like mine. Then all of a sudden, I become my father and the little boy becomes me.

Fuck, I wake up with sweat pouring from my brow. I look out into the ocean in an attempt to calm down. I couldn't sleep, so I moved out to the deck early this morning to listen to the sound of the water crashing against the rocks.

"Ben?" a voice calls from somewhere below me.

My head thunders in pain as I quickly sit up in the lounge chair and look into the sky, assessing the time. The sun is overhead. Looks to be around noon.

"Ben?" the voice says again.

"Up here, Serena."

I can hear the thumping of her sneakers against the weathered wood of the stairs and I see her dirty blond hair, much shorter than the last time I saw her, blowing in the wind. "Are you ignoring my calls?" she asks, taking the last step.

I shade my eyes with my hand. "No, I just have a lot going on. You cut your hair?"

She looks down at me in the lounge chair. "Yes, I did, and don't change the subject. Do the words *let's have lunch tomorrow* ring a bell?"

I throw my head back against the chaise. "Sorry." I grimace. "Your hair looks nice."

She kicks my leg off the lounge. "Thanks. Now come on, let's go for a walk."

I stare at her a beat, but don't move. "Could you turn the volume down a notch?"

Her eyes widen in disbelief. "Are you hungover?"

I slowly sit back up, still squinting to see her through the brightness of the sun. My head feels as if someone is pounding a hammer right in the middle of it. "Yeah."

"Get up. I'm not leaving until you talk to me." There's an angry edge to her voice.

I shake my head and another crack of thunder explodes inside it.

She stretches out her hand with disappointment more than evident on her face. "Come on."

"Let me brush my teeth first at least."

She crosses to the glass doors. "I'll make us a cup of coffee."

"Thanks." I grimace as I stand.

Water gushes from the faucet as I try to scrub last's night drunken encounter from my mouth. I hop in the shower, hoping that will make me feel better. When I head to the kitchen the smell of freshly brewed coffee assaults me, turning my stomach. I'll pass on a cup this morning.

My sister rinses her empty cup and places it in the sink. She turns around. "Are you drinking again?"

"No, not really. I needed a release, so I went out last night."

Her eyes glisten with tears.

"Serena, I'm doing okay. I'm not going down that road again. I promise."

"I hope not," she says, handing me a coffee and heading for the door.

I take a gulp and follow her. The heat burns my tongue and I leave the cup on the deck, taking two steps at a time to catch up with her. We walk the beach for a long while without conversation until she turns to look at me.

She finally breaks the silence. "I went to the cemetery yesterday and saw the seashells you put on Mom's gravestone." I glance over at her. "Yeah, I've been thinking about her a lot lately."

She takes a deep breath and inhales the fresh sea air. "Me too."

"I'm sure she must miss the beach."

She nods.

I stare out into the distance and catch sight of a sailboat going by. I point to it. "Do you ever wonder what life would be like if you could go back and change things?"

She bends down in the sand to pick up a seashell. "No, I don't. There's no sense in doing that."

"Sometimes I do. I think it's the littlest things that could make the biggest changes."

She makes a face of contemplation but doesn't answer. We walk for a bit and then I decide to just tell her. "I started seeing S'belle while you were gone," I blurt out.

She stops to pick up another shell and when she rises she hands it to me. "That doesn't surprise me."

Brushing the sand from it, I examine its beauty and think about its uniqueness. No two seashells are ever the same. I look at my sister. "She told me something yesterday that caught me completely off guard."

"Would you like to tell me what it was?"

I've gone over in my mind who must know about the baby. I'm guessing S'belle's family and more than likely Dahlia. What I'm not certain about is if Dahlia would have told Serena. I turn toward her. "Did you know about the baby?"

Her eyes widen. A look of shock crosses her face. "Do I know about what baby?"

I toss the shell I'm holding into the ocean and watch it hit the water.

She grabs my arms. "What are you talking about, Ben?"

I feel my throat tightening. "My baby."

She stares in disbelief, her mouth open. "Your—your ba-a-b-b-by?" she stutters.

I nod. "S'belle, Bell, I mean, got pregnant that night I spent with her in college. She had the baby and gave it up for adoption."

My sister's hand flies to her mouth.

"Yeah, I was a little shocked too." I try to keep the edge off my sarcasm.

"Let's sit down," she whispers, walking toward the rocks and choosing one. I sit beside her and bend to sift the sand with my fingers.

"How do you feel about it?"

"How do you think I feel?"

"You're upset?" she asks.

"Fuck yes, I'm upset. There's been a kid out there in the world for the past six years that's mine and I never knew he or she existed until yesterday."

She takes my hand. "What did she say?"

"She told me she gave birth on St. Patrick's Day and gave the baby away."

She looks at me for the longest time. "Are you sure it was yours?"

"Yes, I mean no," I stammer.

"But she told you it was?"

"Yes."

"And you believe her?"

"I have no reason to think she'd lie about that. What would be the purpose now?"

She nods, agreeing. "What else did she say?"

"She said she didn't want to tell me. She wanted to leave the past in the past."

"Why didn't she tell you before?"

"She said she tried to contact me, but I didn't call her back."

"Did she?"

"Serena, come on. Yeah, she called me, but . . ." I stop, not really sure what the but is. That she didn't try hard enough, try often enough?

"Where did you leave it?"

I drop her hand and cradle my head. "Nowhere. I left her standing there. I was so fucking pissed. I had a right to know." I glance over at her. "I had a right to know."

"Yes, you did, but put yourself in her place. You were with someone else. She was young and I'm sure she was scared. It must have been hard for her. Shit, it was hard for me when I found out I was pregnant. I was twenty and scared shitless—scared to tell Jason, scared to tell Mom, and so scared to have a baby."

"Yeah, but you had him. And you kept him . . . ." My voice trails off.

"Yes, but my circumstances were different. I was with Jason. He was there to help me through all my doubts."

I run my hands through my hair. "Are you defending her?"

She gives me a stern look. "No. I'm not. I just think maybe you should think a little more about her and a little less about yourself."

CHAPTER 22
Burn

Bell

Guilt chased me for years. Guilt for pursuing a guy that belonged to someone else, guilt for asking a friend to drive me home from a bar and being oblivious of her drunken state, guilt for giving up my baby. It was a domino effect—I chased someone I shouldn't have and wound up pregnant. When I found out, I couldn't wait to tell him in hopes he might be as thrilled as I was and that it might change things between us. But in my haste to get home to meet him, one of my friends died, and the guilt was more than I could stand. How could I raise a child? I was irresponsible and incapable—I was sure of that. And with that realization came the certainty that someone else could give my baby the life I knew I couldn't.

I never blamed anyone for my actions but myself—not my dead father, not my mother, not my brothers, and not any former lover. I just swam in my own self-condemnation. It hung around the fringes of my very existence. For years, it teased me, taunted me. It haunted me to the point that it almost dragged me under. But then something happened, something that made me realize I could let it go. That something was a friendship with a very special person—Dahlia London. Her kindness and understanding helped me see through my pain and made me understand it was okay to move on. With her support and that of my family, I finally found direction in my life. I stopped flailing and decided it was time to grow up.

Don't get me wrong—the constant guilt is still there. Time can never fully heal those wounds. But I had come to accept my decision and because of that, I was able to start anew. It hadn't been easy. My wounds ran deep. Yet somehow I was confident that I could continue to heal. My choices had led me to where I ended up. I had accepted that. When I started down this path, I was a young, immature woman. And once I made my decision, I was a lost girl who looked for love in all the wrong places.

Now I've turned my life around. I'm doing great—well, not great but really well. Sure, my job sucks. Working for Tate Wyatt started as a dream job, but the novelty wore off the more his attention toward me bled into possessiveness. I am handling it, though. And I don't really love living here. However, I'm not home that often and my family stops by or I visit them often.

But the hardest thing about telling Ben is that I'm feeling lost again, and I can't shake the feeling. All the memories keep swooshing around in my head and I can't get them out. I spent all day in bed and called in sick on Monday, but Tuesday comes way too fast. I wake up from a dream. The same dream I always have but this time instead of smiling I yell, "Damn you, Ben Covington, you came back into my life with all your charm and turned my world around one minute, then upside down the next just like you did to me before." My mind keeps repeating over and over, *You should have known better. You did know better. You kept yourself at a distance. You tried so hard to stay aloof. But the more time you spent with him, the more time you wanted to spend with him.* I shake my head, saying to myself, "Yeah, it's all true but it doesn't make it any better."

My legs swing onto the floor and I push myself into the shower, drag myself out of it, force myself to dry my hair, dab on a minimal amount of makeup, and dress as casually and comfortably as I can for work and still get away with it.

With coffees in hand I enter the showroom. Tate is standing at Josie's desk with his arms crossed talking to her. His head snaps up.

I cross the room, stopping at Josie's desk. "Coffees for everyone." I manage a smile.

Tate takes his and with a huff he storms off. His door slams, but before I can say anything to Josie, it reopens. "Bell, I need you in my office in fifteen minutes."

I nod and his door slams again.

"What's going on with you?" Josie asks, clearly concerned.

"Nothing." I take the lid off my coffee.

"You look like shit."

"Jeez . . . thank you."

She laughs. "Seriously, where have you been and what's the matter? I left you a message and yesterday Tate was the biggest asshole that ever walked on the planet. Did something happen?"

I don't want to break down at work. "Oh, Josie, so much has happened, but Tate is the least of my worries. He showed up at my event on Friday with Romeo." I lower my voice. "I think they may have been having a threesome."

"With you?" she asks, shocked.

"No!"

"Holy shit, those are two hot men. I bet they both have big—"

I cut her off. "Ewww . . . don't say it. I am not interested in either of them and definitely not the two of them together."

"But you'd be in between." She tips her coffee cup in my direction.

I start to walk away. "Not interested."

"What happened to Glow Boy?"

"Glow Boy?" I toss over my shoulder.

"The one who had you glowing brighter than a firefly for the last few weeks."

"He dumped me."

"So you were shagging him," she says, not exactly quietly.

"Shhh . . . And I was not."

"Well, whatever you were doing it's better than what I'm doing."

"And since when do you say *shag*?"

She smiles and shrugs. "Seemed appropriate."

I toss my stuff on my desk and flop in my chair. "Hey, are you doing okay?"

"Me? Ha! Me and Bob are doing great."

"Bob? Who's Bob?"

"B.O.B.," she spells out.

"Oh." I laugh, thinking I haven't used mine in so long I kind of forgot about it.

"Oh is right," she says, turning around.

I turn on my computer and think that at least work will take my mind off Ben for a little bit.

"Bell, are you coming?" Tate's voice booms from his office door.

"Yes, let me grab a pad and pen. I'll be right there."

Josie turns around. "Just remember, big . . ."

I cover my ears. "Don't say it."

She doesn't know we dated, because I ended things before she started work here. And although I never actually had sex with him, I am very well aware how big he is from the couple of times he shoved my hands down his pants during some heavy make-out sessions. The thing was, I've never needed more than first base with a guy. I do like to feel wanted, but the actual sex part isn't important to me—until Ben. Don't get me wrong, I've slept with my fair share of men. Any boyfriend's end game is to score, but I don't always let them win. Sometimes I cut them loose because I just don't feel any connection, but there are times when I've drunk enough to get myself in the mood and then I feel something, and something is better than nothing. But those times are past.

I keep my eyes down as I pass Josie's desk for fear she'll make me laugh. Tate's door is cracked open. I knock. "Can I come in?"

"Yes," he says in a cold tone.

I step in and leave the door open.

"Shut the door and take a seat."

I inwardly roll my eyes at his dramatic behavior, but I do as he says.

"What the hell were you thinking? When a client asks you to come meet him, you don't say no. Was it because you didn't want to run into that boy toy of yours so you didn't come?"

Boy toy? I have no idea what he's talking about, and the blank look on my face must register with Tate.

"Romeo told me he saw some guy's name on your phone and that same guy was at Beck's with his face buried in another girl."

Tears sting my eyes and any energy I had managed to muster up this morning is depleted immediately. Ben already found someone else? I should have known. I sit up straight, knowing I am not going to allow my boss to see my weakened state. "No, Tate, that's not what I was thinking. I was actually thinking how inappropriate it was for you to tell our client where I live and for said client to call me at the last minute and expect me to drop everything to come running."

He clears his throat. "Well, moving on, the Johnsons are having some issues with the florist. Can you see if you can help them out?"

I jot it down on my pad, trying to control my furious shaking. He continues with a list of items that need to be taken care of and I write them down, never once lifting my head to meet his scrutiny. About twenty minutes later he finishes.

I stand up. "I'm still not feeling well, so if you don't mind I'm going to take care of these issues from home."

He nods. "That's fine."

I walk out of his office on trembling legs and go to my desk, collect my things, and make my way to the door. As I step out onto the sidewalk I realize I never said good-bye to Josie. I didn't even notice if she was at her desk.

My grandmother loved to go places but hated to drive. She didn't think it an extravagance that she had a driver take her where she wanted to go, and neither did any of us. My grandfather used to joke that she was like *Driving Miss Daisy*. I own that movie now and watch it whenever I want to be close to her. I stop it and rewind before it gets to the sad part, though. I don't like sad. My grandmother had her license and she could drive; she just chose not to. She told me she liked to ride in the car and look out the window—that was why. In fact, the only time I remember her being behind the wheel was the night my father killed himself. She came to pick up River and me, but I didn't know why at the time. It wasn't until much later that night that my mother and brothers told me my father was dead. I blamed myself, Xander blamed himself, we all blamed ourselves for our fractured family, but we stayed close, maybe even closer because of what had happened.

My father's death made River and Xander stronger but not me. Somewhere along the way I let everyone shelter me, coddle me even—after all, I was the baby of the family, the younger sister to two older brothers, the girl who couldn't make her daddy happy when all he wanted was for her to play the guitar, and the young woman who got pregnant and who lost her direction at the same time. I might look like my grandmother—the red hair, the shorter stature, the curvy form— but unlike my grandmother who loved to go places and found an alternative way to get to them, I'm struggling finding my own alternative way in life.

I want so much to find that elusive direction in my life that I'm determined to make this job work even though it doesn't. It isn't just

Tate either, it's me too—I just don't love it the way I wanted to. But Tate's hot-and-cold demeanor isn't helping at all. And now it's Friday and the workweek isn't even over. I have to work with him all day tomorrow. The thought makes me want to crawl back into bed. It's been exhausting trying to push what happened with Ben aside and concentrate on work, so much so I've ended up sleeping most of the week when I wasn't at work.

And just as draining has been my avoidance of my family. They'll know immediately something isn't right when they see me, and I don't want to discuss what happened with Ben right now. So every time one of them calls I blurt out a reason I have to rush off the phone. With my mother and Jack in New York City, avoiding them has been easy. My brothers too. But Dahlia saw through it all when she called me last night and I couldn't help myself—I broke down and told her a little bit about Ben—just that I had seen him and it didn't go well. I left it vague and she didn't pry. I thought it would be awkward, but it wasn't. As usual she listened and gave support.

Peeking through the blinds this morning, I see it's later than I usually get up, but I'm not sure of the exact time. I unplugged my clock because time was moving too slow. I roll out of bed and relocate to the couch. *The Adventures of Huckleberry Finn* draws my attention and I decide to read a little bit more. I've become obsessed with the boy who isn't thrilled with his new life of cleanliness, manners, church, and school. The boy whose life on the straight and narrow isn't necessarily for him but who sticks it out for his friend. It makes me wonder if Ben somehow relates to this character and that's why he loves the book so much. More than anything I wish I could ask him.

A light knock on my door tears me from my thoughts, but I opt to pretend I'm not home. When the knocking turns into pounding and a familiar voice carries through the door, I can't ignore it any longer.

"Bell, it's me, Dahlia. I know you're home. I saw your car in the parking lot."

"Coming," I call as I shuffle toward her. Turning the lock, I pull it open and see Dahlia's shining face.

Her eyes sweep me from head to toe. "Hi, are you just getting up?" She sounds concerned. She pushes past me with a tray of coffees in one hand and a white pastry bag in the other. I step aside and cross my arms as she heads for the kitchen with determination. Today I can tell by the look on her face she's on a mission and I'm having a hard time seeing the beauty that's usually the first thing I notice about her.

I follow her. "Hi yourself. What brings you here on a workday?"

She sets the cups and bag on the counter and pulls out a coffee, squinting to read the side. "Do I need a reason to visit?"

I eye her suspiciously. "No, I guess not." Although I know why she's here.

"Well, I'm going to meet Aerie for lunch and I thought . . ." She pauses, handing me a cup. "Here, this one is yours. Extra cream and sugar."

I smile and remove the lid. Happy to have this delicious treat in my hands, I slurp down a big gulp. "Ow . . . that's hot."

She laughs. "It's coffee, Bell. Of course it's hot. You're supposed to sip it, not chug it."

"I know but usually the cream makes it cold."

She traipses across the tile floor in her high-heel black boots.

"You were saying?"

She shrugs. "I don't remember." She opens a cupboard and takes a plate out—a clear pink glass one. "Charlotte's been to the flea market, I see," she says, eyeing the plate.

"Yep. Came by last weekend with a bag full of groceries, Tupperware, and a few Depression-era pieces."

"It's beautiful," she says, opening the bag and setting some muffins on the dish.

"Yeah, it is," I agree.

Her eyes meet mine. "But you still don't like it here."

I lift one shoulder in a shrug. "It's fine."

"Bell, move in with River and me until you find a place you like better. Jagger stayed with us and it was fine, fun even."

"I appreciate it but I'll be quitting Tate's by the end of the year and then I'll have a lot of time to figure out where I want to live. And besides, I could never live with my brother."

She scrunches her nose. "Why do you say that? He loves you."

"Nothing bad, it's just him and Xander are so overprotective as it is. I couldn't imagine the third degree any date I brought home might get."

She giggles. "Yeah, that might be an issue." She takes the plate and her cup over to the sofa and sets them down on the coffee table. Her eyes dart to the book on the glass surface and I can see what she clearly knows—it is Ben's favorite book. She pulls a leg up and tucks it under her other one. Turning toward me, she asks, "So, do you want to talk about it?"

I sit next to her and take a muffin from the plate. My eyes search hers as I peel back the paper around it.

"I talked to Aerie. She says Ben seems withdrawn but refuses to talk about it." She sips her own coffee through the small hole in her lid.

"You really should take the cover off. It's much easier to drink."

Her lip curls up. "You really should stop avoiding the conversation and your family."

God, she's observant—too observant. I sigh as tears prickle my eyes and I can't hold them back anymore. And as awkward as the face-to-face conversation will be, I decide to tell her some of the things I skipped over last night. Like how I ran into Ben during the summer and then again at his award ceremony. How I was attracted to him and tried to fight it. How he seemed to care about me. How my mother told me I owed him and myself the truth and I agreed with her. And finally how he left me standing alone at the restaurant when I told him about the baby.

She listens quietly without even flinching and surprisingly without judgment. When I finish she says, "Bell, Ben has always been reactive and a bit of an asshole at times and you have to understand that's who he is. Sometimes he just needs time alone."

"Well, he's got it," I say. What I don't tell her is he was out with some girl the very same night, not because she'd care but because I do.

"Hey, listen to me. I know you're upset right now, but he'll come around and when he does I just want you to be happy. And if he makes you happy I'm okay with it."

I sigh in relief that the thought of me with Ben doesn't infuriate her, but also knowing there's no future with Ben anyway. "So you don't hate me for everything?" I finally ask.

Her eyes fill with protectiveness. "God no! I'm here for you whenever you need me. No matter what it is you want to talk about. Ben is a part of my past, but that doesn't mean I don't want what's best for him. And if you think he's what's best for you, then, Bell, I support you."

In this moment I can't possibly love her any more. I swipe my tears away. "Well, he's not what's best for me, that's for sure." I can't say anything else as my throat tightens.

She frowns. "However you choose to resolve this, do it, because it's what you really want. I hate to see you like this."

I nod. "I'm fine. Just a minor glitch but don't worry, I'll be back to normal soon."

She eyes me suspiciously. "Bell, did Ben tell you how old he was when his father died?"

"No," I croak.

"I'm not making excuses for him, but he was the same age . . ." She pauses and I answer for her.

"As our child would be now."

She nods and takes a deep breath. "And I think Ben sometimes separates himself from that child who lost his father. . . ."

As she talks it hits me . . . why he likes Tom Sawyer and Huck

Finn—two lost boys. I imagine he likes Peter Pan too. I quickly bring my attention back to Dahlia and shove those thoughts aside.

"He has a softness for kids. He always has. He took Trent under his wing and helped Serena raise him. He was a big brother to under-privileged kids for years, and even when he was in New York City he told me he volunteered as a drug counselor to teens. I'm not saying his reaction was right. I'm just saying I think I understand it."

I nod, absorbing everything she says. I feel a little raw. Looking at the time on my phone, I jump up. "Oh my God, I have to get ready. I have a retirement dinner downtown and I have to make sure the flowers arrived and the tables are set up."

She stands up and hugs me. I hold her tightly for a long time before I walk her to the door.

"Call me," she says.

"I will. I promise. And, Dahlia, please don't tell River about this."

She stares at me. "I can't do that."

"Please," I beg.

She sighs. "I won't bring it up, but if he asks me, I have to tell him."

I understand that and hug her close again. "He won't ask. Why would he?"

She pulls back and narrows her eyes at me. "But you do have to tell him and Xander too. I can't keep this from him forever."

"I will," I promise.

She leaves and I slump back against the door. The thought of it is too much to bear right now. Dahlia wasn't there when it all went down—how River and Xander wanted to confront Ben and I begged them not to. The truth was, I wasn't sure if Ben finding out about the baby would change my decision or possibly change my future and I didn't want it to change at that point. I was too broken to be fixed—or that was how I felt. I wonder now, if I had let them confront him, would my life be different today?

CHAPTER 23
Stuck in the Middle

Ben

I'm focused intently on my computer screen as I search the TRASH folder for Beck's monthly layout that I accidentally deleted. Almost a week has passed since I found out I have a kid out in the world. My sister's words are still swirling around in my brain. *"Maybe you should think a little more about her and a little less about yourself."* The trouble is, she is all I have been able to think about. A memory sweeps through me.

It was October thirty-first my senior year and S'belle e-mailed me and asked me to meet her that night. It had been almost two months since she had left me sleeping after our night together. I replied no. She asked again and that time I couldn't say no—so I said I'd meet her later that night. I knew I was lying to myself thinking I could just see her—I knew I couldn't. I wanted her to know how I felt. I told her that her green eyes were the most otherworldly eyes I had ever seen. That thoughts of her touch excited me. And that her red, almost copper hair haunted me. We agreed to meet at her apartment. She gave me the address.

But I never went that night, I couldn't. Dahlia came back early—I wasn't expecting her. Instead I went the next day to her apartment and she wasn't home. I went back the next five days and she never answered. The next time I showed up, someone answered and said she didn't live there anymore.

A soft knock on the door pulls me back to the present. "Come in."

Aerie enters. "Hi. Do you have a minute? I need to talk to you."

"Hey. Sure. Everything okay?"

She takes a deep breath. "I know you have a lot going on right now, but I have something to tell you and I'm not sure how you're going to react."

I glance over to her and motion for her to take a seat. "That doesn't sound good."

Her eyes meet mine. "Jagger got some disturbing news earlier this week. His father has colon cancer. He's there now with him."

"I'm sorry to hear that."

"It's stage four and it's unlikely he'll live much longer."

I push back in my chair. "I'm really sorry. Let him know I'm here if he needs someone to talk to and let me know if there is anything I can do."

She leans forward. "I've decided to go to New York City to be with him. Jagger's mother, Celeste, is already there, but I feel I should go too."

"How does that impact Jagger's movie role?"

"He's dropped out. The announcement will be made later today."

"And you? What are your plans?"

"The December issue is ready for press. And I can work on January's from New York. My assistant is back from maternity leave and between her and my intern, who I'd like to hire full-time, I know I can do it."

I rub my hands together. "We could bring in someone temporarily to lessen your workload."

"No! Ben, please. This is my magazine. Let me try," she pleads, and a few tears prick her eyes.

I stand up and round the desk. "Hey. Of course. I just wanted to lessen your stress. I know how important *Sound Music* is to you. I'll do whatever you think is best."

She glances up at me. "Thank you. I really appreciate it."

I lean back against the desk. "When are you planning on leaving?"

"Later tonight." She grimaces. "I'm so sorry. I only just decided to go this morning when I got off the phone with him. I'll e-mail you all my information. And I'll be back for Xander and Ivy's wedding."

My eyes flash to hers. "They set a date?"

She nods. "New Year's Eve."

"Oh, that's quick," is all I can say as my mind wanders back to S'belle.

"Are you okay?"

"Yes, I'm fine. Anything else? I was just headed to the gym."

"No. Thanks again, Ben."

I nod. "No need to thank me," I say to her as I usher her to the door and head to the locker room. I need to clear my head.

I'm sweating and biting back grunts as I run like hell, trying to escape my own thoughts. The treadmill beeps three point five miles in twenty-four minutes, my fastest time in years.

"Fuck, mate, are you running from the devil?" Kale asks from beside me, still hammering out his time.

Lifting my shirt, I pat my face. "Some days it feels that way."

"You seem preoccupied this week. You got something going on?"

I gulp my water and look at him. We're buddies but not in the same way I am with Beck. "Same shit, different day."

"That girl whose arse you've been chasing got you in a snit?"

"We aren't seeing each other anymore."

He slowed his pace. "It's about bloody time. Did you find a new piece yet?"

I shake my head. "We aren't all dirty dogs like you. Some of us do have to work."

"Ah . . . don't forget who outchased whom when I met you. And I work, just not night and day like you."

I blanch at the memory of a time when all I cared about was forgetting. Then I force myself to grin at him. "I know you do. Just busting your ass."

"Are you decent?" Aerie calls out to us.

"It's a gym, sweetie, not the locker room." Kale laughs, stepping off the treadmill.

She comes in and shoots him a look. "I'm not your sweetie."

He grins at her. "But I bet you wish you were."

She puts her finger in her mouth, pretending to gag. "Not in this lifetime or any other."

I make a T with my hands. "Kale, cut the shit. You know she has a guy. And, Aerie, he's just trying to rile you and you let him every time."

She glares at him.

"Did you need something?" I ask her.

"Yes, I wanted to tell you that I just found out that Kaye left her job at the radio station and maybe we should see if she could help us out temporarily."

"Kaye?" Kale wiggles his eyebrows.

Aerie rolls her eyes. "Kaye Hudson, or Kimberly as I know her, worked for *Sound Music* magazine when the former owner, Damon Wolf, wanted to expand into entertainment. She left before the first issue was published, though."

"That sucks," Kale remarks.

I shoot him a quizzical look. He never gets emotional about things that don't impact him.

"All that work never to see your first issue go to press. That would suck."

"Wow, so you do have a heart," Aerie says.

"I'm not the fucking Tin Man."

"Language, Kale, language," Aerie says, exasperated.

His lips twitch. "I bet you let that guy of yours talk dirty to you."

She ignores him. "Ben, should I call her?"

"She won't take the job."

"Oh, I think she might. I found out after she left she had been seeing Damon and things ended badly. So with him gone, I don't see a problem."

I take a deep breath, disgusted by that news. Damon is the biggest ass. I wonder if that's who she was crying over when we hooked up. "I thought you said you could handle it."

"I can. I'm just worried about you. . . . What if you need something sooner than I can respond?"

"Let's see how it goes. After the New Year we can reassess and go from there."

"But she might have a job by then," Aerie says.

I rock back on my heels. "Aerie, she and I had a thing while I was in New York City, and we also . . . reconnected one night and things ended badly."

"Oh, I didn't know." Aerie blushes.

"Is this chick that you fucked hot?" Kale asks.

With a disgusted look on her face, Aerie turns and slams the door. "Dahlia, hey, girl. You're early," she says just outside the door.

Kale's gaze darts to me. "Dahlia?" he mouths. "Your Dahlia?"

I narrow my eyes at him. "She's not my Dahlia," I mutter, not hearing the rest of their conversation.

"Yeah, he's in there. I'll be in my office when you're ready," Aerie says.

Dahlia pops her head in. "Hey, Ben, I was hoping I could talk to you."

"Sure, now?"

"Yes, if you don't mind."

"Want to grab a cup of coffee?"

She nods.

Kale clears his throat.

"Dahlia, this is Kale. Kale, Dahlia. Kale manages *Surfer's End* magazine."

His eyes sweep her. "Nice to meet you." He grins.

"You too," she answers, and quickly looks toward me. "Ben, I'll wait for you downstairs."

"Yeah, sure. Let me take a quick shower and I'll be right down."

The door closes and the sound of her boots click on the tile floor.

"She's hot," Kale says.

"You're such an asshole."

He raises his hands in the air. "What?"

"Forget it," I say, and pull the door leading to the locker room. "You're just hopeless."

"What did I do?" he calls back.

I just ignore him.

"Hey, why do you call that Kaye chick Kimberly?"

Again I ignore him and turn the water on, shower, and get dressed.

Curiosity has gotten the better of me. Dahlia couldn't possibly be here to talk about S'belle, could she? I'm pretty sure that even if we've moved past our issues, that would still be one very uncomfortable conversation. We've only seen each other one time since she bailed me out of jail and helped me find my way to the path I'm on today. One where my life doesn't center on booze and chicks, but rather on working hard and trying to make something of myself.

The elevator door dings and, glancing around the lobby, I see her outside sitting on a bench with her face lifted toward the sun. She looks the same as she always does. Her blond hair hangs long, her denim jeans are tucked in her boots, she has on a concert T-shirt and a leather jacket. There's so much history between us, and when I see her like now, carefree and happy, it reminds me of all we shared. Sometimes I forget she was my best friend for so many years. It's times like now that I miss that—just being able to talk to her.

"Hey, what's going on?"

She lowers her head and pulls her sunglasses onto her face. "I want to talk to you about Bell."

My stomach drops. So that is what she's here to talk about. Fuck me if this conversation isn't going to make me squirm. Even though the romantic feelings are gone between us, the fact that I cheated on her has to sting. I know it makes me feel like a real asshole.

I straighten my stance and fix my gaze anywhere but on her.

"Ben, don't be nervous. Come on, let me buy you a cup of coffee," she says, standing up.

"You mean let me buy you a cup?"

"Some things never change."

I grin at her. I don't care if I have ten cents or ten dollars in my pocket, I'd never let a girl pay—ever. Starbucks is only a few buildings over in the Commons and the line is fairly short. I grab our coffees and once she fixes hers with cream we sit outside.

I take a sip of mine. "Sucks that Jagger had to pull out of the movie. Had they started filming yet?"

She holds her cup with both hands. "No, there was some kind of production delay. But I guess Aerie had a suggestion for a lead replacement and the director is meeting with him today."

"Really? Who?"

"Do you know the guy that plays guitar for Ivy?"

"No."

"His name is Leif Morgan and Aerie and Jagger both think he is a shoo-in."

"Hmm . . . sounds like a good plan." I tap my fingers on the table. "So, what exactly do you want to talk to me about?"

She blows on her coffee before slurping a small amount so it won't spill. Her eyes lift toward me. "This isn't really any of my business, but I'm pretty sure I know how you're feeling."

I take a deep breath. "About?"

"Bell. I talked to her this morning and she told me the two of you started seeing each other. And she also told me about what happened last week."

I stare at her for a moment. No need to beat around the bush. "So you already knew? About the baby, I mean."

Seconds of silence elapse. "Yes." She removes the lid from her cup and then looks back up. "I found out the day she told me about the two of you."

My mouth forms a thin line as I try to control the anger rising up in my throat. "And what, you didn't think I had a right to know either?"

"Ben, it wasn't my place to tell you."

I narrow my eyes at her. "No, I guess not. It seems it wasn't anyone's place." I stress the word *anyone*.

She ignores my tone, but then again she always was good at doing that. "Did you know Bell was in a really bad accident shortly after she found out she was pregnant?"

I shake my head no.

"She was. The girl, Stacy, who was driving was killed and Bell was in the hospital for six months. She actually didn't leave until after she gave birth."

The words *gave birth* seize my attention, and any questions I might have had catch in my throat. I've been thinking of nothing but my child for the past week. She searches my face for any reaction, but I don't have one. I'm trying to process what she just said and I get lost in her words while attempting to work through the events in my head.

Dahlia leans forward. "Ben?"

I snap out of it. "When did she get in the accident?"

"It was Halloween night our senior year."

I swallow. "The night you went out with Aerie and came back to the frat house early." It's not a question.

She nods. She's already figured it out. That was the night I was supposed to meet S'belle but couldn't go because Dahlia ended up at the fraternity party instead of having a girls' night.

I push up from the table.

"Where are you going?"

I look down at her. "I don't think I can sit here and talk to you about this. It doesn't feel right."

She stands up and grabs my elbow. "Ben, sit down. Please. I'm not finished."

I inhale a huge breath and glance around and then at her. The look in her eyes is stern but also full of concern and I decide to lower myself back down. When I do the steel toe of my boot starts tapping the floor so fast my thigh hits the table and I can see the black liquid inside my coffee cup swirl.

"This isn't easy for me either, but I'm here because I know you. I know how much learning about the baby must have bothered you." Her voice trembles.

I suddenly feel a swell of emotion for her. The fact that she lost a baby just a few months ago must weigh heavy on her mind with the conversation we're having. "Dahlia," I say, pausing. I reach across the table and give her hand a soft squeeze and quickly retreat. "I'm sorry."

She shakes her head and her hair tumbles around her face. Her lips form a smile that isn't the least bit reflected in her eyes. I don't have to finish. She knows what I mean.

"I want to ask you something," she says, her voice gaining strength and clarity.

I cut my gaze to hers and nod.

She stares at me, holding my attention. "What would you have done if she'd told you? Back then, I mean."

It's a question I've asked myself. I put my elbows on the table and cradle my head in my hands. Then lifting my eyes toward her, I answer with all I have inside me, "I honestly don't know."

The summer heat wave is over, but the brush fires seem even more stoked by the Santa Anas. Hot and dry, the winds wrap themselves around the Southern California coastline as I ride along knowing where I'll end up but not quite ready to seek the answers to the questions I've asked myself over and over. The sweeping air picks up speed as I push through the narrow canyon passes, and the unusually warm temperature reminds me of a short story I read in college. Raymond Chandler described the "devil winds" in "Red Wind" in the most eerie way. He wrote:

> There was a desert wind blowing that night. It was one of those hot, dry Santa Anas that would come down through the mountain passes and curl your hair and make your nerves jump and your skin itch. On nights like that every booze party ends in a fight. Meek little wives feel the edge of the carving knife and study their husbands' necks. Anything can happen.

I furrow my brow thinking, *Anything could have happened. Anything can happen.* Despite the warm temperatures, a chill chases up my spine and then back down as I try to determine what I would have done if S'belle had told me she was pregnant. Would I have been a dick? I'd like to think I wouldn't have. Would I even have believed her? I'd like to think so, that I would have done the right thing, but the more I think about it, the more I know it's a question I will never be able to answer with any absolute certainty—but I do know with absolute certainty that I still want her.

CHAPTER 24
Say Something

Bell

Even though it's only eight in the evening, I feel completely drained. I just want to tuck my thoughts away deep down where I had them stored for so long. I cradle my arms around myself as the clouds gather in the sky and the temperature begins to drop, and I think tomorrow has to be a better day. However, as soon as my foot hits the top step of my building and I look toward my door, I want to run back to my car. He's sitting on the ground with his forehead resting on his knees. The hood of his sweatshirt beneath his leather jacket is pulled up over his head, but I know it's him. Once I'm practically standing in front of him, his head pops up. He looks worn, tired, and the glow in his blue eyes seems diminished.

I know that I'm to blame for that. I cast this spell of pain over the both of us and I know we'll be chained to it forever. For us the only answer is to go our separate ways—I figured that out the minute he left me standing outside Pebbles and ran to some other woman.

He rises and shoves his hands in his pockets.

The pull he has over me is still stronger than ever. All I want to do is throw my arms around him and cry with him for the child we made together but will never know.

"Hi," he says, his voice low and cautious.

I try to speak but can't. Emotion is so thick in my throat that I don't even look at him, because the threat of my turmoil spilling out in a waterfall of emotions is too great. I slide my key in the lock and walk inside, leaving him standing there. But I don't close the door. I leave it open, silently inviting him in.

He enters and shuts the door behind him. "I think we should talk."

My heart pounds loudly in my chest as fear rips through me. I'm not even completely sure what I'm afraid of—maybe that he'll tell me what he thinks or maybe that he won't. I pat my wild mass of curls that I know looks like a mess and drop my purse to the floor. I keep my eyes trained to the floor and my back to him.

"What exactly do we have left to . . ." I don't finish the sentence. I can't. I know what he wants to talk about—the baby, of course.

He steps behind me. His breath blows in my hair. "Look. I'm sorry I acted like an asshole the other night."

I sigh heavily. "It was a week ago," I say, the tears leaking from my eyes.

"Time is all convoluted right now. I'm sorry. But I'm here now and I want to know everything you wanted to tell me last week." His hands grip my hips.

"Please don't," I say, kicking my shoes off and heading toward the kitchen to put some physical space between us.

"Don't what?" he asks, sounding genuinely confused.

I stop at the counter and use it for support. I finally summon the courage to look at him again. Oh God, the look in his face makes me ache to soothe his pain, but my own pain is too great. "Don't touch me."

"S'belle," he says, moving toward me.

I put my hand out. "Don't call me that anymore." I muster up all the courage I have. "I'll tell you what you want to know, and then you need to leave for good."

He stares at me and an array of emotions crosses his face, but I think he settles on anger. Good. That's easiest to deal with.

"I want to know what happened," he says again. This time his voice is sterner; the edge of kindness is gone.

"What? In a nice little package?" I echo his anger because it will be easier for him to leave if we're both upset at each other—and that is what has to take place. It's best for both of us.

He furrows his brow. "No, just like it happened."

I open the refrigerator and take out an already uncorked bottle of wine and set it on the counter. I opened it last Saturday night but never drank any of it. I take a glass from the cupboard and pour a glass. I turn toward him. "Do you want some?"

"No. And I thought you didn't drink," he barks.

I shrug. "I didn't say I don't drink. I said it's better if I don't."

"Then why are you now?" This time his voice is compounded with compassion.

His concern starts to break me down, but I need to keep that wall up. I slam the bottle on the counter and turn toward him, allowing my eyes to meet his for the first time tonight. "Look, Ben, what do you want to know? Where the baby is? Because I don't fucking know."

His shoulders visibly shake and his eyes widen. I feel a tug at my heart. I've never sworn in front of him, but it's necessary to get my point across—that we cannot be together. He continues to stare at me, this time with confusion clear on his face, as I cross the room to the couch, averting my eyes when I can't stand it any longer.

"I just want to understand everything a little better."

He lowers himself on the couch but keeps a safe distance. My eyes cut to the *Huck Finn* book on the coffee table with the bookmark sticking out at about the halfway point, and I notice he does the same. I hesitate a moment and then reach to set my phone and my glass down, drawing his attention away from the book. I pull my feet up and twist my head to look at him, resting my chin on my knees. I search deep in my soul and start by asking him a question. "Have you ever been the reason someone died?"

He bows his head and drags his hand down his face as though pained by my question. Silence hangs in the air for one, maybe two long moments. "Yes. When my mother had her stroke last year, I blamed myself for her death. I felt responsible."

More tears slip from my eyes and I will them to stop. We stare at each other, and the small distance between us suddenly seems like miles. I want him to wrap his arms around me and hold me forever, tell me I made the right choice, the choice that was best for the child with a whole life in front of it, but I shake those thoughts away. That's not what will happen. It can't happen. Being together will only end in blame, and I can't bear that cross. I blink my momentary lapse of misjudgment away. "Well, then, you must know it changes your mind-set. You do things you might not normally do. . . . You make decisions that you might have made differently if you had been in a different state of mind."

"Yeah, I know that well. Too well," he answers, dropping his elbows to his knees.

His forthright honesty makes me suck in a shuddering breath. Blowing it out, I keep telling him what I've held inside for so long. "By the time I had the baby I was in such a bad place I couldn't imagine raising a child. I didn't even want to get out of bed. How could I take care of a baby? I told my family I didn't want the responsibility, but really the pain of what I'd done shadowed any good I thought I had left inside me." My voice cracks on the admission and I have to look away from him.

"What happened? Tell me what happened," he pleads. His own voice sounds pained.

My mind slips back to that distant place. "It was Halloween and you had told me you'd meet me at my apartment around twelve. My brother was in town, so I went to watch him sing. He drove me. He always did. That night my friend Stacy was there and she was after him, but by the end of intermission it was clear he wasn't interested in her. I wasn't paying much attention to what she was doing. I was listening to the band. When the night ended I wanted to get home." I look at him pensively. "Well, my brother wasn't ready. I knew he'd be there for a while, so I begged Stacy to take me home. She was upset over him anyway, so I said we'd talk about it in the car. And . . ." I take a deep breath and more tears fall from my eyes. "I'm not sure what happened, but a semi blew a light and hit us. You see, I made her drive me home so I could see you. I wanted to tell you I was pregnant. And her death was my fault."

He shakes his head. "No, Bell, it was the driver who blew the light. Not yours."

"So everyone says."

He shifts his eyes but leaves his elbows on his knees. At that angle I catch his face in profile. I can see its flaws, the way his nose has a bump on it that looks as if it might have been broken once, his hair so messy that it covers his ears, the stubble on his jawline as though he hasn't shaved in a few days, but to me those flaws make him even more attractive. I try to stop myself from falling, from faltering as his mind works and he pieces the events of the past together. I can see it happening before me but can't stop it now that I started it.

When he asks, "Was your brother unable to take you home because he was with Dahlia?" I pick myself up immediately. There's the elephant in the room that we've only briefly touched on. I swat my tears away and stare in disbelief at him. The anger that rears this time is real, genuine, and I don't have to fake it.

"Never mind, it's not important. What happened after that?" he asks, but it's too late. My wall is already back up.

I purse my lips at him. "Did you even show up that night? Did you go to my apartment like you said you would?"

He sits up and wipes his palms on his jeans. His eyes cut over to the book on my coffee table. The book he gave me because it's his favorite. The book he remembered he was reading the first time we met.

I take his lack of response to mean no, he didn't show up. "What would you have done had I told you?"

He swallows, working his throat.

My phone rings, interrupting this painful admission of guilt, and I seize the opportunity to put an end to the conversation when I see Tate's name flash across the screen. I reach to answer it, but he grabs my wrist.

"You're going to answer that in the middle of this?"

I take a deep breath, then another one. My pulse is racing. "It might be important."

"This is important!" he seethes, letting go of my wrist.

I let it ring.

Suddenly his eyes grow dark and his gaze sharp. "You're fucking him, aren't you?"

His question temporarily stuns me, but I quickly scramble to my feet, needing more distance from him. But even the distance can't contain my hurt. He thinks I'm the one screwing someone? Well, let him. That will work. I know how it feels. With my eyes narrowing at him I yell, "Why do you care!" and a rage flames inside me as I consciously decide to keep silent.

He too rises and moves closer to me. His fingers curl around my upper arms and I blink rapidly, standing frozen in place—love, lust, want, need, and even fear make my stomach tighten and my chest constrict.

His body stiffens and his grip tightens. "You know why I care."

"No! No, I don't! What I know is that you will always do what's best for you!"

He drops his hold on me as he stares in stunned silence.

But I said what I believe to be true. I finally admitted it out loud. It's why I kept my distance for as long as I did. He's proven to me time and time again that he makes the decisions that are best for him and him alone. He could have tried to find me after that first night we spent together—but he didn't because he had a girlfriend. When he saw me at River's house that first time—he could have come after me, but he went after Dahlia because that was what was best for him. Then this past summer when I realized he messed around with someone—it wasn't morals that drove my anger but rather the lack of persistence to prove he was interested in me. And just last week when I told him I gave our baby up—he left me at the restaurant because it was best for him.

I look away from his powerful stare, afraid of what I might see if I look any longer. "Do you have anything else you want to know? Because if not I think we're done."

I dare to look up when he fails to answer, and the stricken look on his face is enough to make me avert my gaze again.

"Was the baby a boy or a girl?" he asks softly.

I cross my arms over my chest in a hopeless effort to protect my heart. "I don't know," I whisper.

My phone rings again and this time I scurry toward it. To put an end to both our pain I answer, "Hello."

My eyes searching the floor, I spot his boots turn and I watch him go. He stops for a moment at the door.

"I'm here," I say into the phone.

The door slams and I jump. And as I strain to hear him pound down the concrete stairs, I feel my heart shrink just a little bit more as tears scald first my cheeks, then my neck, and finally my chest.

CHAPTER 25
Losing Sleep

Ben

Waking up on Thanksgiving morning to the smell of pumpkin bread baking in the oven reminds me so much of my mother. An aromatic wake-up call, the scent is enough to lure me from my old bedroom and out to the kitchen. I pad across the room and pour a cup of coffee that smells recently brewed. Standing at the large picture window in the kitchen, I stare out at the waves crashing against the rocks. Weeks have passed since I've seen S'belle, but I can't stop considering how different things might have been if Dahlia had stayed at the bar that night. And truth be told, I think that had I known about the baby I would never have let her give it up for adoption. But our issues run deeper than just our painful past—she proved that.

"You're awake," Serena says, entering the room.

"How could I not be?" I grin over at her.

She pulls the loaves of bread from the oven. "Did the wafting smell of cinnamon wake you up?"

"I hope you added extra cinnamon."

"Of course. Just like Mom." She grins.

"It's strange, being here on Thanksgiving without her."

"Yeah, it is. I really miss her."

I turn back toward the window and sip from my cup. "So do I."

Serena and Jason both sold their own places and decided to make Mom's house their new home. Trent was home from college and Caleb was supposed to arrive in town last night but had a flight delay. My sister had insisted I spend the night with them since today was a holiday. Trent arrived home last Sunday and has alternated staying with me and staying here.

With Aerie gone from the office, I've been extremely busy at work and although she's doing what she can remotely, there is some on-site work to be done. Well, maybe there isn't, but I've volunteered to take it on nonetheless to keep myself busy. But with Trent's arrival I actually took the week off. We've surfed, gone to the movies, and hung around talking about how college life is treating him. He really loves it.

"Caleb called. He's on his way from the airport," Serena tells me.

I turn. "Great fucking news."

"What's great fucking news?" Trent asks, standing shirtless in the doorway.

Serena shoots me a glare.

I shrug.

"Uncle Caleb will be here soon."

"Oh, cool," Trent says, then turns to me. "Want to hit the point?"

"Sure, just let me finish my coffee."

"I'll pack the shit in the car."

"Trent! Cut the swearing now. I mean it."

He rolls his eyes. "I'll put the stuff in the car," he corrects himself.

"Why are you looking at me like that?" I ask Serena.

She walks closer to me. "First time I've seen you laugh in a while. That's all."

"Really? I hadn't noticed."

"Well, I have."

I sidestep her and place my cup in the sink. "We're off. Will you be okay?"

She laughs. "Like the two of you would be any help anyway?"

"Hey, I help."

"Go have fun."

I salute her. "If you insist."

It's a short drive to the beach and before I know it I've found some peace on the water. Surfing has always helped me rid my mind of everything. Time flies and I'm glad we hit the waves, but it's time to get back. The ocean shimmers in the distance as the clouds move toward us. From where we stand stripping off our wet suits, the sky is bright with the afternoon sunshine casting upon us. A sun shower has already left its marks in the sand, but the tide is picking up in an indication that downpours are imminent.

"Come on, the storm is coming," Trent says.

I smirk at him. "Are you afraid of a little thunder and lightning?"

Trent turns, rolling his eyes. "Fuck no. It's just Mom will be calling every five minutes if we're not home before it starts."

I swing my arm around him. "That's sweet that you're concerned for your mother."

He snorts, shrugging out of my hold. "You were always concerned about Grandma too. And you wouldn't have wanted her on your case for not calling."

I catch his eye. "Yeah. Yeah, I was."

I let Trent drive home and just stare out the window. As we pull onto the gravel of the driveway, the tires spin. My head snaps to Trent. "Hey, watch it."

He grins. "I love this car. It's the shit. And you know, you really need to let me ride your bike."

"No fucking way. Your mother will kill me."

He rolls his eyes. "I call car duty."

"You're a little shit."

He shrugs.

I carry the boards around back to the deck as Trent unloads the gear.

"Hey, man, how the fuck are you?" Caleb calls over the railing.

I toss the boards on the sand as he rushes for me and we collapse into a flurry of backslapping.

"Fuck me, you made it."

"I sure did. And not just for a day. The week."

I slant him a look. "A week?"

"Well, I think so," he says with a cocky grin.

"Fucking awesome. Where are you staying?"

"I was hoping I wouldn't have to crash with the newlyweds," he says with a laugh.

"So, are you asking to stay with me?"

"Well, I was hoping . . ."

I save him from groveling and push him into the sand. A headlock, a few rolls, and sand sticking to us everywhere don't stop us, but my sister's voice makes us freeze.

"What the hell are you doing?" she calls from the top of the steps.

I rush to my feet.

Caleb one-ups me and rushes toward her. "Need help, Serena?"

She narrows her eyes at him. He shrugs. "Fucker jumped me."

She sighs in deep exasperation and turns on her heel.

I catch up to Caleb. "Just a little piece of advice, fucker. Keep the swearing to a minimum around my sister. Trent's picked up the same nasty habit and Serena is not happy about it."

"You could have warned me!"

"When? Between you begging me for a place to stay and using all your new fancy moves to beat the shit out of me?"

His grin widens. "I did learn some cool shit."

I shove him up the stairs. "You'd better have time to teach me how to kick your ass, then."

An hour later the table has been set, the game is on, and Caleb, Trent, and I are sacked out watching it. I look up and see Serena gazing around the room with a peaceful look on her face.

"Want some help?" I ask her.

"Suck-up," Caleb mutters quietly enough that my sister can't hear.

"Could you help me bring out the food? Jason's busy trying to find the carving knife."

Trent clears his throat. "The one with the black-and-silver handle?"

"Yes," Serena answers, casting her piercing gaze his way.

"Let me help Dad with that." He glares at me.

She looks at him.

He points to me.

I shrug. "We had to clean some fish the other day before we cooked them over the open fire."

Surprisingly she laughs. "I like having everyone home."

I give her a smile, happy to be here but feeling as if a piece of me is missing. I'm just not sure what piece.

During dinner we all eat as if we haven't eaten in years, and before I know it the sun is setting and I'm ready to head home, stuffed with turkey, mashed potatoes, cranberries, and apple pie. Serena hands me a bag to take home.

"Hold on, I forgot the pumpkin bread," she says, hurrying toward the kitchen.

"I'm coming with you, Uncle Ben. Hold up for me," Trent says from the top of the stairs.

"You sure? I think your parents might want you to spend the night here."

"I'm ready to scrub my eyes out from all the kissing going on in the kitchen earlier. I have to get out of here."

276 | KIM KARR

"Fair enough. Let's go."

Three hours later we're at my house with Trent sacked out on the couch and Caleb and me flipping through the channels.

"Let's get out of here," he says.

"Nah. I don't feel like it."

"Well, I do. I haven't gotten laid in months. The no-fraternization policy is killing me."

I bow my head and drag my hands down my face, feeling exhausted.

"Hey, what's going on with you? I noticed when I was home in October you weren't drinking and that today water bottles replaced beer bottles. What have I missed?"

I mute the television and then spill everything I neglected to tell him whenever we talked on the phone. The picture of a playboy fantasy life I had painted was far from reality. I had told him Dahlia and I were talking, I just didn't tell him how it happened—that she had to bail me out of jail. While I was at it I went ahead and told him about Bell, the baby, and how I walked out on her—twice. The second time because I figured out she was fucking her boss when she wasn't fucking me.

He slumps back on the chair and runs his hands through his hair. "I'm sorry, man. You should have told me. What are you going to do?"

"Nothing. Move on. What else can I do?"

"Seems like you care about her,"

I hiss a breath through my teeth and shrug.

"You could go after her, you know?"

"Sloppy seconds aren't my style."

"What are you, Danny Zukko?"

I raise an eyebrow. "You think I'm quoting *Grease*?"

"Yeah, I do. What are you going to do about it?"

I lunge at him and this time when we wrestle on the floor I emerge the clear winner. I head to bed as he makes his way to the door and I call out, "I don't need to learn your fancy martial arts moves to whip your ass."

"I let you win," he says under his breath.

"Fuck you," I call.

He turns and grins. "Love you too, brother."

I leave Trent where he is and take the steps two at a time, thinking about what Caleb said about S'belle. I fall asleep with her on my mind just as I have done every night since I saw her across the ballroom.

My phone rings before I'm even fully awake. "Yeah, this better be good," I answer without even looking at who it is.

"Ben!"

I sit up. "Beck?"

"Sorry to wake you, man, but we have a problem."

"What is it?" I flop back on my pillow while I'm checking the time—nine forty-five a.m. Fuck, it's late. I never sleep this late.

"There's a glitch in sending January's issue of *Surfer's End* to publication."

Cradling the phone to my ear, I scrub my face. "Did you call the systems analyst?"

"Can't reach Eric."

"Any idea what's going on?"

"It has to be the new encryption program Australia sent us when we went live last month."

"Fuck! I'll be right in."

I hop out of bed and take a quick shower. When I head downstairs it's quiet. There's a note from Trent saying he went to have lunch with Dahlia, and it looks as though Caleb never came home. I rush around looking for my keys and accidentally knock Caleb's backpack off the coffee table. The contents spill and I spot it immediately—the flash drive I gave him over a year ago. The same one he supposedly gave to Agent Bass during the drug cartel trial that the detectives said had a phone-book directory on it. I pick it up along with everything else but shove the drive in my jeans pocket before running out the door.

Traffic is light and I make it to the office in record time. When I reach Beck's door, I can see Eric Ryan sitting at the desk with Beck hovering over him.

"Well?" I ask.

They both turn their attention to me.

"Found Eric." Beck grins.

Eric drops his gaze and pounds the keyboard ferociously.

"I see that. And?"

"I'll have the syntax corrected as soon as I can concentrate," Eric mutters, his baseball cap blocking any view of his face.

"So, is it going or what?"

"Should be sent within the hour. Minor delay. Sorry I called you in," Beck answers.

"I'm going to grab a coffee. I'll be back in a few." Neither one of them acknowledges me.

When I enter the break room, Ruby is sitting at the table reading on her iPad.

"Anything good?" I ask her.

She looks up. "Just the latest on government health care and fiscal crisis."

"So early in the morning," I joke.

I grab the pot and tip it toward her. "Want a cup?"

"No, I've had a few."

"What hour did Beck drag you in?"

"It was supposed to be a two-minute stop over two hours ago."

"Well, I think it's under control now, so hopefully not much longer. Got plans? Christmas shopping?"

She laughs. "I wish. Actually we're going to visit my parents."

I nod.

"I've been meaning to call you," she says. "I went to the address I had for my birth mother."

"Oh yeah. Did you meet her?"

"No, I changed my mind once I got there. I decided I am happy with the life I have. She gave me up for a reason, and honestly not knowing just seems better than knowing now."

I nod again. Not sure of what to say.

"I love my parents. I don't need any other parental figures in my life. They're enough."

I stare at her for the longest time and it suddenly hits me—I have to believe that my child, S'belle's and my child, is just as happy with his or her life as Ruby is with hers. I have to let that go.

"Hey, man, Eric is a wizard. Whatever you pay him he's well worth it," Beck announces as he enters the room.

"You dragged my ass in here on a day off to tell me my computer engineer came from Oz?" I smile at him.

"Something like that."

I grab my coffee and clap him on the shoulder. "Now get out of here. I'll talk to you later."

I head to my office, figuring while I'm here I might as well get some work done. But after an hour or so I head back home. When I arrive home at two p.m., Caleb's car is here, so I can ask him about the flash drive that looks suspiciously like the one I gave to him. I'm glancing up just as Trent begins to pull in, but then he slams on the brakes and backs up, opting to park off to the side of the road rather than in the driveway. He rushes out of what used to be my car—my beloved BMW M5 Touring. Dahlia had given it to him and there was no way I could take it back.

"Hey, Uncle Ben, I need to talk to you," he huffs, bending down to catch his breath.

I raise an eyebrow. "What's so important that you're running, kid?"

The wind shifts direction as he swipes the back of his hand over his forehead. "I had lunch with Dahlia today."

"Yeah, so you told me in your note." I motion toward the house and walk toward the door.

When we reach the garage I turn toward him.

"Now, don't be pissed," he says.

My eyes narrow on him. "Come on, let's go in."

I open the unlocked door and we both walk in. As we enter the family room, my attention turns to Caleb sacked out on the couch with a few containers of Chinese food scattered on the floor and the coffee table, but I quickly turn my attention back to Trent. "Go on."

"Well, I mentioned to Dahlia that you thought the girl you like is fucking someone else."

I stare openmouthed at him. This is the first time his mouth has caught me off guard. "You did *what*?"

He repeats himself and Caleb bolts upright.

I flop down on the couch and rub my palms on my jeans. "I heard you."

Trent picks up one of the take-out boxes and a pair of chopsticks and slurps some noodles in his mouth.

"First of all, why the fuck didn't you tell me you were awake? And second, why would you say anything to Dahlia?"

He shrugs and settles into one of the oversized chairs across from the sofa. "I wasn't asleep last night when you were talking to Uncle Caleb and I heard you telling him about Dahlia's sister-in-law. You sounded a little desperate."

I squeeze my eyes shut. *Fuck, fuck, fuck.* "So you heard everything?"

I chance a glance at Caleb, who's sitting there with a blank look on his face—red eyes, messy hair, and obviously very hungover.

"Hey, Trent, what you heard, I'm not like that anymore."

He laughs. "I know that. And, Uncle Ben, I'm not twelve. I get we all make mistakes. Come on, you of all people know I get that."

"He's a pretty smart kid," Caleb finally chimes in.

I shoot daggers his way.

"So, do you want to hear what I have to tell you or lecture me on how not to behave?"

"Keep being a smart-ass and I'll call your mother," I threaten.

"I'll take the lecture," he jokes, biting into an eggroll.

I run my hands through my hair. "Okay, what did she have to say?"

He grins. "That the guy you were talking about is a complete douche bag."

My eyes widen in disbelief. "Dahlia called him that?"

"Well, no, she called him an asshole."

"Go on."

"Anyway, that douche bag still has the hots for her. I guess she dated him for like a month almost a year ago. Dahlia thinks he keeps coming on to her. And don't worry, I didn't tell Dahlia you were heart-broken or anything."

I ignore his smart-ass comment. I already knew Bell had dated Tate. Fuck me, obviously I was letting my anger about the baby impact my reaction. But why didn't she correct me? I guess because I was being just as big a douche as her asshole boss. Wanting to hear her voice, to talk to her, I pull my phone from my pocket. When she doesn't answer I send her a text.

Where are you?

Her reply is immediate.

I'm at work.

I need to talk to you.

She doesn't reply this time.

"Well?" Caleb and Trent say at the same time.

"She's at work."

"Well, go get her," Trent says.

I look at him, exasperated. "This isn't a movie."

"Oh, I thought you were Danny Zukko," he says, laughing.

Caleb laughs too and they both are almost crying in a matter of moments.

I leave the assholes sitting here and stride into the kitchen. Today is the day after Thanksgiving and I remember her telling me something about where she'd be.

"You know, I think you're actually over her?" Caleb says as he's tossing a few containers in the trash.

Distracted by trying to remember where Bell had said she'd be, I look at him quizzically. "What?"

"Dahlia—I never thought you would get over her. But you call her Dahlia now. And there's no spark in your eyes when her name is mentioned."

I hadn't noticed that before but knew I had gotten over everything as best I could a while ago.

"Hey, Uncle Ben, I'm serious as shit. I think you should go after that girl," Trent chimes in.

"You know what, I have to say I agree with the kid," Caleb says.

I open the refrigerator and grab a water bottle and toss one to him. "Here, man, you need this. You look like shit."

He runs his fingers through his already disheveled hair. "I feel like it too."

Ignoring the fact that Caleb and I are having a completely different conversation, Trent pulls us back to the previous one. "Where does she work?"

"She's an event planner. I know she's been coordinating that asshole Romeo Fairchild's wedding. But I have no idea where it is."

Trent turns on his heel and leaves the kitchen.

"Where are you going?" I call to him.

"You're the investigator. You figure it out."

I follow him into my office. "Don't be a smart-ass."

He sits in front of the computer, taps a few keys, and then looks up. "Bingo! It's breaking news. Governor's son's wedding set to take place at Adamson House canceled at last minute."

"Looks like you're going to Malibu. My guess is she's still there. Last minute sounds messy to me," Caleb says, high-fiving Trent.

I glare at him. "You told me she was forbidden fruit."

"Yeah, but you weren't walking around looking like your dog just died then. You wouldn't even go out with me last night. That's unheard of. You don't have to drink to go out and have a good time. And when was the last time you got laid?"

I cringe at his question. No way I am telling him that and besides, there are just some things a nephew doesn't need to know. "Let's just say it's been a while." I leave it at that.

"Come on, man, you're miserable. If you want her, go get her," Caleb prods.

I lean against the doorway. "You act like it's that easy. It's complicated."

Trent pipes up, "It's only as complicated as you make it."

He has a point. I did say I wanted to leave the past in the past.

Caleb lowers himself on the corner of the desk. "When have you ever backed away from something because it wasn't easy?"

Trent pushes back in my chair. "I can drive you."

I grin at him. "I'm a big boy. I think I can go after a girl myself."

The ride should be fairly short, but the worsening weather conditions are making the drive tougher. The palm trees bend from the strong winds, and the county has issued the highest wildfire threat it's seen in years. I finally spot the sign at the road that reads CALIFORNIA STATE PARK NATIONAL HISTORIC SITE. I turn in and immediately notice the wildflowers that line both sides of the narrow drive. They lead me all the way to the end, where I see a building that must be the Adamson House. I've never been here, but I have read the book written by the original owner, Frederick H. Rindge. *Happy Days in Southern California* provided a detailed history of the region and it was something I had picked it up at the library last summer when I had too much time on my hands and was reading every historical book about California I could find to help cement my decision to stay here.

There are no cars here and I hope I'm in the right location. Standing in front of me is a very large Mediterranean-style house with hand-carved wooden front doors. Detailed filigree ironwork covers what looks to be lead-framed bottle glass windows. I walk around the side of the building, where I catch sight of Malibu Beach as well as the lagoon and the pier—it's one gorgeous view. I loop to the back and spot her car and the Tate Wyatt catering van immediately. She's here.

Excitement combines with nervous energy as I finally allow my mind to consider what the hell I'm doing here and what the fuck I'm going to say. All of a sudden I feel like Richard Gere from *An Officer and a Gentleman*, and that couldn't be any lamer. Now I need to consider my options:

1) Go home

2) Call her

3) Text her

4) Just go the fuck in.

I decide on texting.

I'm outside and I want to talk to you. So
you either come out or I'm coming in.

I wait for a response—one minute, two, three. Fuck it, I'm going in. I pull open the rusted metal door that has been painted chocolate brown in an attempt to cover up the corrosion marring it. As I step inside, a musty smell fills the air. The room is dark and I flick on the light switch. I'm in a closet of some sorts that's been turned into an employee entrance with a time clock machine, a few lockers, and coat hooks. I push through the door in front of me and end up in a hallway. It's quiet and I follow it to the end, where the next door opens into the banquet area. It's partially set up with place settings, flowers, and candelabras on each of the tables, but it's also empty of any people. A number of other doors line the walls and I walk the perimeter of the large space, peering into them. They are all dark inside and I can't find her anywhere.

CHAPTER 26
Sundown

Bell

Romeo Fairchild's wedding has been canceled without any explanation and Tate and I have been cleaning up what we had already set up. The weather may have kept everyone away anyway. I've been out in the main room for a while when he calls me into the kitchen area.

As I push through the door I notice a bottle of scotch and a glass on the work area. "You're drinking?"

"Celebrating is more like it." He grins at me.

"The biggest wedding we have all year cancels and you call it a celebration?" I raise an eyebrow.

"He wasn't ready for marriage and neither was she. It's the best thing for the both of them."

I'm actually impressed with his insight.

"How much more do you have left?"

"I'm more than halfway done."

"Put the flowers in here," he says, holding out a bucket. "I'll drop them off at my mother's nursing home. The ladies love getting flowers."

"That's sweet of you."

Something flickers in his eyes that I can't decipher.

I reach for the bucket, and his hand catches my wrist and he yanks me to him. "You like sweet, don't you? I can give you sweet. Just give me a chance."

"Tate, come on. We've talked about this."

"Yes, we have and I think you need to stop fighting the attraction between us."

I push at his shoulder. "I think you've had too much to drink."

I keep trying to extricate myself from his grip, but instead he cages me. I try to remain calm because I know he won't hurt me; he's just had too much to drink. "Tate, please move out of my way."

"Bell, I'm tired of this game," he says with a warning in his voice.

I shove at him again, this time harder. "I'm not playing a game. Now let me get back to work."

In an unexpected move he takes my wrists and pins them to my side, pressing himself into me. I scream from the pure shock of it.

Suddenly the door swings open and Ben is standing there wearing an anger like nothing I've ever seen before. "Let her go," he seethes.

Tate turns. "What the fuck!" he yells.

My eyes desperately seek his, trying to tell him I'm okay. I can practically see the hatred pumping through his veins as though he wants to kill him. With my chest heaving and my heart pounding, I scramble toward Ben but twist my ankle and stumble to the floor, hitting my head on the corner of the counter. Ben slams into Tate, who falls back but catches his footing. Tate's eyes darken as he lunges toward Ben. He swings at him and Ben tries to duck but falls into a crate on the floor.

He yells, "Get out of here, Bell."

But I can't move. I can't believe this is happening.

Tate looks down at me. "If you want to keep your job, tell this dick to get out of here."

"Leave her alone!" Ben shouts as I get to my feet.

I take a deep breath and prepare to tell Ben it's not what he thinks, but I can see he's not listening. His fists are clenched and he rams into Tate, who starts to fall to the floor, and Ben swiftly kicks him in the gut. Tate lands on the floor and Ben straddles him, ready to deliver a punch to his face.

"Stop, Ben! Please stop!" By now I'm screaming.

He cuts his eyes toward me and looks at me for a few long seconds before he moves away from Tate.

He rushes over to me. "Are you okay?" he asks, stroking my cheek, and I can see the blood dripping down it onto his hand.

A sob escapes my throat and I suck in a breath to stop the hysteria. My heart hammers against my rib cage when he tenderly says, "Shhh . . . don't cry. Shhh . . . don't cry, Bell."

I look into his blue eyes and murmur, "I don't like it when you call me Bell."

In the midst of everything that's going on, a smile flits across his lips. He lifts my chin and finds my eyes. "Don't cry, S'belle."

I hear a rumbling from behind as Tate approaches us. "You'd better get out of here before I press charges for assault," he threatens.

Ben turns ever so slightly. "You ever touch her again and I will kill you."

Tate straightens his shoulders and turns around, storming out of the room.

Ben turns back to me and pushes the hair from my face. "Let me see your forehead."

"I'm okay," I whisper.

"No, you're not. You're bleeding."

He reaches for a stack of clean towels near the sink and wipes my face. "You have a gash just above your eyebrow," he says softly, and presses the towel to it.

I can see the blood soaking through it.

"Come on, we're going to the emergency room."

"I'll be fine. I don't have to go to the hospital."

"Where's your stuff?"

"My stu-stuff . . . ," I stammer.

"Whatever you brought in the building with you. Where is it?"

"In a locker in the entrance, but I can't leave. I have to finish cleaning up. I'm almost done."

Applying pressure to my gash, he frowns at me. He sucks in a deep breath and squats down so that we're eye level. "You are done working for that asshole. Do you hear me?" I can tell he's controlling his tone.

"I have to keep my job," I cry.

"You don't have to do anything."

"I can't fail at something else. I fail at everything I do." The words come out without thought.

He swallows. "You are beautiful from the inside out. Failure is never anything you have to worry about. And what happened today is just proof of that."

My eyes fill with more tears.

Pressing a kiss to the top of my head, he holds me tight to him. Once my sobs are under control, he pulls away. "Give me your hand."

I just look at him in confusion.

He lifts one of my hands to where he's holding the towel. "Keep this tight to your head."

I nod.

He lifts me off the floor and cradles me to him.

"What are you doing?" I yell.

"I'm getting you out of here."

"I can walk."

"I can walk faster," he says. "Just hold the towel."

I band my arms around his neck.

He makes his way down the hallway and stops in the employee entrance. "Which locker?"

I point. I'm not sure if it's my head, or what happened with Tate, or the fact that he's here, but I'm feeling as though I'm in shock.

He manages to open it with me still in his arms and grabs my bag and carries me to his car before setting me down.

I look up at him, a little dazed. "I can't leave my car here."

"I'll send someone to get it."

When he gets in the car he pulls up his GPS and selects the nearest hospital. After watching him for a minute, I sag back against the seat and shut my eyes.

His hand squeezes mine. "Hey, don't fall asleep, S'belle. Not that I think you have a concussion, but you never know."

I glance down at his hand and give him a slight smile.

"I think I should call your mother."

"No!"

My panicked reaction seems to surprise him and he glances over to me. "Hey, you didn't do anything wrong. You know that. Right?"

"Please don't tell my family."

"S'belle, he attacked you. You have to call the police."

"He didn't attack me."

"I saw him."

"It wasn't an attack. He would have left me alone."

"I'm not sure of that and I don't care what it was. He's a fucker!" Ben yells, and slams his hands against the steering wheel.

I flinch.

"I'm sorry, I didn't mean to yell." He moves his hand to the towel. "Press a little tighter. Okay?"

I do. We both stay silent the rest of the drive.

When he pulls into the hospital, he puts the car in PARK and turns to me. "S'belle, I really think you should call your mother."

I sigh, knowing he's right, and pull my phone from my purse where I tucked it when we got in the car. "Will you call her? I'll just cry and she'll think it's worse than it is."

He nods. "Sure. But let's get you inside first."

CHAPTER 27
Counting Stars

Ben

Charlotte and Jack Tyler arrive just as the doctor finishes the last of S'belle's five stitches, both of them speaking at the same time.

"Bell, darling, are you okay?" Charlotte exclaims.

"What happened?" Jack questions her.

I release S'belle's hand. "Hey, I'm going to arrange to have someone pick up your car."

"You don't have to leave," Charlotte says to me.

I give her a slight smile. "I'll be right back."

Jack extends his hand and I shake it.

When I get out into the hallway I lean against the wall and bow my head, noticing there's blood smeared across the corner of my shirt. Tate Wyatt has obviously been harassing her for a while even if she didn't see it. Who knows what he would have done to her tonight? The situation could have been so much worse. And I accused her of sleeping with him. I take a few more deep breaths and squeeze my eyes shut, cursing my own stupidity.

After a few moments I pull out my phone to call Trent and Caleb and ask them to pick up her car. After explaining what happened and that I tucked the key in the wheel well, I get off the phone and make my way down the hall. Jack is standing outside the door of her room. When he sees me he starts walking my way.

He claps my shoulder, the one without the bloodstains. "Bell told us what happened. I think she's downplaying it. What did you see?"

"What did she tell you?"

"She said he was drunk and that he didn't really mean anything by it."

I stare at him. Eye to eye. Man-to-man. "That could be the case. But he was being forceful with her and she was trying to shove him back." I can feel my stomach lurching.

His face heats in anger. "Oh, Christ."

"I don't know how far he would have taken it. I don't know if he's done anything like this before. But I know she was scared even if she won't admit it."

Jack runs his hands through his hair. "She's worried he's going to press assault charges against you."

I shrug. "Let him. Let him try to explain why I had to shove him off her to begin with."

His eyes glisten with unshed tears. "I worry about her, you know. She wants everyone to like her. She wants to make everyone happy. But I never thought this guy was like that. I got her the job, for Christ's sake."

I take a deep breath. "I don't know what he's like. But I saw him with her over the summer and he rubbed me the wrong way. Of course he didn't push himself on her then."

He clasps my shoulder again. "I don't know what you were doing there, but I can't thank you enough."

My eyes find his before I respond. "You don't have to thank me."

"I will make sure Wyatt knows I'm aware of what went down. You can be sure of that."

"I hope he gets what he deserves—one way or another."

He bobs his chin toward the room. "Come on, let's get back in there before Charlotte has a breakdown. The doctors ordered a CT to rule out a concussion."

"Did they do one?"

"They took her down when I was waiting for you."

My pulse pounds as concern courses through me. She's sitting up drinking a small container of apple juice, making a slurping noise, when we enter the room. I feel slightly uneven as I slow and take the last steps toward her bed, but when she smiles at me around her straw, it eases my worry.

"What did the doctors say?" My voice comes out hoarse.

She sets her drink down, but Charlotte answers, "They said there were no signs of a concussion, but they want her to stay awake for at least the next six hours and—"

"Mom, I got all the instructions. You don't have to repeat each one," Bell says.

My palms are sweaty and I wipe them on my pants.

"You should come home with us tonight," Charlotte says.

"I can make sure she gets home," I blurt out, not wanting to be away from her.

S'belle's eyes dart to mine.

"If she'd rather be home, I mean," I add, not certain what she's thinking.

"Oh, we appreciate that, but I think she needs to be with us."

"Charlotte, why don't we go make sure the front desk has the correct insurance information?" Jack takes her hand.

"Oh yes, of course." Charlotte picks her purse up off the table.

They both leave and I sit beside S'belle on the bed.

S'belle's eyes search mine. "You don't have to stay with me. I'll be fine."

I take her hand. "I want to stay with you."

"What if I'm not sure I want you to?"

"S'belle, why do you always to have to fight me?"

"Why did you run into the arms of another woman the night I told you about the baby?"

I blink at her in confusion. "I didn't. I haven't been with anyone since you."

"Tate told me he saw you at Beck's that night."

"I did get really drunk and some chick talked to me, but Beck and Ruby brought me home. I swear."

"So you were going to sleep with her?"

I shake my head as definitively as I can.

She searches my eyes. "Why did you come tonight?"

I draw in a ragged breath. "I wanted to talk to you. No, I wanted to tell you I was sorry, S'belle, sorry for the way I acted when you told me. I was an asshole. And you were right—I do seem to always think of myself, but I promise . . ."

Her eyes drop to the white sheet on the bed. "Ben . . . we can't do this. Just go."

"I'm not leaving without you."

"Just go home!"

"I can't do that."

Her gaze lifts to mine. "Why?"

The question makes me laugh a little, under my breath. I have to think for a moment how to explain my feelings. I lift her chin in my hand. "Some part of me is drawn to you. No matter how long we're apart, I can't stop thinking about you. I know you feel it too. And I'm not walking away."

Silence sweeps the sterile space around us.

She reaches out her neck and kisses me softly on the lips—and the gesture feels like a new kind of kiss, a new beginning.

I smile at her. "So I'm coming home with you." It's not a question.

She nods. "Yeah, I guess you are."

A strange feeling runs through me as I take her hand. I'm not sure what it is, but I feel the connection I always feel when I'm near her grow stronger than it's ever been.

She pushes some hair from my eyes, and the feel of her fingers on me makes my body burn.

"You have blood all over your shirt," she says.

I shrug and lean closer to her. "I'm just glad you're all right."

She takes my face in her hands and pulls me even closer.

"Okay, honey, that's all set. We can go now," Charlotte says, walking into the room.

I quickly jump to my feet.

Jack clears his throat.

"Mom, Ben will take me home."

"Are you sure?"

"Charlotte, Bell is old enough to make her own decisions. She'll be fine," Jack reassures her.

Charlotte turns toward me and hands me a bottle. "She's to take two of these antibiotics a day, plus Tylenol every four hours, she's not to fall asleep for six hours, and if she feels nauseated she's to go to the hospital."

"I'll take care of her, Mrs. Tyler," I promise.

She seems surprised. "Charlotte."

"Charlotte," I acquiesce.

She steps closer and gives me a little hug, whispering, "Thank you," in my ear.

I catch her eyes and nod. I see her throat working to hold back the tears. Obviously Jack filled her in.

Jack takes my hand and covers it with his. "You call us if anything happens."

"I will," I assure him.

As soon as Bell is dressed Charlotte and Jack walk us to my car and stand in the parking lot watching as we drive away. I did my best to reassure them, but I think the concern goes beyond her head wound. I get that.

We're both quiet as I drive from Malibu to LA. My thoughts keep flipping back to what might have happened to her if I hadn't gotten there in time.

"How long has he been harassing you?" I ask because it's driving me crazy.

She turns toward me. "He wasn't really harassing me. But ever since I ran into you I think he could sense I was interested in someone and sometimes he'd make inappropriate comments, but it wasn't anything I couldn't handle."

"Inappropriate how?" I ask, my stomach plummeting.

"I really don't want to think about it. But I promise, today was the first time he actually got physical."

I shudder at the word *physical*. The thought of anyone touching her sickens me. I take her hand in mine.

"He wouldn't have hurt me. I know what you're thinking."

I hope she's right, but it's over now and we never have to find out. "How about some food?" I say, deciding to lighten the dark conversation.

"I am kind of hungry."

"Good, because I am too." I turn and grin at her and then look down at my shirt. "Takeout okay with you?"

"The Kettle has the best broccoli cheddar," she says.

"You want soup?"

"Yes, when you're sick you're supposed to eat soup."

My head snaps to hers. "Do you not feel well?"

She presses her fingers to her bandage. "I feel fine. You know what I mean."

I try to control my laughter but feel my shoulders shake. "Sure I do."

"I can call ahead."

I grin over at her. "I thought you didn't eat vegetables."

Her eyes light up. "Cheese goes with everything."

This time when I look over at her, I let my laughter fill the car.

CHAPTER 28
Talk Dirty

Bell

While Southern California is being battered by the powerful Santa Ana winds, Ben and I pick up the soups and he takes me to the ridge to look at the city view while we eat.

"Do you believe me about Beck's?" he asks.

"Strangely enough, I do."

I place my spoon in my golden cheddar soup deliciously nestled in a bread bowl. "Want to try some?" I ask, pulling the spoon now laden with soup toward my mouth.

"I'll pass. Even cheese can't conceal the broccoli smell. Brings back nightmares from my childhood."

I think about him as a child for a moment and how cute he must have been. "Did you have to sit at the table until you ate all your vegetables?"

His teeth graze his own spoon slurping in a giant noodle. Once he swallows he says, "Something like that. For me it was more like I had to sit at the table until I could get my dog to eat all my vegetables."

God, he was a bad boy even as a kid. I find that oddly to be a turn-on. Watching him eat has my stomach yearning with desire and not for food. "We had a dog too. A golden retriever named Beat."

He laughs. "That makes sense since your dad was in the music business."

"What was your dog's name?"

A gleam enters his eyes, one I've never seen. "Kahuana. He was the biggest, baddest, chocolate Lab you could ever have seen."

I laugh. "Sounds like 'Leroy Brown.'"

Seemingly lost in his thoughts still, he looks at me questioningly.

"The song 'Bad, Bad Leroy Brown.' He was meaner than a junk-yard dog."

He shakes his head at me again. "Yeah, something like that. Can I ask you something?" His tone changes to something more serious.

"Sure," I say, blowing on my soup.

"That night I came over and you pulled out a bottle of wine, I saw vodka on your counter too. Are you drinking again?"

I tense up while his eyes study my face. "No, I never drank any of what I bought. I thought about it. I opened the bottles. Even poured a glass or two but never drank a drop."

His hand moves to tuck a piece of hair behind my ear.

I jerk away, moving to swat his hand. "I'm not like my father. I'm not an alcoholic, you know."

He catches my wrist and gently closes his fingers around it. "I know that and it doesn't matter anyway. I just want to make sure you're okay."

My heart beats faster, as if it's reaching for him. "I am."

The moment suddenly feels too serious.

"Good, because I'm the jackass that got so drunk that night at the bar I couldn't remember where I parked."

"You didn't drive home, I hope?"

"No, Beck drove my bike home, and believe me, he was not happy."

We finish our soups and talk about fun things we did as kids.

When we're done and heading back, I stare out the windows watching the trees sway side to side. It seems as though so much time has passed since our first dates. But in actuality not that much time has passed; it's more that much has happened between us.

Before I know it we pull up to my apartment building. He puts the car in PARK and turns to me. "You know, I really missed you."

I smile. "I know."

He shakes his head, somewhat amused, I think.

I leave him there pondering my answer and open the door to get out.

He catches up to me just as I'm climbing the steps. Once we hit the top, he grips my hips. "And how do you know that?" he growls in my ear.

I breathe him in—that scent I've missed for far too long makes me feel a little dizzy. I stabilize myself and take my keys from my purse. "Because I missed you too."

Then I turn to face him. He's staring at me, his eyes gleaming. "That strangely makes sense," he says, and takes the key from my hand before leaning in to place a soft kiss on my lips.

The heat between us intensifies and he pulls away, caressing my cheek and motioning for the door. When we get to it, he quickly shoves the key in the lock. I stand behind him as close as I can and rest my chin on his shoulder to peer down.

He twists his neck around to see me. "What are you doing?"

I grin, liking the feel of his body so close to mine. "Making sure you know how to unlock the door."

"You know, I could use a little direction," he says.

I press closer into him. "You insert the rod into the hole," I whisper into his ear. My voice is low, raspy with desire.

His body stiffens and his breathing is rough.

I close my eyes and feel a rush of excitement. "Next you turn it and pull it out."

He twists the key ever so slowly. "Like this?" he asks in that husky voice that makes me throb between my legs.

My own breathing picks up and I'm shamelessly panting. If I never understood kinetic energy before, I do now. He grabs the door handle and quickly pushes it open, ushering me by him at a rapid speed. I take the key from his hands. "Then you—" I start to say as I turn around to lock the door, but I'm silenced when his hard body meets my back.

He grips my hips and his lips find my neck. "Are you sure you're up to this?"

I try to catch my breath, but all my air is gone. I let my head fall back on his shoulder. "I'm sure. I don't want to wait any longer."

He flips me around and runs his hands down the side of my body. "Do you have any idea how badly I want you?"

"Show me just how bad," I breathe huskily over his lips.

His eyes close and he shudders.

"Ben, stop thinking."

His eyes open at the sound of my voice, and they have never been bluer. "I'm trying to figure out if we should be doing this after everything that happened tonight."

I bring my hands to his face. "He didn't attack me. I wasn't really afraid, just startled. I'm okay. This is okay," I reassure him, my body aching for him in a selfish way.

He stares into the depths of my eyes and brings a hand up to stroke my cheek. "We'll take this slow."

I slide my lips to his hand and kiss it, nodding.

And again he stares into my eyes. And then as if he can't take another minute of restraint, he slides his knee between my legs. My chest rises and falls with an intensity I've never felt before. He brushes the hair from my forehead and softly kisses above my bandage. I wrap my arms around his neck and throw my head back as he feathers kisses down my neck. He kisses behind my ear, and a hum of some kind escapes my throat. He groans at the sound. My breath is shallow but fast. Finally he moves to my mouth. My lips part and when he presses his to mine, I slide my tongue inside his mouth and across his lower lip. I want to explore every part of his gorgeous mouth and I want him to do the same, but I know my breath must smell really bad right now.

"Ben?" My voice is shaky.

He pulls away to search my eyes.

My palms flatten on his chest and I can feel his heart pounding. "I need to brush my teeth."

Obviously fighting off laughter, he presses himself into me and kisses me even harder, deeper. "You taste delicious. You always do," he says.

I melt back against the wall and band my arms around his waist. "You sure?"

"I'm sure," he chuckles.

"Okay, then."

"Besides I don't want to wait another minute to see you naked," he growls, and then promptly lifts me off the floor.

I flick my shoes off one at a time and hear each clatter against the floor. Then I wrap my legs around his waist and ask a question I already know the answer to. "Where are we going?"

He slides his hands up and down my sides. "To your room."

"I liked the wall," I purr.

"If I fucked you against the wall, I'm afraid you'd bang your head against it. Let's keep to soft surfaces like the mattress. I told you we were going to take this slow, and besides, we've already done the wall."

I place openmouthed kisses down his neck, tasting him with each lick and suck. "What if I don't want slow?"

"Good thing I'm the one in control, then," he says, and my heart races at his tone.

"Maybe that's where I want to be," I tease and run my nails down his back—hard.

"Fuck," he groans, lowering me to the floor in my bedroom. "You're not going to make this easy for me, are you?"

"Did I tell you I've dreamed about you almost every night since the library?" My fingers trail to the buttons on his shirt and I undo them one by one.

"Tell me what you dreamed," he says in a seductive voice.

"I dreamed about you delivering pizza to my apartment but I had no money to pay you, about you pulling me over and me trying to get out of a speeding ticket, about you being my doctor and me needing a very thorough exam." Okay, so really I dreamed about him and me lying together, naked, happy, just us, but I want my dreams to sound a little sexier than they actually were. And I don't want to scare him off.

His tongue caresses my earlobe. "Did all of your dreams end in me fucking you?"

"Um . . . hmm," I answer, shivering when his tongue slides inside my ear.

His breathing accelerates at a rapid speed. "Good, because your dreams are about to come true."

I fumble with the last few buttons of his shirt, my entire body trembling in anticipation. He looks down at my hands and then rips the rest of his bloodstained shirt off, the remaining buttons flying to the floor. He looks at my pale pink silky top also spotted with blood and with his fingers gripping the V of it, he tears it right down the middle and pushes it off my shoulders to reveal my matching pink bra.

His eyes grow dark with desire and his hair has fallen and lies tousled over his forehead. He has to be the sexiest guy I have ever seen—ever.

The lights are on in the room and although the blinds are pulled down, they aren't fully shut. I want to say something, but when his hands move around to undo my bra and he places both his palms over my breasts, the tingle in my skin is all I care about. He feels me for a bit, thumbing my nipples to draw them into stiff peaks. When his hands drop I immediately feel their loss and want that warmth back. He takes a moment to admire me.

"So fucking sexy," he murmurs.

His voice makes me shiver again. His head dips and he circles his tongue around my nipple, first one side, then the other. He tugs a little on one and traces circles around the other with his thumb. I press into his mouth, loving the way it feels on my skin.

"Touch me," I plead, wanting his hands to move a little lower. Needing to feel them there.

"I'm in control here," he says, letting his mouth drop a little as if teasing me.

I gasp when his lips hit the waistband of my skirt, his fingers gliding up the silk of my hose. In response I thread my fingers through his hair, tugging harder the farther up my thigh his fingers creep. My body hums at his sensual touch and my heartbeat accelerates. He undoes my skirt and as it floats to the floor, one of his hands spans my rear and the other the area between my hipbones. I moan so loudly I almost want to beg him to speed it up, but luckily I don't have to.

He quickly straightens and grabs my chin with my fingers to bring my eyes to his. "I've dreamed about being inside you every night too. My cock has swollen so big thinking about it I've come in my dreams," he confesses.

My hands fly to his jeans and I unbutton them as fast as I can. My need to feel him is out of control. I slide inside his pants, wrap my fist around him, pumping him up and down.

"Does that feel good?" I purr, getting on my toes to nip at his lip.

"Really, really good. So good," he hisses.

"In your dreams were you this big?"

"Bigger."

I squeeze him harder, reaching down to grab even lower.

"Oh, fuck," he groans, and takes a step back, disengaging from me. Then he reaches his hand inside my hose. "Fuck, you're not wearing underwear again."

"I never wear them with hose," I say.

"Sexy as fuck," he mutters again. He cups my sex, sliding a finger inside me so fast the pleasure seems more like pain. "S'belle . . . your skin is so soft and you're so wet. I think you like torturing my cock."

A wicked smile tilts at my lips as I reach to touch him again, but he doesn't let me.

"Take your hose off."

"Take your pants off," I counter.

He grins at me but doesn't move.

Okay, so I'll go first. I slowly slide my hose down and stand naked before him. "Your turn."

He toes off his boots and pushes his jeans and boxers down at the same time. I stare in awe now that I finally get to admire him in all his glory. I want to reacquaint myself with every part of him. I step forward and run my hands over him, under him, around him.

"Oh, fuck," he groans again, this time letting his head drop back when my index finger touches that one sensitive spot. His response to my touch only further ignites the sexual energy between us.

"Still want to take it slow?" I taunt.

"You don't play fair," he manages through gritted teeth.

I rub my palms back and forth over his penis and stop only to squeeze it tight. Tight enough that I can feel an incredible pulsing. It matches the one between my legs. I do it again and then again. Each squeeze causes his face to bloom in a pleasure he can't mask.

His hands move quickly to my sex. The sound I make when he plunges a finger inside me is one I've never heard and only escalates my urge to have him inside me.

"I think we're done with the foreplay." The husky tone of his voice makes a wave of pleasure skip all the way from my head to my toes.

My pulse is racing as we fall to the bed together. He props himself up on an elbow and lets his gaze lazily slide down me, but he stops when he sees the gleaming green shamrock in my belly button. For a moment time stands still. He leans down to softly kiss it and I rest my hands on his head. A spark of uncertainty blossoms between us and I'm almost afraid to look down. When I finally do, I can feel a tear shimmering in my eye and feel another slide down my cheek. He crawls up the bed and with both elbows resting on the mattress he hovers over me and catches my tears with his thumbs.

He swallows hard. "I'm sorry."

I shake my head. "Don't be sorry. I'm not sad. What you did was beautiful."

He kisses my tears one by one and once they've all stopped, he finds my mouth. We kiss for a long time. Soft gentle kisses with tender touches. We share a sadness that we both take the time to mourn. His tongue strokes mine, his hands roam my body, and the flame between us reignites. With each touch my body burns hotter for him. When our kisses turn into hard, deep, soul-searching ones, he nudges my legs apart.

He presses his palms into the mattress, shifting his weight. I run my tongue in a frenzy up and down his chest, letting him know I'm hungry for him. His penis throbs between us until finally he slides inside me. He groans at our contact and my back arches to allow him in—all the way in. He slides deep, so deep. We're both so aroused there's no friction between us. I feel him everywhere—inside me, surrounding me, in my soul even. I lift my hips, curl my fingers around his shoulders, dig my nails into my flesh, all while his body rocks over me. I'm in sensation overload. He's everywhere and I want even more of him.

"You're so wet, so tight," he whispers in my ear.

"You feel so good," I moan.

Everything around us disappears; every part of my body feels licked by flames. He moves deliberately, painfully slow, but it feels torturously good. I don't want this pleasure to ever end. His tongue thrusts into my mouth. I moan when he pulls out and slams back into me. He does it again and I cry out even louder. My hands graze his back, roam down, and push him deeper.

He stills. "The feel of your hands drives me wild."

I become impatient and thrust my hips up. "You drive me wild."

"Not yet," he groans. "I want to stay buried deep inside you."

"Please, Ben." I'm begging him.

He looks at me and then he rocks harder, faster, thrusting in and out in an unrelenting momentum that makes me feel as if I've gone to heaven.

My back arches. "Don't stop. Please don't stop."

"You like that?"

I scream out, "Yes, Ben, yes. Take me to heaven," over and over.

He buries his face in my neck and then I hear my name like a prayer. "S'belle," he calls out, his body convulsing.

I squeeze my eyes closed, seeing stars everywhere as I come harder than I ever have. My body shakes, pleasure radiates throughout it, and I feel him spasming over and over inside me.

"Open your eyes," he tells me.

He thrusts one last time and I watch as pleasure covers his face in a way I've never seen on a man. He falls on top of me, breathless, panting, and completely spent. He murmurs my name against my neck. After a few minutes he rolls to my side and pulls my body tight to his. He cups my chin to look up at him. "That was . . ." He stops and bolts up. "Fuck, I'm so sorry."

I sit up, confused.

"I didn't wrap up."

"What are you talking about?"

"I didn't wear a condom."

Laughter bursts from my mouth. "I'm on the pill. It's fine."

He darts his eyes to mine. "I hope you don't say that to all the guys you've fuc . . . been with."

I push his shoulder. "I haven't actually slept with that many guys and, yes, they've always . . . wrapped up." I laugh even harder.

"Don't laugh at my choice of words. Why don't you tell me how good that felt for you?"

I want to be embarrassed but I'm not, so I decide to answer honestly. "Sex with you is like heaven. Plain and simple."

He grins devilishly and then grabs hold of me and pins me to the bed. "You seem perfectly fine."

My laughter fades as the heat surges between us again. "I told you I am."

He dips his head. "Good," he growls in my ear, "because this time when I take you to heaven, I'm not taking it slow."

CHAPTER 29
Shape of Love

Ben

The creamy white sheet that perfectly matches her skin tone covers our bodies from head to toe as I caress my hand down her back, dusting light kisses all over her face. She giggles and my heart skips every time. I really fucking love that sound.

"That tickles." She laughs from inside our cocoon.

I bury my face in her neck and suck on the spot behind her ear I've already discovered doesn't tickle her but encourages her to make those sounds that drive me insane.

Her breathing picks up the minute my lips apply pressure. She might not be ticklish in that spot, but it definitely turns her on.

"Does that tickle?" I murmur in her ear, knowing already it doesn't. Knowing the more I suck the wetter she'll get.

"No." But her voice sounds breathy.

We stay up most of the night exploring each other's bodies. We fall asleep much later than the six hours she was prescribed to wait and wake up before the sunrise. Aside from water breaks, bathroom runs, and one small food run, we haven't moved from her bed.

I nip at her earlobe, then roll over onto my back, pulling the sheet from our heads. I blink the brightness of the daylight away. "What time is it?"

She burrows out of the sheet and crawls up to lie beside me on the pillow. "When I called my mom it was ten."

"That had to be hours ago." I reach for my phone, but then I look over toward her. With her freckles bright, her smile wide, and her hair a beautiful mess of tangles, I unclench my hand and leave my phone where it is. "You know what, it doesn't really matter what time it is."

She takes a grape from the bowl beside her bed and pops it in my mouth before taking another one for herself. Once she's done chewing she flops back down. "We should probably get something to eat soon."

I raise myself up on my elbow and look down at her. "Let's order in. I don't want you to leave this bed."

"Pasta?" Her eyes light up at the thought.

"You're hungry, aren't you?"

"Yeah, a little."

I pull the sheet back over our heads and entwine my legs with hers. "Okay, tell me what you want."

"You," she whispers.

With a growl I roll her and pin her to the mattress. "I meant what restaurant, but I like your answer better." I let go of her wrists and glide my palm up her thigh. "Tell me what you want right now."

She looks at me and covers her face with her hands.

"Why are you so shy during the day?"

She lifts her fingers from her eyes. "I don't know. I've never really had sex with anyone during the day."

I raise an eyebrow. "Anyone?"

"Other than myself," she confesses.

The things she says are sexy as fuck. Does she know that? "You'll have to show me someday." I offer her a grin.

She flips around so I can't see her. "The first month we dated and you'd call me, all I wanted to do was listen to your voice and touch myself."

For her it was a deep, dark confession. One I could relate to. I'd had to jerk myself off many times after hanging up the phone with her. A surge of some kind of emotion that again I can't clarify flows through me. I push it aside and pull the sheet even higher so we're covered in semidarkness again. And then I press myself into her back and skim my fingers over her clit.

"I'm here now. And if you're ready to touch yourself in front of me, then tell me what you want me to do to you."

Her eyes hood and her lips part. "I like it when you put your face between my legs."

I crawl over her so I'm facing her and place a soft kiss above her bandage. What I feel when I look at her winds me. It's more than just lust and desire—it's a need to make her part of me. And with that sudden realization I kiss her mouth chastely, still trying to skate on the edge of softness. "See, that wasn't so hard."

I watch the rise and fall of her chest as the heat flares up again between us.

My pulse is racing at an uncontrollable level and I take a second to let it slow and to admire how beautiful she is—her fiery red hair fanning out under the sheets of her bed, her breasts full and perky. I draw my lips down her neck and stop at the hollow below it. I dip my tongue in and out of the space. Fueled by excitement, I continue down over the curves of her breasts and stop to suck and lick her already pebbled nipples. Her back arches and my dick twitches in response. But when my lips skate over her ribs and skim down to her navel, I have to stop the seduction and place a gentle kiss there. It's not surprising that her body tenses in response. My own does as well. But I quickly push aside the sadness I feel crawling up my throat and move to nibble on her hip before blowing a breath across her clit. A shiver shakes her body. Her legs part and slowly the tension between us turns into passion, turns to nothing but pleasure.

Her body is completely bare of any hair. Even her eyebrows are faint, lighter than the color of her hair. I had noticed on our dates the smooth skin of her arms, and on the few times she had worn skirts, I noticed her legs were just as bare. But when I felt her smooth, bare pussy at the beach I almost came on the spot. I love this—love the feel of her smooth, soft skin against my tongue. I love the lack of any barrier between us.

A gentle kiss on her thigh, then another and another. I trace a half-moon around her pussy from one side to the other. She squirms and her fists clench the sheets. I feel a grin cross my lips when I see how turned on she is. When I get to the other thigh, I lift my face but quickly descend to cover her clit with my mouth. I suck on it immediately and she cries out, sending adrenaline shooting through my veins. Next I place a soft kiss in the same place I just engulfed with my mouth and suck on it again. She whimpers, alternating between sounds of plea-sure and pain—the pained sounds come when I stop; the pleasured moans escalate with every suck. I take my time, wanting her to thor-oughly enjoy this. When I use my tongue to circle her clit, I can't sup-press my own groan at her reaction. She almost jumps out of her skin.

"Do you like that?" I ask, already knowing she does.

"Yes," she answers through gritted teeth.

"Do you want me to do it again?"

"Yes," she cries out, her legs stiffening in anticipation.

I look up at her. "Do you want to feel heaven?"

I know she wants to roll her eyes at me, but instead she says, "Yes," in a pant.

"Then take the sheet off us."

She peeks down at me. "What?"

"You heard me, take the sheet off and watch me."

I see her fingers let go of the bottom sheet and as she starts to tug the top one down I grab it and pull it off us. With sunlight shining on us I dive down, wanting to devour every single inch of her. Her fingers thread in my hair. And when my fingers move her apart and my tongue dips inside, she tugs on my locks. When her knees pop up and her toes dig into my calves, I know she's close. I look up at her—her hooded eyes filled with desire look back at me.

"No, Ben. Please don't stop," she says, her words choppy, sounding as though she's having trouble speaking.

"I won't. Just tell me where you want to go," I answer, my words coming out with equal effort

"Take me to heaven, Ben. Make me come."

My mouth covers her again and this time I lick and suck at the same time and let her find her release. I want her to feel something she never has. I want to be the one to take her heaven.

"Oh, Ben, yes!" she screams.

My hands find her toes curled into my calves and I clutch them as she rides another wave of pleasure and then another. With my heart pounding in my ears, I crawl up her body and hover over her and stare down at her. Again I have to swallow the lump in my throat, but it has nothing to do with sadness. It's her beauty and I don't understand where these feelings are coming from, but at the same time I don't care. Her hands glide down my face, and the smile on her lips grows wider.

Unable to speak, I simply stare into her eyes. Her hands move to my cock, and her finger goes right to that spot beneath it. Fuck, if I weren't already ready for her, what she's doing right now would make me hard instantly. Finally I reposition myself and slide my straining cock slowly inside her. Her pussy is wet and as I fill her I can't stop from shuddering at the overwhelming pleasure.

Her back arches.

"Oh God," I groan, and bury my face in her neck.

Pleasure strikes immediately. She feels warm, welcoming, and so ready for me that I can't control myself.

She smooths her hands down my back and runs her nails over my muscles. My blood feels as if it's on fire. I push deeper, move faster. She urges me faster with her hips and this time I can't hold on. When she moans louder suddenly, that's all that matters. In this one single moment all I can feel is the need for release.

"Fuck," I call out when she changes the angle of hips by wrapping her legs around me, allowing me to thrust even deeper inside her. I've had sex with countless women over the last three years, but not one of them has made me feel like this right now.

I chance a look in her eyes and I'm done. It's a bolt of lightning crashing through my body.

"Come with me," I plead with her, my voice hoarse.

"I will, I will, I promise," she cries in a ragged tone.

I close my eyes. My muscles tense everywhere. And as we call out each other's name in unison, my body jerks and I feel as if I'm breaking through some unknown barrier I didn't know existed. I open my eyes to look at her as I come harder than I've ever experienced. I feel as if my body is exploding—as if it's separating into smaller pieces and leaving this universe for another. The feeling scares the living shit out of me.

It takes me a few minutes to collect myself. Sweat coats my body, my cock throbs inside her, and finally I collapse next to her, unable to move. I bury my face in her neck and when I feel the air return to my lungs I kiss her softly. First her shoulder, then her neck, her jaw, and finally her mouth. She kisses me back, mimicking my own pattern. She kisses my mouth, my jaw, my neck, my shoulder. I shiver at her gentleness. Maybe that's what's different about her? The fucking isn't just fucking. It's intermixed with tenderness. I haven't felt that in a long time. I think I missed it.

I roll off her, the weight of my odd feelings heavy on my mind. She stays silent and so do I. But I pull her to me and then tug the sheet back over us. I bury us in our cocoon where I don't have to try to figure out what the hell is going inside my head.

I must have fallen asleep, because when she turns in her sleep, it awakens me. Her back nestles into my front and I curl my arm around her. Her skin is warm and feels incredibly comforting against mine. My fingers mindlessly play with the shamrock in her belly button.

"You asked me if I knew if the baby was a boy or a girl," she says, and the sound of her voice surprises me.

My movement stops for the briefest of moments but then I continue to finger the ornament. "Yeah, I did."

"What I said sounded cold. But it wasn't like that."

I close my eyes. "I never thought you sounded cold."

"I loved the baby. That's why I knew I couldn't keep it."

I kiss her cheek and let mine rest on hers. Inside our cocoon we can talk about anything and I know this is something that she needs to share and I need to hear.

"Knowing the sex would have made it all too real. It was better for me not to know. Can you ever understand that?"

I kiss her cheek again, leaving my lips there because I feel the wetness of her tears. Then I turn her around to face me. "I do understand, S'belle. I do." My fingers move back to the symbol of our baby she wears to remember, although I don't think she needs to wear the shamrock to remember. "This is a beautiful thing," I say, circling her belly button. "But you did what you thought was best for the baby and you don't have to take the blame alone anymore. Let me help you."

Her tears fall and her cries grow louder and I let her get it out. Let the emotion she's kept bottled up for all these years spill out onto me. I know we can't change the past. I have no idea what would have happened if she had told me, and that enables me to share in the blame. I want to help her heal the wounds that she hasn't allowed to close. My arms tighten around her and I whisper, "It's time to let go, S'belle. It's time to let go."

I don't know how much time passes, but when I feel her breathing even out, I know she's fallen asleep. I hope when she awakes, the burden she's carried on her shoulders will feel a little less heavy. I carefully lift the sheet and slip out to shower. When I finish I go in search of my clothes, then remember I ripped the buttons off my shirt. I creep into her closet and find a USC sweatshirt large enough for me to wear. It looks familiar and I wonder if it's mine from so many years ago.

With a grin on my face, knowing it is, I grab my keys and hers as well. I open the door to go pick us up some food and come face-to-face with S'belle's brother—Xander Wilde. We were in the same fraternity in college, although he's older. I knew who he was but didn't really know him. Last year I saw him again at Dahlia's house when he pulled his brother off me and Caleb hauled my ass out of the room. Not one of my fondest memories—getting my ass beat. But in hindsight it was well deserved. My cocky attitude and belligerent words were more than deserving of River's anger.

His eyes narrow as they assess me. I feel he's trying to determine if I'm good enough for his sister. Maybe I'm aiming higher than I should. In fact, I'm sure I am because I actually feel he's trying to determine if I'm as big a piece of shit as he believes I am. It's how I imagine I'd feel going to pick a girl up for a first date and having to meet her father, one that already hated me. But since I dated Dahlia all through high school and I had grown up next door to her, thank fuck I never had to experience that kind of scrutiny, because this is a really uncomfortable feeling.

He steps around me and makes his way in, looking around for Bell. "Where's my sister?"

I take a deep breath and extend my hand. "Xander."

His eyes keep sweeping the apartment. Then he nods, extending his hand in return, allowing his eyes to settle on me for a quick second. At least he doesn't leave me hanging. "Jack told me what happened yesterday. I stopped by to check on Bell."

Fuck me if this couldn't be more uncomfortable. Normally I'd have already said fuck you. But since I've just spent the last . . . I don't how long . . . fucking his sister and she's sleeping naked in the other room while he's here to check on her, and I do want to try to earn his respect, I face his scrutiny head-on. "She seems to be fine. She said her head only hurts around the stitched area."

His face turns red. His fists clench.

I start to wonder if he's going to be the next one throwing a punch at me. I'm not worried for myself. I just want to prove to S'belle that I can handle the situation. So if he wants to pound the shit out of me, I'm going to let him. I need to make things right with her family, and although him throwing a punch at me isn't ideal, it's a start. I brace myself and fight the urge to retaliate.

"I'm going to kill that motherfucker one day," he blurts out in a huff.

I let my tension release and nod in agreement. "My feelings exactly."

"I had a bad feeling about him from the day I met him. I told Bell, but she always sees the good in people and couldn't see it."

I know there was a dig in there for me. I could hear it in his voice.

"Where is she?"

"She fell asleep—"

"I'm right here." She pops up in the doorway fully dressed—thank fuck.

"You woke up?" I smile over at her.

Her eyes dart to my sweatshirt and she grins at me.

Xander crosses over to her and pulls her in for a tight embrace. He leans back to look at her forehead and hugs her again. "Are you okay?"

She nods.

"You sure?"

I place my hand on the door as I witness what I already knew. This girl has been loved, protected, and sheltered her whole life by a family that adores her. There is no bad in her. She's good through and through. I wish I could say the same. A feeling that maybe she's too good for me makes my body tremble slightly. But when she looks over to me from her brother's arms and winks, my stomach leaps.

"I'll leave the two of you to talk."

She pulls away from her brother and frowns at me.

"I thought I'd go grab some food." I quickly add, "Where is the closest Italian spot for takeout?"

She smiles and her eyes gleam.

"Vito's. Around the corner on North La Cienega Boulevard," Xander says.

"Thanks." I turn the handle on the door.

"Hey, man," he says, and I turn around. "Thanks for taking care of my sister."

I nod and as I turn back I catch S'belle's big green eyes shimmering with happiness.

CHAPTER 30
Roar

Bell

The thing about family is—you can love them and dislike them at the same time, and right now I'm torn at seeing Xander. I nod toward the dark clouds massing on the horizon. "Looks like another storm is coming?"

He huffs, "I'm not here to talk about the weather."

My brother's stare is fierce, but I know I can be fiercer, or at least I think I can.

"I know." I smile to lessen the tension.

His brow furrows as though he wants to say something but changes his mind.

"I quit my job."

That earns me a smile.

"Finally," he sighs with relief. "You know I never liked that guy. Bell, I understand you better than you think I do. I know you're determined to prove to us that you can make it on your own. But I came over here to tell you, the thing is, you don't have to."

I open and shut my mouth without coming up with a response.

"You're one of the lucky ones—don't you get it? You have us. We're here for you."

He takes a step closer.

I breathe in, willing myself not to cry. "I know that."

"Do you? Do you really know that no matter what, we love you?"

"I do." My voice is a small squeak. So much for fierce.

"Then the next time you're in a bad situation, I want you to tell me." He looks around the room before continuing.

"Are we getting to the elephant in the room now?" I stand up straight and face him head-on.

His expression grows darker and truth be told, I feel a little scared. Not of him, of course, rather of him judging me. But I believe in Ben and I'm ready to take the first step. You have to crawl before you can walk, right? And Xander is going to be easier to open up to about Ben than River. So I take another deep breath. "Can we sit down? I have some things to tell you, and the first one is something I should have cleared up a long time ago."

We've never spoken about the baby since the day I gave birth. But something inside me feels ready to open up to my brother in a way I've never felt I could before. So I tell Xander that I actually never talked to Ben, that my attempts to contact him and tell him I was pregnant were really not attempts at all. I tell him about this summer and then meeting back up with Ben a couple of months ago. I tell him that I want to see where the relationship will go. I stay strong. I tell my brother how I feel. And surprisingly he handles it okay. He isn't thrilled, but he isn't disappointed in me either.

When I finish, his look is unreadable.

Then he reaches across the sofa to squeeze my shoulder. "You know all I really care about is that you're happy?"

I nod.

"And you know if you ever need me, no matter what the circumstances, I'll be there for you in a heartbeat?"

I nod again. "I love you."

"I love you too. Now I'm going to get out of here." He grins at me.

I fly across the couch and hug him. "I don't say this often, but you're the best brother—ever."

"I won't tell River you said that," he jokes.

"Oh, I tell him the same thing." I laugh.

He just shakes his head at me in amusement.

After Xander leaves I hop in the shower. Then I decide a quick cleanup and a mood enhancer are just what we need for the night. Twenty minutes later there's a knock at my door.

"Who is it?"

"It's me, Ben."

"Ben who?"

"S'belle." He sounds a little annoyed.

I'm sure he's worried about what Xander had to say, so I cut him some slack. "Come in."

He opens the door carrying bags of delicious-smelling Italian food. He looks around. I've really outdone myself. Soft music is playing in the background, candles are lit around the room, and my green bikini is lying over the back of the sofa. He raises an eyebrow. "Déjà vu."

I'm in the kitchen slicing lemons with two glasses of sparkling water in front of me. I drop them in the glass and smile at him. "You didn't have to knock."

"I wasn't sure if your brother was still here."

"Nope, he's gone."

He takes the bags and walks back out to close the door.

Did he forget something? There's another knock on the door. Now I'm curious. I walk over and open the door just a smidge. "Yes?"

He raises the bags. "Delivery, ma'am." He grins.

My smile grows wide and I throw open the door. "Come in. You can set the bags on the counter, but I'm not sure I have any money to pay you."

"Ma'am, I don't take cash anyway."

"Oh, good, because after we eat I know just how to pay you back."

"After?" he questions.

"Yes, sorry, but I'm starving."

He laughs. "Me too." He crosses to the kitchen and deposits the bags on the table.

I can't restrain myself and I throw my arms his neck.

He pushes my wet hair to the side and kisses my neck while I press the weight of my body against him. "You smell so good," he says.

"I wasn't sure you'd come back."

He takes my face in his hands as he reassures me, "Nothing would keep me away from you, even your brother camped outside the door."

I lick the lemon juice from my fingers while giggling. "He wasn't that bad."

He takes my hand and sucks one of my fingers still sticky with lemon juice. "No, he wasn't," he agrees, moving to the next one. "If I was looking to get my balls served on a platter, he'd be just the guy I'd go to."

The laughter is uncontrollable and I start hiccupping from the hysteria. Once I've calmed I tell him, "I called everyone else while you were gone, so we should be visitor free."

"By everyone else I assume you mean your other brother, the one who isn't going to be even a fraction as unimpressed as his older brother."

"What did you get us to eat?" I ask, pressing against him in an attempt to change the otherwise awkward subject. And then before he can answer I lift my arms and snake them around his head. "Kiss me."

He finds my mouth and kisses me deeply before pulling away and walking over to the table, where he set the bags. He takes a round container out. "Spaghetti and meatballs." He takes out another. "Chicken Parmesan." And then another. "Rigatoni."

"Yum, but are you feeding an army?"

"I just wanted to make sure you were well fed."

I look up and catch his glance. His face looks perfectly content and I feel the same way.

CHAPTER 31
Start of Something

Ben

I have been with many women over the past three years, but I have never spent any real length of time in their places—enough time to fuck and move on and that's been all. So to say lying on the couch with S'belle and flipping through television channels after we've both stuffed ourselves with pasta, garlic knots, and salad feels unfamiliar would be telling the truth. But in a sense there is something familiar about it, in terms of the only relationship I've really ever had in my life, the one with Dahlia.

It isn't that I don't know how to be in a relationship, because obviously I do. I had been in one, the same one, for ten years. And I think for the majority of those years we were both happy together. But after that I have never wanted to seek out another relationship. It takes a lot of giving, and I think I have already proven to myself I am a taker. So why when I look at S'belle lying in front of me do I feel that at last I have something to give?

The sound of the rain outside is calming even though my thoughts are swirling around my mind. I reach for the book on the coffee table, noticing that the bookmark is gone but the book itself still has a place on the table.

"Did you finish this?" I ask her.

She turns around. "I did."

"What did you think?"

She smirks. "That I'll stick to romance novels."

I gently bump the book on her head. "No, really, what did you think?"

Now she giggles.

My heart pounds a little faster whenever I hear that sound.

She sits up, waving her hand in front of her face until she settles. "Sorry, sometimes I'm just so witty."

I withhold my own smirk at how fucking cute she is.

"Okay, okay, so . . ." She takes a deep breath. "Here goes. At first I kept resisting the context, which made me dislike the book."

I raise an eyebrow. "I did mention this is my favorite book. Didn't I?"

She pouts her lips. "Let me finish."

I blink at her. "I just had a vision of you as a teacher."

She bends down and kisses me. Running her tongue along the inside of my lip and then catching it with her teeth. "I can be your teacher—later."

I'm sure my eyes widen in delight.

"Now let me finish."

Excitement starts to build within me because she's turning me on. "Please do."

"Okay, so once I surrendered myself to the time frame and fictional virtuosities, the story finally captured my heart. I could picture a circus of events as everything came to life in my mind."

I raise my hand like the good student I never was.

She squares her shoulders. "Yes, Ben, you have a question."

I bite my lip to keep from laughing. She really would be a good teacher if I ever gave her that control. "Can you explain what you mean by fictional virtuosities?"

The corners of her lips tilt up. "I can tell you're surprised. Believe it or not, I paid attention in school."

My laughter rasps. "I believe it."

She continues. "A variety of personalities are portrayed in the text, including children who are smart, women who are full of grit, strong old ladies, men with confidence, fools, drunks. The book is just a cornucopia of complex characters."

To be honest I am rightfully impressed, but I continue to play along with our little charade. "So you enjoyed it?"

"Students' hands should always be raised."

I pull her to me to say, "I thought we were doing this later, but if you're ready, I think we should take it to the bedroom, where I can show you just the kind of student I am."

She nods, breathing heavy, and then pulls the strings of the sweatshirt I'm wearing and yanks me up toward her. "You found your sweatshirt."

"I thought it looked familiar. Was it your choice of contraband sweatshirts back then?"

She pushes me to the couch cushion and tries to hold my arms down, but fast as lightning I flip her on her back and pin her wrists above her head. "Are we moving from student/teacher to submissive/dominant? Because I'm up for that too," I growl. A rush of arousal floods me at the thought of tying her down.

Her eyes burn into mine, lust looming in their depths. "Are you staying tonight?" Pressing my raging hard-on into her belly, I return her stare. "I didn't realize there was a question as to whether I would."

"Kiss me," she purrs, and ignores my statement.

"You understand I'm the dominant, right? That means I take control, not you."

"Kiss me, please," she repeats.

And I do that and so much more.

I stare at her for the longest time, trying not to breathe so as not to wake her. She stirs and flips around. Fuck me, my cock lies pressed against her ass and I don't know if she's awake and doing it on purpose or if she's sleeping.

I kiss her head and slide my leg off the bed. Obviously not on purpose since she doesn't stir.

"Where are you going?" she asks. So—maybe on purpose.

Before leaving the room, I bend down and kiss her head. "I'm going to go get us some coffee."

"Oh God, I love you," she says sleepily.

I freeze on the spot, but she doesn't say another word as she settles her head into the pillow and falls back asleep.

I pass her comment off as what it was, gratitude for much-needed coffee, but I can't keep her words from echoing in my head the whole drive to Starbucks and back. Love is the last thing I'm looking for right now. I just got myself together and I'm not looking for overly serious.

When I walk back into her apartment, I check my thoughts at the door the minute I see the green bikini still lying on the back of the sofa. I pick it up and with my tray of coffees I head into the bedroom, but she's not in the bed. I hear the shower and walk into the bathroom.

Setting everything down, I lean against the wall to look at her through the steamed glass. The shape of her perky breasts, the curves of her perfect-sized ass, and the contour of her legs couldn't be more defined. I find myself biting my lip as she lifts her arms and scrubs her hair, then squeezes body wash into her palms and rubs it along her body, but when her hands rub circles across her tits, I can't suppress a groan.

She opens the door and peeks out from the shower. "Are you watching me?"

I pick up my coffee cup and sip from it. "I was going to join you, but you looked so good from here I got caught up in the show."

She shrugs. "Finish your coffee."

Fuck, I almost choke. How could anyone not love her? I go back to watching and sipping my coffee. But the minute she lets her fingers wander to her pussy, I have to jump in. "I'll do that."

The shower water is hot, but nothing feels hotter than the feel of her skin against mine. I can't get enough of her. We've spent two days together, had sex more times than I've had with any one person in a forty-eight-hour window of time, and I still want more.

"The water's getting cold," she whispers to me.

I reach to pull the lever and turn it off. "We're clean enough."

She shivers and I reach for some towels, wrapping one around her shoulders and then dropping to my knees to pat her body dry. Once her legs are dry, I make my way up her body to the areas I want to concentrate on the most—the silky skin between her legs and her breasts. When I stand back up, I wring the water from her hair and take a moment to stare at her. "Leave your hair curly today."

She nods. Her palms are flush to the tile wall and her chest is visibly rising and falling.

So I drop back down to my knees and flick my tongue against her clit. Clutching her ass, I pull her closer to me. I work my mouth eagerly, loving the feel of her beneath my tongue, the taste of her, how wet she is. Her hands clasp my head and I can feel the muscles in her legs tighten. I clutch her ass tighter as I consume every inch of her sweet pussy. Tension coils in my own body. But the sounds she makes practically make me come on the spot—her stuttered sighs followed by her soft moans that become louder as she calls out my name.

She looks down into my eyes as she comes, and the picture is one of perfect bliss.

Afterward I slide up her body and bend to kiss her. My hands move slow and easy over her flesh. My lips press softly against hers. "Did I say good morning?"

Her eyes catch mine, and a fierce glimmer of light shines in them. "Good morning," she says, a little breathless.

In a move that takes me by surprise, she pushes me back against the shower wall and drops to her knees. I close my eyes at the feel of her warm breath against my already bulging cock. The one thing we haven't done, she hasn't done this weekend, is suck me off. I haven't asked. I haven't pushed. I wanted her to be the one to decide. Before S'belle I had always been a taker, but with her I want to give.

Her lips wrap around my tip and I tremble at the first contact. She draws me in an inch at a time steadying herself by holding on to my thighs. A grunt I didn't mean to make leaves my throat. I open my eyes to watch her—watch as her hand moves from my thigh to fist my base and her tongue flicks down my hard cock. I suck in air at how good it feels. Fuck me! My legs are shaking by now.

I hiss out the air I forgot to exhale. "Fuckkkk."

I can feel her lips form a smile, but she doesn't stop.

There's another harsh intake of breath when my cock hits the back of her throat. I'm not even sure it's me standing here right now. I feel as if I'm watching this sweet girl blow me in a way no one ever has.

I put my hands in her hair.

Her eyes flick up.

"You're so fucking beautiful," I mutter.

With her palms now flat on my hips, she takes me all the way in until her lips brush my stomach and then she slowly drags them back. She does this again, sucking a little harder. And again—stopping to suck the head of my penis.

"S'belle." I moan her name as I push my hips forward.

Her response is to fist my base again, but this time her hand follows her mouth's trail and overwhelming sensations after sensation start to race through my body.

Never feeling this sexually possessed by a woman in my life, I struggle to maintain my control as the pleasure flares through my body, but when her other hand cups my balls and her tongue trails along the underside of my cock, I give in to it and let it devour me whole.

"S'belle," I scream. "I'm going to come."

I give her a warning through gritted teeth, letting her decide what comes next. When she doesn't pull, I thrust into her, trying not to push too far or too hard so I don't choke her, but fuck, control left me a while ago. Warmth floods my body as my orgasm hits unlike anything I can remember. An animalistic cry I don't recognize as my own leaves my mouth as my cock throbs against her tongue. Her warm mouth stays wrapped around me even after I've come. I slip my hands under her arms and when she slides her lips down my cock she stops to suck on my tip one last time, causing a shudder to chase down my spine.

When I pull her to her feet, blinking uncontrollably at her while clasping her arms to steady myself, I stare at her, unable to speak for the longest time. She licks her lips with her tongue and I take my thumb and wipe them for her.

My thoughts finally clear and I steady myself in front of her. "Wow." It's the only lame word that comes to mind, but there are so many more phrases catching in my throat—words like best blow job I've ever had, you're fucking amazing, I want to feel that over and over, but they all seem to belittle what just took place.

My hands glide down her naked body and I hold her as tight as I can for a long time. When she shivers I know she's cold and I pull away to gather the towels we discarded earlier.

"Lift your arms."

As soon as she does I wrap the towel around her and draw her to me again so I can kiss her on the lips, soft and gentle. The kiss quickly deepens as I suck on her tongue, her lip until neither of us can breathe and I pull away with a quick kiss above her bandage before I do.

"We need to change that."

"I can do it."

"I want to."

She points to the supplies the hospital gave her behind me on the counter.

When I turn to retrieve them, I spot her green bikini. I turn back to get her attention. "Come to Laguna with me today. We have to get your car anyway and I really need to shave."

She rubs her fingers over my face. "I like the way your face feels against my skin."

My pulse races. This girl is going to kill me. "Oh yeah, where particularly do you like the way it feels?"

She points to her lips. "Here." And then she points between her legs. "And here."

"Fuck, you're hot as hell."

She shrugs. "Just being honest."

"What happened to the shy girl under the sheets yesterday morning who wasn't sure she could tell me what she wanted during the day?"

Her eyes meet mine. "You helped with that phobia pretty quickly."

I laugh and pat her bandage. "There, all done."

She laughs. "Thanks for the help."

I bow and say, "My pleasure."

A look I can't quite decipher crosses her face, but she doesn't say anything. And I don't ask but instead hand her the green bikini. "I'm going to see you in this one way or another, and since I'm taking you to Laguna today, I want you to wear this under your clothes," I growl in her ear.

She playfully pushes me backward. "I didn't say I'd go home with you."

I feel a corner of my mouth turn up. "I have food, lots of food, at my place."

"I can be ready in ten minutes."

. . .

What you can learn about a person in a short period of time when you pay attention astounds me. I've learned so much about S'belle Wilde over the past couple of months and even more in this block of time we've spent together. I've learned she loves to eat but never keeps food in her apartment—I'm pretty sure she doesn't like to eat alone. I've learned she's really smart and thinks long and hard about things— but likes to come across as being more aloof or maybe even scatter-brained. Which she's neither. I've learned she likes sex dirty and she likes it clean. And I've learned she knows how to turn me on and she does it on purpose.

I glance over at her fingers as they tap the screen of her phone. "Did you check in with your mother?"

"She's texted me every four hours around the clock. I told her I'm spending the day at the beach and Xander and River too. I don't want them to hunt me down."

I laugh. "Or me."

She laughs back. "That too."

I reach out to caress her bare leg. She's wearing a pair of denim shorts with an eighties type of sweatshirt that hangs off her shoulder, exposing the golden threads of her bikini top. My heart beats a little faster at the thought of finally seeing her stand in front of me in it—just the bikini top, that is, nothing else. I quickly chase the thought away.

"I need to give Josie a heads-up too," she says, tapping her fingers on her phone again. "She'll be worried when I don't show up for work tomorrow."

"She's Wyatt's assistant, right?"

She looks up at me from over her sunglasses. "Yes. So you do pay attention."

"You think I don't?"

She looks back down. "No. I just wonder how much people hear when I talk because sometimes I feel like I never shut up."

I smirk at her—she's definitely quirky and it's a breath of fresh air from all of the other women I've known. "Speaking of work, I wanted to ask you something."

"Okay," she says, dropping her phone in the cup holder and twisting in my direction.

"The night Wyatt saw me at Beck's he was with that arrogant SOB."

"Romeo?"

I nod and go for broke. "He told me he'd seen your phone, that he saw a message from me. Why would you show him that?"

She frowns and reaches up to brush some fallen hair out of my eyes. "It wasn't like that."

I glance over and lift her sunglasses so I can see into her eyes; the green is even deeper than usual with the sunlight streaming through the window. "What was it like, then?"

"Why do you hate him?" Her voice is soft and full of curiosity.

My fingers tighten back around the wheel. "For a shit ton of reasons. Because he was captain of the football team and I was a surfer, because he lived on the bluff and I lived on the beach, because he was a jock and I was . . . well, I was more of a rebel, I guess, but most of all because from what I saw that night he's still a prick."

A laugh bursts from her. "I think that has to be one of the most honest responses anyone has ever given me."

I shake my head at her and grab her hand.

"It's true."

I raise an eyebrow. "You haven't answered my question."

"I'm not interested in him."

"I didn't say you were."

"No, but I can tell what you're thinking. You're not going to like this, but I was late for work and when I got there Josie pulled me into the break room. I set all my stuff down, including my phone, and to make a long story short, Tate and Romeo came looking for me and since we use the break room as a meeting room sometimes, I left Romeo in there while I grabbed something from my office. You texted me and he saw the text."

"See, he's a prick," I mutter under my breath.

She leans over and kisses my lips. "I'm not interested in him."

"So you've said."

Her hand runs up the leg of my jeans. "I am interested in you, though."

I flick her a glance and the honesty I see in her expression puts a smile on my face—and her touch, well, it's doing exactly what she intended. Trying to push sex out of my mind for a bit, I say, "Tell me something about you that I don't know."

She picks up her phone, looks at the screen, then drops it in her bag before pulling her sunglasses down from atop her head and back onto her face. When I hop on the freeway she presses the button for the window and it slides down. She inhales as the wind blows her mass of red curls all around her face. Then she turns back to me. "I love the feel of the wind in my face. I love riding on the back of your bike. And I love the Santa Anas."

The sun is shining today and the winds have died down, but they're still stronger than on a typical day. She points out the window to the smoldering smoke in the distance. "But I hate the destruction they cause."

"You know surfers think of them as heaven and hell mixed in one?"

She cocks her head in my direction. "Do explain."

"When they hit the surf head-on they hold up falling lips and hollow out pitching waves, making for an unbelievable ride. They turn reef breaks into emerald green tube-riding playgrounds. It's fucking awesome. But at the same time they can knock a foot or so off any incoming swell and can actually flatten an otherwise small but rideable wave. That fucking sucks."

She smiles at me. "You really love surfing, don't you?"

"Yeah, I do. I hated living in LA and not on the beach. It really made me miserable."

She seems to ponder this for a long time.

"But I was asking about you. Tell me something else I don't know about you."

My fingers caress circles on her leg and she glances down. "I used to think I had superpowers."

A huge grin crosses my face. "Oh yeah?"

"It's stupid."

"You tell me and then I'll tell you how I used think I was Aquaman."

"Aquaman?" she squeaks.

I shake my head and shift my eyes her way. "You first."

She inhales a deep breath. "Don't laugh."

"I can't promise that. But, S'belle . . ."

Her eyes cut to mine.

"You . . ." I stop, not sure of what I want to say or how to say it. "You know what, never mind. I promise to try my damnedest not to laugh."

She narrows her eyes at me.

I pinch her leg. "I said I promise."

She jumps in her seat at my touch.

"Ah . . . I think you might be ticklish."

She grabs my hand. "I'll never tell."

"You don't have to." I grin and pull her hand to my lips to kiss it.

"Okay, so when I was little I noticed that I could mix words up or say things I knew didn't make sense and people would give me what I wanted."

I nod, thinking about what's she's saying.

"As I got older it worked even better. One time just after I got my license, I got pulled over for speeding. I honestly didn't know I was speeding. The police officer asked if I knew how fast I was going. I answered that I was going sixty. He stared at me. I said, 'Sir, my car won't go any faster than that unless I really jam the gas down, so I'm sorry if I was going too slow.' He looked at me flabbergasted but only gave me a warning and explained I had crossed into a residential area and three miles ahead the speed limit would increase again."

Clutching her hand on top of her leg, I roll my eyes at her. "He just thought you were cute."

"No, really it was my silver tongue."

"Your silver tongue?" I burst out laughing and drop her hand to cover my mouth.

She sits up straighter. "Yes, I used to believe my superpower was that I had a silver tongue."

My mind wanders back to sex at that comment, but she doesn't seem to notice and continues with her anecdotes about her silver tongue. When it's my turn I tell her my story about how I really believed I could grow gills and breathe underwater if I stayed in the ocean long enough. She laughs just as hard at me as I did at her.

CHAPTER 32
Burn

Bell

The glorious Pacific and the serene Catalina Island on the horizon are the only view from the floor-to-ceiling windows in the living room. A hand-forged copper-shingled roof engineered by a master ship-builder to weather the worst of storms protects it. Ben's house, built on the bluff and jetting out over the ocean, looks like a physical paean to light, sky, and sea. I can make out sweeping views of the city and the surf breaking on the coastline.

He'd told me all about it, but nothing could have prepared me for how beautiful it is in person. I look over at him. "This is supernice."

"Thanks. I haven't lived here that long, but it really feels like home."

A sadness washes over me when I see the waves rolling onto the shore.

"Where are you going?" he yells.

"To see the beach up close."

He chases after me around the side of the house and down to the back.

I kick my shoes off as soon as I hit the sand and look out into the calmness of the sea.

He catches up with me and grabs my hips. "You're crazy."

"No, I just love the beach. My dad used to take us all the time when we were kids. He'd put the Beach Boys on in the car and sing along and eventually we all joined in."

He dips his head and skims the skin of my neck with his tongue. "Do you miss your dad?"

"Sometimes I do. Sometimes I don't. The good times blend with the bad and it's hard to figure out which were more real."

"I'm sorry for what you had to go through when your dad died. My dad died when I was really young too and I don't really remember that much either," he says.

I look up at him and that's when I see it in his eyes. The same look I've seen before but haven't been able to place. I think it's a longing for family. The thought makes me even sadder.

"How do you know how my dad died?" I'm not upset, just curious. I really never talk about it.

He scratches his head. "I did some research earlier this year for Aerie."

"What kind of research?"

His silence has started to alarm me. "Ben, what kind of research?"

"You know what? I think you should talk to your mom. I shouldn't have said anything." He says it delicately, not angrily, but his refusal to tell me something about my own family still stings.

"Ben," I plead. "Tell me now."

He grabs my hand. "Come on, let's walk and I'll explain."

I nod and try to hide that my heart is beating abnormally fast with worry.

He leads us up the steps to a deck that looks out onto the ocean, offering a perfect view. I take a seat in one of the lounge chairs, pulling my legs up and tucking my chin on my knees, and he does the same.

Ben squints into the sun. I can tell he's teetering on whether to tell me what he knows or not.

"Ben, please." I say his name softly, prompting him to tell me what he knows.

He takes a deep breath. "I was investigating Sheep Industries' finances for a story Aerie had me working on after I left the paper this past summer and I came across books for Little Red Records."

"My father's label before they let him go?"

"Yes—Little Red is one of the holdings of Sheep Industries. Anyway, what we found proved the sales records had been severely altered and that he was let go under false pretenses."

"So who altered the records? Damon Wolf?"

He sits up and leans toward me with his arms on his thighs. "Yes."

"Because he was jealous of my father?"

"I don't know the answer to that."

"Does my family know?"

"S'belle, I don't really know who knows what. I only know what Damon told me the day I yanked *Sound Music* from his hands."

I stand up and head toward his glass doors. "How about a tour?"

He pulls me onto his lap, his arms banding around me. "Hey, what's going through your mind?"

I swallow a few times as I start to cry. "That my father spent his whole life chasing the dream of being famous, and he thought he lost his chance, but in reality he never lost it. Someone stole it from him. Why would anyone do that?" My cries grow louder.

He cradles me in his arms. "Because so many people in the world don't understand what it is like to be good."

I bury my face in his neck. "I failed him, you know?"

He lifts my chin to look into my eyes. "What do you mean?"

"The day he killed himself all he wanted me to do was get better at playing the guitar. I hated playing. I was never any good at it. He picked me up early from school that day. Xander always got me. When I asked him why he was there, he had a haunted look in his eyes. He told me he wanted to have more time for us to practice, but I knew something wasn't right. Then when I couldn't do what he wanted, he made me do it over and over. Xander came home and heard me crying, saw my fingers bleeding from strumming the strings over and over. My father and Xander argued and River brought me to the neighbor's house. All I knew after that was that my father had shot himself. My brother blamed himself for the longest time—and I think he still might—but if I hadn't failed my father they wouldn't have fought and my father might still be alive."

He holds me, rocks me, soothes me but doesn't judge. "S'belle, what happened is not your fault. Your father was in a bad place."

I shake my head no. Why couldn't I just do what he wanted?

"Hey, look at me." His voice grows louder. "There is nothing but good inside you. You should never think anything different. Your family loves you so much. It's evident by the lengths any of them would go to protect you."

He holds me for the longest time. Silence fits comfortably between us as the only sounds I hear are the ocean, the sky, and his breathing—all of which calm me down. I know he's right. I've been through this so many times. I'm sure that's why my family didn't tell me. I'm not even upset that they didn't. I know Xander and River and my mother must feel the burden of the information and they didn't want me to carry it too.

I don't blame them for not telling me what they had learned. The truth is it's over, but in a way it makes me proud that although he'll never know it—my father did succeed.

Once my internal emotional battle settles, I pull away and smooth my hands down his face, but I see that his face looks haunted too. "What are you not telling me?"

"S'belle," he says hoarsely, and I feel that this conversation has stirred up something. "I've never said this out loud to another person before. But I think my father killed himself and made it look like an accident and I think my mother knew. That's why she never told us his body was found or about the settlement money."

Our eyes meet and my heart splits open at his confession. The emotion that echoes the loudest is written on his face. He had already told me that his father was hanged by a sail rope that was said to have malfunctioned, leaving his mother with a ten-million-dollar settlement payout. But now he has chosen to confide in me with what he believes is the truth behind the accident. "Why would you think that?"

"When I was going through some old papers, I found his business bank statements and foreclosure notices. I think his business was collapsing and the need to take care of his family drove him to it."

We sit with our arms wrapped around each other for a long while.

When he pulls away, I know he's had time to compose himself, but I didn't mind seeing that side of him—in fact, I liked knowing we're both a little frayed.

He clears his throat. "Hey, I've never told anyone my theory. It's just what I think, but I'm telling you now because I believe everyone makes their own choices and your father, my father, they made theirs. Don't blame yourself. Your father wouldn't want that. Is that why you didn't quit when Wyatt's harassing started? Some kind of need to succeed?"

I nod.

"Hey, you are not a failure at anything. Do you hear me?"

I'm still nodding, but words escape me.

Suddenly the sliding door flies open. "You finally decided to come home," Trent yells, and stops in his tracks when sees us. "Oh, fuck, sorry."

"You okay?" Ben whispers in my ear.

"Yes," I whisper back. I wipe away my tears and stand. "Hi, you must be Trent."

"And you must be Bell." He grins and his eyes, just like Ben's, rove over me from head to toe.

Ben stands up and walks over to him, knocking the side of his head.

He rubs it with hand. "What was that for?"

"You know what it was for, kid."

I giggle. Like uncle, like nephew. Isn't that a saying?

"Well, I'm leaving at five to go back to college, so I wanted to stop by and say good-bye."

Ben looks at him with a pride I find endearing. "You know I hate to say this, but I'm going to miss you."

Trent snickers. "I'm starving. You making lunch?"

"Yes, I'm starving too and you did promise food," I remind him.

"I make a mean stir-fry."

"Vegetables?" I make a face.

"I ate Chinese for two days with Uncle Caleb while you disappeared."

"I didn't disappear. And where's Caleb anyway?"

"He left you a note. It's in the kitchen."

"What's it say? That he loves me?"

"Yes, that he's pining away for you," Trent jokes. "No, I guess something came up at work, because he was called back early. He said he'd be in touch when he could."

Ben pats the pocket of his jeans and then shrugs. "He could have called me."

"We both decided we didn't want to bother you."

He taps his head again. I like seeing this side of Ben with his family.

"Cut it out or I'm telling Bell how I had to tell you how to find her."

"Oh, do tell," I say.

Ben glares at Trent and takes my hand. "I owe this beautiful lady a tour. When I'm done I'll run out and get us some flatbreads from the Loft."

Inside, Trent flops on the large sofa and grabs the remote. "Sounds awesome."

The entire place is stunning, but my eyes keep going back to the towering ficus tree. "It's beautiful," I comment as we climb the stairs that lead to the second-floor balcony.

Ben follows me, hooking his finger in my belt loop and staying very close. I like him there. I reach the top stair and turn around. "Everything here is perfect. I can see why you can call it home so quickly. This place reminds me why I hate my apartment."

He steps up so that we are nose to nose. "Why?"

"It's so small and claustrophobic. My living room only has two windows, one door, very little direct sunlight."

"I can understand that. Why don't you move?"

I crane my head toward the skylight above us. "I thought I just hated living alone. I never understood why . . . until now."

His hands coast down my sides. "Let me show you my room."

"Please do but remember your nephew is downstairs." I wave my finger back and forth. "So no monkey business." But honestly I want him, all of him. Now. But I know we have to wait.

"Like that's what I had in mind," he says as if appalled, and tugs my hand.

I squeeze his—hard.

The door is open, so he steps aside. I walk in and scan the gallery of graffiti-style artwork that lines the walls. It's just how I'd have pictured his room to be. "I love it. It's so you."

As he laughs he starts walking us toward the bed. "What do you mean?"

"The whole place screams *low-key beach living*, but it's also got style."

Turning me around, with his body pressed against mine, he lowers us to the bed and hovers over me. "Go on."

I look up into his eyes, smell his familiar scent, feel his body, and I know—I have fallen for him. I try to control my crazy emotions. We haven't known each other long enough for me to be feeling like this. But the pull I feel toward him is so much stronger than what I felt in college, so much stronger than I've felt for anyone.

"Earth to S'belle, earth to S'belle. Have you gone to heaven?" he laughs.

I smirk at him and try to shove him away, but he doesn't move. "I don't know. I feel like it has a barefoot, carefree beach vibe that is all you."

His mouth finds mine. "I've never had a girl in my room before."

My breathing picks up. "You've already got me on your bed. You don't need to feed me any lines."

He raises himself up on his forearms. "I'm not. I've never had anyone here with me. In fact, until you I haven't been with anyone since March and I certainly never took anyone to heaven in these sheets," he adds with the biggest, baddest, devilish grin.

I laugh hard and long because if I don't I might confess the depth of my feelings for him.

"Spend the night here with me tonight. Be my first."

I grab his face in that way I know drives him crazy and crush my lips to his. I want to taste his mouth, feel his tongue, touch his body for hours. I want to hear him call my name.

"I'm starving and I have to go soon, so could you hurry it up?" Trent calls from downstairs.

Panting, I smile up at him.

He shakes his head. "I'd kick his ass out if he wasn't leaving today."

I lift myself onto my elbows. "I'd love to spend the night."

He hops off the bed and we head back downstairs. Ben goes out to grab food while I sit down with Trent and talk about college and Hawaii. Before I know it we're in Ben's office at his computer and I'm showing Trent just how to accomplish one of his biggest wishes.

"What's going on?" Ben's voice carries from the door as he eyes us curiously.

"She's fucking awesome," Trent says enthusiastically.

"Yeah, she is but tell me what specifically makes you say that," he says with a smirk on his face.

"So, you know how I never know what time of day is optimal to hit the waves until the morning tide rolls in?"

Ben nods and moves closer to the desk.

"Well, Bell took all the factors I use to determine when I want to ride and developed a formula she's going to use to create an app that can forecast over the next week the optimal times of day to hit the surf at whichever beach is selected."

He rounds the desk to stand behind me. His hands rest on my shoulders, squeezing them in the most delicious way. When I turn my head he's staring at the screen in amazement. I feel a slight sense of pride that I could put that look on his face.

"I already knew you had a talent with apps, but you never told me you were a math whiz," he says.

I shrug. "I was a biology major. Math was just a prerequisite."

"She's fucking brilliant," Trent says in awe.

"That and so much more," Ben responds.

"Come on, let's eat. I'm starving."

Ben's eyes devour me as if I'm what's for lunch—and the way he looks at me makes me wish I was.

As soon as we've finished eating, we say good-bye to Trent and then both fall on the couch in a post-meal stupor. Naps on Sundays are the best. But naps in Ben's arms, on a sofa that is beyond comfortable, with a view of the ocean, well, that's almost heaven—almost.

The ocean calms the chaotic and tames the wild in anyone who dares allow it. And I do. And I can tell Ben does.

When we wake up, the sun is just starting to set and he builds a bonfire on the beach so we can sit eating s'mores for dinner while we talk and listen to the sound of the waves as time slows around us. At first we merely kiss and touch each other, but once the touches intensify, we hastily take our clothes off. I even prance around him in my bikini—finally. And with only my top on, we have sex in the sand near the fire.

The entire night is magical in a way I've never experienced. Eventually we make our way to his room and he takes me in his bed too. Afterward he holds me tight as I nod off with the same calm I felt on the beach when I first arrived.

CHAPTER 33
Best Day of My Life

Ben

My alarm goes off way too early. The sun is just beginning to rise.

"What time is it?" She pulls the sheet over her head.

"Six," I say, flopping back on the bed.

"That's illegal."

I laugh. "What is?"

"Getting up at six in the morning."

I shift to my side and press against her before lifting the sheet to find her head so I can nuzzle her neck. "Take a shower with me."

"It's too early to get up."

To persuade her, I run my hands down her sides and across her hips to settle between her legs. Her body jerks and she moans. My fingers play with her folds. She tries to act as though she's going back to sleep, but her movements give away her excitement.

I dip a finger inside her. "Take a shower with me."

She doesn't answer, but her body does as it arches in response to

354 | KIM KARR

my touch. I plunge another finger inside her and go deeper. My other hand fondles one of her breasts. Then just like that, I take my hands sway and slide out of bed. "Shower with me."

She lifts the covers off her head. "You play dirty."

"You have no idea." I'm sure my grin tells her how much I love getting up in the morning and getting ready for work like this.

By seven we're both dressed and drinking coffee out on the deck.

"You can stay here today."

She draws in a deep breath. "I have to get home and figure out what I'm going to do with my life."

"What do you mean?" I ask, raising an eyebrow, thinking that's a little deep for the morning when the girl sitting across from me is not a morning person.

"My own event-planning business isn't going anywhere and Josie tells me Tate plans to blacklist me from every big event."

"You talked to her?"

"She texted me back last night."

"Did she say anything else?"

"No, only that Tate contacted her and told her to clean out my desk first thing in the morning, that he had fired me for insubordination."

"Fuck him. And you don't know for sure that he'll blackball you."

She shrugs. "I'm sure he will if he can. Besides, honestly my own business has turned into more of a catering company than an event-planning one. And the truth is, I enjoyed the whole thing more when I did it for fun."

"Come work for me." The words just come out without any fore-thought or warning.

She quirks a smile and turns to look out toward the ocean. "Right!"

I reach across the table and turn her head to face me. Planned or not, it's a great idea. "I'm serious. You're brilliant. I need someone like you. My goal is to bring my publications into the modern era. Beck is working on the technical side of things—development, computer support, links, servers. But I need someone who can handle the social media. You'd be perfect."

"I don't even have a college degree."

"Hey, stop selling yourself short. Come in today. Spend the day with me. Tell me what you think at the end of it. If you don't like it, no harm, no foul."

She takes her hand in mine, kissing each finger one at a time in the most provocative way. "If you're my boss does that mean we can't . . . you know?"

"Fuck?"

"Yes." She drops her chin.

I lift it and lean across the table to whisper in her ear, "Baby, it means absolutely no such thing."

Her smile grows bright and with a lift of her shoulder she says, "Okay, I'll give it a try."

An hour later I'm sitting at my desk waiting for her feeling a little nervous. On one hand, I think her talent is a match, just what I need. On the other hand, I can't get her off my mind and having her close isn't going to help that at all. I can't forget the weekend—threading my fingers in her hair, kissing her neck, sucking on the skin behind her ear, letting my teeth graze her skin, and those sounds that drove me wild.

My phone jolts me from my erotic thoughts. "Hello." My voice comes out a little hoarse.

"Ben, it's Aerie. Are you okay?"

"Yeah, I'm great. How are you? How's Jagger's father?" I realize I never asked S'belle this weekend.

"I'm hanging in there. Jagger's dad is doing as well as can be expected."

"Don't forget, if there's anything you need make sure you let me know."

"Well, that's why I'm calling. The January issue is ready for press, but the social media column is still blank. Have you had any luck finding someone to fill it? You said you wanted to launch that piece in January and we're getting down to the wire."

A slight tap at my door snaps my head up. I cover the phone. "Come in."

The door cracks open and a very prim-and-proper-looking S'Belle Wilde walks in. She insisted she go home and change before coming to the office. My grin grows as large as the tent in my pants. Fuck me, working with her might be a bit more of a challenge than just getting her out of my mind.

"Ben," Aerie calls from the line.

"Yeah, sorry. I've actually been trying to fill that position all morning. Let me get back to you in a few hours."

"Okay. Thanks," she says.

I disconnect the call, my eyes trained on S'belle's every move. I can't help whistling a catcall. "You look fucking incredible."

She has on a black pantsuit with a white silk blouse unbuttoned just enough but not too much. Her hair is done in curls, but they aren't wild; they are somehow tamed. I prefer wild, but I'll save that for the bedroom.

She twirls around. "Do you like it?"

I push my chair out and pat my lap. "Come here so I can tell you how much."

Her eyes are cautious and slide to the door.

"Lock it," I tell her.

"But I thought you had to work and wanted—"

I don't let her finish the thought. "Lock it and come here. We'll start the workday after I get a better look at you. After we do a little boss/secretary role exploration."

Her eyes gleam, and I know she's intrigued by the idea of some dirty role-playing. She sits on my lap and I peel off her jacket. My lips find her mouth, and my tongue dives in. It's only been a few hours since we left my house, but I'm starving for her, for the feel of her lips on mine. I want to devour her. She shifts her weight to straddle me, and desire flares hotter than ever between us. I slide my hand inside her blouse and under her bra to thumb her nipple. My other hand finds the center of her thighs and I circle her clit through the fabric of her hose. "No underwear?"

She shakes her head no.

"You're so fucking sexy."

She pushes her clit against my palm.

"You like that?" I ask her.

Her head drops back and her body arches into my touch. "Yes."

"Do you want me to fuck you?"

"Yes," she moans.

With my teeth grazing the skin of her neck, I stop at her ear. "I want you to come to work for me. You're going to be my social media correspondent."

She doesn't answer.

"Would you like a job like that?"

She nods.

"Then you'll work for me."

"I can't do that." Her voice is ragged as my thumb continues to work her clit.

I apply a little more pressure, bringing her to the edge, and then I stop before starting again. "Why?"

"You don't have to give me a job." Her green eyes meet mine.

I lift her breast and drop my mouth to suck on her nipple. I pause and feel her heart beating faster and faster. "I'm offering you something that I need. Please help me out. Give me a month."

"If I work for you I don't think we should do this in the office."

My mouth skirts up her body to her lips. "You can start at noon. Now be a good secretary and do as I say. Stand up and take your clothes off so I can fuck you on my desk."

CHAPTER 34

Dark Horse

Bell

Three weeks later

"How about this one?" Josie asks, picking up a large crystal bowl formed in the shape of a heart.

I shake my head no. Josie and I have kept in touch, having lunch every now and then. She told me Tate replaced me with a hot young guy who seems to jump every time he says fetch. Whatever works, I guess. Today her blond hair is tied back in such a way that none of the blue streaks are visible and her makeup seems lighter. She's also in jeans and a simple top. Her punk rock edge isn't visible. She looks really pretty, not that she's not anyway. But it's a softer look that I like on her.

"Why the change in style?" I ask with a smile.

She pats her hair and laughs. "Oh, my parents are in town for

Christmas. They would die if their little girl didn't look like the beauty pageant queen they raised."

"Really? Well, I like it, but why not just let them see who you really are?"

She blows a piece of loose hair from her eyes. "Says the girl who won't bring her boyfriend around to meet her family?"

"You know it's more complicated than that."

"What I know is something has you all worked up this week. Has Glow Boy's glow diminished?"

"No, and stop calling him that."

"Well, I'd say you got it bad, but I'm afraid you'd bite my head off. Bad case of PMS or what?"

She may be onto something. I can feel my mood shifting constantly but can't stop myself. I laugh. "Yeah, maybe."

"If Midol doesn't work you might want to check yourself away from everyone for the week, because you've got crazy written all over you right now."

"That's enough. I get it."

"Hey, you know I'm a good listener if you need one. After all, I have no life, so listening about yours is better than nothing."

I nod in her direction. How can I talk to her about it when I don't understand it myself? I deflect the conversation from me. "What about Hot Boy in the office?"

"I wish."

"What does that mean?"

"He doesn't even know I work there."

"I find that hard to believe, Josie, since, A—he has to pass your desk to get to his and, B—you're beautiful."

"He usually goes straight to Tate's office."

"Brownnose."

"Ha, right."

"Why don't you ask him out?"

She makes a face. "No."

"Okay, then."

"This one?" she asks, picking up a red-lacquered square dish.

"God nooo!" I exclaim as I squish my nose.

"Now, what exactly are we looking for? After all of yesterday's nos, I'm not sure I can help you." She moves closer, standing at least a head taller than me.

"I don't know. Something that looks like magic."

She rolls her eyes. "Okay, then we'll keep looking."

Eclectics is a small boutique featuring blown-glass items where I always find unique centerpieces or table accessories. Xander and Ivy's wedding is just over a week away and I still haven't pulled together the table décor. All I know is I want them to look like magic. My eyes flutter to the shelves laden with vases of every shape and size, and then I see it—magic in the shape of a fishbowl. I place my order for two dozen silver-and-gold-star-etched glass bowls and hug Josie good-bye.

"Call me if you need to talk," she reminds me

"At least think about asking him out," I chastise her.

She ignores me. "Oh, I almost forgot, mouthwatering boy Romeo stopped by this morning asking about you. I guess Tate didn't tell him anything after all."

I shrug over Tate and the job. I'm over it. I have a new job now. In fact, Kale asked me to join him and Ben for lunch today, but since I'd already asked Josie to help me shop for the centerpieces, I told them I'd meet up with them. Ben doesn't mind if I take an extended lunch as long as I get my work done. He's like that with all his employees. I've made sure he doesn't show me any favoritism. Yet today even his generosity seemed to irk me.

But in general working at Plan B has been the best decision I've ever made. I love my job. Love, love, love it. I get to tweet, surf the Web, go on Facebook, post on Instagram. I'm building the company's social platform—me! My career is finally just that—a career. But my relationship with Ben has not been so easy to define. I've tried to keep things casual between us, I really have, but I know we're so much more.

Together I feel we're magical, more alive, two halves made whole. We have no obstacles left between us. He knows about the baby. I've told my family about him, even River, although that wasn't fun. River stayed silent, looked agitated, but didn't say anything bad, that I could hear anyway. Still, I haven't brought Ben to see my family, because I'm concerned he might not be as committed to the relationship as I am. And the reason is stupid. I shouldn't be thinking about it so soon—I shouldn't be thinking that those three little words I want so badly to say to him will make him run away.

As soon as I step onto the sidewalk, I spot his mop of dirty blond hair. He's sitting at an outdoor table with Kale.

"I don't know, man, but I'd say that's an easy one," Kale says to Ben, removing his black sunglasses. His light eyes almost disappear as he squints against the sun.

"You're a lot of fucking help," Ben says.

"What's easy?" I ask as I approach Ben from behind.

His head snaps around. He looks a little guilty about something. This past week I have felt that something's going on. My mind might be reading too much into everything, but I can't stop myself. He seems to be pulling back.

"Hey, you made it." Ben stands up.

I glance over at Kale to see if he'll answer, but obviously he isn't going to either. He's wearing khaki cargo pants, canvas slip-on shoes, and some kind of terry-cloth sun-blocking shirt that buttons up the front. His hair is long but swept back. And he's a man who calls it as he sees it. Sometimes I get nervous around him, but I try not to let him intimidate me.

"Sorry I'm late."

"You're not late," Ben says, lowering his head.

I turn my cheek so his kiss lands on it.

His eyes sweep me in my short skirt and jacket and I know he has sex on his mind. He always does. Not that I don't, but I'm also starting to feel that maybe that's all we have. I didn't go over there last night and we still had sex—phone sex but sex nonetheless.

"Don't like kissing the boss?" he jokes, and pulls my chair out.

When he leans down to place my napkin on my lap, I whisper, "You know I do."

I'm full of mixed signals and even I know it. If it's driving me crazy it must be driving him crazy. I should tell him—tell him that I love him and maybe that will set my mind at ease.

Kale sits there with an amused look on his face.

Ben rolls his eyes. "What?"

"You're different when you have a girlfriend."

Ben flinches at the use of the word *girlfriend*. I see it. How can I tell him how I feel when he can't even call me his girlfriend?

"Hi, Kale. Thanks for inviting me," I break in, wanting to change the subject.

"Hey, sunshine, anytime," he answers. "You ever have wheatgrass before?" He opens one of the menus on the table.

"No." I twist my head around to look at the restaurant name again—Sprouts. I've never heard of it until today.

He waves the waiter over and points to the menu. "Three to start."

"I'll get those right away, sir," the waiter answers.

"What kind of restaurant is this anyway?"

"Raw food," he answers, licking his lips at his choices.

Ben opens his menu. "Kale chips, sunchokes, seawitch? Are you kidding me? What kind of food is this?"

I look at him with a *zip it now* look. "I've never eaten here. What's good?" I ask Kale.

Ben bursts out laughing. "Let's just say you'll want an early dinner."

I glare at him again.

He tosses me a questioning look as if he doesn't know why I've reacted that way. Conversation during our meal is strained and once we've finished I feel a little impatient to leave. I stand up.

"Where are you going?" he asks me.

"I have a lot to do."

"I'll walk back with you."

"I have some stops to make before I go back to the office. I'll catch up with you later."

"Okay." He lowers his head to kiss me.

Again I turn my cheek.

"What the fuck is wrong with you?" he whispers.

"Nothing. I just have a lot to do. See you, Kale," I say, and turn and walk away. Tears leak from my eyes and I can't stop them. Okay, so PMS it is.

About an hour later I feel really guilty for my behavior and for what I haven't told Ben yet. I pick up my phone and use the intercom to call him.

"Hey, sexy. I've been thinking about you. I was hoping you'd stop in when you got back."

"I have work to do, Ben." I stress this, but the truth is I really want to see him. I want to feel the touch of his skin on mine.

"Well, come in here and let me see what you're working on."

"I can't. I'm just calling to see if you want to meet me at Pebbles tonight."

"Sure. We can go together."

"I'll meet you there. I want to stop by my mother's first."

"I'll go with you," he says, and I know he's trying really hard to help me bridge the distance between my family and him, but I'm not ready for that. I mean he flinched today when Kale called me his girlfriend.

"I have a bunch of other stops to make. Can you just meet me there?"

"Sure thing, but anything I should know about ahead of time?" he asks, sounding a little annoyed at me.

"No. I'll see you then." I hang up as more tears prick my eyes.

Six hours later I'm sitting in the dimly lit restaurant that seems extremely crowded for a weeknight and I can't help wondering if I've turned into a sex addict. All I can think about is him—having him, wanting him, touching him. I even send him erotic messages. A few days ago I sent one that read:

```
Went to spin class at lunch and got wet
thinking of you.
```

And another one that said:

```
Have you ever done it in an elevator?
```

With just one look from him as he joins me at the restaurant, it's stronger than ever. Now as I stare at him across the table, I can't help wondering how he feels about me. Does he feel the same?

He clears his throat. "So, are you going to tell me what this is about or make me suffer through dinner trying to figure it out?"

There is an incredibly long silence before I push my plate aside. I take a deep breath and exhale, deciding I can't do it. I can't tell him how I feel. I'm too afraid he'll leave me sitting here again. So instead I tell him the other thing I needed to let him know. "My whole family is flying to New York City to be with Jagger for Christmas and they want me to come with them."

He looks at me a little blankly.

"Did you hear me?" I snap, wanting to see that he at least cares he won't see me for Christmas.

He waits another moment before answering, "Are you going?"

I can't tell how he feels about it. "Yes."

He reaches across the table and grabs my hand. "Stay here with me."

"I can't," I say, lowering my voice so I don't cry. I knew he felt more for me. But why won't he tell me that?

My phone rings and at first I'm grateful for the distraction. But then our eyes dart to the name Romeo Fairchild on the screen. I ignore it and all is silent until Ben says, "Why is he calling you?" His voice is edged with anger.

"I don't know," I answer truthfully.

A text message scrolls across the screen.

```
I'd really like to talk to you and ex-
plain things. I'm not sure I've made the
best impression. Things at the release
party weren't what they looked like.
```

"He was at the party?" he hisses.

I bite the inside of my cheek, feeling nervous. "Yes."

His eyes narrow on me. "Why didn't you tell me?"

"I'm not sure. I guess I never thought of it."

"What's his message mean?"

I look at him.

He has daggers in his eyes.

"I'm not sure."

His brow furrows. "S'belle, I have a hard time believing you have no idea what he means."

My eyes meet his before dropping. "Well, maybe he wants to clear something up."

He doesn't say anything. His stare does all the talking. He waits for me to explain.

"I thought he and Tate were having a threesome with some girl that night."

His hands grip the table. "And how would he know what you thought?"

My voice grows small. "I told him when he called me and asked me to meet him and Tate."

Fury blazes in his eyes now. "Fucker," he says a little too loudly.

"Why don't you two like each other? There has to be more to it."

His jaw is stiff, his body rigid. "Because he wanted Dahlia in high school and he didn't care that she was mine. And now he obviously wants you and once again doesn't care." His words come out laced with resentment.

"Am I yours?" I ask him.

His eyes dart to the table and something shifts in his gaze. "What's going on with you? Are you playing some kind of game with me? You've been so hot and cold."

"No!" I sound offended because I am. But the disappointment I feel that he won't answer the question rises again. "When Kale called me your girlfriend today, you flinched like you didn't like him using that word."

"No, I didn't."

"Yes, you did."

"It wasn't why you think."

"Then why was it?"

He seems at a loss to come up with an answer.

"Do you consider me your girlfriend?"

"Yeah, I do. You know I do."

"No, I don't."

"What's all this about?"

"Never mind, forget it." I'm afraid I'm losing him.

Shifting in his chair, he asks, "When do you leave?"

I swallow. "Tomorrow. I already planned to take the time off work anyway until the wedding."

"You leave tomorrow?" His voice rises.

"Christmas is in two days," I say incredulously.

"I know when Christmas is," he blasts.

"Oh, I wasn't sure. You hadn't mentioned it."

"How long have you known you were going?"

"My mom asked us all last night at dinner. Jagger's dad has taken a turn for the worse and Mom wants us all to go to be with Aunt Celeste and him."

"Shit, S'belle, I'm sorry. Do you know how long you're going for?"

"A week, hopefully less." Not that I don't want to be there for Jagger, but I need to get back and finish getting everything ready for Xander and Ivy's wedding.

"Do you want me to come with you?"

"Do you want to?"

"I wouldn't have asked if I didn't. I'm getting a little tired of asking you to be honest."

"Then I'm sorry to inconvenience you."

"What's with the attitude, S'belle?" He grabs my hand. "Talk to me."

I search his face. "What's going on with us?"

He pauses a moment as if trying to figure out where this outburst is coming from. "Do we have to define it now, here in the restaurant?"

"No. But the mixed signals and blank stares are getting to me."

"My mixed signals? Are you fucking kidding me? This week you've been all over the place."

I motion between us. "What is this for you? Just sex?"

He hesitates before saying, "No."

"Is this about Dahlia, then? Are you not over her?" I can't believe I'm asking him that, but the Romeo comment must have brought it to the surface.

He glares at me. "No, I mean yes, I am. You know I am. This has nothing to do with her."

The hurt and shock are evident on his face and I want to take it all back, but it's too late. Maybe I'm not just ready for this. I can't handle these kinds of feelings. That has become very clear. I stand up and toss my napkin on my plate because something that feels an awful lot like finality courses through my body.

"Sit down and let's talk about this," he says, trying to keep his voice controlled.

"I have to go. I don't think I can do this anymore."

He stares at me in disbelief and even though I know I'm being irrational I lay it all on the table. "Look, Ben, I'm not looking for forever, but before I bring you home to my family I need to feel like there's more than just tomorrow. And I'm not sure you can give me that."

And then I leave him sitting in the dining room at Pebbles two days before Christmas. He doesn't come after me and I remind myself that I knew something like this would happen eventually.

What did I do? Why am I ruining this for no reason? I'm unable to answer any of my own questions. The valet pulls my car up and I get in. As I drive home I try to figure out why I didn't just tell him the truth—that I want him to come with me, to be with me, that all I need to know is that he wants the same. I think about my actions the whole way home—maybe I'm just self-destructive. When I drive down Sunset I stop at a light and look around. A purple sign flashes MISTY'S WORLD. She's a fortune-teller; I've passed the place many times but never gone in.

I find a place to park and walk down the street. When I get to Misty's I take a deep breath and walk in. A bell rings and I look around the tiny room with green walls, fluorescent lights, and stars hanging from the ceiling. A smiling woman opens a beaded curtain and I nod to her.

"Fortune," she says in broken English.

"Yes."

She goes back behind the curtain and returns with a tiny cup of coffee in her hand. "Drink."

"Cream?" I ask her.

She shakes her head no and I drink it quickly, not liking the taste at all and even more disgusted by the grinds at the bottom of the cup. She shakes her head at me, disappears, and comes back with another. "Drink it slower."

I sit down on the tattered chair and take sip after sip. Once I set it down she points at me and then turns and goes back into the room behind the beads. I follow with my cup in my hand. I question what I'm doing here, but the second thoughts are fleeting.

"Your cup, please," she says.

I hand it to her.

She stares into the cup, and without asking me a single question, she begins to talk. "You will find love, but it won't make you happy. Be patient and let it come to you and you will find true happiness."

I roll my eyes because that's a little generic.

"Your job has changed in a big way. You have two bosses. Listen to them both."

How could she know that? She doesn't know me from Adam.

"You will find yourself in a situation you have been in before, and you will handle it much better this time."

Another generic statement, but the one about the job still makes me want to believe. She stands and leaves through a door, making it clear she is done with me. When I push the beads aside, a younger girl is waiting for me.

"Forty dollars please," she says.

I open my purse, a little dumbfounded, and hand her two twenties. "Can I ask her some questions?"

The young girl shakes her head.

I leave there laughing that I just wasted not only my time but forty dollars. I pull out my phone and send Ben a text.

```
I'm sorry but I knew this wouldn't work.
Please give me time. I'll contact you
when I get back.
```

I press SEND and resolve to push him out of my head until I have to go back to work.

CHAPTER 35
Say Something

Ben

One week later

Don't be stupid—my own words echo in my head. I'd heard the statement from many different people and in many different contexts in my life. Mostly from teachers when I was growing up. I was far from an A student, but they knew I wasn't dumb. I just didn't know how to channel my energy. Fuck, I could never keep my mind on one task. How could I when I couldn't even sit still? And right now I feel like that same fifteen-year-old kid again. I haven't been able to concentrate, my leg is perpetually tapping the floor at high speed, and I feel I want to throw something, anything.

The office is closed but I came in anyway since I didn't have anything better to do. I've been sitting here for hours alternating between staring out the window and glaring at my computer. I turn back around in my chair and this time I fixate on the keyboard. It's been just over a week since she left me sitting at Pebbles and then sent me a text to give her time. And I have. She has family responsibilities. I understand those. What I don't understand is what went wrong. Nothing that we talked about makes any sense. I drop my head to my hands. Fuck, fuck, fuck.

I haven't spoken to her. Not because she asked me not to but because I can't figure out what happened. I've typed a few texts but never hit SEND. I've dialed her number more than a few times but never let it connect.

Christmas came and went. Serena and Jason went to Hawaii to spend it with Trent. He had a surfing competition over the holidays that he didn't want to miss out on. I could have gone but wasn't really in the mood to be jovial. So instead I spent the day with Beck, Ruby, and Beck's dad. I ate with them and called it an early night.

Today is New Year's Eve and I find myself even more agitated than I've been all week. I switch to staring at my phone, trying to figure out what to say to her, but I just can't find the words. Can I tell her that being without her is fucking hell? That I'm miserable? That I miss her, and not just the sex? I'm not sure any of those will work. Still tapping my toe, I grab a pencil, break it in half, and throw it across the room. "Fuckkk . . ."

I push up in my chair and decide to hit the gym. Running always helps. I change quickly and yet as soon as I hit a steady stride she's back in my thoughts. Having her at Plan B has been a real asset and I hope she comes back to work here. In the past month she's created a comprehensive social media strategy to increase magazine visibility, membership, and traffic across both publications. She's experimented with new and alternative ways to leverage social media activities. And she's been monitoring trends in social media tools as well as trends in applications. Together she and Beck have successfully launched Plan B into the social media network.

I kept my promise and after that first day of a little boss/secretary fun, we haven't stripped down in the office again. However, one late night she did pretend to be my secretary again, push me back in my chair, and suck me off. And one morning when we had to be at work really early and she was extremely grumpy, I did punish her by lifting her skirt and slowly licking her to climax. But other than that I have really behaved while at the office. Our relationship was—is, I'm not sure—incredible. Hot as fuck, fun, and engaging. I thought it was almost perfect.

There may have been a few flaws and I was working on them. She'd spend most nights at my house except for Thursdays and Sundays when she went to her mother's for family dinners. Even then I'd usually met up with her at her place later. She hadn't invited me to go with her and I hadn't asked to join her until the night at the restaurant when I knew she just wasn't going to let her two worlds collide. That's why I let her go. I don't know how to break that barrier between us.

"Running from the devil again, mate?" Kale says, pulling my earbud from my ear.

"Something like that."

"Must have to do with our girl."

I ignore the *our*. "What makes you say that?"

"You were on top of the fucking world and now that she hasn't been around, you don't seem happy about it. Did you break up?"

"I have no fucking clue. I don't know if we were ever really together."

"I'm not sure about what you Americans call together, but to me it looked like you were definitely together."

I slow my pace. "I can't figure out what we were."

"So you'd be cool with me asking her out?"

I slam the STOP button and the treadmill slows and I get ready to pounce on him.

He raises his hands surrender-style. "Whoa, mate, I'm just mess-ing with you. See, there's something more there you're not seeing. I'd try to figure that out if I were you."

Even though it pains me to admit it, he's right. I know that. "Have a great night," I say to him, and head toward the door.

"I'm headed out if you want to join me."

"No, thanks, man." I hit the shower.

On my way home from the office, I stop by Blondie's to say hi to Noel.

"Just a fucking brilliant way to expand the merchandise," I say. I say it every time I walk in because I'm so impressed.

He beams from behind the counter. "Hey, Benny boy. What brings you by?" And he says it just as he always does.

"Wanted to check on you." But that's not the truth. I want someone to talk to. Someone to help me figure out what the hell is going on in my head.

"Getting ready to close up and take Faith out for a night on the town. I might even swing for a hotel suite if she's up for it. Walk with me."

I follow him outside. "Where are you taking her?"

The breeze pushes his salt-and-pepper hair in front of his eyes. He swipes it away. "I don't know," he says.

I bend down to pick up one of the boards lying in the sand.

"I was thinking about one of those fancy hotels in downtown LA where they have what they call the heavenly beds."

I glance over my shoulder toward him. "Yeah?"

"What do you think?" he asks, pulling the shutters closed over the windows.

I shove the board under the shack. "I think you should let me spring for it. Call it a late Christmas present."

He sits on one of the broken steps and looks up at me. "Anything you want to talk about?"

I put my hands in my pockets. "What makes you ask that? Because I offered to do something nice for you?"

"No, Benny, because you look like shit and your leg is moving a hundred miles an hour. Now come sit next to me and tell me what's going on."

I give him a tentative smile, but it quickly cracks. The breeze picks up again and as the metal chimes surrounding the run-down shack sing in the wind, I tell him everything—everything from my first conversation with S'belle in the library to our last one in the restaurant.

He looks out toward the water once I've finished to where the sun gleams off the waves. "I'm going to be honest with you. I think you're scared."

"Scared?" I feign indifference.

"Yeah, I do. And I'm going to give it to you straight. You had one girl growing up. She was your life. When you lost her, something in you changed and that's to be expected." He pauses to look at me, but it's without the smile he usually wears, then casts his eyes back out toward the horizon. "Did I ever tell you about my first love, the girl I married in Hawaii?"

My eyes dart to his. "No."

"Her name was Keilani. I met her when I moved to Hawaii to train. I was eighteen. I had never been in love, but I thought I was with her. I asked her to marry me right away. Needless to say, it didn't work out. We divorced two years later. But then I met Faith. And what I felt for her was so different from what I felt for Keilani it took her telling me how I felt to realize I loved her."

I grin at him. "I could see her doing that."

He rests his hand on my shoulder. "Do you love this girl?"

I look at him stunned for a minute. "Love her?"

"Yeah, love her. You don't have to answer me. But you need to figure it out for yourself. I think you're afraid to admit your feelings for this girl because they're different from your feelings for Dahlia. But it's okay if they are."

He stands up. "Think about it, Ben. And if I'm wrong, then you need to let her go because it sounds to me like she really loves you."

It hits me then that I've never really thought about it from her point of view.

He locks the door to the shop. "Call me and come over for dinner next week. I want to finish this conversation after you've had time to think."

I rise to my feet, my legs a little wobbly. I try to ignore what that means. I start walking toward my bike and turn around. "Noel, head over to the Beverly Wilshire. It's on me."

He shakes his head.

"I mean it. I'm calling now. Tell Faith I said Merry Christmas."

Even from a distance I can see the old man's throat working. "Thank you," he calls out hoarsely.

I jump on my bike, and as I drive, every single minute I've spent with her pops in my head. Things she's said, things I've said. And fuck me if I don't see it clear as the sun descending on the horizon—all she wanted from me was to acknowledge that I have feelings for her—was it really that easy? Because if it was—why didn't she just ask me? Am I really that thick that I didn't see it? *Yeah, you are,* the devil that's been sitting on my shoulder waiting for me to fuck up announces in my ear. Fuck that— I'll show him. I slow down and quickly turn around to head home to change. I know exactly where I plan to spend New Year's Eve.

Although the scenic stretch of moonlit highway between Laguna Beach and Los Angeles is forever etched in my mind, it still captures my attention every time I drive past it. The exhilaration I feel when I see the crashing surf or the transcendent vision of the jagged shoreline is something I'll never get tired of. It's easy to lose yourself in its beauty—in fact, the sight helps to calm my racing nerves. And the panoramic ocean view off to my right lit by streetlights overhead always seems to put things in perspective for me.

When I left the house I was still trying to figure out exactly what I was going to say to S'belle when I saw her. But now looking out to the distance, I know I'll do whatever it takes to make her understand I'm looking past tomorrow.

Sequestered behind iron gates, the SLS Hotel is perched on a secluded coastal bluff. The guard waves me forward with a pass of my ID. My car makes the mountainous climb and when I reach the top I valet it and head to the sixth floor. S'belle managed to score exclusive access not only to the rooftop pool but also the hotel's restaurant conveniently located on the rooftop. The elevator dings and my palms start to sweat. When I exit the doors the wedding party is in full swing. Looking around, I notice right away what S'belle had been so excited about—the place looks magical. The pools have been turned into usable space. With pieces of Plexiglas covering them and lights shimmering from beneath them, one pool has been turned into a dance floor and the other a stage for the band.

I take deep calming breaths and search the space for her. My eyes land on the restroom and I decide to slip inside there first. *What the hell am I so nervous for?* I splash cold water on my face and when I look up to straighten my tie, I'm staring into the reflection of the face of the man I haven't seen in over a year. The man who for far too long I thought stole my girl from me. The same man Dahlia chose to marry. And up until today I didn't realize she must love him in a very different way than she ever loved me. And right now, strangely enough, I'm thankful for that.

River Wilde's green eyes narrow on me as he takes another step inside. His resemblance to Bell is unbelievable. Their facial features, skin tone, and eye color are so much alike it's uncanny. I've recognized it before, but right now I see it clearer than day.

"What are you doing here?" he asks. His tone is even and controlled.

Trying not to let my nerves rattle me and not wanting to upset anyone, I look at him and say without pretense, "I came to talk to your sister."

His bow tie is undone and hangs to either side of his collar. His eyes look slightly glassy as though he might have had a few drinks. His piercing gaze makes me feel we are in some kind of silent stare-down. But I don't avert my eyes. Instead I allow him to study me. I get the feeling he's trying to gauge my intentions. I'm okay with that. Then I notice his fingers tighten into fists and think, *Fuck, I'm not here to fight with him.*

Finally he says something. "Did you tell her you were coming?"

"No." I'm trying not to let his attitude get to me.

"Then I think you should leave."

"I need to talk to her." I'm not sure what she told him, if anything, about what happened, but I don't like the impression I'm getting from the way he's glaring at me. Silence hangs between us for a few long moments.

His face is like stone. "If you hurt my sister—"

I don't give him a chance to finish, because the words leave my mouth without a thought. "I would never hurt her. I love her."

My knees start to shake and I grab the counter to steady myself as it occurs to me that I need her in my life because I love her in a way I've never loved anyone. The part of me that I thought died a long time ago didn't. I just couldn't find it.

That's how I feel about her. She's my missing piece—my Rosebud.

Those are the emotions I've been feeling that I haven't been able to figure out. *Fuck me.* It's not the same kind of love I felt for Dahlia. What I feel for S'belle is somehow different—deeper, more consuming maybe. I don't know, but I do know Noel was right. It's not something any man wants to think about. Comparing the love for one woman to another seems wrong.

I shove all these thoughts aside, knowing all that matters is making sure she's in my life, because without her I don't feel whole.

The shock on his face has to mirror mine.

"I'm going to find your sister now," I tell him in a surprisingly even tone. Then I walk past him and out of the room without a second glance.

Ivy plants are scattered through the room, and twinkling lights are strung beside paper lanterns. Banners reading HAPPY NEW YEAR and CONGRATULATIONS, XANDER AND IVY are wrapped around the chairs. Champagne bottles, party hats, and noise blowers decorate the tables along with white candles of all shapes and sizes. But what I notice most is the sheer amount of gold and silver confetti that dusts the floor and all of the wedding guests. It looks as though they might have celebrated midnight a little early.

When I drag my eyes over to the couples dancing on the clear platform over the pool that makes them look suspended in air, I spot her parents first. Charlotte has her arms around her husband but gives me a wave and Jack nods hello. My breath hitches when my eyes dart to a couple dancing beside them. I immediately spot the mass of red curls tumbling down her back.

Time stands still as I stand frozen in the glow from the dance floor beneath me. She's all I can see as I drink her in. A vision of beauty, she's wearing a long silver satin dress that skims her body to perfection. Her back is bare and her skin looks soft and smooth. As my eyes drop, so does my heart. Someone else's hands are wrapped around her waist, resting just above her ass. I nearly jump out of my skin when I see his fingertips caress the dip at the bottom of her spine.

As if she senses me, she turns in my direction. Her green eyes flash in surprise, but her gaze catches mine and holds it. In that moment I see what I've somehow known but not understood. I remember thinking so long ago that she looked at me as if she got me, understood who I am. I've thought that since the first time I laid eyes on her. But it's not until right now that I really understood it. It has to be because she loves me as I love her.

The guy with his arms around her is tall, with dirty blond hair and a spray of freckles across his nose. He's wearing a white T-shirt with a screen-printed bow tie on it, black scuffed boots, and a tux with his jacket unbuttoned. His skinny downtown biker look makes my blood boil. *Has she already moved on?* I take a few slow breaths, trying to calm the jealousy erupting within me.

The music changes from a slow ballad to an upbeat tempo and more people rush the dance floor. I keep my eyes pinned to her, and when I'm sure I can handle whatever the situation brings, I slowly make my way toward her. Thank fuck she pulls away from the guy who still hasn't removed his fingers from her back even with the start of a new song. She pops up on her toes and whispers something to him. He nods and finally drops his hands.

She moves off to one side of the dance floor. I can't help staring and begin to move closer and her eyes widen as she watches my every step. People cross the space between us, but I don't notice their faces; I only see her. She runs her hands down her arms as though she's cold. I increase my stride to be by her side faster. But once I'm standing in front of her, my words catch and stick in my throat.

A mix of emotions crosses her face, but she seems to settle on confusion. My mind, on the other hand, is still spinning with what to say, how to say it. Shit, Casanova I'm not.

She's the first to speak. "What are you doing here?" A tear leaks from her eye and flows down her cheek. Her voice doesn't sound accusing or angry; it's soft as though she's genuinely surprised to see me.

My hand goes to her face and I gently wipe the tears away. "You invited me." I give her a slight smile, trying to make light of the situation, make light of the fact that I haven't called her in a week, that I'm about six hours late, that I didn't pick her up—that I'm an asshole.

"I can't do this," she says, and rushes away.

When I follow her exit with my eyes, I also notice we've got the attention of her mother, stepfather, brother, and Dahlia. Her mother starts toward the door, but I step in front of her and say, "Please let me."

Jack takes her hand.

"Let me make this right."

Charlotte steps aside and with all eyes on me I head toward the closed door of the bathroom. My stomach is in knots as I lightly tap on it.

The door cracks open.

"What are you doing?" I ask her as I take a step in and she takes a step back. It's a small bathroom just like the men's—two stalls, one sink, and a mirror.

"Why are you here?" she asks again, dropping her eyes.

I move closer still. My pulse pounds so fast I can hear it in my ears. "I wanted to see you. I missed you."

"Why? I was such a bitch. I don't know what came over me. I feel ridiculous about the way I acted. Pushing you for more that wasn't there."

I lift her chin toward me. "S'belle, look at me."

I continue speaking once she raises her eyes to me.

"You were not a bitch. And there's more. I was the dumb ass who didn't understand what you needed because I couldn't see what I needed. I let you walk out because of it. But I've had time to think about it and I know what I want."

Her eyes sharpen. "What?"

"You. I came here for you." Finally I manage to say something that makes sense. Sweat coats my brow and I draw my hand back to loosen my tie because I feel as if I'm suffocating. I'm so fucking nervous. She's not saying anything. Maybe I'm too late?

"What do you mean?" She steps closer to me. Her warm breath whispers across my skin. The heat from just that slight contact makes my body buzz.

I press my forehead to hers. "Can we talk?"

She nods but quickly pulls away. Her eyes flash over my face and I'm certain that what she thinks she sees isn't how I feel. This has to be one of the hardest things I've ever done. I've been so closed off in my own life I haven't really allowed anyone in. She's the closest I've come, but now I know it wasn't enough. Obviously it wasn't.

I look around at the small space. "Somewhere that isn't the women's bathroom?"

Her slight smile gives me a little bit of hope, but it gives way to a swallow, as if she's trying to hold back the tears. I try to pull her to me, but she pushes me back. It takes all of my willpower not to struggle with her. I want to comfort her, just hold her. But I'm not sure how she'll react if I push. I know my chances are running out; they should have been up already. I want to do this right, so I opt to guide her out of here. My hand finds the dip in her back and with just that slight touch I'm electrified. Every inch of her seems to draw me in. She fills me—my body, my mind, my soul, and my heart.

I open the door and try hard to avoid the stares of her family huddled together on the edge of the dance floor. I whisper in her ear, "We have an audience."

She shakes her head. "Give me a minute. I'll meet you at the elevator."

With my hands in the pockets of my suit pants, I rock back on my heels and wait for her. She's just a few feet away with her family gathered around her. My breath comes in stuttered pants until I see her hug her mother and head toward me.

"I'm ready," she says, her voice surprisingly much calmer.

I press the DOWN button at the only elevator servicing the rooftop. We enter along with two other couples. I stand behind her, and heat fills the large gap between us.

"You did a beautiful job planning the wedding," one woman compliments Bell.

"It was breathtaking," the other throws in.

"Thank you," is all she says, and I notice her hands are trembling.

I grab one and then the other as I stand behind her. She doesn't flinch or pull away until the doors open. When they do, the four older people in front of us vacate the space quickly, calling good-bye over their shoulders. I follow right behind them, taking the lead in front of her, and finally feeling my stride, I slink back to grab her hand.

"Where are we going?" she asks.

"I want to show you something."

"I thought you wanted to talk."

"I do," I say.

Pulling S'belle to my side, I reach over the valet stand and grab my keys. "I'll bring them right back."

"But, sir, you can't do that," the valet calls.

S'belle turns. "He locked his keys in his car."

I laugh and bend to whisper in her ear, "They're in my hand. How could I have locked them in my car?"

She shrugs. "I know that, but he's still trying to figure it out."

"Silver tongue," I joke. *God, I missed her.*

A slight giggle escapes her and when I stop at the car I have to take a moment to admire her. This girl has occupied so much space in my mind for so long and I had no idea why. But I do now. It's because she's perfect for me—we are perfect for each other. I just hope she feels the same way.

I pop my trunk and pull out the large red box that I loaded before I left my house. "This is a little late, but Merry Christmas."

Her expression falls. "I can't take this."

"Please, S'belle, just open it. It will help me explain."

She sighs and sets it on the ledge of the hatch. "Ben, I think we need to talk."

"And we will as soon as you open this." I push it toward her.

Her hands hang at her sides.

I lift her chin and stare at her with an intensity that I hope conveys just a little bit of how much I care about her. "Please."

She looks down at the box and then back up to me.

I nod, my eyes pleading with her.

With resignation she pulls the box toward her and lifts the lid.

I breathe deep as she stares inside the box and pulls out its contents one after the other—red, black, white, green, gold. Cloth napkins from every restaurant I've eaten at since I saw her stash in the parking lot of the Biltmore Hotel.

She glances up at me with a puzzled look on her face.

I pull her closer to me. "You said you wanted more than just tomorrow. I'm shit with explaining my feelings, but I had this gift ready for you weeks ago. I want you to see that I never only thought of you in terms of just the next day. To me there was always more. I just didn't know how to tell you. S'belle, I think about you all the time. Everywhere I go, everything I do. Fuck, I even steal napkins because they remind me of you. Look, I know I can be an asshole, but I can promise you more than just tomorrow if you let me."

She crushes her lips to mine.

I close my eyes and savor the sensation of her body pressed against mine—soft, warm, and tender. Then I wrap my arms around her and pull her as close as I can so I can feel all of her—every single inch. When we're both breathless I lean back. "There's more in the box."

She reaches for it and removes the rest of the napkins before pulling out the shiny key from the bottom. She looks up at me. "A key?"

I nod. "To my house. I want you to move in with me. That's what I was talking to Kale about that day you overheard us. How to ask you."

Her mouth drops open in shock. "I can't do that."

"Why?"

"I—I—I've never lived with a guy," she stammers.

I grin at her. At how fucking adorable she is. I open her hand and place the key in her palm before closing her fingers one by one. "Lucky for you I'm not just any guy. I love you and I want you to live with me. Say yes?"

My breath stops as I look down at the myriad of emotions crossing her face.

Her hand slides up my chest to my cheek. Tears glisten in her eyes and she closes them tightly.

"S'belle, open your eyes. Did you hear me? I know I'm really shitty at this relationship stuff. I'm nowhere near perfect and I never will be. I'm not a heart-and-flowers kind of guy. I don't even know how to be one . . . but I'm the guy who will love you with everything I have.

"I can't bear to be away from you. I want you near me all the time. Not just in my bed but I want you sitting across from me at dinner, I want to go to the market with you, I want to do everything with you. I want to be the one who makes you smile for no reason. I want to be the one you can't stop thinking about. I want to be the one who rocks your world."

She opens her eyes. A shiver passes through her before she finally speaks. "Ben Covington, you've rocked my world from the first time I laid eyes on you. I love you too," she says, her words hoarse and soft.

Bending down closer to her mouth, I whisper, "Is that a yes? You'll move in with me?"

"Yes." She throws her arms around my neck.

"Yes!" I crouch down so we are eye to eye and grin at her. My hands move to her hips to hold her close against me.

"I can't believe Misty was right."

"Misty?"

"A fortune-teller. Never mind, you'd never believe me," she giggles.

I kiss the corner of her lip, taste it, tug on it. "You're crazy. Just the kind of crazy I need in my life."

She laughs.

Then her expression turns serious. "I'm sorry for bringing up

Dahlia. I never really thought that at all. I don't really know what was going on with me."

"Shhh . . . ," I whisper, and place my finger over her mouth. "We can talk about all that, talk about everything, but first I want to kiss you."

Her lips part and I lower my mouth to hers. I kiss her more softly this time, sweeter, maybe full of love. When she moans I can't hold back my own groan. I want her so much. I need her so much. But instead of throwing her in the backseat of my car and taking her here as I really want to, I decide we should go back upstairs. I have to make things right with her family. I know it isn't going to be easy, but I also know I love her enough to do it.

"So I saw your brother in the bathroom before I saw you," I confess.

"Xander?"

"No, River."

Her eyes widen. "How'd that go?"

"Let's just say it went better than could have been expected," I whisper in her ear.

"Oh, that's really good."

"It's going to be okay. They don't have to love me, but I'll make you feel comfortable enough that we can all be together—I can guarantee you that."

I pull back to look at her. Her smile is wide and bright—just the way I like it. There is no fear or concern anywhere on her face. Also the way I like it.

"I believe you."

I step closer. The heat in her eyes flames, proof of the passion that's always between us, and I reconsider the backseat plan. I stare at her lips but quickly raise my gaze back to her eyes. They exude such innocence and trust they make me remember I'm really trying not to always take. But fuck, this isn't easy. With my mouth now hovering over her lips, I grab her hand and say, "Come on, let's go up to your brother's wedding. I'd like to say congratulations."

She yanks my hand and pulls me back to her, flush to her body. Close enough that I can feel the hardness of her nipples through her dress and my shirt. She grips my tie and pulls the knot from it. "The festivities were just ending when you arrived. Xander arranged a private fireworks display for Ivy and whisked her off on some yacht to watch the show alone. They're actually headed to Mexico on that boat for their honeymoon."

"Does that mean you're mine, all mine, for the rest of the night?" I lick my lips.

"I am," she purrs. "I even have a room on the fifth floor. Would you like to see it?"

"See it? Oh, baby, I want to do more than see it," I growl in her ear.

The sound she makes in response sends my body into overdrive. My hands are skimming down her body and around to her back when the unpleasant memory of that guy's hands in the same place as mine comes to the forefront of my mind. "Who was the guy with his hands all over you?"

"Leif?"

My eyes drift down her body and back up. "I'm asking you."

"That was Leif Morgan. He's the guy I told you about that took Jagger's place in the movie."

"Oh yeah, right. Lucky for him I didn't punch him out, then."

"Ben, we're just friends."

"I've told you I'm jealous as fuck, haven't I?"

She nods, biting her lip with an amused smile on her face. "Have I told you that turns me on?"

Fuck me.

CHAPTER 36
Our Song

Bell

Three weeks later

Happiness fills me, all of me, every part of me. I never thought two people so lost in this world could make each other feel found, but we have. I slip back into bed as the sun makes its way up on the horizon and look over at Ben, his bare back tan from our time out on the beach teaching me how to surf, his head buried in his pillow, and his hair a rumpled mess—he couldn't look any hotter. I know he's tired but I can't resist letting my tongue draw a line from his neck down.

In a flash he has me on my back. "What time is it?" He shifts a squinting eye toward the clock.

"Six."

"In the morning?"

"Yep."

"That's illegal for a Sunday."

I laugh. "That's my line."

His mouth travels down my neck with a lick and a suck. "I like your lines."

A throaty moan escapes my throat and I shift beneath him.

He lifts his head. "Why are you up so early?"

I arch my back, pressing my body into his. "I had to pee."

He pulls away with a grin.

"What?"

"Nothing," he says, rolling us so he's on his back and I'm straddling him. "Nothing."

I moved into Ben's house two weeks ago. It was the week after we got back together. He kept his promise, doing everything he could to make things with my family comfortable. And moving day couldn't have been a bigger testament to his desire to make things work. It was definitely a family move. My whole family insisted on helping and so did Ben's. My mom and Jack were of course really easygoing and more than welcoming toward Ben, but I already knew they would be. River, well, he and Ben didn't actually speak to each other, but they didn't fight either. And Ben and I both agreed we could live with that. At least they proved they could be in the same room together without killing each other. I even think I heard River mumble, "Nice place, cool tree," under his breath when Ben was in his proximity. I got a laugh out of that. They'll come around with each other; I know they will—someday.

Once we finally leave the bed, we spend the day out. We meet my mom and Jack at the Farmer's Market where we buy a few things for the house as well as some groceries. Once we get home and get our bags unloaded, I turn on the music, pour two glasses of sparkling water, slice a lemon, and suck on a wedge. I notice Ben's stare as I do and a wave of relentless desire sweeps through me. I can feel my pulse racing and my breath quicken with every move around the kitchen he makes. He can feel it too, I can tell.

I lean back to watch Ben make dinner—stir-fry. He finally convinced me to try it, but it wasn't that difficult. I've had a weird need to eat carrots. It's as if I'm Bugs Bunny lately. I would never admit it to Ben, though, because if he knew I wanted to eat vegetables, God knows what he'd have me eating. So instead I wrinkled my nose at the idea and hesitantly agreed. But first he had to promise a few sexual favors in return. That part was fun. And since Ben's always telling me what a whiz with a wok he is, I really did want to see him in action.

I stand back with my arms against the counter watching him as he dices the onions, chops the peppers, and juliennes the carrots.

"Show-off," I mutter as he slices perfect rectangle wedges out of the last orange stick.

I take a sip of my drink and move closer. "I think you need an apron," I whisper in his ear, and then nibble on it.

"I have to concentrate and with you doing that, it's hard."

I giggle.

He picks up the cutting board and pours all the perfectly cut vegetables into a bowl. I lean over and grab a carrot, popping it in my mouth.

He turns and looks at me, raising an eyebrow.

I shrug. "They look edible the way you cut them."

He shakes his head.

I squeeze his butt. "Don't you want to know why I think you need an apron?"

"Sure, I'm dying to know."

I let my hand trail between his legs to that spot I know he likes me to touch.

He sets the knife down and turns. He grabs my wrists and lets his tongue slip out of his mouth, wetting his lip. I'm getting wet just thinking about what I want him to do with that tongue.

"I thought you were hungry and you wanted to eat," he growls in my ear.

"I am and I do. I just wanted to say you might want to wear an apron the next time you cook because I think you should be naked and this"—I rub myself against the erection I saw bloom the minute I sucked on the lemon—"might stand out."

He grins, unashamed. "You noticed, did you?"

"Yep."

He walks me backward away from the island and toward the bank of cabinets behind me. His hands go first to my waist, then my hips, and farther down. I wish I wasn't wearing jeans. "Next time we cook together, you're going to be wearing one of those little black-and-white maid outfits."

"I don't have anything that resembles an outfit like that."

"You will," he says with a sexy smile that sends tingles all the way down to my toes.

He kisses me a few times, on my mouth, my chin, my ear—a taste here and there.

"Ben."

He doesn't stop. My shoulder, my collarbone, my other shoulder. "Hmm?"

"You have to finish dinner," I manage to say.

We have been taking turns cooking and sometimes we cook together. The problem with cooking together is we usually end up eating cold meals because we have a hard time concentrating on the food, like right now.

His mouth quirks up. "Okay, but you distracted me with the whole apron thing. And I know you just really want to wear one."

I scoff. "How do you manage to always turn things around?"

He looks over at me, his eyes heavy lidded. God, what he can do to me with one look. I draw in a breath, squeezing my thighs together to control the pulsing.

He moves back to the island and turns the stove on. I want to tell him let's skip dinner, but I'm also starving. He avoids making eye con-

tact as he moves around. I've figured him out—it's the only way to accomplish his task without distraction. I go about my own business.
Back to the cutting board, where I continue slicing lemons.

When he looks up he sees me holding a lemon under my nose. His
stare grows curious. "Okay, spill it."

I give him a smile. "What?"

"Why are you smelling the lemon?"

I breathe it in again, but this time the smell I've always loved hits
me in a sour way and almost makes me want to gag. The oil crackles
from the wok and he momentarily drops his gaze and lowers the heat
so he doesn't notice. When he looks back up I outstretch my hand.
"Here, smell it?"

His hand covers mine around the yellow oval. He inhales with an
exaggerated whiff. "Okay, I give."

I drop my hand and make a little noise, trying really hard not to
sigh. "Argh . . . don't you smell the lemony scent?"

"Yes, I smell it. I smell you. You know I love that scent, because I
tell you that all the time. But if you want to know if one is ripe, you're
supposed to squeeze it, not smell it."

I peel the skin back with my nails and toss it in the sink. I slip the
tip of the wedge in my mouth, hoping it doesn't make me gag again.

"Um . . . so good," I say.

"I bet," he teases, flinching at the thought of eating a lemon.

"Ben, it doesn't matter what it tastes like. Don't you know that
when you eat a lemon it's readily absorbed into your body and acts as
a natural perfume? That's why I always smell it before I eat it to make
sure that's what I want to smell like."

"Fuck . . . sometimes you actually can make sense out of your
nonsense," he teases, grabbing another from the bowl and quickly slicing it into quarters and offering me the wedge with skin on. My lips
circle his fingers and I put the piece in my mouth. I take my time,
sucking all the juice, hollowing out my cheeks as I do. I know what I'm

doing. He stays close even after I drain the liquid from the lemon. He puckers his own lips and I know exactly what he's thinking. When I finish I take another quarter and hold it up for him to eat.

"I'm good." He holds his hands up.

"Please try it. It tastes like lemonade." I lick my lips.

He sighs in exaggeration. "If I do you're going to owe me."

I pop up on my toes. "I'll let you pretend to be Tom Sawyer."

"Huck Finn and you have a deal," he counters with a devilish grin.

"You got it." I hold the fruit to his lips.

With my fingers so close to his mouth, my breathing only hitches higher and so does his. The oil crackles and splatters from the wok, but neither of us moves as his hands find their magical way down my body. Drawn to each other as we always are, the magnetic pull gets stronger with each day we spend together. "I love you," I say softly.

Suddenly there's a tap at the glass doors from out in the family room. I turn with a jump and a screech to see the shadow of two people standing out on the deck—a silhouette of a man and a woman.

"You're so fucking adorable," Ben whispers in my ear.

He makes his way toward the door, obviously knowing who it is.

"Who is that?" I'm wondering why they wouldn't just ring the doorbell.

Ben slides open the door. "Caleb, where the fuck have you been?"

The two guys slap each other's back in a semblance of a hug. I've met Caleb a number of times. However, I've never met the girl. She's stunning. Dark hair, dark eyes, and very fit, much like Caleb. I walk toward them.

"I knocked, but . . . ," Caleb starts to say but stops when his eyes cut to mine. And with his grin wide asks, "Bell, how are you?"

Ben reaches out and takes my hand.

I give Caleb a smile. "Good, really good."

"This is Gemma. Gemma, this is my best friend in the world, Ben, and his . . ." He pauses for a brief moment.

"This is my girlfriend, Bell."

My heart chases itself in circles at his introduction. "Hi, nice to meet you." I smile like an idiot.

"We're just making dinner. There's plenty."

Caleb glances in the kitchen. "Ben's famous stir-fry—I'd love to but Serena and Jason are waiting dinner for us. I just wanted to stop by and say a quick hi and talk to Ben."

He rocks back on his heels and tucks his hands in his pockets, obviously feeling uncomfortable.

"Well, how about something to drink?" I ask.

"I'd love a glass of water," Gemma says.

"The same." Caleb smiles.

I head to the kitchen, staring back at them. I see their gestures but can't hear anything. Ben keeps staring at me and once I put ice and water in two glasses I hurry back in to figure out what's going on. When I hand the waters to Caleb and Gemma, Ben opens his arms to fold me into them. With my head tight against his shoulder he kisses me and says to Caleb, "You know what, I'm good the way things are."

There was a time I would have been eager for the story. But I went down that road once and I don't ever want to go down it again. I know he'll tell me as soon as I ask.

I look up. "What's going on?"

He smiles down at me and kisses the tip of my nose. "Nothing. Caleb was just looking for some advice, but I can't really help him."

Caleb nods.

"I'll be right back," Ben says, and when he comes back he hands some kind of flash drive to Caleb. "Good luck, man."

"Thanks. I'll be in touch."

We say our good-byes and once they leave through the front door, Ben looks over to me and sees my puzzled expression.

"He just needed some information that I had of his."

"Okay." It feels as though there's more to the story, but Ben's body language says it all. He's quiet, serene, and I feel he needs me to just be here for him. Next, he pulls me close and holds me tight for a very long time. "I love you," he says.

"I love you too." I relish it when he tells me that because it isn't often, but I know he means it, so I'm okay with that.

He pulls away. "Dinner can wait."

I nod my agreement because there's a different kind of hunger I'm feeling all the way to the depths of my soul.

He extends his hand and leads me up toward our room.

We start to make love and when he slowly slides inside me the only words out of mouth are "I love you."

CHAPTER 37
Come to Me

Ben

We all want second chances. Perhaps we even all need them. But we don't all get them. I know I'm one of the lucky ones. Caleb showing up last night proved it to me beyond any doubt. I'm happy with my life—more than happy. I open my eyes before the alarm clock goes off with those thoughts floating around my mind. I lift my head and reach for her, but she's not lying beside me.

"S'belle," I yell.

When she doesn't answer I sit up and that's when I hear it. The sound of her puking. I pull my boxers on and hurry into the bathroom. She's wrapped up in her short pink robe kneeling in front of the toilet.

"Are you okay?" I squat beside her and hand her a towel.

She takes the towel and wipes her mouth. "No. I think those vegetables you made me eat gave me food poisoning."

I try not to laugh. "I don't think the vegetables would do that to you. Maybe the chicken, though? We did leave it on the counter a little longer than we should have. But I'm fine."

She looks up at me. "Your stomach is probably used to it."

This time I have to laugh at the pout on her face. "Come on. I'm putting you back to bed." I feel her forehead. "You're not warm, but it could still be the start of a bug. Stay home today."

"I can't stay home."

"Yes, you can. If the boss gives you a free pass, you take it. If you feel better later, come in then."

Once she falls back to sleep, I shower and take off for work. I call her when I arrive and she sounds really groggy. At noon I shoot her a text.

How are you feeling?

She responds:

Better. I'm going to stay home today, though. I'm trying to figure out something that Misty told me.

Misty?

The fortune-teller.

Oh, right. Explain to me later.

I roll my eyes at her craziness but smirk at the same time. Then I look over at Aerie. It's her first day back in the office and there is a shit ton to catch up on. Sadly Jagger's father passed last week. I accompanied S'belle to New York for the funeral. She had never met Jagger's father and although I hadn't either, being able to be there to support her cousin made her feel better and me feel a little closer to her family.

The funeral did bring back many painful memories of my own mother's death and so I spent a lot of that trip talking to S'belle about her. I think S'belle got to know the woman who loved me regardless of my flaws a little better. Then again I guess now that I think about it, S'belle has done the same thing.

"Okay, what's first on your list?" I ask Aerie.

She pulls out an organized stack of folders and I know we'll be here for a while. Around four in the afternoon she pulls out the March layout. As I stand up and walk around the room to stretch, my phone buzzes. It's another text from S'belle.

Can you meet me at Pebbles for dinner?

I look up at Aerie. "Can we finish this tomorrow?"
"Sure, I have a ton of other things to do anyway."
"Thanks." I quickly look back down to respond.

You have to be joking!

Please.

Not if you're going to break up with me!

No! I'm not. Why would you think that?

Never mind. You're not going to tell me the world will end tomorrow, are you?

No! And I think I get what Misty was talking about.

You're crazy. You know that. Right? See you soon.

If I said my nerves weren't back in full force, I'd be lying. By now I've really begun to hate S'belle's favorite restaurant. But I make it there by six. She's already seated at a table by the window with her back to me, and her red hair hangs in curls. The restaurant is by no means busy, so the atmosphere is tranquil and the room is somewhat quiet. Bending down, I swipe her hair to the side and kiss her neck. "Hi, sexy."

She twists and her lips meet mine. "Hi."

I take a seat and pull my chair right up to hers. When I glance at the tabletop I see two glasses of sparkling water and a dish of lemons as well as a wrapped package that looks a lot like the one I brought her from Fiction Vixen the last time we were here.

I grab her hands. "Let's cut to the chase. Please don't torture me by making me wait until after dinner to tell me why I'm meeting you here."

Her innocent green eyes shine, although she looks a little peaked and a little scared.

"Are you still sick?" I ask, concerned.

She shakes her head. "I have something to tell you and I'm really nervous."

"Why, have you been bad?"

"No," she says quickly, and looks more sickly with each passing second.

"Shit, I thought I was going to have to spank you," I say, trying to ease her nervousness, but honestly my stomach feels as if it might fall at any second, so I'm not sure I'm doing a great job.

But when a slight smile crosses her lips, I think I've succeeded. She twists and pulls a brown paper bag out from her purse and hands it to me with trembling fingers.

"What's this? Nothing that's going to jump out at me, I hope."

She stares at me, looking scared shitless.

My own hands are shaking as I unfold the bag. What the hell could it contain that makes her look like that? I pull out a purple box that reads EPT, with the words *early pregnancy test* written out below it. My eyes widen, my heart pounds, and my pulse races as my head snaps to her.

"Are you pregnant?" I ask in shock.

"I don't know but I think I might be," she answers. All the color has left her face now.

A million different emotions pass through me, but I settle on one— pure elation. I jump from my chair and take the box and her hand. "Well, let's find out."

"Now?" she asks, completely taken aback.

"Right now." I grin at her.

"You're not upset?" She sounds surprised.

I pull her flush to my body, not caring that we're in a restaurant. "Upset? Are you out of your mind? Now come on, you have a stick to pee on."

She tugs on my hand.

I turn around.

"What if I can't go?"

I stride back to the table and pick up both glasses of water. When I return to her I tell her, "Drink these, baby."

She smiles in a way that lights up her eyes and gulps both of them down.

"You can't come in here," she says when I push open the door to the restroom.

"Fuck I can't."

She shakes her head and enters under my arm.

I shakily open the box and hand her the stick.

She stares at me.

"You have to go in there," I say, pointing to the stall door.

"I know."

"Then go!"

"So bossy," she says as she takes the stick.

When she comes out we both stare at it as she sets it on the counter.

"The instructions say to wait two minutes to read the result. Be sure to read the result before ten minutes have passed," I tell her.

With my hands gripping the counter, my eyes are locked on the stick as the time slowly passes by. S'belle is pacing the room. My foot taps the floor at a hundred miles an hour. When a blue line appears in the square window, I twist toward her. "It's turning."

She looks at her watch, the one I finally had fixed for her. "It says wait two minutes. It hasn't even been thirty seconds. You shouldn't be looking yet."

"I'm impatient and never follow instructions. You know that."

She gives a little giggle. The one that makes my heart flip.

I decide I'll pick up the instructions to see what the window means.

"I thought you didn't follow the instructions."

"Shhh . . . let me figure this out."

She rushes over to me and pushes her way under my outstretched arms.

I read out loud with her cocooned inside my arms, "If a blue line appears in the square window within ten minutes, the test has worked." I continue reading the instructions. "A plus sign in the round window indicates a pregnancy result—"

She pulls the folded paper from my hand.

"Hey, let me finish reading that."

She holds the stick up. It has the biggest, bluest plus sign displayed in the first window.

Every part of my body hums with a kind of happiness I've never felt in my life. "A baby?" Shock takes over.

She nods.

"How?" I ask her.

She grins. "Well, the birds and the bees . . ."

I pull her to me and kiss her, soft and gentle. I can't believe this is happening. I can't believe I got a second chance at life.

After a few moments she leans back. "I think this explains my mood swings and my puking. My mother told me taking antibiotics makes the pill less effective. I had no idea—"

I shut her up by putting my finger over her lips. "Shhh . . . I don't care how it happened."

Her hands go to my cheeks and she holds them there. "Are you sure?"

I nod with emotion clogging my throat. Is she kidding me?

We stare into each other's eyes for a long while and then I drop to my knees. She follows my movements as I lift her shirt and kiss the shamrock she wears to never forget our first baby. I look up at her and then glide my mouth to kiss above the gleaming green symbol of remembrance. And this time when I look up again I say, "S'belle Wilde, I love you and I promise you forever."

CHAPTER 38

Happy

Bell

Seven and a half months later

You might be a little horny were the first words I read when I opened a pregnancy book to a random page many months ago. It made me laugh because the description fit. I had bought Ben two books from Fiction Vixen the day I thought I might be pregnant—the first one *The Modern Kama Sutra: An Intimate Guide to the Secrets of Erotic Pleasure* and the second *Finding Out You're Pregnant*. It was the latter that shared that helpful tidbit with me. Once we both calmed our racing nerves in the bathroom, we went back to our table and decided food to go would be best. I was ready to leave my refuge and go home. I just wanted to be alone with Ben.

Sex with Ben has always been . . . well, amazing. And in the past several months my need for him has been off the charts. When we were first together I knew that what we had was different. I don't know how I knew—I just did. And no one I was with after him had ever made me feel the way he does. Everything about him, every touch, caress, word, and whisper, makes my body come alive. It still does. And now even though my belly is swollen beyond belief as I enter my ninth month of pregnancy, I want him more than ever.

Ben doesn't mind at all. He's happy to indulge my every need—whether it's a slice of triple-crusted pie from Four & Twenty Blackbirds at midnight, or my weird craving for vegetables, especially carrots with lemon juice drizzled over them, or of course my constant arousal. He likes that my breasts are bigger—a fact that amazes him on a daily basis. The Kama Sutra book has come in handy because as my body has changed, our favorite sexual positions have grown uncomfortable and some aren't even feasible.

We've had to get very creative and experiment with different ways to please ourselves. We take turns picking new positions to attempt. It's been so much fun.

After showering, I tug the towel off my head and let my hair dangle in curls, patting the water from it.

He picks up the book as I walk into the bedroom and with complete focus looks through it.

I point to one of the drawings. "That one."

He strokes his chin. "You think? I'm not sure about the leg placement."

I giggle and toss the book aside, throwing myself back on the mattress and bringing him with me. "Let's make something up."

Both of our towels come undone. "Sounds like a plan," he growls.

It's not an exaggeration that we have sex at least twice a day. I made the mistake of telling my new girlfriend Summer from Lamaze and I don't think she believed me. We took a spin class together and when we went to the juice bar afterward, I told her my vagina was really sore and I wasn't sure if I was going to be able to have sex tonight.

Her head snapped to mine as she rubbed her own swollen belly. "You're still having sex?" She went on to say, "God, that's the last thing I feel like doing." And then she laughed.

I didn't answer but laughed along with her even though that couldn't have been further from the truth for me. I love Ben and we do it a lot. Obviously I'm very attracted to him and with him I've discovered I love sex, I really love it—a lot. And I know he definitely feels the same.

When he rests his head on his elbow and moves one hand to caress my stomach, I'm pulled back to the here and now. His lips trail down my neck, over my breasts, and stop to kiss the shamrock in my belly button, then just below it. He kisses the baby like this all the time. It gives me butterflies.

He looks up at me. "So we agree. We'll name the baby Huck?"

We found out the sex of our baby at my four-month prenatal visit, and ever since then Ben has been relentless about naming him Huck. I peer down at him. "No, we did not agree. Remind me when we had the conversation where I said yes."

His fingers drift down to circle me.

I let out a long heavy breath, knowing soon my body will be hovering on the edge waiting for the crashing pleasure to peak.

"This morning," he murmurs as his tongue licks a path down the curve of my belly to join his fingers.

I raise myself up on my elbows. Still breathing heavy, I try to see over my stomach. "Do you mean when your mouth was"—I point to where his fingers are—"there and you were whispering things I couldn't even try to understand in the frenzied state you had me in?"

His devilish grin widens. "Yes, when I had my tongue on your clit and you were screaming my name and calling out to heaven—yeah, that's when. You said yes."

"I love you, Ben Covington, but we are not naming our child Huck."

He stares at me and pats my cheek. "Maybe once you see him you'll change your mind."

His eyes gleam whenever he talks about the baby. It's so cute. His thumb strokes my face and he kisses me gently before he moves his mouth to that spot behind my ear that makes my body dance on its own. When I arch my back and moan, I feel the grin that forms on his lips. I knot my fingers in his hair, feeling more than a little ready to do this again. His hand moves back down to caress my belly as we lie in bed naked getting ready to make love for the second time since I got home. I can't even wait until tonight.

His hands move quickly as we lie on the bed both still lightly damp from our shower. One chaste kiss on the mouth and before I know it his lips are sucking on one of my nipples and his hand moves to cup my sex and I'm aroused all over again. I close my eyes as my body soaks in the pleasure of his touch. A loud moan escapes my throat and I lick my lips, but when he stops abruptly and jerks up, my eyes fly open.

"S'belle, there's a lot of, um . . . water on the bed."

I sit up and look. Oh my God, I feel it.

Ben is staring down—petrified.

Once I realize I haven't lost bladder control, I almost laugh at how scared he looks. Calmly I say, "I think my water broke."

He bolts off the bed and pulls a pair of boxers from his drawer. "You're not due for two weeks."

I shrug. "The doctor did say anytime now."

"We have to call the doctor."

I pat the bed. "Ben, sit down. Let's see if I have any contractions."

I try to be calm, summoning all my willpower to not crumble and have him rush me to the hospital, because I know what to do—what the classes taught me.

He looks at me as he lowers himself down onto the bed, his leg tapping up and down with his foot on the floor. "How long does that take?"

"I have no idea." I laugh.

"What do you mean you have no idea? We went to all those classes."

"You were there too."

"Yeah, but I was always a shitty student."

I have to laugh at that. How can I not? I slide my feet to the floor and rise from the bed. As I slip into one of his button-up shirts, I feel a cramp and I slump over.

Ben rushes over to me. "Let's go to the hospital."

"Let me call my mother and see what she says first." I sit back on the bed, taking a deep breath.

Ben quickly hands me my phone from the night table. "Did you pack a bag yet?"

"No. I thought I still had time."

He strides over to the closet. "I'll do it."

I call my mother.

"How far apart are your contractions?"

"I've only had one."

"Jack and I are on our way. You should be fine until we get there. Just relax, okay, Isabelle?"

Isabelle? She only ever calls me by my real name when she's nervous. Great. "Yes, Mom."

I hit END and look up to see Ben standing in utter sexiness in the doorframe. He is disheveled and so handsome—his jeans are unzipped, his shirt, the frayed one that I love, is unbuttoned, and his feet are bare.

He lifts his eyes to me. "Do you think we made a mistake?"

My mouth drops. "Why would you say that? It's a little late now." My voice breaks.

He furrows his brow. "I mean that we didn't get married before we have the baby. What did you think I meant?"

Relief courses through me at the same time as another cramp bites from my lower gut. I wince and he flies to the bed.

"What can I do?"

I grab his hand. "Just stay with me. I'm scared."

"I'm not going anywhere."

"Why are you second-guessing our decision?" I ask as I look down at the large radiant-shaped diamond that adorns my finger.

The sun shining in the window reflects against the ring's cut edges. He proposed to me a week after we watched the white stick turn to a plus sign. It was so romantic—like a scene out of an old film. He took me back to Hearst Castle. No one was there—it was just the two of us. Before we entered the large exquisite doors, he dropped to his knee, called me his "Rosebud," and told me he wanted to marry me. Whoever said he wasn't romantic? He told me I was his missing puzzle piece—a guy couldn't get more romantic than that. The gesture made my heart skip beat after beat. But later when the adrenaline rush slowed, we talked about it more. We agreed that we would get married . . . but only when the time was right. Plus, I would need time to plan the wedding.

"I don't want to be that couple that gets married only because they're having a baby," I reminded him.

"Does my name still go on the birth certificate? Will the baby have my last name?" he asks.

His voice is full of concern. I muster all of my energy as another cramp hits. Once it passes I straddle his lap and take his face in my hands. "This baby is yours and mine. Yes, your name will be on the birth certificate and, yes, he will have your last name."

He slides his lips to kiss my hand and takes them in his. "I love you."

"I love you too." Then I know what he needs. "Ben, just so you know, I did put your name on the birth certificate that just read baby." I can finally talk about the baby, our baby that I gave up, and feel that I did what was right.

His eyes glitter with tears, but before they can spill I let out a scream.

He takes my hand. "Let's go. They're coming too close. We need to get to the hospital."

"Did you pack my bag?"

"S'belle, I can't find shit in there. Tell me what you want to wear to the hospital and I'll get it. We'll worry about the rest later."

"My white top with the . . ." I gasp for air.

He's really in a panic now. He shoves his feet into his boots and zips and buttons his clothes.

When the contraction stops I stand up. "Let me show you."

"Okay, but make it quick."

"Ben, you have to put socks on."

"What?" he asks, confused.

"You didn't put socks on before you put your boots on. Your feet are going to smell."

He laughs and grabs a pair from the dresser as I make my way to the closet. I can see what he's talking about. Huge mess of clothes everywhere. I point to the items I want. Ben throws them all in a bag along with some of my toiletries. Then he helps me slide on my panties. Next I shimmy a pair of jeans on and decide to wear his shirt with no bra. I don't really care at this point.

Once I'm ready he takes my hand, but a knifelike pain radiates from my hipbone to my pubic bone and I can't move.

Sweat coats his brow.

I look around the room as I ride the wave out and spot the book with the blue spine. When my gaze swings back to Ben, his eyes are so wide with fear I can almost feel it. I take a step forward but stop again. "Wait, can you bring that book?"

He looks confused but grabs it and shoves it in the bag.

"So you can read to me while we're in the hospital," I tell him as we leave the house.

He looks down at me and stops to hold me; then he says, "You're so fucking adorable."

From the car I call my mother and tell her to meet us at the hospital. My insides feel as if they're twisting inside out at this point. At the hospital I'm quickly whisked to a room, given an IV, and asked if I want an epidural. Ben and I already decided I would take the epidural. My mother and Jack arrive just as it takes effect. Shortly after that River, Dahlia, Ivy, and Xander show up. Ivy is three months pregnant and still experiencing morning sickness morning, noon, and night. They all pop their heads in before going to the waiting room. When the nurse calls the doctor and time approaches, my mother leaves as well. And it's just Ben and me.

The doctor comes in and I begin pushing. At first I think I might throw up—the pressure I feel everywhere is too intense. But once it subsides, I push again and again. My hand is gripping Ben's so tightly, but he doesn't care. He wipes some hair from my eyes and I look up at him and see amazement and wonder on his face. My eyes drop to where his are locked and I see our baby's head crowning. Intense stinging radiates from my core as I push harder and scream louder. Then just like that, our baby emerges into this world.

His cries are hoarse but steady as if he's having little tantrums.

"I'll do that," Ben says to the doctor as he prepares to cut the cord.

"Can I hold him?" I ask with tears of pure joy leaking from my eyes.

The nurse lays him on my chest for only a brief moment but long enough for me to feel the beat of his heart.

"He has red hair," Ben says, his voice strained with emotion as he tries to hold back his own tears.

The nurse takes him from me. "The doctor just has to examine him and we will have him right back to you."

Ben squeezes my hand and presses a kiss to my forehead before he follows her. When he turns around he's grinning ear to ear, holding our baby bundled in a blue blanket.

"Is everything okay?" I ask, unable to wait another minute.

"He's perfect," he says as he crosses back over to me.

I turn away for a brief moment with relief seeping through me to sip on the ice water by my bedside and catch sight of the book Ben had been reading to me just an hour earlier. Ben carefully places our baby on my chest and I study his little face—the shape of his cheeks, the slope of his nose, the fullness of his lips. Suddenly he opens his eyes and lets out a loud cry. That's when I see his perfect dimples and blue eyes so much like his father's. With tears of joy I look up at Ben and say, "Finn. Let's name him Finn."

Ben's grin is wider than I have ever seen. "Finn is perfect." He smiles down, resting his hand over mine. And as my eyes shift from the baby to Ben and back to the baby, I think this has to be the single-most beautiful feeling in the world. It's a feeling that reaches all the way into my soul and takes my breath away. And it's a feeling I know will never leave me.

Hours later when I awake, I know Ben is nearby because I can hear the sound of his breathing, but this time my senses are heightened. As my eyes flutter open his soft lips are on mine, and although he is barely skimming them, I can feel the heat that sears me every time he touches me. My eyes lift to see Finn in Ben's arms. In looking at them together, observing the bliss I see on Ben's face, I know that what we have isn't perfect, but it is our own version of perfect. And even though the edges of our relationship may be frayed much like the hem of his shirts, the framework is solid and in the end . . . that's all that really matters.

See where it all began in

CONNECTED

the first in the Connections Series by Kim Karr!
Available in print and e-book from New American Library.

We walked through the open door to the University of Southern California Campus Bar and Aerie pulled her tail up. "At least they aren't playing that Halloween crap in here," she yelled a little too loudly. As my ears adjusted, I heard a velvety-soft voice singing an unfamiliar yet captivating song.

Aerie stopped to put her devil horns on, and I glanced around the large room, recognizing a lot of students, while trying to get a look at the band. I shouted directly into her ear, "They sound really good. Have you heard them before?"

She was on her toes trying to see over the crowd. I laughed at how short she was until her pointy devil horn hit me in the eye. "No, but I love their sound," she responded, still trying to see the stage and almost falling over.

I had been coming here for the last three years and couldn't ever remember it being so crowded. I could barely see the long wooden bar to my right, and with the mass of bodies bumping and grinding on the dance floor, I couldn't even catch a glimpse of the stage.

"Do you know their name?" I asked Aerie.

"I think they're called the Wilde Ones." She hiccupped and laughed. She winked at me as she started to dance her way toward some friends on the dance floor and yelled over her shoulder, "By the way, I love them! Great name and an even greater sound."

"I'll get drinks and meet you out there in a bit," I said to no one since she was already gone. When the bartender acknowledged me, I ordered two beers, one with ice and one without, and tacked on two shots to help Aerie drown her misery.

The live music stopped and typical Halloween songs were blasted through the speakers. I turned my back to the bar and scanned the crowd for Aerie. You would think she would be easy to spot in her red sequin devil costume. She said she was out for vengeance, and if her outfit was any indication, she would be vindicated.

I didn't see her anywhere but I did spot an attractive guy. He was still too far away for me to zero in on any specific feature, but something—no, everything—about him drew my attention.

I watched how he moved; his confidence captivated me. He seemed relaxed, like he knew exactly where he was going. And as he headed in my direction, I became mesmerized. Biting my bottom lip, I was unable to focus on anything but him. My head was still a little foggy from the three beers I'd consumed earlier and I was clearly not thinking straight when I made eye contact with him, and then slowly studied his body from head to toe.

As the distance between us narrowed, I could see that he was alarmingly attractive: long, lean, and muscular but not bulky. He wore a black beanie hat with his light brown hair sticking out. When I looked into his eyes, they undid me. Although I couldn't see their color, I could feel their intensity. I almost feared that if I looked into them for too long, I might never walk away. His eyes aside, the words *handsome* and *gorgeous* weren't strong enough adjectives to describe this man.

My mind wandered to where it shouldn't. Knowing better than to compare this guy to my boyfriend, I did it anyway. I felt incredibly guilty, but I couldn't help myself. Ben was all surfer. He was attractive, hot, and sexy with an ego to match. This guy was equally as attractive, hot, and sexy, but there was something else—something more. I couldn't quite put my finger on it.

Easing his way through the crowd, he removed his beanie and ran his hands through his hair. When our eyes connected it felt like minutes, but only seconds passed. Suddenly I felt an electric pull forcing me to keep looking at him. Everything I felt indicated he was dangerous. I knew I should look away, walk away, but I didn't. I couldn't. He was just too alluring.

He was finally close enough that I could tell his gleaming eyes were green. I was instantly drawn to his smile. It wasn't a full smile, more like a half grin emphasizing his dimples. His skin was smooth with no facial hair and that made me weak in the knees. His full lips were begging for a kiss. I'd never looked at a guy like this before, not even Ben. So why was I eyeing him this way, and why was I unable to avert my gaze?

Aside from his overall sex appeal, his clothing made him even more irresistible. He wore faded jeans, a black Foreigner concert T-shirt, and black work boots. I had to laugh a little when I saw the concert T-shirt because I was wearing one, too—my dad's U2 T-shirt, knotted on the side, hanging off my shoulder.

Having made his way through the crowd much better than I had, he was now standing in front of me. His face was breathtaking; he had a strong chin; a small, straight nose; perfectly shaped eyebrows; and long eyelashes. He was a vision of utter perfection and I couldn't help but smile.

The bar was crowded and there was no room on either side of me. Putting both hands in his pockets, he smiled back at me. Then, running his tongue over his bottom lip, he asked in a low, sexy voice, "Were you staring at me?"

I pouted my lips and rolled my eyes. I took a deep breath as I straightened my shoulders and placed my hands on my hips. "No, I was just looking for my friend while I waited on my drinks. You just happened to be in my line of vision."

He chuckled a little, then said, "That look was hot."

I huffed out a breath and tried not to laugh. *Did he really just say that?*

When the bartender brought my order and set it in front of me, my phone started ringing in my pocket, but I ignored it as I continued to stare at him. "Why would you think I was looking at you, anyway?"

As the person beside me settled her tab and walked away, he moved to fill the empty space and tossed his beanie next to my drink. His proximity caused my pulse to race and my heart to pound harder. Leaning sideways, he rested his hip against the bar. With his eyes still locked on mine, he answered, "Because I was staring at you, hoping you were staring back."

I looked directly into those powerful green eyes, so full of intensity, and I instantly lost my train of thought. With the electric pull only growing stronger between us, I feared I wasn't going to be able to get out of this encounter unscathed.

He dragged his teeth across his bottom lip and his eyes scanned my body. The expression on his face told me he wanted to do more than just talk. I wanted to do more as well.

A moment of comfortable silence passed before he cocked his head to the side in the most adorable way and grinned. "With all this talk about who was staring at whom I think we forgot the basics. I'm River," he said as he extended his hand with the most devilish grin on his face.

Feeling bewitched by him, I put my hand out to shake his but quickly pulled it away. Unfortunately, I also bumped into the person standing next to me and accidentally spilled his beer.

He gave me a dirty look and swore under his breath. River's grin quickly turned into a frown, and he gently moved me away. In a clipped tone he apologized, "Sorry, man. Just an accident, but let me buy you another."

The now drinkless man with a wet shirt looked at him and nodded. River pulled out his wallet and handed him a ten. "Buy two." The man took the money and walked away, muttering something under his breath. River immediately returned his attention to me, and I bit the corner of my lower lip and smiled at him.

There we were, standing face-to-face, with only a few drinks separating us. Sliding one of the beers toward him, I took a sip of my own even though the ice had melted. "Thank you. That guy sure as shit wasn't happy with me. In fact, he kind of acted like an asshole."

Taking a sip of his drink, he started to laugh, almost spitting it out. Skimming his finger over my bare shoulder, his eyes locked on mine. "You're more than welcome."

Quivering from his touch and intense gaze, I took a step back, fearful of where this might lead.

Moving forward, he traced my last step. He was not going to let the distance widen between us. He stared intently into my eyes. "Now, where were we? Do we need to start over?" He waited for my response as he watched me swallow my drink.

I pulled my lower lip to the side with my teeth and smiled playfully. "We were introducing ourselves."

"Okay, so let's try again. I'm River and you are . . . ?"

"I'm not sure you need to know that information right now. I'm kind of thinking you might be a stalker."

His eyes widened as he laughed. "You're not serious—are you, beautiful girl?"

Unable to control my own laughter, I simply said, "Maybe I am," but my laughter subsided when I registered the sweet name he'd called me.

Leaning toward me, he was close enough that I could inhale his fresh scent. It was a soapy, just-out-of-the-shower smell.

"What? If you're not going to tell me your name, then I get to call you whatever I want."

Averting my eyes from his gaze, I looked down.

After taking another sip of his beer, he set the mug down. He hooked my chin with his finger and tilted my head up toward him. His touch seared my skin and left it tingling. He stared at me with his intense green eyes and chuckled. "Can we talk about you thinking I'm a Jack the Ripper type? I just want you to know, I'm definitely not. In fact, I think it's safe to say you were staring at me first, but in no way do I think you're a stalker."

My mouth dropped open. I was unsure of what to say. I knew he was right. I had stared first.

"So we can get past this, let's just say I was staring first. Not that it really matters."

We were looking into each other's eyes as the bartender passed me my bill. When I turned to pay for my drinks, our connection was broken. Handing my money to the bartender, I thanked him and told him to keep the change. This distraction gave me some time to think about how to handle this potentially dangerous situation.

I watched River as he ordered two more beers, and realized I had to work out my conflicted feelings. I pushed my guilt aside and handed him one of the shots.

"Cheers."

"It's a beautiful day," he replied before shooting back the shot.

I tried not to show how turned on I was that he had just quoted lyrics from one of my favorite songs.

Setting his shot glass down, he put his hand in his pocket. "So, does this mean you forgive me?"

His voice was strong, but soft, and made him even more tempting. I found myself thinking that he was not only adorable, but unlike anyone I had ever encountered before. I knew I shouldn't be doing this. I had a boyfriend who I loved waiting for me.

I raised an eyebrow and asked, "Forgive you? Forgive you for what?" I was having a hard time concentrating on the conversation and honestly had no idea what the apology was for.

He shifted on his feet. "You know what? Never mind," he muttered in my ear. His warm breath brushed my neck and I wanted to feel it everywhere.

Looking me up and down, he changed the subject. "What, no costume?"

Continuing our dangerous flirtation, I glanced down, motioning with my hands from head to toe. "How do you know this isn't my costume?"

While tugging on my T-shirt and pulling me a little closer, he seductively whispered, "If that's your costume you're definitely taking first place in the contest because it's the sexiest one I've ever seen."

We were silent for a minute, not even our heavy breathing could be heard. The noise from the bar and the crowd around us had quieted, but his words, his touch, they inflamed me, excited me, and sent fire through my veins.

"Where'd you get this, anyway?" he asked, tugging at the knot on my shirt, pulling me closer.

It felt like the room was spinning and I wasn't sure if it was him, the alcohol, or the fact that he had just asked me a question I didn't want to answer. "My dad managed the Greek and was a collector of concert T-shirts," I said, trying to push back the emotions welling up inside me.

He seemed to understand my hesitation before nodding, clearing his throat, and he once again changed the subject. "So, have you ever seen Foreigner play?" he asked, now pointing to his own shirt and grinning.

As I looked at the bold white letters across his chest, I pushed aside my sadness and refocused on our conversation. We were just two people who had a lot in common—or at least that was what I wanted to think. When our drinks were gone, he ordered another round. As I finished the shot, I accidentally slammed the glass on the bar, and the bartender glowered at me. "Sorry," I mouthed.

River reached out and grabbed a strand of hair that had come loose from my ponytail. He very slowly tucked it behind my ear, sending shivers down my spine. Circling his index finger around my ear, he lightly tugged on my lobe. He sparked a fire in me that never before existed.

Gulping the drink I didn't need to be drinking, I hoped to extinguish the flame. I hoped no one had seen him touch me that way. Ben would be fucking furious. He was ridiculously jealous. We had had many arguments about other men, all unjustified. At least until now.

As the strobe lights started to flicker and I leaned my hip against the bar for support, he put his hand on my waist and turned me so my back was against the bar. I wondered if he noticed me almost lose my balance from the flashing lights and drunkenness. Moving to stand directly in front of me, he put his hands on either side of me and pressed his palms into the bar. He was enveloping me, but I didn't feel trapped. I didn't know what I felt, but I knew my heart was pounding out of my chest, my stomach was doing flips, and I became light-headed as goose bumps emerged on my skin.

I thought he was going to kiss me as he stared intently into my eyes. I closed my eyes, preparing for it, but I felt him abruptly pull away. Immediately, I heard a high-pitched voice squeal, "River, don't forget we're leaving right after the show," and before I could catch a glimpse of the girl, she bounced away.

Smirking at me, he said, "My little sister has the worst timing."

I was going to respond when I heard a drumroll echo through the bar. Glancing around, I tried to figure out what it was for. Amused, he rolled his eyes before looking at the stage and then back to me. "That would be for me," he laughed, leaning in so we were face-to-face. "They want me back onstage. I've gotta go unless you'd rather I stay and we finish what we started? Because that certainly would be way more fun."

I really hadn't heard anything he said, but everything seemed to finally make sense. He was the voice I'd heard when I came into the bar. He was so charming, so captivating, and so aware of me. I was pretty sure I was drunk because I was feeling things I should not have been feeling. As I stared into his powerful green eyes, I knew I should've been trying to escape them.

Before I could say anything in response, he moved his head slightly back, lifted my hand, and slowly kissed it. Then he leaned into me and whispered in my ear, "Guess not. Not yet, anyway." My hand was on fire, my ear scorched.

That same drumroll rumbled through the sound system again and he quickly turned his head back to look at me. "I gotta jet."

He was still holding my hand, as he looked straight into my eyes. "You'll wait for me until after the show."

It wasn't a question. It was a statement. And then motioning between us, he added, "Because this isn't finished."

At that moment I realized that what had started as harmless flirting had turned into a situation that had gotten way too dangerous.

He placed his hands back on the bar and waited for a response. Since he hadn't asked a question that I wanted to answer, I just smiled and said, "If you're in the band, you'd better go. You shouldn't leave your fans waiting."

He gave me one last heart-stopping grin and then leaned in and kissed me. My body reacted strangely; a rush of something I couldn't identify surged through me. At first he only lightly touched my lips with his; then for a few short seconds he pressed a little harder before pulling away. I didn't kiss him back, but felt light-headed.

"I hope you've become a fan," he said, winking at me before grabbing his hat. Then he turned and walked away.

I brought my fingers up to my lips and watched as his silhouette disappeared through the crowd. I became vaguely aware that "Superstition" was playing, but my mind was focused on him.

I shook my head, trying to rid myself of the thoughts that shouldn't be there. I knew I had to leave, or I would end up doing something I would regret. I loved Ben, and Ben would fucking kill River just for looking at me the way he did. And then there was the kiss; yes, Ben would certainly kill him.

Knowing these things, I wondered why I hadn't walked away in the first place. For a moment there, I felt as though I believed in love at first sight, which I didn't. And how could love at first sight even exist when you were already in love with someone else? I didn't want to keep thinking about what happened because I was confused as hell, and I knew the meaning of it all wasn't what I wanted it to be.

I smiled about our encounter. He definitely was not a stalker. He was adorably charming and utterly charismatic, a guy who had a simple ease about him that I really liked, and a guy I didn't ever need to see again. This I knew for certain.

With thoughts of River swirling through my head, I made my way through the crowd to the dance floor, where I found Aerie with some kind of pink drink in her hand. "We have to leave. Now!" I shouted at her while pulling her off the dance floor.

"What? Why? Are you sick?" she asked, struggling for words. Then she turned and pointed to the stage. "Because if you're not, I want to see that hot guy sing first."

I turned to see where she was pointing and sure enough it was him, River. I then realized I'd never even told him my name.

Pulling Aerie through the crowd under protest, I heard the audience chanting, "River Wilde, River Wilde." I glanced up to the stage just in time to see him grab the microphone. Before the live music started we exited through the door, and Aerie started yelling obscenities at me. As we walked away I found myself thinking I had just had the most magical encounter and might never be the same because of it.

Photo by Studio One to One Photography

Kim Karr lives in Florida with her husband and four kids. She's always had a love for books and recently decided to embrace one of her biggest passions—writing.